CW01481364

Escapade

SEAN FRASER

Zoë

or,

On the Clockwork Sphæres
of Paradise

{ Escapade }

Éditions Láthebiosas
Los Angeles
1913

© 2020

All rights reserved. No part of this publication may be reproduced, stored in a retrieval system, or transmitted in any form or by any means, electronic, mechanical, photocopying, recording, or otherwise, without prior written permission from the Author.

978-1-7352707-2-2

@TheatreSean

To My Son

ACKNOWLEDGEMENTS

Diana Gallardo and Mary Frances for critiques, diverse et al;

Frank Garrett l'Immoraliste for his expertise with Latin, "The Devil's tongue," by reminding me that word-use taken out of context may have voluminous interpretations;

Peter James for his generous permissions for the use of his photographs to be the covers of the second state of the individual chapters of this work;

David Southwell for graciously allowing the County of Hookland and a few personages found therein to be included;

and, Jennifer Gryczkowski for her extraordinary skills of and patience with proofreading this Tale.

& Carolyn Fraser.

"We cannot assent to a rook or a crow: thoughts which suspend the sense of Reality illustrate that the state of Existence often resides in the different realms of Chaos."

—Sean Fraser

9

Hookland

Interlude: France, 1913 – The Melancholia influent had passed and those who would set intrigues from Orbis paradisiacus were silenced; the arrangements of Change originating in 1871 were concluded by those of Orbis limbus; and, so it was that Life continued as before in Praesentis vagus as Humanity waxed obsolescent by Man's contrived magnificence and mores.

The small asteroeides from Perseús and Aries were gone returning to their realms in the Celeste.

†

It was a dirigeable of construction in the design of Dupuy de Lôme tethered on a green in the county of Hookland.

†

Zoë was seated in her barge ferried by Charon. She had spoken with the Wihttyde Serpent in the tunnel of the Ashcourt canal proposing how it abetted by kith rid the sewers and lakes of Hades from the troublesome common serpents of vermin. The Wihttyde Serpent agreed; it and it's kith would be in Achéron by the Autumn quarter.

"I must thank thee again for thy service," said Zoë.

"It has been rare I have been able to provide it and this was an interesting lark for me," said Charon.

"How so?" said Zoë.

"As far as hydras go, it is an intelligent wight well-versed in Greek comedies who happens to speak fluent Malebranchese. A pleasure to have met her."

They continued on the canals conversing pleasantly.

†

Hooke had met Morgause la Fey when she arrived by carriage. They went and entered his cabinet adjacent to the library. The cabinet was of an Art Nouveau design by Bing.

"Thank you for receiving me," said Morgause. Hooke gestured his slight annoyance. "Madame, you are most welcome at any hour you could choose to be in my house."

There was a knock at the door.

"Yes," said Hooke.

Three servants entered: one had a large tray of pastries; one had cutlery, saucers and cups; and one had the coffee-press. They arranged them on the table. They took exit.

"My afternoon's sustenance," said Hooke pointing to the stands of various heights of the trays: "Blackberry and custard tarts, plum profiteroles, clafoutis and pain au chocolat."

"You have all these?" said Morgause amused.

"No. Commonly, it's blackberry custard tarts," said Hooke; "I could not remember your preference, so these are what were guessed."

"All of these are preferred," said Morgause as she made her selection and sat on the davenport.

"May I?" said Hooke as he offered her coffee. "The kitchen will be happy."

She held her cup by the saucer as he poured.

He sat on the davenport placing his cup and saucer between them.

"I like that painting," said Morgause. "Themis Grey-Witch showed it to me several months after standing for it." She smiled. "This is where it went."

"This is the original from 1886," said Hooke. "Collier painted a copy for exhibition in 1887." Hooke fondly laughed. "I was in Los Angeles when it arrived. Reynaerd believed I should not be troubled and thus he had it hung in this chamber." He reminisced. "I felt as if I were being watched—when entering this room numerous years after—and she herself were waiting for me: I turned to see that—Indeed—she was.

"I never knew."

Morgause smiled.

"Madame," said Hooke thoughtfully, "as wondrous as this painting may be, that is not your reason nor intent for coming. Pray tell me."

"She's in danger," said Morgause la Fey.

"No." Hooke smiled saddened with sweetness. "She has no banes."

"Please, Sir, do not make jest," said Morgause la Fey.

"My pardon, Ma'am," said Hooke as he bowed from his shoulders; he stood. "It was not said in jest. Malevolences and Malevolences as Titans are appearing against all witches and sages and wights of Fey. L'Éminence malus seeks his vengeance, as you know, by the advent against Elfriede de Vienne; he may seek others in his wanton acts of retribution. Malebranche are murdering all they chance upon wandering. Lesser demons and fées are marauding in these days of Mayhem." He sat, on the arm of couch, next to her. "They are none banes because all would greet their Death by her."

"You have seen this?"

"No. I have seen her in a great formidable state of resolve that itself was lurking until 'twas found by her ere to the realm of Tenebris King we went."

"Greater than Persephone and her immolating those asylums?" asked Morgause la Fey. Hooke nodded. "Persephone told me she was eventually overwhelmed by Themis during the last one; she could barely walk from it."

"Far greater," said Hooke. "Dame Hades, on that final day, witnessed Themis la Grises's prise de conscience — her Réalisation — of that which she was able; yet still she remains as ever she was since that eve at Phlegethon House."

"You did this?"

"'Twas she herself."

†

The Blériot XI-2 Hydroaeroplane in the distance could be seen on the grass plain.

†

"I have not been these many years."

The house was of Greek style constructed with Doric columns and encased with external wood structures of Japanese design from the Edo period.

It had two floors with a peristyle courtyard filled with white sand.

"It was pirates, wasn't it?" said Zoë as she admired the woodwork of the interior spaces.

"It is from 1607," replied la Grise grinning. "It came with me to Hookland on the Umi'no'akuma and as cartage was brought from Brighthaven.

"I had forgotten these," said Zoë as she watched a butterfly as it approached her and led her outdoors to the courtyard of multitudes of Phengaris albida butterflies flying.

"Yes, they came with me too from Chine on the route returning from Japan."

†

William Hooke and Themis la Grise watched the Ocean of Dark in it's tumultuous calm as the waves were towering and deliquescent seen by illumination from the falling umbrascence above the Sea.

"Where are we?" asked la Grise.

"We are standing at the edge of the Palisades where Reason ceases," said Hooke: "All things beyond are beyond Reason.

"That is Chaos." He pointed at the dark before them. "We are standing on the Palisades that watch the Sea of Chaos." He turned and pointed at the dark before them. "If we should venture that way it would be the Palisades at the Edge of Nature éternelle."

"How far is that?"

He shook his head and shrugged. "It is neither as close nor long as the raven flies."

She peered at him.

"I haven't a clue," he replied smiling.

"You have walked there?"

He nodded. "Often." They returned to watching that ocean which was Chaos.

"I cannot see. All is dark before me."

"Set your eyes upwards and watch."

La Grise turned her grey-blue iris's hidden so that only the sclera of her eyes would see.

"It's beyond beautiful. I have no words. I'm senseless." She viewed the seascape for an untold length of moments. "I saw a spire."

"It is a single monument of stone; an obelisk constructed before Chronos."

"The Dark changes," said la Grise.

"The dark of Nature is Past returning is what you see behind us. Known existence. Dark at Night.

"The dark of Chaos is pale by comparison. Hence, of the Pâle."

They turned.

"What is that faint light in the distance?" she said as she pointed at the pale illumination.

"Venus," he said hesitantly with a grand Melancholy fallen across him beset by Sorrow. "Shall we walk to the edge of Nature?"

She nodded frowning at his disingenuous reply.

They went.

†

Merle, Caroline d'Eirene, Dilys d'Euphrosyne la Cramoisie, and Hélène Eunomia la Jaune were riding along the avenue with gas lamps faintly illumed at intervals of lengths but was lit by light of a wavering green which rose from the lane itself.

"What is this light?" asked Caroline d'Eirene.

"Goblin-light," said Merle. "They refer to it as Earth-light because it shines when Sky-light shines and Dark's revealed by moonlight even if Moon should not be illuminating seen."

"'Dark at Night, Moon well-lit: Farce and Felicity are all that's it,'" said Caroline d'Eirene.

Merle laughed.

"My Granny."

"Well spoken," said Merle.

The lane was becoming filled with brilliant Earth-light as they approached the end of the lane.

The landau carriage went faster for the horses were now galloping. The horses began flying with unfurled wings in the lane; and, the carriage ascended.

†

Shiretoko-hantō Miyabiyaka – the Brown Witch – and Gwendoline had gone to Coreham for an excursion of the town; they would return by mid-week.

Zoë had spent the Night listening to stories and tales told by all who were their attendance invited though it must be noted it was Old John Wren who spoke longest because he was implored for another tale to be told by all; he obligingly did.

She was departing for the country house of Charon.

†

They entered an underground chamber.

"The Terminus français," said Merle. "We are twenty-seven leagues beneath lands of the surface. It is a Cavum terra, 'Hollow of the Earth.'

"Hollows are of various widths. This is a common hollow of seven miles in diameter. Most are three or seven miles. The larger gares are nineteen."

And, as they continued ascending, there below them was the cacophonous pageantry of the hollow: steam locomotives hastening across suspension bridges of iron chains and ropes from tunnels in the walls of the chamber; boulevard traffic not unlike that seen on the avenue des Champs-Élysées was crossing on the numerous trestles from tunnels in the walls of the chamber; horse-drawn carriages flying; travellers waiting on platforms; solicitous pedlars of red bean paste buns, of cinnamon sticks, of shaved-ice cones, of blood pudding, of pickled eggs, of jellied-eels, of fruit cakes, of triffles, and tarts; travellers walking and scampering between platforms on the hundreds of flights of stairs and walkways zigzagging raised from the lake at the bottom of the hollow; carriages exiting lanes; station masters, attendants, porters, platelayers, iron workers tending all things in that gare; steam whistles shrieking arrival and departure; three moon bridges, for travellers, with stone arched bridges beneath where horses were trotting carriages; lifts between platforms; pamphleteers, cardsharps, cigarette girls, matchstick girls, flower girls, alchemists, bootblacks, tipsters, and touts were plying their trades; funicular cars, trams électriques and tracks rising between stations.

"The carriage lanes are from centuries ago; they were made by barrow-wrights. The trains are recent."

All was fused by the green Earth-light.

"What are those?" asked d'Eirene pointing at the glass tubes bound by Art Nouveau iron-work on red brick viaducts as a train of elongated lozenge-shaped cars went through one of the glass tunnels.

"Trains pneumatiques," replied Merle. "Inter-Continental and Trans-Continental lines. The train pneumatique from Lyon to Paris arrives one hour and one-half after departing. Trans-Continental lines, after leaving the larger gares, descending are set 130 leagues below. They travel much faster."

They ascended entering the lane for Lugudunon.

†

Merle and Hooke were speaking with the Archbishop in the cathédrale city, Weychester.

The Archbishop

The Archbishop was about to be pontificating on Virtues and Vice when there came a voice. "Sirs!" Hooke gestured for the Archbishop to be silent.

Merle and Hooke peered passed the Archbishop: the gentleman was of wolf form with gryphon's wings and a serpent's tail walking on his hind legs towards them.

The Archbishop gasping frowned.

"Majesty," said Marquis Marchosias.

"Marquess," said Merle.

"I was informed you were present and because I've naught else engaged I offer amanuensis service," said Marchosias to Hooke; "I so little write these days."

"Of course," replied Hooke cheerfully.

"'We cannot assent to a rook or a crow,'" said Merle to the Archbishop. "You misquote Ockham — 'We cannot assent to a rock or a cow' — but I prefer this and so shall use it. Regardless, my reply is simply Swift's line—

'When a great genius appears in the world you may know him by this sign; that the dunces are all in confœderacy against him.'

"The sentiment applies over idiot-savants and all folk who are different from thee, Monsieur Grégoire l'Archevêque. That Dunces appear cannot be argued nor can it be known the heights to which their malevolence may be raised by their ignorance but—Still—thy confœderacy flourishes."

Merle nodded to Hooke and Marchosias. "Gentlemen." He exited.

"You speak English, Mister Hooke, but His Majesty never has. Or, any other language," said Marchosias.

"He speaks Brythonic and Gaulish languages in the company of those who do and there are many who choose that language when speaking; but—as has been said—he hasn't need for the English language. He speaks French.

"I prefer to speak whatever language of the place I am or those speaking.

"Why?"

"Your name arose during our earlier Conseil. You are one of very few of them who speak Malebranchese when addressing us even if it is Old Malebranchese, which is sometimes difficult for us to understand you. Nevertheless, we all appreciate it. We thank you."

"My pleasure."

†

The horses trotted and then stopped. Dilys d'Euphrosyne la Cramoisie, Caroline d'Eirene, Hélène Eunomia la Jaune and Merle had arrived. They rode on the funicular car rising to the station while others went on the staircases.

They took their exit from a door at le gare Perrache. They hailed a taxi.

They would take supper while awaiting Night.

†

Theresa Aurélia de Phaenna and Marcelle were seated in the Library in the third and lowest undercroft of the cathédrale in Weychester. They had been let into the chamber of chained works where Aurélia la Violette was explaining that texts were often written for two audiences; but yet there was a third.

Marcelle placed her hand on the first tome—*Maleficium Obscuris*—and said the words Aurélia la Violette had spoken: "Maleficium Obscuris vera involvens."

"Wonders never cease," said Marcelle as she began reading the third version, the text of Truth.

†

They had walked. Merle lead them to the two boys seated on the kerb on le quai Saint-Vincent in Lyon.

"Gentlemen," said Merle. "I would like you to meet Dilys d'Euphrosyne la Cramoisie, Caroline d'Eirene and Hélène Eunomia la Jaune." He introduced them to Edmond Thierry and Pierre d'Aydie who wore a hat. "We have met but were not introduced."

"When?" asked Pierre.

"That very large fellow endowed by Magic phenomena."

"I told you!" Edmond slugged Pierre on the arm. "I saw you but did'n't see you. If you understand my meaning."

"Yes," replied Merle.

"Where's he gone?" asked Pierre rubbing his arm.

"Mister Tetch has things to do. He's very important."

"We figured," said Edmond with self-satisfaction.

Dilys d'Euphrosyne la Cramoisie, Caroline d'Eirene and Hélène Eunomia la Jaune intently stared at those two which made them very uncomfortable.

"Cueilleuses d'Orphelins?" asked Edmond with concern.

"No."

"Anges-gardiens?" asked Pierre sarcastically.

"No."

"We concur," said Dilys d'Euphrosyne la Cramoisie to Merle.

"What?" said Pierre.

Caroline d'Eirene held her hand towards the boys. "Have you seen one of these?" She held two small grey stones each having a hole in the center with faint scratch-marks over the surface.

They shook their heads.

"Do you guess what they do?"

They shook their heads.

"Please," she said as she gave them one stone each.

They examined them. They looked at each other and shrugged.

"What are they?"

"Dusios stones," answered Eunomia la Jaune. They shrugged. "Seers." They shrugged. "Druides." They shrugged. "Goblins." Their eyes lit. They peered closely at them. They each held their stone with thumb and forefinger held them up to the sky.

They briefly wavered in greys.

"What happened!" shouted Pierre.

"Gentlemen," said Merle, "these Ladies are – If you will – Fées marraines; and, if you should like, Madame la Cramoisie would be thy Fairy Godmother who may explain that which to thee has happened."

"What'll happen?" asked Edmond.

"I leave you in their care to explain what'll happen. They know these things," said Merle. "Mesdames." He turned and walked back the way they had come fading in the shadows.

Eunomia la Jaune and d'Euphrosyne la Cramoisie sat on either side of them as d'Eirene sat between them.

"You're not really Fairy Godmothers, are you?" said Pierre.

"No. But it does suffice when speaking with others."

"Does any one see you?" said Edmond.

D'Eirene nodded.

"Does any one see him?" said Pierre.

D'Eirene smiled broadly with her eyes widened, mirthfully.

Pierre leaned behind d'Eirene and hit Edmond with his hat. "I told you he was different!" He faced d'Eirene replacing his hat on his head. "Apologies."

"You will see us; some others will," said la Cramoisie; "We would like, for your own sakes, if you did not speak about us."

"If we do?" said Edmond.

"Do you know anyone who would believe you?" said d'Eirene, "or, would they think you loony?"

"Yeah," replied Edmond. "Loony."

"What's in it for us?" said Pierre.

"Wonders," said la Jaune.

"That's it?" said Edmond.

"That's it."

"What'll happen to us if we refuse?" said Pierre.

"Nothing will happen," replied la Cramoisie. "It would not anger nor sadden; and you'd be thought loony if you should happen to speak of having met us. It would not hinder us since there are two fellows very much like you in Paris who met the King of Hades; we are assured they'd be willing."

"Excuse us," said Pierre. They stood and wandered several paces in conversation. They returned. Pierre doffed his hat. They bowed.

"Done," said Edmond as he and Pierre extended their hands to la Cramoisie.

The Witches stood. La Cramoisie shook hands with them.

"Done," said Pierre.

"Have you visited parc d'Or in the Dark?" asked la Cramoisie.

"At Night, yeah," said Edmond.

"May we show you how it looks in the Dark when we visit?" asked la Cramoisie.

"Why?" said Pierre.

"Marvells."

They nodded. Edmond Thierry and Pierre d'Aydie were apprehensive but excitedly enticed.

They went.

†

Hooke turned to the Archbishop who was in a state of attempting to regain his composure but failing.

"The death of the mother is to be performed so as to preserve the life of an unborn child," said Hooke.

"Certainly," replied the Archbishop.

"Then you would harbour that orphan as your own?"

"Heavens, No!"

"He speaks as statesmen do," said Marquis Marchosias.

"Un petit Richelieu," said Hooke.

Marquis Marchosias did nod. Marchosias began writing. Hooke peered over the shoulder of the marquis; he read and began forming letters and script with the index finger of his right hand as if he were conducting.

"The embellishments and ligatures are elegant. Very musical!"

The Archbishop interrupted.

Marchosias pin-pricked with his pen the priest who flinched; he bled slightly.

"Thank ye, Sir."

"May I request thee future hence?" said Hooke.

"Honoured," said Marchosias.

"Done."

They shook hands.

†

Fille d'Achéron was strolling from the glade of la Grise. She had come to the lands far beyond Barrowcross which were not of the county of Hookland as she went northwards until she alarmed paused as it was a fairly large ghoul head which had risen from the ground ten paces before her in the fields.

"Your father would be displeased if you should have gone to harm come," said Shiretoko-hantō Miyabiyaka who appeared beside Fille. "We were concerned when you had not returned by the hour as you promised; I followed your way and so find you here."

Shiretoko-hantō Miyabiyaka led Fille twenty paces back from the ghoul.

"Who is your father, dear?" the ghoul asked in two voices: one voice was that expected of a ghoul but the second was harshly melodious which seemed as an echo from the far distance.

"My..." began Fille but could no longer speak. Miyabiyaka la Sorcière brune had placed her hand on the shoulder of Fille.

"My dear," la Sorcière brune gently admonished as she shook her head. "She would be insulted by the station of your father as a mere ferryman on an oft-forgotten river, if we continue. She prefers nobility and heritage."

"Thank you for that considerate interruption," said the ghoul. "We have not met."

"No," said la Sorcière brune indifferently. "There are those you know and one you have met who gave you your scar but I'm not either."

The ghoul raised itself to the shoulders and stared.

"Please stand and allow mademoiselle that she may see yourself as you doth be."

"I prefer this," replied the ghoul who raised itself to the waist.

Miyabiyaka la Sorcière brune withdrew two thorny canes. She inserted the canes in the earth and drew an ensō about them; and, a second ensō she drew around the head of the ghoul. Briars began growing serpentine. The ghoul began shrieking as the briars grew encasing it as winding sheets; but the voice heard was from below the surface of the field.

"If you please," said la Sorcière brune.

It rose. A naked Titaness. She had a long gruesome scar on her neck; from neck to waist were teats seeping pus; the legs and feet were gangrening. The shrouded ghoul was impaled on the tallest point of her radiant crown of iron.

The Titaness took the crown from her head with the hand of her good arm and held it with the hand of her withered arm. She removed the head of the ghoul and cast it aside as the body decayed into ash; and, said with the voice of the ghoul: "What have you done!"

"Rubus allegheniensis," said la Sorcière brune. "They are blackberries from a mythical land in the kingdom of Allegheny."

"We have not met," said the Titaness with terrible menace.

La Sorcière brune shook her head and pursed her lips.

"My new fine embassadour," said the Titaness disgruntledly as she donned her crown.

"Pray?" replied la Sorcière brune.

Fille could not speak because of the charm placed on her by la Sorcière brune.

The Titaness bent and took a single step as she extended her hand towards them. Fille would flee but la Sorcière brune held her by the sleeve of her gown with her left hand as she stared at the Titaness, drawing a third ensō with her right hand around the body of the Titaness.

The Titaness could not move her legs for thorny canes of various sizes were ascending as vines entwining her legs; and, as they rose, they grew larger until numerous were the size of great tree trunks. And, as they grew larger, they rose from many places further than the first vines had sprung. She was bound. The thorns from those vines tightening were piercing her flesh as she struggled frantically, enraged and helpless.

"Biancaea decapetala," said la Sorcière brune. Fille nodded absently.

"If you would but be still, they shall eventually one day loosen and fall," said la Sorcière brune as she retrieved her twigs.

The Titaness screamed and struggled greater as the vines had reached her arms: the vines began tightening receding pulling her closer to the ground as the Titaness labouring raged; they ceased receding into Earth when bowed—her crown toppling from her head—was she, panting. They remained tightened.

"We shall away," said la Sorcière brune.

They went strolling as Miyabiyaka la Sorcière brune led Fille d'Achéron from that place of Umbrage.

"One thing you must learn is to reply inappropriate questions with a riddle or couched truths. One does not know what another may do on being told of who you are." She laughed. "Nor what they actually are."

"Who was that?" asked Fille.

"A Malevolence," replied la Sorcière brune unconcerned. "They are known by Nature; and—in Nature—they do reside: they wish to know all knowledge of things that they then may Horrors do."

"She was a Titaness Monsieur Hooke mentioned," said Fille: "'*Le Titanomachie colosse* – Titans and Titanesses – are those entombed by Earth' were his words."

"No," replied la Sorcière brune. "She is a Malevolence who has merely taken form inhabiting the corpse of that Titan. What you saw was the corrosive corruption of the corpse by her malevolence."

"What will happen to her?"

"She may solve her conundrum," said la Sorcière brune; "or else she won't."

They began walking.

"I shall if you would be so kind to let me illustrate her conundrum when we get back."

Fille d'Achéron was beset by wonders as she went.

✝

The Archbishop muttered "Ahem!" and was stabbed.

"The prostitute who voluntarily took that life so her siblings would have education and her family would not continue to live in poverty? Her is life sacred?"

The Archbishop adamantly shook his head.

"They should revel in Poverty for to live in abject Poverty is to be closer to absolute Piety. Sins of monies taken from blasphemous harlots are many."

The Archbishop was stabbed.

"You write in blood," said the Archbishop alarmed holding his hand over that newly pen-pricked wound.

"No. Blood oxidizes and fades," replied Marchosias. "All those fanciful notions of writing with blood. Or, signature in blood."

"Though, if the papers were appropriately treated – alchemical and charmed – so 'twould absorb blood into itself thus disappearing from the surface of the paper, that document is fully binding," replied Hooke.

"True. So seldom properly done mayn't as well sign a Papal Bull with piss."

"Piss!" exclaimed Archbishop.

He was stabbed.

"That child born with misfortunes of appearance who shunned enjoys companionship with other Unfortunates in side-shows until side-shows are abolished for the Safety of those so born; and, thus they are left to die in poverty. Their Life is sacred?"

"They should revel in the Safety we have given them far from public scrutiny for to live in the safety of Poverty is to be closer to the sanctity of Piety. Sins of monies taken by Unfortunates are many."

"Do all these Unfortunates tithe?"

"Sadly, they do not. Impoverishment, their excuse. Tithing insures they sit in Kingdom Come as honoured guests and when they cannot they are placed in Debtor's Quarters until that day they are released by the benevolent payment made by family.

"And, much like residence in a cemetery requires an annuity for continued burial, so too are those deceased required tithing or Heavenly Annuity so they may remain as honoured guests in Kingdom Come."

"If Heavenly payment lapses?" asked Hooke.

"They're simply removed to Hell."

"Covetous fuck isn't he," said Marchosias. "Simply."

Hooke shrugged.

The Archbishop would protest but the demon squinting held it's pen at the ready: he remained silent.

†

Snježana de Pasithea the Blue Witch and Félix Trique were strolling in the cathédrale city of Weychester.

"Why are there no arcades?" said Félix. "I haven't seen one since we've been here. Not anywhere."

"It's different," replied de Pasithea. "Arcades are unnecessary. Do you know where Elysium is found?"

"Hades," said Félix.

"Do you not think it odd that that land of Peace should be there?" said de Pasithea.

"Yes," said Félix. "But there it is."

"The locus obscurus that is the county of Hookland is the same," said de Pasithea. "It is a sphære located in a kingdom where it aught not to be; but here it is."

†

"Those who assistance give and tend State-deemed Unfortunates are considered anarchists against pastoral Nature which does not condone anomalous appearance even if all are made in the images of thy deity.

"Interesting how you say that. Thy deity has pale appearance as attested to by paintings. Therefore, all who assist those not following Strictures are indeed anarchists against the norm instilled by Piety in appearance. They are treasonous and so hanged.

"Benevolence does not extend to they made Unfortunate by birth in the poisonous age of Industry; or, heritage."

The Archbishop frowned.

He was stabbed.

"Law 22," said Hooke; Marchosias concurred.

"Heavens! We do not use such antique works. A Modern edict for all or none: *The Laws for the Paradisiacal Progress of Humanity by Which All Mysteries of the Æther Shall be Bestowed unto Them Being for the Benefit of Those Suffuse with Piety*."

Hooke nodded.

They continued speaking – on Colonialism, Suffragettes, Indulgences, Slavery, Sovereignty, Veteran-Unfortunates, Illiteracy, Dominion, Lunatics, Eminent Domain; and, Murder by poisoning from negligence feigned – until Moon had set and risen.

The Archbishop was weak from loss of blood.

"Nine-hundred and seven exclusions," Hooke noted.

"The lives of importance are defined narrow by station and class," said Marchosias: "Most novel."

The Archbishop collapsed.

†

The small asteroeides were gone returning into the constellation of Pegasus.

†

Oana la Verte and Octavien Trouvère were in Romania wandering the streets and alleys of Portul Pădurilor with Madame Lechuza as guide.

†

Caroline d'Eirene, Mary la Toute-Douée, Theresa Aurélia de Phaenna and the three Grace Sisters were paused walking passed the Saint Bryvyth Cemetery in the east of Barrowcross. They were reading a signboard set leaning against the wrought iron fence,

IT HAS OFTEN BEEN SEEN!

Prayer cards, bread dolls & ribbons nailed to trees
as an appeasement
of the Minor Gods!

BEWARE!

All manner of villainous Evils shall befall those who do—
These may appease Minor Gods but most certainly will they
enrage the Great
and

Lesser Gods bound to Earth and Air

ϯ ϯ ϯ

SALTINE & Sons Since 1673
Of All Minor Gods offer
Prestidigitations
Annulments
Removals
&c.

ϯ

Alfred Sleigh Saltine was seated at the gate of a cemetery; he was having lunch.

The ancient oak was deceased but stood over all in the cemetery. It had bread dolls, ribbons and cards written with wishes tied to it's branches with dead vines from years ago; and, those that had fallen were as withered leaves scattered on the earth.

They viewed auræ and sylphides in the branches.

Alfred Sleigh Saltine spoke about Man's monuments after dying; and, concluded: "Effigies. They would not think to desecrate these stone pieces, their monuments to the Dead but they will desecrate Old Taranis with hammer and nail."

"This oak?"

"Old Taranis," replied Saltine. "It is a monument and a testament of Nature, is it not?"

"Oh?" said Mary as she placed her hand on the trunk of the great tree.

"Fell things have happened when it had been pinned with nails. Sprites, they say. I've not seen one myself. Don't believe I need to. But if I should happen across one, howe'er fancyful that would be, I would thank them standing them stout."

The auræ and sylphides frowned.

"And, if they should perchance prefer ale?" said Caroline d'Eirene.

"That I would do. In this Age, Man is in Nature but not of Nature as they were once long ago." He had concluded his al fresco dining and donned his boards before he would be going in the direction they had come. "Progress."

"Then, if you wish to thank them from yourself, a bowl - not too large - of an ale set in that crook would do," said Caroline d'Eirene. "They would bring their own spoons."

"After rounds, I'll be back with their bowl of ale," said Saltine. "Queer. I feel less forlorn, if that's the word to use." He peered at the tree with a vague happy expression and went on his rounds. "Ladies."

They decided a stroll of the monuments to be a pleasant minor excursion; and, they did.

"Some remember," said Aurélia de Phaenna.

†

Hercule was strolling on the High Road from Ashcourt to where he would go to a place between Barrowcross and the Sea.

He paused and watched an air balloon with a carriage-car flying overhead. He thought he was watched from above.

He was wearing his finest blue serge suit, his white starched shirt with patterned silk tie, his onyx cuff-links and his boots which were polished until they were obsidian black.

He continued.

†

They had returned from their repast in the Parc de la Cerisaie and were seated in Merle's parlour.

"The Modern Age – The Victorian – brought Spiritualisme. Many were disgusted that such lowly beings were able to summon seraphs; demons and devils were of their station. Spiritualisme with it's ghosts.

Mediums instead of erraunts fortunes telling or a spiritualist with a deck of cards instead of inconvenient methods of divination, scrying and sacrifice.

"Spirit-summoning from those set in banded-circles alternating between clockwise and counterclockwise rotating for an ever-infinite number in those nine choirs which some may see as Divinity; and for others, Subjugation.

"This Modern Age was, for d'Aquitaine, Paradise while the Middle Ages and Renaissance and Enlightenment were Hell and Purgatory for him. He did not approve the coarseness yet the brutality of those epochs was acceptable.

"Divine Subjugation was his plot with all kneeling gratitude for his beneficence unto them. Le Saint malveillant exploited it.

"The Messenger – l'Émissaire maleficent – and l'Invalide – l'Éminence malus – are the same but in two different Essentiae-wights: they are the Shade of the other; they are halves of the same eternal divine malevolence: le Saint malveillant.

"They walk without shadow. That defies Logic and Reason of the Laws of Nature. L'Invalide knew so it's shadow is a ghôle imprisoned."

"Vampyres," mused de Vienne.

"A marvellous conceit was it not. Things that cast no shadows have no soul because the soul resides in or is the shadow.

"There is no known reason for it's existence; there is no known logic for it existing; but exist it does.

"All of the species likened unto Humanity.

"L'Invalide came centuries ago. 1794 but earlier. It partook of all Earthly Sins as merriments; it continues so.

"It could not come as it's true self for it's true self—le Saint malveillant—would have destroyed all things: it was not allowed. But by one shadow arriving, it could pass in the zones between."

"It feeds on the pain of others," said de Vienne.

"No," replied Merle. "It does not take nourishment from those states of emotion, if that is your question; merely pleasure in causing them."

†

They were strolling on the highway far from the Archbishop in the cathédrale city, Weychester.

"He was — in Life — a lighthouse for those who wished the Sanctity of Life," said Hooke.

"Death comes," said Marquis Marchosias; "and, he offers a noble shrine for those in need for they could not feast on his words but with his very being he does continue that Sanctity of Life."

Hooke stared wryly.

"Maggots and flies; mice and rats; foul and fell. Those sorts. They need Theocracy sustenance, too."

Hooke smiled.

"Le Maréchal and Misses Tetch — *Misses Tetch* — requested you join them for an intimate supper party this evening," said Marquis Marchosias.

"Where?"

"Phlegethon House."

"Delightful."

"Then allow me."

They went.

†

The small asteroeides from Capricornus were begun arriving.

†

Zoë, Morgause la Fey, Megan la Fae and Morgan le Fay were seated in the gondola of the dirigeable picnicking. They were listening to Admiral Paul-Pierre-Clément Duplessis —the captain of the air-ship—regale them with tales of air pirates and his adventure with the Great Meteor Procession as it occurred on the 9th of Fevrier in the year of 1913.

Zoë peered over the edge and viewed the Gentleman wearing his finest blue serge suit ambling on his way on the High Road.

†

Themis la Grise had sought and found Merle as he was standing in la parc de Saint-Cloud as he did watch the sky. She had explained her grief and entreated Merle for him the reason to expound, who replied: "Come."

†

"We stood here," said la Grise as they stood on the Palisades. "I asked him what that light was but it is not here. He changed. His sadness was unbearable. Please tell me."

"What did he say?"

"Venus."

He smiled; and, it was a sad smile.

"Please," beseeched la Grise.

"All celestial objects—from these Palisades—cannot be seen by you from here," replied Merle: "It was not Venus."

Themis la Grise would speak interrupting him but Merle gently shook his head.

"It was not Venus because it was not of celestial objects but origin; yet it could be seen by you while you were standing beside him here."

She nodded.

"We are standing in this place while we are remained standing in la parc de Saint-Cloud where you found me skywatching; we are conversing on *Time*."

She was confused.

"There are three sets in the laws of Nature. There are but two sets in Chaos: laws that have been documented but for which no empirical evidence may been found in this Modern Age; and, laws which shall remain unknown eternally.

"The laws of Chaos are suffused tincturing those of Nature.

"Time was invented by Man in Nature; Time exists not in Chaos. We remain in that parc because of time in Nature. We are standing here in those same hours but of a *different* time, if you will. If thou wouldst consider that a person presently sleeping in their bed in this the year of 1913–in Lyon–is presently dreaming of fishing from the banks of the Saône in–unbeknownst to them–1736. They have not left their bed but yet are fishing."

She was confused but uncertain comprehending.

"You saw that light of his Venus because he saw it. He is able to see you as light in Dark. And, since he was here with you, and you and he were remained in Lyon, you saw it, too.

"You were looking at what he sees. I do not see you as that which he does, therefore there is not light of you to see."

She stared at him.

"That light thou spied was thee."

†

"I do not understand the Library not having any doors before I was shown them," said Milot.

"Locus," replied Merle; "You were shown the door by Hiolle. You wandered in the aisles. What did you see?"

"It was old," said Milot. "Very old. I cannot but guess the year. 1700. I felt as though I was in that year as I walked in the library. I cannot explain. It was unseen until my visit but it seemed quite familiar. The airs in it were different from the hall and those from the boulevard."

"The windows at the West and East ends you peered. What did you see?"

"I was dumbfounded," said Milot who shook his head remembering his disbelief. "I saw the surroundings to be unchanged; they were the same as I passed them coming here."

"This residence has locus and Sense. The library is locus. It was not hidden; it was not disguised; it was not *magically* appeared. There exist loci—neither common nor sacred—which are Locorum obscurorum. You were shown entrance. That's all."

†

The bodies of seven children and one of the staff were strewn in the hall. All of the children and staff in Eden Hall, established by the Children's Friendly Society, had been wounded; nearly all were fatality. All had many small puncture wounds. All had bled.

A single boy with a cherubic face sat against the wall sleeping in a stuporous state.

The headmaster was conversing with two officiates of authority when suddenly it grew bone-chilling cold on that sunny day of l'Automne.

Hooke entered walking directly to the cherubic boy; he roughly held the boy by his throat lifting him from the floor. He slept still.

They protested.

Hooke with fierce anger stared at them.

"We have authority dating back to the Madhouses Act 1774," said the first gentleman of authority.

"You are?" said Hooke.

"We are Masters in Lunacy," said the second Master in Lunacy.

"That child was witness to this carnage," rejoined the first Master in Lunacy. "This was the work of a madman."

"He arrived a few days ago," said the headmaster.

"We must keep this child from further reminders of this event else he goes lunatic. His spirit must not be damaged."

"He's become comatose from the horror," said the headmaster.

"There have been other murders," said Hooke: "the Lost Sisters of St. Joseph, the Home for the Orphaned Blind, Deaf and Dumb, and the Agatha King Institute for Foundlings. Have you not been?"

"We have," said the first Master in Lunacy. "This poor child was found wandering Ashcourt and was sent to Coreham. That madman followed him to Coreham and struck again. He was brought here for safety. He is mute. He cannot speak. He has not ever opened his mouth. He is unable to tell what occurred in those places."

"You did not confront the possibility this was the villain."

"We did not! He is not capable of using a Maxim gun."

"What!" said Hooke with seething incredulity. "There aren't bullet holes in walls nor casings on floors."

"We have taken that under advisement."

"Such a child with a cherubic countenance and angelic eyes cannot be villainous."

Hooke with his left hand held the boy by the back of his neck with his face towards them and slowly Hooke did, with his right hand, pull the mask of flesh from it's face: it had no mouth; it had no teeth. The mandible was suture-fused with the calvarium. It's eyes opened; it began flailing. Hooke crushed it's neck: the body was paralyzed. Three-foot long black serpentine stems fell from the cavity in it's chin. The stems softly hissed.

"Putus inexplebilis."

Hooke extended his hand: the first Master in Lunacy was bewildered as he gave his fine silk hat to Hooke.

The body of the putto was slowly consumed by brilliant flames of light beginning with it's feet. The eyes of the putto shown with terror. The stems shrieking thrashed wildly. The putto was consumed until the hat of the first Master in Lunacy contained ashes: wisps of wreathing vapours entwined did rise from the ashes; but did not exit from the hat.

"It's spirit," said Hooke as he brusquely returned the hat of the Master in Lunacy.

He did exit.

The cold lingered long after he had left.

†

Themis la Grise and C. L. Nolan were strolling on Kensington High Street.

C. L. Nolan commented on the variants of those in the Fées milieux he had read about or seen in art pieces.

"Where are they? How does one find them?" he asked.

She paused. She peered the length of each direction of the boulevard.

She directed him to stand far from her and watch studiously the persons passing on the pavement approaching from the West. He did. He noticed nothing different.

Then he gasped. Nolan's eyes grew large. He gaped. He began laughing.

He saw a noble woman whose head had stag antlers; she was clothed in a green gown with it's long trailing train; and, she was followed by dryads and fauns.

They passed and none paid him notice; one did turn her head briefly in his direction but shrugged and continued. They did notice Themis but did not react except for those who smiled.

He returned to where she stood.

"May I speak with them?"

"Eventually. Perhaps. Though, they may not wish to speak with *you*," replied la Grise. "You did notice that it was but a single dryad who took notice of you staring even though she did not know what she saw.

"They are of a different populace which cannot see." Themis la Grise explained that since Nolan was imbued with Fey he may see these folk but they cannot see him; and, a few may briefly notice something fleeting in passing but not realise what is was they saw.

"It is the reverse of Man seeing faeries!" exclaimed Nolan.

She smiled. "There are those born Feyish. Some understand while others recognize us as simply another figure in the Masses. They see us and they know us. They may forget that Sense; or, reject all such knowledge of it, if they choose, because all beliefs of faerie, as they have been told, even in this Modern Age, are signs of Madness. There are those few who are born Fey-like chosen for permanency by an inoculation colloquially named the Fairy's Kiss. It was once — Perhaps, it still is — thought the Witch's Mark." She laughed cruelly. "Simple nævus, nævus with hair, lentigo: all birthmarks and moles are Witch's Marks believed." She composed herself. "And, so— enchantments and voyages ethereal may be learned."

He with furrowed brow thought.

"Still," laughed la Grise: "take heart, Monsieur Nolan, for the Queen did see you but, since you are merely one of the lowliest of creatures, she would never deign acknowledge you with her condescension."

"How is this possible?" asked Nolan.

"They are amoungst you but not of this time," replied la Grise.

Nolan stood confused.

"You must have that question addressed by someone who will give a proper reply," said la Grise: "I cannot."

Nolan pondered.

"Chaos's mad humour is unrelenting, isn't it," said she.

They continued.

†

Hercule would pause and unselfconsciously reconstruct the small shrines to Saint Ellen—Empress of the Land—he found disassembled by the whims of Nature on the wayfares as he trod.

†

Zoë was walking with Merle in Ashcourt on Clore Street. Several young girls were following on their way to the park.

Suddenly, an elderly gentleman ran on to the street from one of the Regency town houses.

The Apothecary diplômé

Honorius the Elder—commonly known as Henry Marleye-Hearse, Apothecary—was clean shaved and balding with a toupee balanced on the top of his head. He was of normal height and standard portly weight for an elderly sort of gentleman.

He was dressed in a plain brown dress coat with blue breeches and a white blouse; and a waistcoat of crimson cut silk velvet and yellow lace over which he wore a green Victorian cape with capelet embroidered with sigils and seals in red threads; he wore mauve velvet slippers.

"Cease!" He ran directly to Zoë. "My dear, I must insist you are to be my witness! for the marvells and wonders of my doing!"

Zoë turned to Merle who smiled and said: "Black Molly's." He wandered.

"All persons come to this place," said Honorius the Elder. "It's not un Maison de Tolérance. Enter of your own free Will freely!"

She entered.

It was a common Georgian house but most of the rooms were destitute: furniture was covered with muslin; mirrors and paintings were covered with black cloths.

He led her through the rooms until they had come to his atelier which was the entire second floor. The atelier was sparsely furnished. All of the four walls were covered with theater drapes.

The Solomonic circle had been drawn. Runic glyphs had been scrieved. Candles had already been placed and lit. She was made to stand at the East.

"Prepare to be amazed, my dear child." The conjuration was made and a demon appeared facing at the West.

The demon went to the drapes in front of him; he pulled them aside and admired the view from the window for several minutes. He turned and he glanced around the room until he saw Zoë—standing behind the fellow who stood in his circles—who was smiling very much to his surprise. He walked around the circles and stood before her. He bowed. "Ma'am?"

"I was asked as particular witness," she replied to his confused expression. The demon pointed at the Alchemist with his left arm crooked and his palm held upwards; his face perturbed. She nodded in her charming fashion. The demon bowed from his shoulders. "Witness," he chuckled but continued with serious tones: "He offered you neither couch nor chair?"

"No," Zoë replied.

"Civility has truly died." The demon—Aguarès le Duc—walked around the circle. "Very artistic," he said addressing Zoë. "I've always liked this design." He peered at the Apothecary. "It's a pleasure to find one who isn't from the Tourist class of alchemists."

"Tourists?"

"Dilettantes," he said as he looked around the chamber. He dragged a chair near the circle. "All these circles. Bogia, radius of spheres, concentric. Quadrants. Compass points. Runic glyphs mumbo-jumbo cryptically scrawled. False temenos. Those." He offered Zoë the Victorian chair in which to sit; she graciously shook her head. He sat. "Spheres are good. Columns are novel. You've got a fine column here."

Honorius the Elder worried.

"No," said Aguarès le Duc reassuringly. "It's a column. A very tall one. The diameter isn't wide enough to be a useful sphere. Nine feet needed; seventeen foot's best." The Apothecary was confused. "You've not invested with Geometry, are you?" Honorius the Elder shook his head. "If it was spherical, your knees and feet would be all which are protected. Oblongs are'n't spheres; hence, not used. Touch it."

Honorius the Elder hesitantly extended his forefinger and touched it.

"See. Column." Aguarès le Duc was gesturing with his right hand as he slung his left arm over the back of the chair. "Those three rings are proscribed widths, but the innermost ring should be wider." He turned to Zoë and said: "Aesthetics." She smiled. "Did you know columns from circles on planes are problematic?" She shook her head slowly still smiling.

Honorius the Elder screeched. The demon's arm had grown in length and disappeared into the floor and his hand was clutching the Apothecary's ankle.

"Invocation was good. Spell was'n't. Simple misdirection engages you." He shook his head while staring with piercing eyes at Honorius the Elder. "Disappointing conjuration. Very common but — Still — disappointing that you incanted a common Cavum column and neglected amending a Terra inexpugnabilis clause in your scripture." The demon released his hand; his arm returned to it's normal length. "One must be very careful with Columnas tubulosae. They never seem to go down. It's always up but never down. Spheres are better but again everyone makes the diameters so small. A few do large ones. Few of them go under floors. And, people wonder why so few alchemists." He pointed at the column. "Did not you know that very nearly all columns incanted are hollow?" Honorius the Elder was speechless. "It's true," he said reassuringly. "Has none other addressed these deficiencies?"

Honorius the Elder slowly shook his head.

"Ah, well." He stood. "What'd'ye want?" Aguarès le Duc said as he replaced the chair in the corner.

Honorius the Elder declined the offer with a horrified expression.

"Certain?" asked Agares le Duc interrogatively. "Your conjuration was for a young girl to seek you — however modest she may be" — He bowed from the shoulders towards Zoë who nodded graciously. — "for the experience of the marvellous power of the intelligences supérieures you possess which if followed by an incanted request would make that young girl dance in the naked before you." He turned to Zoë and chortled: "An *unexpected* witness."

Honorius the Elder nodded.

"I don't mind, if you'd want something."

Honorius the Elder shook his head.

"Absolutely certain?"

He nodded.

"Well, I'll be off then." He went to the chamber door, and, he opened it. He turned to Zoë and said with a courtly gesture: "Majesty" and was gone.

"Please hear my wish," said Zoë; the candles were continued flickering but the shadows did cease their undulating dance on all surfaces of the room. She faced Honorius the Apothecary. "You may ask whatever thee desire; but not this nor malevolence of any sort against hapless and innocent are to be done." She gestured about the room. "They'll know."

Zoë departed.

†

Honorius the Elder remained standing long in his place after for from that moment he knew shadow and shade would stand motionless and stare watching him where ever he should be in those his years remaining.

†

Zoë exited from the house to find Aguarès le Duc leaning against the cast iron fence waiting on the pavement.

"A most generous lesson you have given me," said Zoë laughing. "Most kind."

"Ma'am," replied Aguarès le Duc. "Where ye off to?"

"Someone you know is waiting for me at Black Molly's."

"Molly and him and thee in a single evening would be enchanting. Might I accompany you?"

She assented.

They went strolling as he continued his lesson on conjurations; and, specious tomes written and circulated by djinn and imps; and why charms should never be used when summoning harpyiae.

†

Hooke was strolling with C. L. Nolan and Louis-Aldonse Milot. They were walking leisurely on a lane through the woods to the manse of la Grise.

"Monsieur Milot, do you remember that single charm once taught you?"

"Yes," replied Milot.

"Mister Nolan, do you still know the words of that particular curse from the Alkonost and Sirin visiting Hookland last month?"

"Possibly," said Nolan.

"It's written in your book," Hooke suggested.

He quickly found it.

"Yes."

They went a mile further.

A league of wood sprites appeared brandishing cutlasses, daggers and pikes.

"Gentlemen," called Hooke to the sprites. "I shall stand here and do naught to hinder you their murders done." He placed his hands in his trousers's pockets. "Monsieur Milot. Mister Nolan. If you would, your lines recite."

They did.

"It's you again! We told you!" shouted the Head Sprite, Bad Knocks.

The noses of the sprites were grown to seven feet by Milot; they were grown with wings and began flying by Nolan. Sadly, since their noses were longer than their height, the sprites were flying upside down not of their own free Will. All weapons fell.

"Most amusing," said Hooke. "And, I told ye—Birdie—I would not be troubled by thee and thine if ever again we should meet on this lane."

"Birdie?" said Nolan. Several of the hooligan sprites were intrigued as evidenced by their sniggering.

"Bertram Trevor Potts is his birth name," replied Hooke as he turned to Nolan. "'Bertie' was his affectionate name even after delinquency befell him. An upstanding heritage besmirched."

"Birdie!" said one of the sprites with giggles.

"Indeed," said Hooke as he faced that sprite which had flown and bounced on it's nose closer to them. "Sadly, during his entrance into l'Académie militaire, where his registration was made as Bernard T. Potts, he was soon thereafter known as *Birdie Teapots*. Birdie."

The sprites were hilariously laughing 'Birdie Teapots' between his shrieks of indignation. "Bastard!" screamed Knocks.

"Mister Nolan, you are familiar," said Hooke as he idly went to Knocks; "Monsieur Milot, you're not. They are my guests. And so, as such, they are not to be troubled by thee if they should pass your woods. Ever."

Hooke, Nolan and Milot continued with the wood sprites flying in circles and gyres; a few did bounce on their faces from the weight of their noses.

"How long do they fly?" said Milot.

"I haven't any idea. I've not ever used it," replied Nolan astonished.

"You do see, Milot," said Hooke, "that you do have an effective curse. Well done, Nolan. I'm certain the dryads in the woods will soon tire of their screams and cure them." He thought. "Or, gag them."

†

It was late afternoon before they had come to expanse of heath on which was found a structure. It stood thirty-one feet high and was thirteen feet in width. It was a single wrought iron grille of intricate design set in a single piece of Volvic stone.

"This, Mister Nolan, is your reply," said Hooke: "the Mirror of Persephone."

There was a figure standing beside the iron work.

It was Jean-Marie Jules.

"Queerest thing. I was compelled," said Jules as he replied to the stares of Nolan and Milot. "What might you be doing?"

"Purportedly, it is all that remains of a temple for Persephone," said Nolan. "Her mirror." He strode with determination to the structure as if to pass like Alice through the glass; but, bruised his nose.

"No," said Hooke. "Nine after l'Aube if you stand in the West."

"I found it years ago but never understood what it was. A monument, I thought," said Jules. "Didn't know it was named."

"Yes?" said Milot.

"It is late afternoon. The shadows are falling East. Helios-orb opens the mirror at nine in the morning when it's shadows are falling West."

Hooke went to a particular spot near the West side of the mirror. He brushed aside the heather with the toe of his boot where a small iron plate had lay hid.

"I do not understand," said Nolan.

"This isn't a Station nor all that remains of a temple," said Milot

"No, it is assuredly not a Station. The single Station is in Chiswick next to a cemetery," offered Nolan solemnly; "It is in the basement of a house which was once a baker from the Middle Ages. Horse-drawn only. There was a caravan vendor on the high road but it's gone. Folk often went with passing voyagers but they are not in this Modern Age." He faced Hooke. "It is not ruins?"

Milot peered at Hooke who nodded at Milot.

"It is a gate," Milot replied. "There are no ruins because there never was a temple. The shadows cast at that precise hour are the words which open the gate. Those designs are words. The gate opens if one or no one is standing. But to enter, one must stand on the plate. The shadows align with the person standing on the iron plate. It is of a conductive design."

Nolan wandered on the heath peering stooped for stones and detritus of the remains of the ruins.

"If you do come in the morning, you should wait for the bells ringing knowing it is the correct hour," said Hooke.

"There aren't steeples nearby," replied Nolan who had abandoned his search for ruin.

"The bells sounding from the Sea of Redemption are heard in this field," said Hooke.

"How do you get back I should like to wonder," said Jules.

"During the full Moon," said Hooke.

"Sea of Redemption?" asked Milot.

"How do you know when it's a full Moon in Hell?" queried Nolan.

"Hades," Hooke corrected.

"Schedules are posted," said Milot; "They are pictographs for those who do not read Malebranchese."

"Full Moons are seen in Hades," said Hooke. "It is a field - this same field - when you arrive. Simply, remember your way back to this gate in Hades which shall return you to this field in Hookland.

"Gentlemen, you seem to be under delusion regarding Hades. That it is a commune in a département – a chamber – in Earth. Hades is an orbis that lends credence to Hollow Earth, if Hades were resided in Earth; or, it could be an orbis of a circumference less than Venus but greater than the star of Judgement of the Fate of the Dead – set in Æther."

They were silent.

"I do not know that language," said Nolan finally.

"You shall if ever you should visit," replied Hooke.

"Payment?" asked Milot.

"'My gladdened tidings of Will I give' said kindly," said Hooke.

"Who is Will?" asked Nolan.

"Free Will," said Hooke smiling.

"If I don't say that?" said Milot.

"They send you back the long way."

"Long way?" said Nolan.

"You are sent walking—one-hundred and seventeen leagues—on the embankment from Achéron Quay to the Pearly Gates," said Hooke, "where you will be identified as an interloper: documents typed; signatures required; stamps obtained; photographed, front and left; wax seals affixed. All of which may take several quartets of the Seasons. Then—escorted blindfolded far from the Gates which may be in walking distance of your home or on a different continent depending on where one has residence; and, afterwards from there, here."

A barouche harnessed with two black horses was approaching. It was driverless.

The horses stood near Hooke. Hooke greeted the horses; and, Hooke sat as the driver.

"Gentlemen, perhaps," began Hooke, "a Society could be formed: you each seek things different than the others but those things often are sought by all for different reasons.

"Jules finds things: he found this gate many years ago but has never known it's meaning; Nolan knows things: he heard tell of the ruins many years ago but never found it's place; Milot surmises things: he has never heard of the ruins nor mirror before but has wished to visit that place which lies beyond. He knew it's worth when approaching.

"I leave you gentlemen to your thoughts for I am required away in Ashcourt."

"Sir," said Nolan; "Why have deceased Faerie not ever been found?"

"They are found," replied Hooke. "By kithfolk; and, Mortality Brigade."

He departed with the horses trotting.

They in their bewilderments stood.

†

Louis-Aldonse Milot was taken by Consul-Secrétaire Javelle to the cathédrale in Weychester. They were let into the chained library. Javelle directed Milot to the volumes he would be in the best of his interests to read. Milot entered memoranda in one of his cahiers d'écriture.

They were led and entered the Black Library in the first undercroft of the cathédrale where Javelle directed Milot to the volumes it would behoove him to read. Milot entered memoranda in one of his cahiers d'écriture.

They exited.

†

Minister-Cardinalis Taberd was standing in the foyer of the Hôtel Parthénon. He had dressed with his jacket over his blue and white pin-striped pajamas; he wore a single shoe.

Merle expressionless, for a great length of minutes, had silently observed the misfortunate Minister-Cardinalis in deliriums from fever and fears pleading his life to be spared from harm.

"I beg you!" cried Taberd. "I cannot suffer like this! Lord-Chancellor comes for me at Night in dreams. The Holy Invalide with Dark things lies waiting for me in the shadows of the day."

"Omnes monuit sunt," said Merle. "And, were you not admonished on the value of thy life?

"Thy play is done; actors, deceased."

Minister-Cardinalis Taberd began incomprehensible whimperings of the Dark until he was screaming collapsed on his knees.

"Please inform l'Hôpital Coulmier," said Merle as he passed the front desk and went walking up the stairs.

†

Louis-Aldonse Milot and Javelle were visiting the Museum of Curiosities in Hook.

An old gent was reading scissored newspaper articles from the *Hookland Standard* pasted into a scrapbook dated 1873.

Milot noticed a separate case of blackened small figures and would ask Javelle but was interrupted as he began listening to the old gent speak.

"Various bureaus, years ago, deduced that two visitations are made: those by spirits; and, by those taken. Further, that visitations from loved ones are simple manifestations of Terror, Horror, Despair, Fear or Love."

* * *

"Mr. Frederick Hills was the beadle in Hook until 1838. He was last seen, according to the written accounts of witnesses interviewed, speaking with a regal woman dressed in red on Thorn Street at approximately nine o'clock that evening. In 1911, an apparition briefly appeared walking on Thorn Street; it was dressed in a peculiar fashion, striking a staff on the pavement. After a strenuous investigation, it was determined that this was the ghost of

Beadle Hills who, every night thereafter, would briefly appear at approximately nine o'clock. He was last seen in 1917."

* * *

"It is not merfolk of the Fælgroves water-meadow and not the Grey Witch who bathes in the Lake to be feared for it is the Lake itself that takes travellers beneath it's surface."

* * *

"All Hookland gardens are tithes to the forests and woods to wit all residences have had gardens since St. Agilbert was consumed by fire in 1723."

* * *

"Mary Elisabeth Carter, 12, was last seen being led from St. Mary Magdalene's Church in Albury by a regal woman dressed in green."

* * *

"Mrs. Edmund Pilford, 47, was last seen entering the abandoned Queen of the Woods stall in Luna Park, Blaxwich."

* * *

"The unfortunately named Samuel Hayne was hung in Albury in 1711."

* * *

"'We live in Umpteenth times.' Viscount Oliver Laurel. Letter to the editor, Hookland Standard in 1803."

* * *

"The High Gallows Pyre last seen in 1880 was attended by all manner of fiend in debauched merriments who were witnessed flying in a location that could not be accessed. It was later recounted by several stout fellows how the blackthorn hedges and trees of Barrowcross were altering paths and alleys against those not of Faerie wishing to pry for which constables credited merely as drunkenness."

* * *

"1917?" whispered Louis-Aldonse Milot.

Javelle replied nodding.

†

They had ridden in the elevator behind the twelve-foot-high door in the middle of a large basalt structure in the Queen Anne Revival mansion.

Anne Felkin and Antoinette Vaïsse were seated in the galerie of Persephone at her place set in the Parc de la Tête d'Or as their guide—Guenevere de Sens—was speaking with Madam Frood who was suffering hysterics.

"It's complicated," said Miss Felkin. "Guenevere de Sens was once la Sorcière rouge who afterwards has traveled in various guises. She was previously engaged in one of the small chambers behind those doors you saw when we were in the atrium because she enjoyed unfettered solitude in the regimented bureaucracy of this place; she also watched Madam Frood. She was Kleodora, a small woman who dressed like Clochards and smoked pipes. Kleodora recently left her position here and returned to being Guenevere de Sens due to the state of malice in the world. All of les Treize past, as you may have noticed, assist when need rises."

"Are you one of the Thirteen?" asked Antoinette Vaïsse.

"No. I did not wish to be. I am afforded privilege which suits me fine; I do not wish that honour."

"Madam Frood knows about Kleodora?" asked Antoinette Vaïsse.

"No; but, since de Sens is smoking the same pipe Kleodora used, Madam Frood is suspicious of malfeasance and does not remember ever having seen de Sens before though she has seen her before she became Madam Frood."

"Kleodora was la Femme laide?"

"No. Madame Frood is the Loathly Lady. Except, she does not know she is the Loathly Lady."

"I'm confused," said Antoinette Vaïsse.

"Guenevere de Sens and Madam Frood are sisters," said Miss Felkin as she would continue her lengthy explanation of the complications surrounding Frood.

†

Louis-Aldonse Milot and Javelle did exit from the Museum of Curiosities.

"The Grey Witch," commented Louis-Aldonse Milot.

"She's often here," said Javelle.

"Are there parishes of Hell?" asked Louis-Aldonse Milot.

Javelle nodded.

"Do you suppose Nolan has visited Hell?" mused Milot.

"Perhaps," said Javelle. "I know of those who would have offered their services as Guide. Though, if you ask him, he will wish you be gone from him and falls silent. He shall not ever speak with you again. He knows there are things which must never be acknowledged because once done so — Yea or Nay — Life will irreparably change."

"I've heard tell tours are booked and taken," said Milot.

"Virgil-revenants — from Virgil's Fabulous Tours — are not to be engaged," Javelle replied with the gravest disdain. "You have seen them hawking, wandering with their signboards. Those tours are very like these Civil Prosperity omnibuses filled with the idle vain Aristocracy amusing themselves o'er the plights of the Common you see travelling about the countrysides."

"You mentioned others who offer services."

"They would not take you, Louis-Aldonse Milot, l'Encyclopédiste," said Javelle. "That all things exist does not signify one need view them. They may be discerned from different avenues. Those others would guide but not protect you: stench; unpredictability of violence from all who raging dwell on those continents of the realm; unceasing oppressiveness of it's atmosphere; maëlstroms of emotions felt and sensed by all; malevolencies of Envy, Fear and Hatred seeping into your thoughts; collusion of evil and kindness; collisions of the Damned and the Saintly. All of those reign titanic; they reign beyond your present understanding.

"You are steeped in the knowledge of the tomes others have written with empirical knowledge: they have witnessed; you have read. 'Tis your safety others would keep by refusing your request. The subject of your work is far different from that of Mister Nolan."

"I confess myself disheartened by your words," said Milot after long contemplation, "but, as you said, I shall continue gathering knowledge from those who have written of their voyages."

"'Tis far better for your services, Monsieur l'Encyclopédiste."

They continued.

"Of course," said Javelle, "if you should be shown an entrance, it may behoove you to enter."

Milot l'Encyclopédiste stumbled stunned.

†

"Frood," said Guenevere de Sens. "Sit!" Frood sat as de Sens went to the side bureau and did dial a number with the telephone. "Her Highness." She waited. "Frood." She listened. "Thank you." She handed the receiver to Frood. "Her Highness wishes to speak with you." Madam Frood stood and listened for several minutes until she handed the receiver back to de Sens; she remained standing. "Yes?" De Sens listened. "Of course," she replied pleasantly. "It's been ages since I last visited you and Misses Tetch in Phlegethon House. Wednesday would be fine. I look forward to it." She replaced the receiver.

"Madame Frood has been instructed that you two have been given privileges and are not to be bothered," said de Sens. "Madam Frood and myself will continue our conversation in the parc."

Guenevere de Sens and Madam Frood took their exit.

"Complicated Madam Frood," said Antoinette Vaïsse.

Miss Felkin nodded.

†

"Those blackened imps from Hades?" said Milot; and, Javelle nodded but frowned.

"These imps are of the hundreds found after the Great Conflagration in the year 1816," said Javelle. "These devils are believed having been originated from in those dark places nearest Barrowcross consumed by Satan's flames. Did you notice their features and carriage?"

He nodded.

"They were not imps."

✝

Hercule went idly ignoring the blasphemes and curses from the head of the ghoul he found in a field of Barrowcross and was kicking down the path.

✝

Javelle had taken Milot to the south of the county. They were in Brighthaven standing on the alley in front of Thinne's bookshop.

"All manner of occult, Western mystery tradition, devils and myths and loons," said Javelle as he held open the door for Milot.

"Mister Javelle," said Hugh as he came from behind the cases and stacks of books, ephemera and roughly printed manuscripts.

"Hugh," said Javelle. "This is Mister Milot. He wishes to view your fine selection."

Hugh showed Milot those particular works Milot had wished to find. Hugh showed several books as well as others he believed Milot would like to purchase. Milot found one other. The works were wrapped in brown paper and tied with twine excepting the one Milot was reading. Milot attempted to pay but Javelle refused.

"I'll have your coin delivered this evening at closing," said Javelle.

"Very well, sir," said Hugh.

Milot was flustered.

They exited.

"All of the works found in the Black Library, all works in the chained Library, all works in the Museum of Curiosities I was able to sense those which were needed; but not there. They were found by Hugh but I could not sense them."

"I cannot explain," replied Javelle as they walked; "Let's find one who shall. What is that you read?"

Milot showed him the front.

THE RAVENS LIEGE

Or, Tyrany found from the Woods of Ignorance

where in the original rise, extent, and end of the natural rights, freedomes and properties of Mankind are discovered, and undeniably immured by Ignorance; the late oppressions and incroachments of the Truths which are borne by noble servants of All-Knowledge.

and included

The Grey Queen's Gambol

An Treatise on the effects occurring when visited
by Her Majesty.

Written by A. LATHEBIOSAS

Imprinted at Weychester, for *David Southwell*, and are to be
founde at his shoppe, at the Singe of the White Ship,
in *Albion Lane*, 1731.

"He's written many," said Javelle.

They went.

✝

Hercule had arrived at the estate of Themis Grey-Witch.

†

"All Victorian Era assemblies of Belief are thus shown to be that Spiritualisme is the Victorian practice of Necromancy," said Hooke as they entered.

"Yes," said Milot confused; but, he continued; "I can sense arcane: Theourgia, Sorcellerie, Nécromancie, l'Alchimie, Spiritualisme, Spiritisme, Mesmérisme, l'Ésotérisme, Hermétisme, l'Occultisme, l'Astrologie, Magie; all manner of works when entering bookshops, houses and stalls but those works printed after 1863 are difficult sense-finding."

"Theourgia should be included in Goëties," said Hooke, "since it is performing rituals with Magic and Sorcery conjuring spirits or demons and lesser deities under provenance of the Divine as Saint Augustine of Hippo noted they are both bound by rituals of demons: Goëtia under the names of demons; Theourgia under the names of seraphs.

"'Magia naturalis is precise."

"I'll amend my work," replied Milot.

"They're feeble," replied Hooke: "Whose have you found by sense?"

"Hargrave Jennings, Frederick Hockley," said Milot; "Allan Kardec published several works: *Le Livre des Médiums* in 1861; *L'Évangile selon le Spiritisme* in 1864; *Le Ciel et L'Enfer* in 1865; and, *La Genèse* in 1868. Baroness Vay's *Geist-Kraft-Stoff* in 1869; *Studien über die Geisterwelt* in 1874; and, Madame Blavatsky published *Isis Unveiled* in 1877. A few anonymous pamphlets but no others."

"What thou asks lies in History," replied Hooke. "It is thy profound knowledge of Victorian Goëtia that was the avenue for your research of Sphæres."

"Yes," said Milot. "I began with the elements of Goëtia familiar. I continued and so was versed until I understood acutely how Modern Age has invented new subcategories from before Antiquity."

"Precisely, Milot l'Encyclopédiste," said Hooke: "You are at this crossroads exiting Modern Age where six ages in History may be viewed for particular significances as regards thy question— The Medieval Age: the Early Middle Ages from the 5th to the 10th century, the High Middle Ages from 1001–1300 and the Late Middle Ages in the 14th and 15th centuries; the Renaissance from the fourteenth to the seventeenth century; le Siècle des Lumières from the years of 1685-1815; the First Industrial Revolution—the Early Age of Industry—was from 1760 and 1830; the Victorian era commonly believed to be from 1837 until 1901; and, the Second Industrial Age—the Modern Age of Industry—with it's coda of the Machine Age, was 1870 and 1914.

"What significance do you find in those dates, Milot l'Encyclopédiste?"

Milot read his notes. He shook his head and read again as he did write marginalia of the years.

"An acceleration!" said Milot: "The Middle Ages lasted ten centuries; the Renaissance was three centuries, le Siècle des Lumières — one century and thirty years; the First Industrial Revolution — seventy years; Victorian era — sixty-four years; the Modern Age of Industry — forty-four years."

"And, Humanity's la Belle Époque is from the cessation of the Franco-Prussian War in 1871 to the beginning of the First Great War in 1914: 43 years," said Hooke.

"Odd, by Chance, how le Siècle de Lumières happens to be identical to the years of the Enlightenment," said Javelle.

"By Chance," said Hooke smiling.

Milot uncomprehending shrugged.

†

Hercule left the head of the ghoul at the edge of the forest. He wandered into the glade. It was a cold day but, once he had stepped into the sphere of the land, the temperature was pleasantly clement. He went to the front door. He knocked. An attendant came who led Hercule to the main room where several folk were situated in conversation.

He was pleased. He marvelled at everything. He standing waited.

"Master Hercule," said la Grise as she went directly to Hercule on his entering. "I was informed you would be coming but expected you earlier yesterday."

"I went lost but found a fellow who knew the way," said Hercule as he bowed.

"None of that, dear Sir," said la Grise. "Have you never visited in this county?"

"Never."

"This country?"

"Never."

"She was here but has gone to Hook. We are going to Weychester and could take you to her on our way to there."

Elfriede de Vienne appeared.

Hercule was woefully embarrassed but said softly: *"J'eusse aimé vivre auprès d'une jeune géante, comme aux pieds d'une reine un chat voluptueux."*

"This is unexpected," said de Vienne pleasantly albeit surprised to see Hercule.

"I was asked to retrieve an item from Hook," said Hercule.

"Mister Hooke?"

"My apologies," replied Hercule. "It is from the city of Hook I wish to go."

"Oh," replied de Vienne.

La Grise asked Elfriede if she could take him because her steed was much stronger. She agreed.

Hercule protested weakly.

"Yes," said Hooke; "An acceleration. The Modern Era—la Belle Époque—actually began in these years preceding occurred during the 5th century and 1800s: thirteen centuries. All are set in a thirteen-year fin de siècle of la Belle Époque in this year 1913."

Javelle nodded.

"Cher Milot l'Encyclopédiste," said Hooke: "When did you deduce we are set in fin de siècle?"

"It has been several years I suspected but it was deduced in Avril in the early morning on that day His Lordship met with me in Saint-Étienne."

"Secrecy encased," said Javelle smiling.

"Sir?" asked Milot.

"Clockworks," replied Javelle.

"It was in the third decade of the First Industrial Revolution," began Hooke, "that sense of Fée and things imbued with Fée was wane begun. I shall digress from further in History.

"All of devils and demons were influenced or purloined from d'Abano's *Heptameron*."

"Perhaps, we are fortunate d'Abano moved to Paris in the auspicious year of 1300 and not, say—" said Milot hesitantly, "1299."

Hooke and Javelle laughed.

"He jests!" Hooke announced.

"Levity appears," said Javelle.

Milot meekly smiled as he blushed at receiving such attention.

"I noticed solving your riddle," said Milot, "that dates do have meaningful significance but the years between *and* the dates themselves have - Seemingly - an absolute significance when the number 13 appears.

"It was many years ago when I became curious about the significance of numbers in antediluvian tomes, after trudging with my studies, distinguishing prime numbers appear oftener than Probability accepts."

"And?" said Hooke.

"I have yet to learn that part," replied Milot.

"And to learn what did influence d'Abano in Paris," said Hooke

"I shall," Milot said pleasantly.

✝

Jean-Marie Jules arrived carrying the head of the ghoul Hercule had met in the fields. He had stumbled into the woods of la Grise's acreage as he had done that once before but could not remember how he came to be there even though he remembered being on the greens of her house.

He was escorted by faeries of the Woods where Themis la Grise was waiting; the mouth of the head of the ghoul was gagged.

They were greeted.

"What is consumed by flame
but never shall die
whose plumes are seen
in raven-filled sky?
Answer me this, and you may pass
if you answer me not, Alas!"

Jean-Marie Jules stood silent but the head of the ghoul was shrieking it's reply muffled by the gag.

La Grise nodded. They entered. The head of the ghoul was perplexed.

𝔗𝔥𝔢 𝔖𝔢𝔠𝔯𝔢𝔠𝔶 𝔆𝔞𝔯𝔱𝔬𝔤𝔯𝔞𝔭𝔥𝔢𝔯

Merry Jules, as he was commonly called when traveling in the woods and forests of places where things arcane were to be found, removed the white glove from the hand which carried the head of the ghoul.

The ghoul spied Hercule and scowled.

"That?" asked Hercule.

"A map," said Jules as he handed the glove to Hercule.

Merry Jules placed the head of the ghoul on the lawn and removed the apothecary cabinet from on his back. There were numerous drawers with sigils on paper pasted to each; the drawers held his neatly folded gloves; opera gloves were for his longer travels.

He explained he had different cabinets of gloves for all places in Europe which are not written on maps for reasons practical and secret.

"The gloves are coded. They are for those places where loci are very dark, very dangerous and very secret."

He offered a short soliloquy of avenues and paths of things in secrecy.

Hercule had studied the map on the glove while Jules spoke. He walked slowly in a slight easy way as he read the map. He peered at the clouds. He went South several paces. He viewed the horizon beyond the trees. He stopped. He thought and nodded his head as he was counting paces he had taken from the High Road.

All were silent watching.

Hercule shrugged. He went to Jules offering him his glove, saying: "If you went lee of the stele past the blackthorn hedge by thirty paces, it is the arch of the allée leading." He pointed to the meadow which was the entrance of the green. "There." Merry Jules stared at his map. Hercule pointed at the helical mark representing the stele on the map.

"You are welcome to meandering visit with a Guide touristique as you did before," said la Grise.

He thanked her absently as he stared at Hercule who went wandering off. He spoke with his guide about inspecting the oppidum foundation of her house; he was staring at his map as they went.

†

"Ritualistic conjurations performed in the chamber of those summoning are master-and-servant," said Hooke. "Conjuring rituals performed in Nature are requests: l'Évocation absolue. Those may be ceremonial; or, offers as simple as placing a Saint-honoré on a decorative plate at the base of an ancient tree."

"I read - in a 1427 manuscript - the Pope's Slippers have magical properties," said Milot.

"They haven't," replied Javelle. "They are slippers; but, to wear slippers, thieved from His Holiness's bed quarters, while he is sleeping, gives that thief admiration due to their daring, for which deities, as well as kings of Hell, duly amused accept and invariably will do that which ever is asked of them.

"Prestige."

"Of course, those asking must still request proper and civil wishes," said Milot.

"Yes," said Javelle.

†

La Grise mounted her Pegasus lepidopteran.

De Vienne stood in épaulement beside her Pegasus gomphidae then seated herself on her's. She assisted Hercule who would sit behind her. "It would be safer for you if you placed your arms around my waist." His arms reached but to her sides; he clutched her tunic. She protested. "This shall'n't be!" She had Hercule step down and she lifted him so as to sit in front of her. "You assuredly would have fallen. You are safer here."

Hercule was aghast, embarrassed, mortified, and serene all in a matter of moments; la Grise who had watched their proceedings was intrigued; and, happy.

They began flying towards Hook.

Hercule softly spoke:

> «Les soleils mouillés
> De ces ciels brouillés
> Pour mon esprit ont les charmes
> Si mystérieux
> De tes traîtres yeux,
>
> Brillant»

†

"The end of the First Industrial Revolution — assuming it did end in 1837 — and the beginning of the Victorian Age in 1837 are of particular significance because that year was fin de siècle—as of one era ending and the beginning of the era which follows—in which Nature as entity would cease.

"Industry was paramount; Nature was become merely servant of Industry.

"Nature debased was tapering.

"Barrett's *The Magus* in 1801 has been considered by some the final work with Goëtia significance albeit slight though it was a compendium — an aide-mémoire — of earlier works.

"It wasn't.

"The *Dictionnaire Infernal* of which there are several editions of the book of which the most famous is the edition of 1863. Fifty years ago! during the era of Victoria. It too was an aide-mémoire of earlier works. It is true de Plancy's book was taken from *Clavicula Salomonis Regis* which was based on works *Heptameron* in 1287, *De Occulta Philosophia libri III* in 1531 and *Magnum Grimorium sive Calendarium Naturale Magicum Perpetuum Profundissimam Rerum Secretissimarum Contemplationem Totiusque Philosophiae Cognitionem Complectens* in 1620; but to have it printed in the Machine Age is remarkable.

"*Dictionnaire Infernal* was the final work."

"Did de Plancy access the library south of Achéron Quay?" asked Javelle.

"I did suppose that," said Hooke; "but, after speaking with Charon, and we two visiting the Library, it remains mystery." Milot would speak but Hooke replied: "We could not, No. All visitors were accountable and above suspicion for an intrigue of that form; and, none were found after sleuthing by Charon and myself. None. Lord nor Lady, Chancellor nor Minister, Man nor Fey."

"Titus?" said Javelle.

"We considered his part but could not find reason," said Hooke. "Titus has Logic and Reason before he begins; No."

"And, yet *Dictionnaire Infernal* is popular," said Milot, "which begs the question of intent by de Plancy in that it appears in format as a work printed in the 18th century."

"*Dictionnaire Infernal* was novelty: devils and demons were thus by 1863 become spirits and ghosts with the attributes of dæmon and demon engaged with benevolence or malignant acts against Humanity."

"Novelty?" said Milot.

"Yes," replied Hooke. "Epilepsy was once considered—as you are aware—demonic or angelic possession of the person afflicted. Masses were delighted at viewing these Citizens-in-Fits — with their expressions of horror, of terror, of movements as if by wire, and words spoken but not of their voice — as they would view side-shows and arcades of atrocities they believed committed by Nature on human carriage until it was published that epilepsy was a condition of the human Psyche. Dementia praecox, too. They were no longer Mystery but Man himself it's cause.

"Science and Church proclaimed Fée were unexisted therefore superstitions. Psychiatrie informed all that Demon and Fée were superstitious hallucinations of the mind. Madhouses and asylums of lunatics as side-shows for paying-tours by Wealth and Bourgeoise diminish.

"Fickle Humanity — once novelties are made banal in explanation; or, made commonplace or superstition — shall engage a new novelty: to wit, Spirit."

"Why are there such few works on Fey?" asked Milot.

"Fey - in the main - are like felines whereas demons are most similar to Man," said Hooke.

"That History you would speak?" asked Milot.

"We shall continue our colloquy later," said Hooke. "The Great Mystery and Vodouisants are of more interest to me." He stood. "However, the later decades will have a small Renaissance of works — Blavatsky, Olcott, Judge from the Theosophical Society; Crowley from the Hermetic Order of the Golden Dawn, and Ordo Templi Orientis; Mathers from the Hermetic Order of the Golden Dawn, and his own Alpha et Omega; and, Jörg Lanz von Liebenfels and his Ordo Novi Templi founded in 1907: his are vile yet they must be read to know the guise la Malveillance absolue has taken and shall have essential influence in years yet come. They are of this Modern Age; they're of Theourgia.

"So, Nature ceases."

Hooke departed.

Milot was composed but fraught with queries and wonder.

"There are none to be sensed," said Javelle; "other than those you have."

Milot would have spoken.

"He rages," replied Javelle.

†

Hélène Eunomia la Jaune and Fanchon Colombe were wandering the town of Provenienţă in Romania with Bassompierre as their Guide touristique.

†

Zoë and Hooke were haphazard wandering in Lyon.

"There are numerous dark Gentlemen. Numerous and different Gentlemen. It could have been Verge or le Maréchal or al-Jinn or l'Invalide; or, Titus or His Lordship; or, me. Those first three you would have known; l'Invalide was cautious though Titus would have appeared as himself.

"The papers have written about several who were seen over the last few years. Hiolle had mentioned over those years other appearances. Javelle had noted appearances on all continents when the Mortality Brigade was involved by summons. Those were homunculus fashioned from men by l'Invalide. Or, by Titus."

"And, I've spoken to you about your erratic behaviour of fleeing my approach," said Zoë

"I had forgotten," began Hooke; "My apologies." Hooke bowed before her. "It was Titus. Idiot Titus! Three years ago, you mentioned you had seen me while you were strolling about Palmyra but, when you approached, I turned with great haste as if I had seen ghosts or remembered a previous engagement at the Century House."

"Yes?"

"I had been delayed by Astolpho so came after you were departed from Palmyra. Yes. A Titus entertainment against the Ministry from which they do not know what has become of their Dupe. L'Invalide may even be conspiring himself with these others. Those who have spoken of seeing Devil were those created by l'Invalide. Titus created the other dark Gentlemen after learning of l'Invalide's resurrection. Titus created those named assassins; those who kept brothel tokens, those who spoke of a mysterious person were created by Titus." He grimly laughed.

"How many of you are there?" said Zoë merrily.

"I haven't evidences nor clues," Hooke cheerfully replied. "Some were found; some are missing. One-hundred? Two-hundred? The Ministry cannot understand nor comprehend all of the malice done by their single Malefic; however, they are pleased nonetheless with their presumed Machiavellian grand design even as it has resolved itself into bedlam."

"For what purpose?"

"L'Invalide for anarchy," replied Hooke absently as he shook his head; "Those homunculi fashioned from men were of Titus's design for amusements against l'Hallow Malveillance, and Ministry."

They continued strolling.

"Please do not speak of this when Astolpho is about," said Hooke as they strolled. Zoë looked at him amused. "Astolpho conspires with Titus. Titus would be displeased knowing that all of his amusements are known; and Astolpho would be embarrassed knowing that his own intrigues were found out."

"As you wish; but you do know all of the plots laid by Titus and those set by Astolpho," said Zoë.

"Astolpho was protecting someone who has become very dear to him since his first sight of her decades past in Persia," said Hooke kindly. "They do know that I do know."

Zoë nodded sweetly.

†

They were flying.

†

Hercule recited:

> Vois sur ces canaux
> Dormir ces vaisseaux
> Dont l'humeur est vagabonde;
> C'est pour assouvir
> Ton moindre désir
> Qu'ils viennent du bout du monde.
> — Les soleils couchants
> Revêtent les champs,
> Les canaux, la ville entière,
> D'hyacinthe et d'or;
> Le monde s'endort
> Dans une chaude lumière.

"What is that you're speaking?" asked de Vienne.

"*L'invitation au voyage.*"

"That's lovely," said de Vienne; "Did you compose it?"

"Another did," replied Hercule; and, said the last lines quietly to himself.

> Là, tout n'est qu'ordre et beauté,
> Luxe, calme et volupté.

†

William Hooke had been requested to accompany a member of the Historical Occult Society for the Preservation of Goëtia as Geoffrey Humphrey Cooper went his rounds seeking spirits who would not keep to their places of sacred residence. They were walking in the woods and hamlets around Holdhurt.

"Quite often one will be seen traversing," said Geoffrey Humphrey Cooper, "when it should be stayed in it's room at the place it died. It is my avowed sacred obligation to return them from whence they came."

"Why do you wait until Dark for prosecuting these apprehensions?"

"They arrive at Dark," said Geoffrey Humphrey Cooper amused at Hooke's ignorance. "How else?"

"They are simpler seeing them in Dark?"

"Naturally," said Cooper.

Hooke viewed him with his left eye closed; he frowned.

"Forgive me," said Cooper, "but I was informed you were knowledgeable in all manner of the Occult of ghastly things."

"I have been told that, Yes?"

"I must say, sir, you are lacking."

"I've been told that, too." Hooke gestured across the path as a spirit entered the woods. "Should we follow?"

"We must regardless of what horrible Fate awaits us!"

"Your lantern?" asked Hooke.

"They cannot see it."

"Ignorance profound," said Hooke as he turned on the lane. "You deign that none were died in battles nor murdered on street or land; but rooms. Rooms. Ghosts existing sôlely in rooms is treacly ignorance." He shook his head. "I shall meet you at the asylum in late morning when shade falls from it's structure."

He left Geoffrey Humphrey Cooper annoyed standing with his lantern shining brightly in the Dark as auræ gaily sent his hat flying ever higher until it was gone.

†

Dilys d'Euphrosyne la Cramoisie was walking hand-in-hand with Edmond le Silencieux and Pierre le Courageux, as they had christened themselves, on the lanes of Proveniență.

They were pleased.

†

Hooke was standing on the pavement beside the abandoned asylum set in the woods at Holdhurt when Geoffrey Humphrey Cooper arrived in a contemptuous fit.

"Come," said Hooke as he went to the gate of the asylum and stood in the shade of it, leaning against the wall. He gestured Cooper to stand in the shadows.

"You say spirits and ghosts are best seen in the Dark because your lantern cannot be spied in Dark by them. That ghosts and geists are bound to a single locus from which they may not be removed by Will or Fate. That geists and ghouls seen wandering are lost for which your services must engage returning them to their rightful sacred locus. That ghosts and geists, spirits and ghouls are seen at Night because it is only in the Dark when they wander sojourning."

"Yes," replied Cooper.

"Thy ineptitude's remarkable," said Hooke. "They do wander when visiting during Sky-lit hours as they did when residing in this realm." Hooke pointed with his forefinger at a couple arm-in-arm faintly seen as they did exit in the shadow of the asylum. "They are Spirit. Though, they are oft auræ in blustering hours."

"Heavenly Saints!" Cooper shrieked as they passed by him.

The gentleman shook his head; the gentlewoman amused did laugh.

"They can be seen in the shadows but become vague forms when beneath skylight," said Hooke.

The Headmistress was leading a column of school children on their Tuesday outing from the asylum. Hooke tipped his hat as she passed; but Cooper, who had once thought lit days were safe passage from spirits, fled screaming.

The school children giggling were hushed by their mistress as they went up the lane.

Hooke took his entrance into the asylum.

✝

Thirteen malebranches in the Marshwood Forest were standing a small distance from the large barrow while several of Mister Tetch's Flying Squad brutes were idly nearby conversing.

One of the malebranches approached them.

"What are they doing?" it asked.

A squad member shook his head and shrugged. "It's best not asking that," he replied. "They tend towards upsettednesses over these things. Most unpleasant."

The malebranches nodded forlornly.

"I only asks since it's over an hour they're at it."

"Hour's normal. It's the ones which take longer you need worry about," said Bill. The others agreed with shudders and breathy whistles. "We'll see."

They waited.

They heard le Maréchal's laughter growing louder from the barrow.

"He's laughing," said the same malebranche, frightened.

"He's a Happy Gent," said Bill.

"Excepting when he ain't," said Oleg, "he gets displeased."

"Displeased's good," offered Bill as he nodded to Oleg.

The squad laughed to the dismay of the malebranches.

Le Maréchal did exit from the barrow laughing still as Merle followed after.

"Who would like to explain this?" asked le Maréchal; and, when none replied, he nodded to Bill who walked over to the malebranches and gestured with the index finger of his right hand at the one who had spoken. "Name?"

"Theodosius Hallow," answered the malebranche as he strode paces towards Bill and stood before him.

"Well, Theodosius Hallow," said le Maréchal: "Please begin."

Merle was softly laughing.

"Sir?" asked le Maréchal.

"An appropriately vindictive name," said Merle; "Flavius Theodosius Augustus condemned all such religious peoples and aspects of impious divinity that were not of his beliefs and so all such things were extinguished."

"My father chosed it," said Theodosius Hallow.

"Well chosen," Merle replied; "Please."

Theodosius Hallow explained at length how they learned of haruspicina years ago but the Greeks were the modern parishioners who influenced them. They found exta under Etrusca Disciplina to be particular in foretelling; they began exclusive use of this procedure since the beginning hours of Frederick-Kings, as haruspices. It was then they began hearing rumours of a superior vessel they could use. He concluded, saying: "So we did."

"How often have you engaged this?" asked Merle.

"We heard tells was when we'd come," replied Theodosius Hallow: "Wars and kings and strife."

"Vesuvius," said one of the other malebranche.

"Right! Always volcanoes we come," said Theodosius Hallow.

"Godly flatulences!" said another.

Le Maréchal and Merle slowly simultaneously turned their heads to the fellow, puzzled.

"Meteor streams," offered Bill.

"This is your first voyage here," said Merle as he gestured to the barrow.

"It has taken us very long to find this place like this," said Theodosius Hallow. "A gent with gloves helped."

"There are few like this," said Merle. "These arrangements which seemingly are recent – perhaps, 1600s – were likely fashioned by Tyrrhenians from those originally documented by Gaius Suetonius Tranquillus. The labyrinth, tools, drawings, tomes of interpretation, all these things are exceptional. Those older specimens are commonplace as one could see from viewing mummified corpses and bones."

"They were here. Abandoned we guessed ages."

"It is now as once it was originally done," said Merle as he turned his head to Tetch; "Meticulous reconstruction from abandonment in 1850s." He continued. "Those corpses decomposing have been collected over twenty nine full Moons." They nodded. He faced le Maréchal. "They are using common methods of Anthropomancy."

"Humans choosed animals but, as we've mostly been told by them, *they* are the superiorest beings. Superiors are better accurate telling. We've come here since those we marshal haven't any entrails."

"La Supériorité humaine," laughed Merle but continuing said with a subdued terrible menace of tone: "A single flaw." He looked at the malebranches. "Those were taken by opportunity. Those who speak of their superiority are not amoungst them: common folk are ill-informed; children are not yet old enough; elderly infirmed are yet too old. Please cease their abduction."

They nodded slightly with wide eyes of fearfulness.

"Statesmen speak highly of themselves," said Merle conversationally; "Nobility, too. There are other sorts which may be of interest for some. They shall suffice."

"What should be done?" asked le Maréchal. "I didn't see fit to punish them for the deaths since they believed the rumours but they will be punished for sneaking. They were on leave."

"We not sent in shackles with Prometheus?"

"No," replied Merle. He turned to face le Maréchal. "It's temporarily Sisyphus-like, is it not?" Le Maréchal nodded. "It is not for these divinations but for being sneaking caught."

Le Maréchal laughed.

"Bill! You and the lads take them," le Maréchal said; "They can spit-shine scrub the tiles of Augean Stables after that other lot's finished spooning them. They haven't been cleansed these fifty years."

A few groaned.

"You'd rather take spoons with deserters breakfasting with them there!" bellowed Bill.

"Brushes're good!" they loudly rejoined.

"Off ye go."

"A final word," said Merle. They paused. "You are viewing individual incidents and events that may occur by selecting single objects when using this divination practice but, if you take all previous samples and view all, including the latest, things become more accurately seen.

"It is the same with History. The more one knows of the Past, the more one knows what lurking shall then thence come."

Le Maréchal and Merle departed.

†

They arrived.

†

"Who was that?"

"Majesty," said Bill.

The malebranches stood wide-eyed silent as the Flying Squad began walking.

"He's a scary Gent."

"Le Maréchal d'Empire's a *scary* gent," replied Bill nonchalantly. "He's scariest."

"Mister Hooke?" asked Oleg.

"Him. My wager's he's scariest scarier scary of them all," said Bill. "Heigh-ho."

†

It was a large lawn of the Palladian residence by design of Inigo Jones set amidst landscape and gardens by André Le Nôtre. An airship with a carriage-car was anchored on the lawn.

Hercule dismounted.

"Isn't that dangerous?" said Hercule.

"No," replied la Grise gaily: "They believe those so voyaging are great winged demons."

He thought. "I cannot recall ever seeing great winged demons with butterfly or dragonfly wings. They've pointy wings. Don't they?"

"Always pointy wings," said la Grise; "but we should not discourage their imaginations, should we."

Hercule shook his head.

"Did you enjoy your passage-flight?" asked la Grise.

Hercule nodded as he slightly blushed.

"Take thee well," said la Grise as they ascended in their flight to Weychester.

Hercule watched as they—Elfriede Marie-Thérèse de Vienne and Themis la Grise—did fly away until they were not seen.

Hercule stared at the house. He began walking. He recited as he staggered on his way on the gravel lane to the house,

> Du temps que la Nature en sa verve puissante
> Concevait chaque jour des enfants monstrueux,
> J'eusse aimé vivre auprès d'une jeune géante,
> Comme aux pieds d'une reine un chat voluptueux.

Hercule was marvelled at the residence for it had doorways and windows but not door nor glass. Two sylphs were standing on the steps. They led Hercule inside.

> J'eusse aimé voir son corps fleurir avec son âme
> Et grandir librement dans ses terribles jeux,

Deviner si son cœur couve une sombre flume

Aux humides brouillards qui nagent dans ses yeux,

They walked through the halls. Hercule was marvelled at the residence as they went for it had not roof nor skylight glass.

Parcourir à loisir ses magnifiques formes,

Ramper sur le versant de ses genoux énormes,

Et parfois en été, quand les soleils malsains,

He concluded his last stanza as he entered where Zoë stood in the main room waiting for him.

Lasse, la font s'étendre à travers la campagne,

dormir nonchalamment à l'ombre de ses seins,

comme un hameau paisible au pied d'une montagne.

"You recite Baudelaire," said Zoë.

"My thoughts are flummoxed," said Hercule as he stood before her.

"Blueberries in neige de lait we have if you would care to join me," said Zoë as she gestured to the couch by Atelier Bing. They sat; they were brought bowl and spoon and serviette; and, they were served their blueberries.

"I was informed you are fond of this," said Zoë.

"It is my favorite since childhood though I seldom sup it," said Hercule. He ate absently.

"Are you well, Sir?"

"I am lost." He sighed prodigiously. "My Life's forfeit."

Zoë smiled.

"I have seen her from afar," began Hercule: "I have seen her before accompanying others like yourself. Her sapphire eyes. Her opalescent skin. She appeared as Régence and Art Nouveau." He paused with his spoon he idly held staring at it for several minutes thinking. "She was elegance of her person that my congenial thoughts of her were made. Very amiable was she. She's pretty. We never spoke. We never acknowledged." He sighed. "We spoke. She remains as Venus luciferous. Moreso."

"Does thy Venus luciferous know of these affections?"

"I dare not," said Hercule. "My Life is forfeit because I cannot speak in her company. Her presence. Properly speak."

"What shall thee do when she comes to be speaking in thine company only to speak with thee?"

"Wonders and marvells never do cease, will they?"

"No," said Zoë as she gently shook her head, "nor endearments absolute."

Hercule sat quietly as he held his bowl of blueberries and stared at the late afternoon sky. "Her eyes are like that. When she is happy and laughs her eyes are like that but light."

They sat quietly. Zoë finished her blueberries; Hercule held his bowl on his knees as he watched the Skylands become evening.

"Are you always happy?" said Hercule with serious tone.

"No," Zoë sadly replied.

"Are you ever angry?"

"No," Zoë replied with a reflective smile.

Hercule nodded. His eyebrows pursed and forehead wrinkled. Hercule stood. "I should go," said he.

She gave him a small decoratively wrapped box with a note attached to the ribbons on which was printed,

Do not open until then

"My coach shall take you safely to Dover. This is your passage ticket," she said as she placed it in his jacket's side pocket. "There will be a coach waiting for you at Le Havre; it will take you where ever you would wish to be."

"Lyon."

"Then it shall take you to Paris for the train to Lyon. You'll be met at the gare."

"Her safety once I have gone?" asked Hercule as he stood.

Zoë introduced Mary la Toute-Douée the Red Witch as she wandered into the room.

"I remember her from the Salon," said Hercule as he scrutinized Mary. "No others?"

Mary la Toute-Douée smiled as she took the newspaper she had left behind and exited flouncing from the room.

"Mademoiselle de Vienne accompanies me most often in these days of change," said Zoë smiling.

Hercule blushed.

"Secrecy encased," said Zoë earnestly.

He bowed low enough for the tip of his beard to touch the carpet. He stood and turned but turned abruptly to face her; and, he smiled.

He abruptly turned and went.

†

They were continued strolling along the sea-side cliffs of Santa Monica Hooke preferred as they watched the Ocean of Dark from the Palisades.

"You see me as light."

"Yes."

"Light?"

"I've told you that before."

"The light from dead stars cannot reach the Palisades but mine does?"

"Full Moon," replied Hooke as he bent his arm at the elbow pointing skywards with his forefinger. "Thy phénomènes magiques."

She would be angry, but laughter caught her unawares.

"Shall we?"

"Yes."

"It is always enthralling how thoughts from long ago Past return quite unexpectedly," said la Grise. "I remember my first rendez-vous; it was terrifyingly wondrous." She smiled. "I remember my formal introduction with you when nineteen. Of course, I had heard rumours of your visits with Father in his library but never saw you enter our house. Or, depart from it. Very mysterious."

"If I may," said Hooke interrupting her: "I preferred entrance and exeunts from your Mother's garden's acres which were remarkable by any standard set by Nature."

"They remain so," she replied nostalgically. She laughed. "How very unmysterious."

"Please," said Hooke smiling.

"I had seen *him* before but never you since he always strolled up the drive to the door.

"It was that one Night, when he had come, and I passed my Father's library, when I heard your voice. That hadn't happened before: the two of you together speaking with my Father. Most strange. The two of you were so seldom seen together. I sensed nothing. I listened as I would often do which appears that all of you knew I did.

"Then no one was speaking. I listened closer and was horrifyingly startled by a knock on the door from *inside* of the library.

"I opened it; and, it was you!

"He was gone; you stood there; and, my Father sat at his desk: he giggled. He only did that when he was in high spirits which was exceedingly rare." She thought. "He's done so more since then."

She sighed.

"You asked me inside. I tried my best nineteen years old and well-practiced womanly elegance on entering. I was terrified.

"We three spoke. I was astounded as I sat in that chair knowing that, if I stood, I would fall collapsing and my lack of elegance would be exposed. All astonishment it was. You spoke not slightingly; you spoke not dismissively. You were generous with your replies to things my Father had earlier refused to explain. Until that Night. He then after would tell me what I *wanted* to know. He had before told me what he *needed* me to know."

"Lady Constance was appalled," said Hooke, "I was informed by your Father many years after."

She paused smiling and so reminisced at Hooke.

"You thanked me. You shook hands with my Father and were gone out through the library door and went strolling down the allée into Night.

"All constancy changed that Night. I changed!

"My Father came and sat on the arm of the chair.

"We spoke. I remember nothing of what he said except for a single line,

'The most revered are bound by both the infinite and the finite—Nature and Chaos—where their supreme strength is shown in the absolute gravity of Praesidium; and, levity.'

"He told me I should thank you one day for it was your suggestion, agreed by them, I be engaged with learning all that was to come by me. He returned to his desk and dismissed me with grandiose waves of his hand all the while humming happily to himself.

"I went into the gardens which I had seldom and lesser and less done as I grew older; and, wandered for hours."

†

They stood at l'Obélisque du phare.

†

"I've never thanked you."

"On many occasions you did by thine acts and deed," replied Hooke; "and, with thy laughter.

"The poignancy of remembering shared memories befell me and there—from those ancient Souvenirs by emanation—stood before me Vénus blanche.

"Those Souvenirs of Mysterium Magnum—Orbis infernum, Orbis terrae, Orbis limbus—staged since Chronos engaged by All: la Luminance sublime, les Ténèbres pâle; les Lumières pâle, les Obscurités pâle, Spirit-immortalis and Ghost-spirit and Spirit-objet, and Spirit of Existence; Noblesse d'Existentia, Noblesse du Pâle, Noblesse de l'Illumination, Noblesse des Ombres, Noblesse de l'Obscurité; and, all for those in Essentiae:—

"but 'tis e'er thee."

†

Hieronymus Virge le Maître was seated with Zoë.

He had made his farewells with her for he and Charon were going visiting those sacred places of centuries before Antiquity as well as those arcades newly established since they each last did visit.

"Charon wishes to visit Bucarest," said Virge. "I shall meet my daughter before we—myself and Charon—depart."

"Our voyages part for but nineteen years," said Zoë; "A game of cheating Chance when we again are in company?"

"Assuredly."

†

Caroline d'Eirene, Madame Gallardo, Mary la Toute-Douée and Dame Hinojosa were wandering les Arcades latérales during the third Exposition universelle de Paris on the Champ-de-Mars.

They were dressed in the fashion of 1878: Caroline d'Eirene in variant shades of orange; Mary la Toute-Douée in variant shades of red; Madame Gallardo in Indigo blue; and, Dame Hinojosa in Cardinal red.

"Why are Hooke and Themis not attending?" asked Dame Hinojosa.

"They are taking an amusement they have not had for a wearying length of years," replied Caroline d'Eirene.

"Al-Jinn?" asked Madame Gallardo.

"He accompanies them," replied Caroline d'Eirene. "I was told it was his suggestion."

"I would like to see how they've damaged Francisco's fresco before we leave," said Mary la Toute-Douée.

"It is a travesty," rejoined Dame Hinojosa.

"I know; but I would still like to see it," said Mary la Toute-Douée.

They agreed they would view the fresco before returning to meet with all of the others.

†

"Titus sought and found that shade of l'Hallow Malveillance. It had been nearly drowned during the Horse-races of the Steles. They argued. Titus fought him.

"It was Titus's act which caused him to be found incoherently Mad and sent to Saint-Lazare of Reason. It was when he viewed Fanny's scrawls of Extase he remembered. Titus was aware it had been resurrected in Saint-Lazare but his boredom was sufficient to no longer concern himself: l'Invalide was spoilt.

"L'Invalide was he who seduced the Lord-Chancellor. It was in that hour when Titus began his intrigue. The Messenger came to retrieve his half-self once it became aware of it's resurrection in Saint-Lazare so that they could cause Anarchy in all of the realms in Nature thus fulfilling the Ministry's fear of Pandæmonium unknowing it would be for all realms, all sphæres and in all loci under Chaos.

"Titus, l'Éminence, l'Émissaire, d'Aquitaine all conspired; d'Aquitaine la Dupe believed himself exalted, inveigled by those conspirators plotting 'gainst all.

"There is an irony. L'Éminence, l'Émissaire and d'Aquitaine la Dupe believed they would cause the fall of Humanity. They did not perceive Humanity had begun it's fall needing not assistance with Dégénérescence.

"The Messenger in true shape confronted Lord-Chancellor after d'Aquitaine's plots were ended which caused Lord-Chancellor's fear and terror.

"L'Éminence knew of that Messenger's fall. He was panicked. That reason was his courtship of you." He looked at de Vienne. "All purpose was gone. Vengeance. Revenge."

"Hercule," whispered de Vienne.

"Hercule knew he would lose his duel. That concerned him not. It was an act of Honour he must do."

✝

Themis la Grise and Hieronymus Virge were standing on Machapuchare. They had been speaking until Night was begun descending from the sky; and, they would depart.

"Your Mother did not wish to know what was waiting," replied Virge; "I cannot myself see what waits."

"Balance exists for all things. I have told you this. For every joyful moment, there tragedy follows; for every tragic moment, there joy follows. Immediately or much later but they always appear. *Always*. It is these small mysteries that, after having been, are understood as balance. Some lives begin in Tragedy; others, Happiness. Those who find Contentment unwavering are those who begin with each in equal measure, as you did.

"You have seen him since seven years. He soothed your dismaying anger when you were seventeen; but you began to know him in your nineteenth year of age. It was in 1809 that you parted which after has been one century and four years in which he wonders about you each day." He laughed gently. "When you are twain, he wonders still. He will not forget you; he shall always be with you.

"You saw how he thinks of you when you were standing on the Palisades. It is not light traveling from a long dead star but light from a lamp."

"What becomes of that lamp if I should cease?"

"The light he sees shining would still shine and he will follow it to be with you. He's a very clever fellow." She sighed. "Marvells and wonders have been everlasting thine."

"I miss him as he turns and goes away from me."

"As he does you." He smiled. "The trysts you have? Their length?"

"I don't know." She smiled as she shook her head. "He will depart and no lengths of hours are remembered; I'll be told it was weeks and days but I'll remember it as months. We have done things in a few months that could only have happened over four Seasons."

"It too is how he remembers them and you," said Virge. "Nineteen years remain until Themis la Juste returns from le Conseil des Treize to tend to her marvells and wonders and grace."

"No," she replied as she smiled at him: "Themis la Fey shall be she who appears."

"You're a very clever fellow, too," said Virge, "aren't you." He kissed her on her head. He laughed. "Your mother and her sisters will be made joyously happy."

"My aunt Constance?" asked la Grise in fine humour.

"My sister!" said Virge with gaiety.

They embraced.

✝

Hooke and Themis la Grise were strolling on the route de la Grande Chartreuse entrée du désert in Dauphiné. Hieronymus-Baleberithe-Seere ad-Din al-Jinn in his full height was holding a large umbrella which covered them with an umbrage suitable for their performance. They were reciting with operatic gestures *La grande danse Macabre des Hommes et des Femmes*, from the printing of 1641, for amusement. Hooke was in recital of the characters les Hommes et les Femmes; Themis, La Mort.

Al-Jinn was the delighted audience taunting and cat-calling characters of dubious worth.

✝

"It was a lovely funeral party," said Zoë; "It was in Brighthaven met at the Jenny Hanvers. Regulars and guests of the bride and groom were all very boisterous with happiness, merry and mirth.

"It lasted until Moon was setting.

"Every and all went to the shingle shore making fond farewells watching as the bride led the groom by his hand beyond the surf where other nereides were waiting.

"It was reported he drowned happily ever after."

†

William Hooke and Themis la Grise with her wards were wandering in the woods of Barrowcross for la Grise had wished Hooke to show them an object on a subject of which they had been musing.

Les Mademoiselles—Marcelle, Félix Trique, Fille d'Achéron and Gwendoline—were straggling far behind with Elfriede de Vienne who had been requested by Zoë to accompany them offering replies to their curiosity.

They walked on the road to a basalt water-marked obelisk encrusted with the remains of barnacles which ceased at the ten-foot height; and, from that place, they then went northernly in the woods of Barrowcross.

Hooke was explaining of an event in the last year he was walking northwards on Spring Street in Los Angeles. He was approaching the barber shop he preferred. The barber pole changed to light: flame-like light and particles of light were inside the large glass tube, floating. He stood and watched it for a few moments until it vanished.

"Were there others, Sir?" said la Grise.

"I was strolling along the Palisades in 1895. A column of light from the surface raised hidden by storm clouds suspended as proscenium arch appeared in the far distance on the ocean." He paused. "I stood remaining still until it had slowly and slower disappeared for the vagues of Night had fallen.

"This Fevrier, I was standing in the library candle-lit seeking *Ethica, ordine geometrico demonstrata*—seemingly having misplaced it—when the room was illumed but as quickly as it was, the illumination flew away into the Woods casting shadows of light through the trees. It waited. And—ere 'twas gone—erupted igniting blindly all of that which one could see.

"There have been other occurrences but those I remember dearly."

"How do you know?"

"I knew," said Hooke. "A voice unspoken was heard. My recognition of that light itself." He smiled. "My senses."

✝

They had come to the large long hill where they were asked to wait. They waited.

✝

"Le Gardien de l'Obscurité," said la Grise.

"The Dark Warden," said Hooke.

It appeared from the woods. It was followed by numerous Punchinellos and Joans amoungst other manifestations of the characters from Commedia dell'arte: all were of diminutive stature.

It stood nine feet tall. It's head was a skull from a stallion in the lineage of Pegasus; it was hooded clothed in black shrouds with a long train. It had no arms nor hands; it's legs and feet were shrouded by cloth.

It spoke. Hooke replied at length with a respectful tone as he gestured toward les Mademoiselles. It nodded slowly. It spoke to la Grise in a kinder tone. La Grise smiled; and, she bowed from her waist, eyes cat-like closing. It nodded.

It peered long at the five mademoiselles each in turn: it would bend towards the one it did study and tilt it's head slightly; then, stand erect and move to the next. They could not see it's eyes but they knew they were examined by the darkness where it's eyes had been. They knew it was not a ghost but a creature of greatness and foreboding.

It spoke to Hooke who nodded and replied speaking as they began entrance into the woods of Barrowcross led by the Dark Warden.

†

"The Woman in Orange wishes her regards and that to thee all are well," said la Grise to the imp-goblins before entering. They bowed low and stood in that pose until she had entered and was gone.

The imp-goblins did remain standing at the Crypt.

†

They walked on an unseen path through undergrowth and trees of Antiquity.

†

"Wait!" cried Marcelle after they had walked several miles. "These woods!"

Les Mademoiselles stood surprised; they peered about them. The Dark Warden, la Grise and Hooke paused: Hooke and la Grise turned.

"These woods are not from whence we've come, are they?" said la Grise. "These woods are of the ancient forest from Albion which remains unfound because it was withdrawn from notice to all Humanity and Fey unless given passage."

The Dark Warden spoke; and, Hooke replied: "She truly is."

"What if we were not given passage?" asked de Vienne confused.

"We would have taken a pleasant journey," replied la Grise, "on the countryside with it's grasslands and heaths and vales."

The Dark Warden began walking; all followed. They walked for several leagues until the forest path began widening and was become stone beneath the detritus and flotsam of the forest.

†

They were at the staircase at the foot of the hill in the forest. The staircase was stone steps of great width and length but shallow.

"Have you ever thought," said la Grise, "while strolling in a dream that you are strolling in a dream?"

"What?" said Fille.

"Were you conscious of taking entrance into this place?" said la Grise.

"Dream state," said Gwendoline.

"Sleep is the dream state for some; sleepwalking for others. Catatonia," replied Hooke; "But there are other entrances than sleep supposed."

"These steps?" asked Fille.

"You would ascend them?" said la Grise.

"Why would we not?" asked Gwendoline.

"Some steps seemingly leading to nothing are actually an entrance to a different place. There are places favorable and kind; and, places malevolent and vile. There are places truly terrifying which are neither Evil nor Good.

"Fille may find a locus delightfully nostalgic and Elfriede may find that same locus morose whereas another may find that very same place filled with the malevolences of terror."

"That place changes," said Fille.

"No," replied Hooke sternly: "Entrances never change. Places never change for the benefit of visitors; but, the perception by visitors does change."

They stood silently.

"We should go," said Marcelle resolutely.

The Dark Warden stepped and stood on one side of the staircase as they began ascending the steps.

They had reached half-way when Fille ceased and peered at her feet. "Do you feel something?" Les Mademoiselles were then made aware of what they unconsciously felt.

"It's like water running down these stairs," replied de Vienne.

"Sunlight creeping," said Félix.

"Faint wind," said Gwendoline.

"Breathing," said Fille.

"Ocean's Winter salt-spray," said Marcelle. They found her reply very specific and were curious; Hooke spoke before they could ask her.

"The stairs have been fashioned by Gaels, Gaules, and Romans," said Hooke.

They continued in silence until they had arrived at the second step where Hooke gestured for them to stand.

A large barren clearing of withered grasses and putrid lichen growing on the ruins of a structure in the center of the clearing was their view.

"What was this place?" asked Marcelle as she pointed to the ruins.

"Gaels, Gaules, and Romans set differing structures during ages. The original structure was unknown to them and so no one remembers what this place originally once was," said Hooke.

"No one?" said Gwendoline with doubting suspicion.

"None who'll tell," replied la Grise.

"We stand at the entrance," continued Hooke, "of a locus which has been noted by others to be favorable and kind; malevolent and vile; and, truly terrifying being neither Evil or Good. There are things sensed from those who laboured here and those who were found deceased in this place."

"It is interesting that 'En transe' when pronounced sounds similar to entrance," said la Grise, "in the English language."

"Verge would be pleased," said Hooke.

"Pardon but I've been curious," asked de Vienne: "That language it speaks?"

"It speaks in Brythonic languages," said Hooke; "but includes Gaulish with words from the vulgar: Sermo Vulgaris and Langues d'oïl."

"Les Enragés?" asked de Vienne.

"They — Mademoiselle de Vienne — are radicals in the Here-After," replied Hooke most amused. "They are not who you mean to say. I'll reply your third query when we are at Sea."

She blushed.

All were curious as to what would occur if they stepped on to the clearing except Marcelle who was agitated. Hooke turned to Marcelle. "They do knowests not what thou dost know to be."

She nodded.

†

"Odd ages ago," began Marcelle and said:

The Divinity Tale

It was Night.

I was walking down a very tall huge staircase of black blocks. They reminded me of the stones in Clermont-Ferrand. It was very odd. My first visit, when I looked back at it, the steps ascended and ended: it led to nothing but the sky.

The back entrance would be shut as it was done on earlier visits so I went around the building until I was at the entrance.

The structure is large and not looking unlike it was made with those black stones, too. It is imposing. Prison-like. But it has many windows and glass doors. That night many of the windows were lighted. The staircase to the entrance was made with those stones, too.

A gentleman was walking on the gravel path to the stairway of the main entrance. He carried a valise.

At the landing, a well-dressed gentleman stood waiting and smiling.

'Good Evening, Monsieur de l'Eure. I am le Directeur. Your luggage will be placed in your room.' He gestured to the orderly. 'Please take monsieur's case to his room.' The orderly nodded; he took the valise and parted.

The bronze plaque at the side of the entrance read,

L'Hôpital de la Divinité Bienveillante

CONSTRUCTED by The Society of Psyché the Eternal
1527

They went inside and I followed them.

Several people looked in my direction, but they could not see me. This happened before. I was frightened those first encounters but it does'n't affect me now.

Once le Directeur looked directly at me. He had not done that before. He looked at me. He tilted his head slightly but smiled unpleasantly until he turned and continued his conversation with a company of porters.

The first floor was offices, nurses room, orderlies room, dining hall though patients were allowed to take their meals in their own rooms, solarium, other places I haven't seen. I've been in many of them before.

The main hall had rows of stands of wax-works heads detached from busts. It felt as if they were watching me. If they saw me. They were strangely repulsive for some reason each visit I went they made me ill.

The second floor has rooms for the servants and rooms for the poor to lie.

'I must remind you and request that you do not visit the third floor. Our more *troublesome* patients keep rooms there,' said le Directeur. 'And, as before, you may see other visitors. Most prefer to remain in their rooms. If their doors are shut, please do not disturb them; they shall not disturb you, when your door is closed.' I had been on that floor, too.

They went to his office and sat. I do not remember ever being inside of it. I may have - it seems likely I would have - but I don't remember. There was a placard on the wall behind his desk which read,

Le Tératologiste psychique secours ceux qui entrent
avec des malformations de Psyché.
—Tabella defixionis

'Your psyche has been damaged. Not severely but it was traumatic. This was caused by a mild psychosis. Exhibiting insipid schizotypal traits inspired by neurasthenia.'

Monsieur de l'Eure nodded.

Le Directeur cheerfully spoke of the modern treatments and the recuperative benefits persons would once again enjoy. Physically and mentally. 'You had been at l'Hôpital for several months before you left us. You may not remember but this will be the third departure and return to your rightful residence. You had your treatments but your insomnia—Sadly—continues.'

'It is not the lack of sleep,' said Monsieur de l'Eure. 'My problem is I cannot dream. It is that I cannot dream because I do not sleep which is causing my psychoses. I may dream but I cannot remember them which is the same as not dreaming, isn't it? I can no longer nap in the afternoon. Not even here.'

'Yes, I understand but you are a special case. We do not allow sleeping during the day because the others would continue sleeping at all hours. We shall see.'

Monsieur de l'Eure continued to explain these things, including his visit to where the stile led him, to le Directeur.

'Yes, you had spoken with others who enticed you to jump from the stile but we must not allow that to happen and so you are to be carefully watched by the staff to prevent you from abandoning your treatments.' Le Directeur talked of the folklore that anyone who crosses the stile will be taken to a physically different place: magical, paradisiacal, serene. 'A few of our guests have described it as thus; but they do not know that dangerous and malevolent things may be waiting for them. It is not safe. There are some things inexplicable and unknown by Nature.

'I have read all reports and files from the doctors; they all agree that unless you rest your episodes will continue, and they will continue until rendered psychotic in catatonia.'

They were discussing the dangerousness of his diminishing lucidity, and those things that would occur should he lose all sanity. Le Directeur explained that these visions were manifestations of his growing psychoses. There was a knock at the door. Le Directeur opened the door: he began discussing the gentleman's sanity to a Head Nurse, and cautioned her; the gentleman overheard.

The nurse entered.

He became psychotic. He began running down the main hall; he wanted to return to the stile. He wanted to return to his world. He wanted these terrors to end. He stopped running. He was crying saying all of the staff, all of the docile patients, all of the poor, all of the violent patients: Everyone had changed! They were all malignantly hideous. He thought their bellowings were laughter.

'Monsieur de l'Eure,' said le Directeur from behind him: 'Please.' Monsieur de l'Eure turned; and, he began screaming.

He collapsed.

'He's catatonic,' one of the nurses said.

Le Directeur gestured. An orderly picked up the body. The others shuffled and stumbled to the théâtre.

'Night-Terrors have bound you,' said le Directeur as he went to the body. 'I did warn you after all.' Orderlies placed him on a gurney. 'You *were* told not to visit the third floor but you did before you left.'

They took him to the operating théâtre which I did not see before. It was filled with patients. They sat attentively.

The théâtre had nine circular aisles for seating observers. It had a row of busts on stands lining the alcove of the highest circle. I remember that.

The third-floor patients were standing around a body lying on the table. It had been flayed and eviscerated seemingly during vivisection because all of the nerves were meticulously displayed, and all organs shown but the person was yet alive. I could only tell if it was a woman or a man because the head was virtuously immaculate.

The head was sawn at the neck.

It was set on an empty column-stand. It was a bust. All those rows of busts in the main hall were the heads of people.

They pushed the body off the table and it fell on to all the other bodies in the bottom of the théâtre. There were many bodies. Rats and carrion birds were feasting but they weren't really birds or rats but things. And, there was something else. Something beneath the bodies. Something horrible. Something that knew I was standing there. It was waiting.

'Night Horrors, Monsieur de l'Eure, are those who wait you. They seldom come downstairs. They were intrigued by you when you visited them before you left.'

The gentleman's body was set on the table.

Then! from the main door, a fine mist began descending down the steps to where I was. It was ocean's Winter salt-spray! I could not smell it but I knew. I simply knew.

I could not tell but it seemed to me the théâtre was growing cold; all were speaking of something coming.

The entity under the bodies was writhing in pain as soon as the mists had settled in that stepwell disturbing all above it. The carrion things abandoned their dining: the rats scurried up screaming and went; the birds cursing flew up in a hurry and flew out through the windows. The mist filled the bottom circle. It began creeping up the other circles.

The doors opened. I heard a voice. 'Marcelle.' I went up the steps. Dream-like.

It was a Gentleman waiting for me. I knew him. I could not see but I knew him. 'Please,' he said as he offered me his hand.

The mists were like ground fog except they weren't because they went creeping up the columns and walls of that place. All things were dissipating as he went silently but with a grim expression; they were aware but terrified and could do nothing but fade.

We walked through the grand hall. I looked back. Le Directeur was standing in the doorway staring at me and smiled hideously before turning and walking back into the mists.

The back doors were missing.

He led me to the gnomon - which is what he called it - the stile - and we began walking upwards but I noticed we were walking up the steps of the hôpital. Docteur Guise was waiting. He was very grey with worry.

'She is safe; she is well,' said the Gentleman I could not remember. 'Mademoiselle.' He departed.

I told Docteur Guise it seemed like a terrible dream.

'It may have been a terrible dream,' said Docteur Guise: 'Do you believe it was so?'

I replied, 'No.'

'This way,' he said as we went inside with his arm around my shoulders.

†

"That was that." Marcelle had concluded her tale.

Les Mademoiselles were astounded by her frightening tale and were full with queries.

"Is this that place you visited?" asked Félix.

"No. It isn't."

"What is a gnomon?" asked de Vienne.

"A gnomon—from the Greek—is one that knows or examines," said Hooke; "And, too—it is the blade on a sundial casting shadow."

"Fascinating," said de Vienne; "By descending the gnomon, you too were a gnomon for those things you saw."

"Did you cast shadows when you were in that place?" asked Félix. Fille, Gwendoline and de Vienne, stunned by her question, stared. Hooke smiled as la Grise titling her head did open her eyes wide smiling.

"I don't know," Marcelle replied to Félix with a thought-filled glance. "Does one cast shadows in those places? Does one in dreams?"

"So," said Félix: "those who do not cast shadows - here - when we see them - are wandering around in a dream - they *are* having."

"So," said Marcelle: "Vampyres haven't shadows which means they *could* be having dreams walking in them with us."

"Ghosts are different, no?" said Félix.

"And spirits," said Marcelle.

Fille, Gwendoline and de Vienne with silent wonder had watched them speaking. All of their other queries about the dark asylum would wait.

"Les Inséparables," whispered la Grise and Hooke did agree as he began leading them down the staircase.

Les Mademoiselles whispered.

"We depart because none wished passage," replied Hooke.

They had come to the plane of the forest. The Gardien had departed; the imp-goblins were gone.

They went returning in a slightly different procession: Hooke and la Grise conversing on newspaper fodder of the coming War followed numerous paces behind Fille, Gwendoline and de Vienne went silenced by their thoughts; and, very much in the rear were Félix and Marcelle walking with arms about waists delighted speaking quietly of passed adventures.

†

They sat in the shoin after their dinner meal where they continued discussing events of the extinguished transpiring hours.

"Passage-ways have entrance," said Hooke in reply: "Doors; windows; mercury-glass, silvered-glass; narrow alleys; and, then there are those Passage-ways whose entrance is not spied but innately sensed; they could be in a barren place or traversing boulevards or bed-sitting room.

"Passage-ways are set in a zone of Passage. That zone may be a glade or hallway or room."

"Or, a road in the woods in Hookland!" exclaimed Fille.

"Or, a road in the woods in Hookland," said Hooke: "Yes."

"You said 'originally' but what was it recently?" asked Fille.

"It was believed to be the Watch House for the Crypt of the Géant."

"What crypt?" said de Vienne.

"That mound at which we waited," replied Hooke.

"Géant tombs?" asked Gwendoline.

"The Old Géant on the way to Coreham," said Hooke. "The Tomb of the Géant in Botassart from which one may ascend steps to a plateau. There be more. It was once said that those who fell during *Le Titanomachie colosse* — Titans and Titanesses — are those entombed by Nature."

"Do you believe it?" asked Gwendoline.

"It does not matter if I believe or no," said Hooke. "It is what you believe that is paramount for understanding all the things you'd wish to know. Do you know how to speak to a Spirit of Locus?"

"You respectfully ask it if you may speak with it," said Gwendoline.

"Then, I suggest, you visit that place of the tomb and respectfully ask it if you may speak with it. If no reply is made, no Géant was ever lain in that place."

"And, if it does reply, I'll know!" said Gwendoline delighted.

"The Gardien?" asked Félix.

"There are others; they have different forms as each is manifested by the lands they walk."

"Folklore," said Gwendoline.

"No," replied la Grise. "The land of the Earth itself was given form by Nature to many things. The Wardens on those continents of Fey where Titans fell were by Nature done."

"They are inexplicable and unknown by Nature," offered de Vienne.

The others stared at her until she blushed deeply embarrassed by her words.

"No," said la Grise kindly. "All things are known by Nature. They are inexplicable by those lacking knowledges of the laws of Nature; but for those who know, and even those who are increasing their learning, the minutiæ of those infinite laws, they will—Eventually—know.

"Thy senses are eidetic remembrances of significant acts in scenes you've experienced.

"Marcelle's ocean's Winter salt-spray was herald in the asylum; it was a warning or herald felt before seen on the Géant's steps. Those things you felt you must decide what significance they hold for you for each of you had sensed things specific to an occurrence, of sorts, in Life.

"All have Sense. Some are affected by significant events like Solstice or cataclysmic fountains erupting on the Sun; or, meteor processions. Others do not require them but may find some significance in their occurrence; and, others still are not affected by Celestial events whether they be so majestic they do not sense them or so Human they are incapable."

"How old were you when you went into the Operating Theatre?" asked Fille.

"Fourteen."

"Only ascension leads to different places?" exclaimed de Vienne.

"If you recall," said Hooke, "Marcelle was descending down the steps of the hôpital before she continued descending that gnomon."

"If I may," said Marcelle; "Why isn't a Southern cardinal point stile on those lawns?"

"There isn't need for you," said Hooke, "even though one does exist which you were not shown."

"It's Hell's!" said Gwendoline.

"No," said Hooke affably. "The Western stile is that which may lead one to an entrance."

"Ma'am, Sir," said Fille as the others nodded encouragingly at them. "We humbly wish to inquire after one salient point of this afternoon."

Marcelle gasped. "I went over that one! Twice!"

"That's why we are in Hookland county!"

"Yes?" said Hooke.

"No," replied la Grise; "The *county* of Hookland is most porous."

"Porous?" mused Gwendoline.

"What did you feel?" asked Fille.

"What happened!" Félix shrieked.

"All of the passions, sentiments and affections over all of the ages that locus has stood," replied Hooke.

"I collected plums!" laughed Marcelle.

"Snow-spray on zephyrs from the lands of Antiquity," said la Grise.

"Mister Hooke?" said Fille timourously, "when did you sense it?"

"All of the ages that locus has been," he replied.

✝

It was the Night of the full Moon.

✝

Hooke was standing in the garden admiring the seascape of sand. All of the others were sleeping.

"May I join you?" came a voice from behind him.

"Of course, Marcelle," he replied as he continued watching the seascapes.

She stood beside him.

"I cannot sleep," said Marcelle. "When this happens at my house, I wander in the hallways looking at those portraits of those directors who came before Docteur Guise."

"What do they tell you?"

Hooke went to the steps and sat; Marcelle sat beside him

"Their spirits appear from their painting joining me as I wander and they speak about my thoughts."

"Do you remember what was done while you spoke your soliloquy of the dark asylum?"

"I was standing. My friends were seated on the third step. You and Mademoiselle Themis stood further steps below."

"Indeed. Do you remember your agitated pacing on that step as you spoke about the Operating Théâtre?"

"No."

"Then you do not remember what occurred when you ceased paces. It was when you related mists."

"No," replied Marcelle with a suspicious but growing apprehension.

"You stepped on to the glade and stared over the forest beneath into a far distance none but you could see as you continued speaking."

Her eyes grew large.

"Nothing happened," said Hooke. "You stepped down from there with the words 'That was that.' They did not notice."

"Then I am one of the monsters."

"No," said Hooke. "Humanity wrote those tomes. All entities to them unknown are monsters."

"I'm different."

"Yes. Very much. You are all each different; but there is another very much different much like you."

"Félix!" she pronounced after deliberative thoughts were made.

"Yes." Hooke smiled. "Her father printed all of those works - perilous works - for her benefit more than anyone else.

"He was taken not because he printed them but because he was printing them for his daughter to read and learn. Knowledge is singularly dangerous when found and used by those who sôlely seek it for learning and protecting Truths. Marcelle and Félix are very dangerous fellows, you know."

"Does she know this?" She laughed but weakly.

"No."

"I should tell her."

"Yes; but not until you and she are older when she then will be able to understand all of the events done and act with absolute resolve sans vengeance. Anger not revenge."

"When?"

"You will know. You and she are safe-watched by those all evils fear. And, others of lesser station watch over thee, too."

"Mademoiselle Themis?"

"And, others still."

"Monseigneur!"

"Did Madame not once accompany you unexpectedly during one of your nocturnal sojourns?" said Hooke.

She smiled as she remembered that adventure in the realm of Morpheus.

"Les Treize are constant in their vigilance of protecting others as well as their own defense against the cruelty of malevolent... things. And, still— there are others."

"You?"

"I am visiting for a while. Causes occurred; events were had. These are forever done but, in this year, all have been loosed because causes were set in motion by fell descendings fallen from their Paradise with malice.

"Still— others watch."

"Are you ever afraid?"

"I know those words—afraid and fear—but I have not experienced them," said Hooke; and, he thought long before continuing his reply. "I remember those scenes as one would observe Humanity passing or as one would witness a three-act play performed on stage; but I do recall it was the unknown which gave them fear. At your age, demons and ghôles and geists are fearsome but one can comprehend them. Things lurking behind closed doors or at the end of dark alleys at Night are terrifying. Comprehensions flee. Does imagination create their horrific form one believes them to be from the terror felt? or, is their form unseen but knowingly imagined that which was created by Nature? 'Tis knowledge lacking.

"Which did you fear with trembling realisation: rats? birds? Le Directeur? or, that entity lurking in the over-filled stepwell of Morbidity?"

"The rats and birds were horrific because of what they looked like." She shuddered. "Le Directeur was something I could comprehend for it's cruelty. That thing lurking beneath the waste of Humanity terrified me."

"It is the unknown which truly terrifies. Knowledge of those things shall—Eventually— remove Fear and the acts which are cause of the unknown. That you could find knowledge from dissolving that state terrifies them."

"Knowledge is Light," said Marcelle.

"No. Light exposes things for them lacking true knowledge and Sense. One need not candles at Night, if one knows with clarity what in Existence lurks."

She sighed heavily. Then, her eyes shown bright.

"Félix's watched, too?"

"Félix too. All les Mademoiselles are under aegis of Les Treize. All are watched."

"May I tell her that."

"Yes, you should relate all what you wish to your conspirators. However, you yourselves must keep safe even if others are watching o'er you. You must learn to accept the assistance of others when it is offered but never sôlely rely on them. There have been those who relied on others to rescue them until that one single instance when others did not come saving them before being were taken."

She nodded.

"Thou art resolved?" came a voice from behind them.

"We're resolved," said Hooke as he watched the pâle lights rise, "and would welcome thee our view of l'Aube ascending."

La Grise sat beside Marcelle who would stand at her entrance but was waved remain seated by la Grise.

"All is well," said la Grise.

They sat silently watching.

They were in the fortification zone of Hook.

La Grise did have brought to her the gentleman — Merry Jules — with maps on gloves who came riding in la Grise's curricle with two white steeds led by Odysseus the black panther.

She asked him to take herself with Marcelle, Félix Trique, Fille d'Achéron, Gwendoline and Elfriede de Vienne to a place of Entrance in a very common well-trafficked road.

Merry Jules selected a glove from his cabinet; and, they began walking. Jules led them in the direction of Coreham on the August Road which was populated by travellers, horse-drawn caravans and carriages; and, an odd occasional motorcar.

They went leagues until he ceased and studied his map. He led them returning back a mile to where the road was dirt with ruin of the Roman agger work barely seen and there was standing an obelisk carved with sigils and glyphs festooned with barnacles. He was annoyed. "They've moved again." He took a small ash-wood box with a glass cover and a wind rose suspended by a gimbal; he consulted his dry mariner's compass. He withdrew a sextant; he consulted. "Stones are moved. Paths are moved. They do that when too many know." He studied. "Entrances never move." He replaced his tools. He bid them remain as he counted aloud seventeen paces from the stone and, with the toe of his slipper, drew a diagonal line in the dirt. He drew a second line perpendicular to the first.

"If one would step over this line in the absolute direction so indicated, one takes entrance."

"We passed this stone but nothing happened," said Marcelle.

"Wrong direction. This road, precisely where we are standing, traverses West by Northwest, South by Southeast," said Jules as he pointed to the lines. "We went walking northwesterly; but this is in fact set facing absolute West. Further, they are not random in that they only appear when the person thinks of that place where this entrance will take them either by thoughts or emotions. The entrance will always be there but sense of it will not always be."

"Are all absolute?"

"No. Mostly. Nearly all are cardinal but all type of rose points are found. Rarely."

"Those rarely used directions have greater significance," offered de Vienne.

"They are Evil places," said Gwendoline.

"Villains wait!" said Fille.

Marcelle and Félix shook their heads.

"No! No! No!" Jules interrupted. He shook his head while scowling. "By my readings and colloquies with others of far greater knowledge than I, all the laws of Nature for these types of events and subsequent effects caused by these events of things are consistent.

"Entrance is found; thought and states of emotions and Sense engage destination on entrance; zone is traversed; Destiny arrived. All set by the laws of Nature. Have you not these things been taught!"

They were silent.

"They have just been so," said la Grise laughing. "Thank you, Mister Jules for their lesson."

"Schoolgirls, schoolboys: all the same," said Merry Jules. "Do you intend I shall ever be given privileges on your estate?"

"No."

"Then, if I am no longer press-gang required," said Merry Jules as he adjusted his dressing-gown, "I should like to continue my breakfast before supper."

La Grise agreed; and, he departed in the curricle which had followed their procession.

"What should we do?" asked la Grise.

They were silent.

†

Mary la Toute-Douée and Elfriede de Vienne were attending an exposition of the deserted Congrès des Royaumes Convergents; their Guide-Conducteur was Merle.

"Le Ministère bienveillant is dissolved," said Merle. "The structure remains as before with a few small changes made in the design of it's interior and in the nature of it's members and processes."

"It isn't so different from my last summons here," said la Toute-Douée.

"Nor my last visit in Avril," said de Vienne. "Where is everyone?"

"Conspirators are dead or imprisoned," said Merle; "and, those who did not wish party in intrigues or plots have taken Holiday. Minister-

Cardinalis Taberd shall be murdered in the coming quarter; Lord Jean d'Aquitaine has secretly fled to his country house in le duché de Guyenne et Gascogne."

La Toute-Douée and de Vienne exchanged smiles.

"It shall ne'er attain to perfection yet it is believed it shall have great operation on the Kingdoms."

†

Zoë and la Grise were at billiards when Marcelle was announced.

"We were expecting you, my dear," said Zoë, "yet not as soon as this."

"Monseigneur Hooke said something to me when he came for me in that asylum. It was about le Directeur. I had not thought of it until recently. So many things are happening to me.

"'He Marcelle knows; Marcelle does he fear' is what he said to me as we went through the great hall," said Marcelle.

"Ah," said Zoë. "A very much different and unexpected reason for your visit." She looked at la Grise; and, nodded.

"He does," said la Grise. "He cannot find you; you alone can find him. One day, you shall find him, and he shall cease by your hand returning to from whence he came. It is you alone who may do this. Only you."

"He knows about me?" said Marcelle.

"It's been foretold so all do know."

Marcelle thanked them; she requested of la Grise that she would like to stay longer in her home and watch the seascapes to which la Grise smiled; and, nodded.

"I shall return by midafternoon next," said la Grise. "I'll send a message presently to le Docteur Guise on your behalf."

"Thank you," said Marcelle as she made a courtesy for each. "My escort waits."

"Escort?" said la Grise after Marcelle had gone.

Zoë led la Grise to the window where la Grise saw ravens and crows and rooks lead Marcelle and following as they went on the allée of the entrance.

"You did not tell her it may be she," said Zoë.

"No," said la Grise as they watched Marcelle walk from the house. "She will learn of that as she ages; but her resolve as she ages shall undo all fears she at present harbours."

"Félix soon shall remove herself," said Zoë, "to the good Docteur's residence where they together shall become most remarkable during their stay and after more so."

"Soothly."

†

They were standing at the observatory that viewed over the metropolis on the volcanic plains as air-ships went meandering in the currents of the black smoke against the prusse-grey sky set with choirs of lightning in disparate regions.

†

"I was very young when my parents were drowned at the sea-side," replied Marcelle; "I survived. All I remember from Winter is the salt-spray."

"What happened?" asked Félix.

"My aunt and uncle cared for me until one afternoon an elderly gent came to their house and spoke with them. He had heard tell about my proficiencies with music and physics. And, *my* Somnambulism. I was twelve. He offered it would benefit them and me if I should take residence in his hôpital which really isn't a hôpital but something else. He explained to me that I was a prodigy so extraordinary others were getting fearful of my abnormal behaviour."

"Teratology," said Félix.

"I learned about that later," said Marcelle.

"How long have you stayed?"

"Seven and one-half years," said Marcelle. "I really don't know what it should be named. All manner of ages make their home there. Hôpital. Conservatoire. Museum. Orphanage. Asylum. Cloister. Hermitage. Palisade. It's all those."

"Sanctuary?"

"Egads, woman!" Marcelle exclaimed. "That's it! It *is* a sanctuary."

"May I visit with you one day?"

"I will ask Docteur Guise immediately after returning. My aunt and uncle visit quite often so you should be able to, too."

"I like Sanctuaries. I miss mine."

†

Zoë was seated in the grand library of Thomas Percivale Kleet, Magnétiseur.

The Magnétiseur diplômé

"No," replied Thomas Percivale Kleet, Magnétiseur: "I have read a few. The titles alone signify my standing. My work is more important than valuable hours spent reading."

"Do those felons you spoke of read these languages?" said Zoë.

"They need not read," said Kleet contemptuously. "The resonances of my library are felt by all. My magnificence! They daren't approach for fear of their undoing by me."

Duke Vapula appeared.

"Ma'am?" said Duke Vapula.

"Duke Vapula," said Zoë.

"My pardon," said Duke Vapula as he bowed. "I was expecting Madame la Fae."

"She was expecting to come but a difficult matter has detained her," said Zoë; "She asked if I could come in her stead."

"My pleasure," said Duke Vapula.

"This Clore Street?" said Zoë. "Occultist Row?"

"I did hear about Henry Marleye-Hearse Honorius the Elder," replied Duke Vapula. "Yes, it does seem that they've gathered themselves about here in this borough: Snavely the Wise née Pericles Waddington-Smythe; Theophrastus Magus née Thomas Jeremy March; Aureolus the Revered née Giles Maybrick is further down by the docks; Basil de Wycombe on Longford Street; Péperkouk the Elder on Wagstaff Terrace; Reginald de Sermisy on Dibben Terrace; Timothy Savoy on Tailford Terrace." He laughed. "You're not intending on visiting all of them."

She shook her head with a delicate grimace.

Thomas Percivale Kleet was stunned silent.

Duke Vapula gestured and was given the book Kleet was holding, *The Spirits of Darkness and Their Manifestations on Earth; or, Ancient and Modern Spiritualism.*

"1886," commented Duke Vapula dryly.

He offered it to Zoë who thanking him accepted it. She began reading.

"*Malleus Maleficarum, Maleficas, & earum hœresim, ut phramea potentissima conterens* was first published in the German city of Speyer in 1487," said Vapula to Zoë as she looked from her reading. He laughed. "1890!"

She continued reading.

"Why does a Magnétiseur collect witchcraft? L'Occultisme or those esoterics so popular these days; Spiritualisme's understandable," said Duke Vapula ambling across the library: he read titles consisting of witchcraft, specifically confessor methods obtaining confession by witches. "Torture, Kleet le Magnétiseur?"

"All things of Spirit must be studied and understood before one becomes informed of nebulous forays into this world," said Kleet le Magnétiseur; "and attending Melancholia and miseries."

"Erotica collectors keep their *120 Jours* in clam-shells with pious names; these gents with pious names," said Duke Vapula as he viewed le Magnétiseur's collection.

"Clam-shells are tell-tale." He selected one with a pious title and opened the case. "*Miss Coote's Confession.*" He took another. "*The Way of a Man with a Maid.*" And, another. "*The Yellow Room.*" He selected others letting the cases fall on the carpeted boards and then the works after viewing covers: "Torture. Flagellation. Flagellation and torture. A fine epochal balance.

"*Les Onze Mille Verges ou les Amours d'un hospodar* and *Le Jardin des supplices* are not finished cut." He offered them to Zoë. "Apollinaire's." She began reading *Les Onze Mille Verges*.

"I'm not surprised. They're not your sort, are they.

"Well kept. Your spiritualist tomes are machine made; your erotica 'tis first printings, first states. Penurious nullity, aren't you."

Zoë laughed. "My pardon." She returned the tome to Duke Vapula who replied, "Is'n't, it."

Duke Vapula took, by one hand, hold of Kleet's collars lifting him from the floor.

"I cannot feel resonances - such a stupid word - since there are none to feel," said Vapula. "All these printed works were done in Machine Age. Blessèd or no, they are only made resonant — Do you feel those resonances of the Moon! Do you feel the resonances of the string section it's use of his Mystic Chord during *Le Poème de l'extase*! Do you feel resonances of Spirits sighing! — by those not printed by machines automatiques and those who keep them in thought. You have'n't either of them."

Thomas Percivale Kleet le Magnétiseur was frightened and confused; he his innocence proclaimed in a bluster of fits.

"I haven't maledicta fit for these conniving Dilettantes sorts," said Vapula to Zoë. She nodded. Vapula summoned a second demon, Mortise.

It was Night.

They approached with their lanterns and torches the Queen of Heaven graveyard in Old Tarling.

†

The graveyard was filled with a century of families. Crosses and headstones and monuments were well tended and cared by the families. The graveyard was visited twice a year by the village in honour of those departed and tending of it's garden of roses.

A fox was seated on a headstone watching them.

The twelve men began toppling monuments and crosses or digging disinterring coffins and bones from the graves.

One was made aware of his being watched and over his shoulder saw a young woman watching them.

"What do you want!" a Purificationist shouted. All of the other thugs paused their merriments and went closer to the young woman seated on the headstone.

"I was asked to meet someone," said Gwendoline. "I am waiting."

"Best leave before something happens to you," said another Purificationist.

"It is wrong," said Gwendoline as she gracefully lept and stood on the ground.

They started.

"What'r'ye gonna do," sneered one.

"Who are you?" asked Gwendoline.

"Resurrectionaries," said another.

"Why do you do this?" asked Gwendoline.

"They don't belong! It ain't their lands they're buried here. Read those." He gestured to the stones.

Gwendoline passed through them and did read.

"Many names. Many countries. They are here buried where they lived. They belong," said Gwendoline.

"Try and stop us?"

"They shall grieve," said Gwendoline.

"Hardly."

"They shall grieve," said Gwendoline.

"They're dead anyway!"

"They shall grieve," said Gwendoline.

"Why should we care!"

"She's wasting our time."

"They shall grieve," said Gwendoline.

An old gentleman was standing beyond the railings of the churchyard; he stood motionless but for his eyes. The trees rustling swayed.

"They tend it. It must be honored. It is their belief," said Gwendoline.

"I don't honour anyone but my own."

"Then you have not beliefs; then you have not honour," said Gwendoline.

"They ain't us."

"They shall grieve," said Gwendoline.

"They're false like them gods they go on about prayering to. We're not!"

"It does not matter who for it is their belief. Their religion matters not to me. Their lives matter not to me. Their bones matter not to me. It is their beliefs which matter to me. They are. Their bodies long ago decayed. Their families will grieve. They have tended these rose bushes to honour their loved ones even after spirits and ghosts have gone. Their families will grieve. The roots of the roses had broken into the wood boxes to succor the bones remaining. Earth accepts those boxes. Their families will grieve. The roses may die. Their families will grieve.

"They shall grieve."

"She's insane!"

"They won't know if you don't tell them when yer dead!"

"Let's just kill her and be done with it. They won't know another body's been included with this lot."

"She'll not be asked if she's dead, won't she," said one of gang as he swung his shovel at her but she delicately stepped aside and, with a wave of her hand, her claws scraped flesh from his face.

He stumbled backwards clutching his face with bloody hands. The men were furious but stunned as six foxes were approaching from the far distance, while they stood silently in rising fears. The men noticed them because their tails were green glowing flames.

The six foxes began running. The six foxes became demons running as they entered the graveyard. They with ferocious vengeance slayed the thugs of the Purification Movement whose blood was seeping into the earth. They cast the pieces of the Purificationists's bodies into the opened graves. They cast bones of the once-buried into the opened graves. They filled the graves and smoothed the soil with their hands; they set aright the crosses and stones.

"Thank you, dear Sisters," said Gwendoline. "I will tend the garden."

The six foxes departed.

Gwendoline gently replaced the rose bushes. She began singing softly in a language of the Ancients. She finished. She knelt on the earth and placed her hands on the blood-soaked soil. Green flames flecked with sparking white light came from her hands; the flames creeping spread over the blood and, when the flames had reached the roses, the bushes exploded heightwards in flame. The grass did grow as a green shroud o'er those earthen tombs.

She removed her hands and stood. The flames burnt but briefly brilliantly more until they receded into the earth. All was as before excepting the roses which glowed green with particles of pale white light until slowly they diminished.

"They will not grieve," said Gwendoline before she turned: "Grandfather."

"We keep watch," said the Elder as the rustling of the trees ceased.

"You are not of they," said Gwendoline.

Themis la Grise arrived. She saw the Elder; and, she smiled.

"Not of them nor of you," said the Elder as he smiled at Gwendoline, "but as one of all who knew."

Gwendoline nodded.

"We thank thee and thine," said the Elder as he nodded to la Grise before he turned and returned into the Night.

"You know him?"

"I know him; he knows me," said la Grise: "Old Wren." She began walking from the churchyard with Gwendoline by her side. "He does not appear often these days. And, then— it is sôlely for something or someone that interests him which seemingly you have done, my dear Gwendoline."

"He seemed different?"

"He should," said la Grise: "He was deceased late in the 18th Century."

Gwendoline and la Grise began walking departing but Gwendoline paused and turned to address the trees.

"They will not grieve."

The trees silently bowed before her.

They departed.

†

Mortise was concluding his recitation: "*An Act of General Oblivion for Treasons and other Offences set forth since 1300.* The Philosophy of Composition. X. Deceit.; Rapes, and carnal Ravishments of Women.; General Offences.; Witchcraft.; Accounts of certain Practitioners and Receivers of Spiritualisme, Occultism, Mesmerism, Esotericism, &c.

"All following deemed treasonous acts are so prosecuted and include the detestable and abominable Vice of Deceit committed by Mankind,

"and also included all Rapes and carnal Ravishments of Women,

"and also included all Ravishments, and all Offences of willful taking away or marrying of any Maid, Widow or Damsel against her will, or without the assent or agreement of her Parents or of such as then had her in custody,

"and also all Offences of aiding comforting procuring or abetting of any such Ravishment willful taking or marrying had committed or done, "and also included all Offences of Invocations, Conjurations, Witchcrafts, Sorceries, Enchantments, Charmes, and all manner of malicious Guile against Innocence, and all Offences of procuring abetting or comforting of the same, and all persons now attainted or convicted of any of the said included Offences.

"Fine print."

Mortise concluded closed his tome; Thomas Percivale Kleet protested.

"'Scuse us," said Vapula as he grabbed and was holding on to an ankle of Kleet turned pate downwards. Vapula bowed as they vanished.

Zoë nodded; and, continued reading.

†

Hooke was attending a conjuration in a Georgian house in Ashcourt on Wagstaff Terrace. He had been requested to observe members of the Historical Occult Society for the Preservation of Goeties in their ritual. He stood in the shadows of the corner.

The Spiritualiste alchimique

The twenty-eight Occult Society members stood in half-circle were wearing masks. The masked Péperkouk the Elder the Spiritualist of Alchemy had conjured a demon of Hell by using his large cheval-glass. They were twenty-nine according to the words of the conjuration.

Gremory Duke of Hell had appeared in the glass. He was clothed as a Plague doctor from Germany.

Péperkouk the Elder protested.

Gremory Duke of Hell removed his hat; he removed his mask: he was Noppera-bō.

Péperkouk the Elder was thus ridiculed: he protested vociferously as the twenty-eight Witnesses were amused and laughing by this appearance from a Duke of Hell.

Gremory stated he was who was requested but had learned this form of appearance from a Noppera-bō, and he had read in the *Dictionnaire* the Alchemist Doctor Péperkouk the Elder wore masks; and, because of that artifice, he would stay the Alchemist's course in mystery.

Péperkouk the Elder protested. He dismissed Gremory Duke of Hell from his intended service.

The glass darkened.

Péperkouk the Elder fumed.

"Dictionnaire?" asked one of the masked Witnesses.

"Dictionnaire," said Hooke.

"He was lowly," said Péperkouk the Elder: "By my knowledge of things arcane and occult, I will summon a King."

He consulted his version of the *Dictionnaire Infernal*.

"Be forewarned," said Hooke.

Péperkouk the Elder scoffed.

†

La Grise and Gwendoline were walking North while la Grise had been speaking tales of Old Wren.

"We are going?" asked Gwendoline. "This place is familiar to me."

"We are in Great Tarling," said la Grise. "We are returning to Hook."

Gwendoline abruptly ceased walking; la Grise paused and turned several paces from her.

"I am confused," said Gwendoline. She thought at length. "You asked me to meet someone in the graveyard and I did walk from Hook to meet someone in the graveyard. It was you who came to meet me."

"No," replied la Grise kindly. "There was another who had asked him to meet with you; and, it was done."

"Grandfather!" said Gwendoline after several moments in contemplation. "I do not understand."

"Old Wren was told of you. He was curious. He asked if he could meet you in a setting of dire circumstance."

"Défi de la valeur!"

"Yes."

"I have never lied."

"No."

"I honour."

"Yes."

"I am faithful."

"Yes."

"Why?"

"How should one judge another?" replied la Grise, "by their words? or, deeds?"

"Deeds!"

"You were mentioned by one you know to be observed by one you did not know until this night. His visit was sôlely for being introduced to you."

"I was approved."

"No! You were not approved," said la Grise admonishing her with a gentle tone. "You were welcomed many years ago. You have not seen malevolence as this before; and, whereas, others who have seen your valeur for all other things you have done were assured by your demeanor and Grace, Monsieur Wren had not. It was for his benefit. He knew of your capabilities and senses of Honour and Justice, but he wished to see them."

"It was he who wished this meeting?"

"The one who first speaks with you in Hook when we meet them will be they who did so wish it."

†

The Alchemist Doctor Péperkouk the Elder summoned Beleth King of Hell.

Beleth's eyes and nose and mouth of face appeared hideously close in the large cheval-glass.

Doctor Péperkouk the Elder was displeased. He went to his *Dictionnaire Infernal* by Jacques Collin de Plancy. He showed the demon the engraving of *Beleth*. "You are not he!"

"I cannot see your face; it is well hidden, Mister Theodore Fould Hypocrite, and you are upset by an engraving yet you see my face whilst shaving!" He laughed. "It was my cousin who sat that portrait."

"My name! It knows my name! I summoned him as Doctor Péperkouk the Elder. I did not say my name!"

Hysterics by all but Hooke ensued.

"I am profoundly inconvenienced by this intrusion," Beleth: "I suggest graciousness on thy part."

"My name! You cannot! I want to view your full form. I demand audience with Beleth the King of Hell."

An arm extended from the looking-glass. The hand grabbed Theodore Fould by the head and pulled him into the glass. Moments later, the body of Theodore Fould was heaved tumbling from the glass on to the floor.

Hooke assisted him standing. He was bruised but not bloody.

"He uses a shaving glass," said Fould.

"That is what one uses when shaving," said Hooke.

"Mister Hooke," said Beleth. "What fools these be."

"Beleth King," said Hooke merry.

"Hookland?" said Beleth; "I have not known you to be in this place many years."

"1816 was my last visit in the county proper," said Hooke; "I've been at la Fae's on many an enchanting evening occasion."

"Mister Fould," said Beleth as he laughed at Hooke's reply: "from John Donne in *Devotions*, 'Ask not for whom the bell tolls; it tolls for thee.'"

"Impossible. He knows not where we are! We are safe."

"Ashcourt, Hookland."

"How?" gasped Fould

"Dictionnaire."

"Dictionnaire?"

The glass darkened.

"Dictionnaire," said Hooke.

The front bell clamorously was rung. It was silent. A metal wrenching followed by a dismal sounding bell rung and a thud on the door.

"Thy bell's deceased," said Hooke.

They heard footsteps in the hallway drawing nearer and near to the chamber until a light tapping on the chamber door was done.

Hooke went to the door as none other could move and opened it.

"We found thy name in a directory of Alchemists," said King Beleth on entering: "A dictionnaire." Hooke and he shook hands. Beleth was followed by two goblins carrying a very large and weighty book between them. Beleth gestured to the table and they set sliding it on to the table standing on their tiptoes. Beleth went to the cheval-glass placing the fingers of his right hand on it's glass.

"Exquisite workmanship. Superior charms. Negligently enchanted," noted Beleth; "Pity."

Hooke approached and beckoned Fould to the book,

Dictionnaire Infernal

ou, une Bibliothèque universelle sur de petits romans, de contes bizarres, d'anecdotes prodigieuses sur l'Humanité, les traits qui les caracterisent, leurs bonnes qualites et leurs infortunes; les êtres, les personnages, les livres, les actes et les causes qui concernent les manifestations et les mendies du trafic avec l'Homme; les divinations, les sciences occultes, les grimoires, les merveilles, les erreurs, les préjugés, les traditions, les contes populaires, les diverses superstitions, et généralement toutes sortes de croyances merveilleuses, surprenantes, craintes, méconnaissances, melancholies, imbécilités, négligences, mystérieuses et surnaturelles leur attribue; leurs amours, et les services qu'ils out pu rendre aux Fae

Beleth selected the page kept by an ornate ribbon and set his finger on a photograph below the typed title:

Doctor Péperkouk the Elder
née Theodore Fould

"Impossible!" said Fould staring at his photographs: full face, left side, and full body each without his mask.

The two goblins hoisted themselves on to the table.

"My compliments on the use of photographs," said Hooke.

"Modern Age," replied Beleth.

Fould the Alchemist read his entry saying every few minutes: "Impossible."

"Odd by Chance, Megan la Fae is having one of her Séances this evening in the Necropolis," said Beleth, "in this very cité of Ashcourt and, as I have not been in this town before, if you would, would you care to join me as guide in a tour of the cité?"

"Of course."

"My hôtel is walking distance from here."

They continued their conversation as they went in the hall and, from the front door, departed for the hôtel.

†

La Grise and Gwendoline arrived at the green lantern-lit where a game of croquet had been set.

Zoë and Hooke were waiting in conversation while Mary la Toute-Douée the Red Witch and Caroline d'Eirene the Orange Witch were standing about practicing with their mallets. Lady Constance watched.

Hooke excused himself and approached Gwendoline and la Grise as they were approaching; Gwendoline and la Grise did pause. Gwendoline was startled as he walked towards them but he passed her and went to Themis who took his arm as they would depart from the green with Lady Constance which caused her distressed confusion as she watched them.

"Do you play?" asked Zoë who had come silently to Gwendoline. Gwendoline turned around surprised in amazements. She turned and stared at la Grise who winked at her before she and Hooke and Lady Constance were gone as Gwendoline stared as they went; and, replied as if to them: "No."

"Come," said Zoë as she took stuporous Gwendoline by the hand; "If Alice could, you too should the game of croquet play."

†

"We shall be obliged to answer any questions you should ask," said the first goblin.

"Impossible," said Fould.

"Conjurations's formalities include introducing yourself. All names spoken are in a dictionnaire, actual and nom de plume. New alchemists are photographed and noted in the directory when first noticed. Then found. Those things," replied the second goblin.

"Impossible."

"Pardon me," said one of the Witnesses; "but how are *they* found?"

The goblins riffed pages. One pointed to a photograph; they consulted whispering. "Very simply, Miss Mortimer. We photograph those in the glass, bottle their fragrance and wandering in an expected location find that person."

Miss Mortimer went silent.

"Bottle?" asked another.

"To speak with one in a glass that other too must use a glass. An équivalence is formed establishing a passage-way betwixt each glass. We use a bellows-apparatus for inhalation of the scent exhaling it in a bottle to be used as authentication."

"If there isn't an *équivalence?*" asked one of the Witnesses.

"*La Belle au bois dormant,*" said the second goblin.

"No. Theren't any glasses in that one." They thought.

"*Schneeweißchen?*"

"Yes."

"I must remember," commented the first goblin. "The vain wicked Queen stares into her mirror but it is only the mirror speaking."

"Impossible."

"Though, if she had not been vainglorious, she may have considered asking her foretelling mirror on the wall if any harm would her befall."

"She would have known about the iron slippers."

"We see, we hear, we smell. Glass mirrors used by Man are made by Man. If Mortal uses one when summoning, there must be a second glass made by Man used by them being summoned. An équivalence. Common sense.

"Further, after being found, an item is selected from the Mortal for future identification."

"Impossible."

"Item?" asked one of the Witnesses.

"Haven't you ever misplaced unwashed delicates? or a stocking? or, a foot folding cloth? or, serviette?"

"Yes."

"A goblin or imp took possession of it. It's safely in a cabinet for any and all who wish to know your scent if they ever should wish to find you. So, as you see, it's not impossible."

"Impossible."

"You have an illustrated work of all who practice arts of the Goeties?" asked a different Witness.

"Yes," replied the first goblin. "You have various works, have you not?" It pointed to the Collin de Plancy *Dictionnaire Infernal.* "We have various works."

"Impossible."

"By using a mirror," said the second goblin: "it remains passage until *each* are darkened: équivalence's broken. If the conjurer, however, concludes the ritual, concludes any ritual, but does not cover the glass, those on the other side of the glass can continually view the chamber in which rituals took place, if they remove the shroud they have used to darken their own glass; not hear nor smell but view. That photograph of you, Miss Mortimer, was taken after a ritual was concluded but Fould l'Alchimiste did not shroud this looking-glass.

"Obsidian mirrors verifiably keep privacy and require no shrouding."

"In point of fact, Fould l'Alchimiste, you have never sought privacy," said the first goblin as it jumped on to the floor.

"Verily!" said the second goblin. "This chamber is most popular evening's viewing when Sunday's Sade's Salons occur."

They retrieved the tome and went departing.

"Good day."

†

Hooke and Themis and Lady Constance were promenading on one of the forsaken lanes of Barrowcross that led to la Grise's estate in the woods when they were come upon John Nottingham-Neville who was standing over the body of a recently deceased raven.

"How do these occur?" John Nottingham-Neville said sadly as they approached, "so far from where they once were before?"

"Perhaps," said Hooke, "it was returning from a pilgrimage made from afar."

Mister Nottingham-Neville pondered and then knowledge of things unknown crept over his countenance. "Possibly."

"If you find a black bird on road or land or path," said la Grise, "take it in your hand before continuing. If any threaten you, show them the bird and say—

I wish this pilgrim from it's journey returning be.

"They will let you pass.

"When you meet the Raven-Lord, say—

I return this to thee what was found by me.

"He will accept it. He shall proclaim safe passage in his name while you for that time take sojourn in Hookland until you depart. Then, express your gratitude; and, he will let you pass."

"And, if I do not make Gratitudes?" asked Nottingham-Neville.

"Familiars may be one who once you knew. The bird shall live by you deceased," said la Grise: "You'll black bird be."

He took and gently wrapped the bird in his handkerchief.

"If I may," said Lady Constance; "John of Nottingham?"

"My father," said Nottingham-Neville. "I was intended to follow family heritage but could not and so include my mother's maiden name on to that of my great-great-great-great grandfather's."

"Your trade?" said Hooke.

"Gardener," Nottingham-Neville replied with a wistful smile.

He went the way they had come on the lane with the raven kept safe in the crook of his arm.

They continued.

"How often it is to be on gallows at rest before knowing one's Fate," said Hooke after.

"Unfortunately," Lady Constance replied.

†

They walked entering la Grise's estate in Barrowcross, Monaglæd. Hooke paused and gestured for them to wait.

All was silent.

He went strolling towards the darkened woods where a darker shape was waiting seated in a gargoyle vulture-pose. It growled; but it was an odd growl which ended with a hiss not unlike that of a serpent. And, there stepped from the shadows a shape the size of a great wolf.

The dark shape ran across the lawn on four legs, lept and attacked Hooke. Hooke and the large black panther each fell and were wrestling on the ground.

Lady Constance was frightfully concerned until she heard two unexpected sounds: laughter and purring. Hooke was laughing; the panther was purring.

"Mister Hooke's cat," said la Grise attempting a somber tone as she led her aunt passed them but it ended with her laughter.

Lady Constance was appalled but less so.

Hooke was seated by the panther which was on it's side as Hooke rubbed it's stomach and chest. Hooke's coat and shirt sleeves were missing from his right arm; he bled slightly.

Hooke stood; but only after the panther was satiated. He introduced with his bloodied hand the panther to Lady Constance; the panther was unimpressed. It turned and faced Hooke and Hooke bent down; and, they touched noses. It wandered off into the woods with the spoils of victory.

"This was definitely not seen," said Lady Constance with unaffected wonder. "Your familiar's name? I did hear."

"Odysseus Aristophanes Diogenes Heraclitus," said Hooke.

"Odysseus is accepted," offered la Grise.

They continued.

"I never!" Lady Constance fumed.

Hooke following after.

†

Zoë was attending a séance in a Georgian house in Coreham.

They had summoned King Paimon for learning secret things but, instead of the king, Queen Dris his consort appeared with several other wives: Madame Barbatos, Marchioness Cimejes, Duchess Eligos, Countess Bifrons, Queen Salix the consort of King Balam, and Duchess Vapula.

The spiritualists as statues sat silent staring.

"Mesdames," said Zoë delighted. "An unexpected joy."

"We were only informed by my husband yestereve," said Duchess Vapula.

"We conspired," said Duchess Eligos.

"The Cortège is a league near-by," said Marchioness Cimejes. "Others are already there, and you should expect more if you do come."

"Shall we remove ourselves there?" asked Queen Dris.

"Let's," said Zoë.

They did.

†

Hieronymus Virge le Maître and Morgause la Fey were arm-in-arm strolling with Megan la Fae and Morgan le Fay on the banks of the Lethe in the far meadows of the valley of Aion.

"Themis la Fey," mused Morgan.

"She was solicited by King Tenebris," said Morgause, "and accepted to be Madame l'Ambassadeur of the Ghôle."

"They've not even ever had an ambassadeur!" exclaimed Morgan. "Ever!"

"How did we not know this?" said Megan.

"Hooke knew," said Virge. "Do you not remember that incident with Titus at Phlegethon House?"

"Themis slightly withered his leg as he fled from her," replied Morgause with a bland tone. "We all saw it."

"We were all concentrating angrily on Titus for what he attempted during festivities of the ball," said Virge; "but it was Hooke alone who had been watching her and perceived her then at seventeen years in age what she could become in later Ages. You read Her Majesty's letter. It was Hooke who petitioned her in her presence."

They sat on the bank of the river.

"I asked him one evening during a visit," continued Virge: "He said she was suddenly shown in fulgent Lumière pâle in the alcove she was standing *before* Titus fled; it was then he turned his attention to her. Titus acted; she coruscated. Titus would flee while she stood sedately with seething anger; and, calmly cursed him. That she could even conceive retribution against Titus was what intrigued him because none had ever before dared. We found her in anguish." Virge laughed. "He said it was because she was attempting all of him to be cursed but lacked the knowledge to do so which accounted for her anguish while we believed Titus caused it."

"That would explain why she was sullenly upset with us for all our coddling," laughed Morgause.

"Yes, it does," said Morgan. She laughed. "All these years!"

"It was he who came last," continued Virge, "the guests all parting before his presence to console her." He paused. "So, we thought."

"What!"

"He took her aside from us so none could see."

"We followed them in our concern for her well-being. Their backs were to us."

"He was giving her that knowledge she lacked," said Virge. "He was adjusting bending spacing her fingers. The right hand higher, the left hand's palm facing outwards held by her thigh. He adjusted her stance. He was whispering in her ear while he did those things. He was telling her words from the ancient languages she would use instead of all these later-day literal translations."

"We could not approach them," said Megan.

"His doing!" Morgause exclaimed.

"He returned to the wall 'gainst he'd been leaning," said Virge; "and, all through it, he kept that same stern expression of his when being in thought the same when he came to her."

"She was *giggling*," said Morgan.

"He showed her how she could wither all of Titus if they by Chance should meet," said Megan. "Of course, she'd be giggling."

"If he taught me this very moment, I'd be giggling," laughed Morgause.

"He did say he sought Titus," said Virge, "and did inform him of his lesson with Themis in the proper method for his decay. After that, Titus employed spies that—To this day—are ever watchful over her. When she was arrived in New York City, Titus went to Africa."

"Why?"

"She's not bound by Gentleman's Agreement," said Virge. "Nor proclamation of any sort since none of les Sorcières were thought worthy of condescension."

Morgause cruelly laughed.

"How he does those things!" said Megan. "He effects an object-lesson for one who wishes to learn by giving them the knowledge they wished for which shall then affect one who will consequently become the object-lesson itself lasting centuries."

"A single simple lesson causes events, delightful or dire, for many who will never know how they were bestowed," said Morgan.

"No, dear sister," replied Virge as he smiled at Megan. "'Tis not Fortune-telling. It is a compréhension: his perceptive abilities to grasp the full meaning of what he has observed and what he already knows becomes that knowledge of how things will come to pass. He that night knew Themis would become like her mother and her aunts."

"And, you!"

Virge laughed; he waved her compliment away.

"It appears greater she's further surpassed us," said Morgan.

"And, still she remains Themis of seventeen years," said Morgause. "He allowed her to understand what we had been waiting to give her."

"We waited too long," said Megan.

"He did not instill in her her courage nor confidence nor any other thing she has of presence and state; nothing," continued Morgause. "It was merely one of practical employment for her intent. He gave her encouragement from that one simple lesson."

"We should thank him."

"That would annoy him no end," said Morgause with a mischievous grin.

"It's agreed. We shall annoy him at first opportunity," said Morgan.

Virge stood. "My dear." He kissed Morgause on the top of her head. "Mesdames." He would go but paused. "He recently said she was christened by King Tenebris, 'Her of the Light of the Dwelling.' So, if you should thank him, you should thank him effusively for his most nurturing manner."

They recoiled in laughter.

He sauntered away, giggling.

†

The black panther was sleeping on the top of the couch where Hooke and Themis were seated.

His wound was bandage-wrapped. He wore a new white shirt with the right sleeve rolled and his waistcoat laundered and pressed, unbuttoned. His trousers were laundered and pressed. His new coat would arrive in the morning.

"My arm was sacrificed which allowed me my other hand to reach his weakness; I tickled him."

"He allows me tending and bathing him," said la Grise.

"Him!" said Lady Constance indignantly pointing her waving finger at Hooke.

"No," said la Grise. "Odysseus allows it."

Lady Constance went to her rooms in a state of high pique.

"She fares well."

"A fine imbroglio you began," replied la Grise. "She has become pitiable. She is contrite."

"Those too shall pass."

✝

Shpresa la Rose — The Pink Witch — and Guillebert Duguillet were seated in the undercroft of the cathédrale in Weychester: he was reading the works she had selected for him to read.

✝

Aglaea d'Olive — The Olive Witch — and Françoise-Aurore Marivaux were in conversation with several of the Guests at l'Hôpital Coulmier.

✝

"Odd ages ago," began Old John Wren and said:

The Fellness Tale

An old woman and an old man lived far from the village in poverty but fed stray cats and they did have their own, a very old and quite plump tortoiseshell named Fetch. They were content with Life. She was a bearded lady of plump and pleasing stature; he was a skeletal gentleman with a top-knot of hair from the crown of his very small head, and bird-faced with large nose and eyes; and, small half-formed jaw. They had toured countries and courts in the side-shows of Marvells. The old woman was cooking supper with an old Fetch rubbing itself on her legs and purring. An Imp appeared at the door after watching the cats being fed; it wanted food. Old Fetch fled. They gave the Imp food. It went away. The old woman was cooking supper with old Fetch rubbing itself on her legs and purring. The Imp was back on the very next day and wanted food but more than they had given. The cat fled. They gave the Imp some food. It went away. The old woman was cooking supper with an old Fetch rubbing itself on her legs and purring. It was back the next day and wanted food but more than the day before. The cat stood and hissed. The old man explained if they gave it more food, they would have none. They gave it the same amount they gave it on the day before. The Imp threw it down furious. 'Misers! Ye more food would have if you didn't give those. Specially.' He pointed at Fetch. 'He is our child since he was a kitten after all these years," said the old man. 'Misers!' The Imp spat at their feet and left. The next day Fetch did not return from it's afternoon wanderings. The old woman began cooking supper when she felt the familiar rubbing on her legs by Fetch except the purring was hissing. It was the Imp wearing the head with the skinned tortoiseshell fur of Fetch. 'I fancied me a fur coat with a head like them folk run in fools at Solstice.' They cleaved to each other began uncontrollably crying and lamenting about their only child dead. 'I want more food than days before.' The Imp lept on the table and took all of the food and left. All of the other cats were dead from bludgeoning, stabbing or poison by the end of the week. It returned still wearing the head and fur of Fetch. It wanted all of the food. 'We have none. You took all we had. We have nothing left to give.' It peered. 'Cape and hat I'll take.' It cut the old woman's skin and took the beard from her face for a cape; it wore it over the cat skin fur coat. It cut the old man's skin and scalped the hair from his head for a hat; it wore it over the cat's head of the coat. It was never seen again.

✝

Old Wren had concluded his tale.

✝

The hooded monk was walking and was come across an old man sitting in the ruins of structure in a circle of burnt trees. Stone steps led to the floor of stone. The old man sat beside a fire with three Dutch ovens stacked in the firebox, wispy smoke rising from the chimney.

"I am waiting. My guest shall be coming soon with stuffs for supper."

"I saw the smoke of your fire." The monk introduced himself as Imago the Hermit Pilgrim.

"An interesting name," said the old man; "I've not had the pleasure of one on a pilgrimage in the county of Hookland before with such a name."

"It is a venerable Moorish name," replied the Pilgrim, "once used by your William Shakespeare."

Imago the Pilgrim offered to tell a tale in exchange for his supper. The old man agreed, saying: "Please begin as I do not wish to keep you."

The Pilgrim sat at a short distance from the old man.

"Odd ages ago," began Imago the Hermit Pilgrim and said:

The Tinker's Tale

Humphrey the Tinker was walking on the lane and he was accosted by a wood sprite barring his way on the lane as he – Humphrey the Tinker – was returning home from a late afternoon visit with the vicar.

'Wither ye go?' asked the wood sprite.

'My supper is waiting so whither I go,' said Humphrey the Tinker.

'All the better,' the sprite replied. 'How far go you?'

'As far as the crow flies I go,' said Humphrey the Tinker.

'All the better,' the sprite replied. 'I am weary and have not eaten for days, and since I am small where you are large, by the Graces, would you let me ride on your back?'

Humphrey the Tinker accepted.

The sprite clutched his hands around Humphrey the Tinker's neck who was caught by the snare of the sprite's lies. No matter how the Tinker fought and clawed at the sprite he could not free himself.

'Run as fast as if the devil de Goule is at your heels.'

Humphrey the Tinker ran three leagues as fast as crows fly when Devil is at their heels. And, there— the old man stood. 'Why did you stop?'

'My wife is crying for she worries the lateness of my return,' said the Tinker.

'Hasten! Hurry! I shall eat her, too.'

He ran three leagues as fast as crows fly when Devil is at their heels. And, there— the old man stood.

'Why have you?'

'My lamentation of swans are crying for they worry the lateness of my return. '

The wood sprite whistled. Two more appeared grabbing the ankles of them before and formed a lengthening chain of sprites.

'Hold tight, cousin! Our feast a-waiting!'

He ran three leagues as fast as crows fly when Devil is at their heels. And, there— the old man stood.

'Why have you?'

'My tidings of magpies are crying for they worry the lateness of my return.'

The first sprite whistled. Three more appeared grabbing the ankles of them before and formed a lengthening chain of sprites.

'Hold tight, cousins! Our feast a-waiting!'

He ran three leagues as fast as crows fly when Devil is at their heels. And, there— the old man stood.

'Why have you?'

'My band of jays are crying for they worry the lateness of my return.'

The first sprite whistled. Five more appeared grabbing the ankles of them before and formed a lengthening chain of sprites.

'Hold tight, cousins! Our feast a-waiting!'

He ran three leagues as fast as crows fly when Devil is at their heels. And, there— the old man stood.

'Why have you?'

'My train of jackdaws are crying for they worry the lateness of my return.'

The first sprite whistled. Seven more appeared grabbing the ankles of them before and formed a lengthening chain of sprites.

'Hold tight, cousins! Our feast a-waiting!'

He ran three leagues as fast as crows fly when Devil is at their heels. And, there— the old man stood.

'Why have you?'

'My conspiracy of ravens are crying for they worry the lateness of my return.'

The first sprite whistled. Eleven more appeared grabbing the ankles of them before and formed a lengthening chain of sprites.

'Hold tight, cousins! Our feast a-waiting!'

He ran three leagues as fast as crows fly when Devil is at their heels. And, there— the old man stood.

'Why have you?'

'My murder of crows are crying for they worry the lateness of my return.'

The first sprite whistled. Thirteen more appeared grabbing the ankles of them before and formed a lengthening chain of sprites.

'Hold tight, cousins! Our feast a-waiting!'

He ran three leagues as fast as crows fly when Devil is at their heels. And, there— the old man stood.

'Why have you?'

'My parliament of rooks are crying for they worry the lateness of my return.'

The first sprite whistled. Seventeen more appeared grabbing the ankles of them before and formed a lengthened chain of sprites.

'Hold tight, cousins! Our feast a-waiting!'

The Tinker went running.

'Hold tight, cousins! I have not eaten in three moon's time and supper's waiting,' cried the Tinker. He ran thirteen leagues though the woods of bracken, brambles and briars as fast as crows fly when Devil is at their heels. The wood sprites could not loose themselves.

They were crying and begging, shrieking and weeping to be let loose but the Tinker laughed and laughed, laughed and laughed.

'Why have you stopped?' cried all of the sprites in fear.

'My home is there, dear cousins.'

'What home do you see?'

He pointed.

They looked and they saw it was the haunted barrow of the Devil Goule who cackled, 'Hold tight! Cousins!' And, with that— old Archimago de Goule took them far deep into the barrow for his supper was ready.

†

Hooke, la Grise, Marcelle and Félix went strolling in the great park of Nemessos in the city of Clermont.

"Can lead—Truly—undergo transmutation into gold?" asked la Grise.

"Yes?" said Hooke with narrowed eyes and a single laugh before he smiled at her.

"Just curious," said la Grise.

"It was noted in a manuscript from Persia, 4th Century," said Hooke. "A very simple process: water, air and iron distilled in a copper retorte over flame of peat and tar; Exhalation; Incantation; Projection. Blood."

"Why was it never done?" asked Marcelle.

"Cryptic interpretation most always wends 'til leading down the avenues of Frustration and Despair particularly when text is written having none of cryptology.

"'Spring Oceanus Water' was commonly translated as 'Ocean water taken during Spring' which succeeded except instead of gold it created small humonculi which devoured them; then it was 'rain water taken from seaside during Spring' but that failed except instead of gold those alchemists were transformed into ten foot tall Cathartes; and, they then attempted using water from the different Seas taken in Spring which all failed except instead of gold they created Æther, and so entered Madness. They thought it may be Oceanus's piss—his water—during Spring but all thought it wise to not ask him. That line has mutated ever since."

"Do you know how to do it?" said Marcelle.

"Yes."

"And, what that line means?" said la Grise.

"Yes."

"Why haven't you?" asked Félix.

"I have," said Hooke; "It was an elementary exercise in the transmutation of metals and objects: an amusement."

"What is 'Spring Oceanus Water'?" asked la Grise.

"You've gone swimming in it," said Hooke smiling.

She thought but could not remember. Her eyes were shining with merry expectation.

"The lake at the bottom of the Sea is kept by a spring," said Hooke.

She grandly laughed.

Félix coughed politely.

"Oceanus. His *spring's* water," replied la Grise.

"Oh," replied Félix.

Imago the Pilgrim was concluded with his tale.

A large fox appeared. It dropped a sack filled with the forest spoils of black fungus, mushrooms and leaves. It eyed Imago the Pilgrim.

"Humphrey the Tinker has finished telling tale," said the old man to the fox.

The fox sat silent staring at the Pilgrim.

"Imago the Pilgrim," corrected the Pilgrim: "Humphrey the Tinker was the person in the féerie."

"A very fine parable," said the old man to the fox. "Do you know of Imago de Goule?"

The old man took the sack and began seasoning the three ovens with the forest spoils.

"It was Archimago de Goule," corrected the Pilgrim politely but irritated.

The fox shook it's head.

"Did your Father? did your Mother? tell Tales to you when you were a wee cub of a cautionary nature?"

The fox nodded.

"Good," said the old man. "They are as delightful as much as they are illustrative. My Mother told me cautionary and bloody tales. My Father told me heroic tales and he spoke tales of clever resolve where knights and weak folk outwitted the mightiest of villains with intelligence. I like those."

He replaced the ovens in the fireplace.

Imago the Pilgrim noticed no wood was burning in the firebox. He stared at the smoke rising.

"You have not wood but smoke rises," said Imago the Pilgrim.

"Very true," said the old man as he turned to the fox. "The Pilgrim's tale was told of malevolent wood sprites who were outwitted by a ghoul. Did you know wood sprites can be malevolent?" The fox shook it's head. "It is an unfortunate trait but true. It was a parable of greed. The ghoul's greed triumphed in the end because it was clever and patient."

"Clever?" replied the Pilgrim aghast. "I believe it was cunning; not clever."

"No, it was clever," replied the old man. "Though, by which cunning did you mean?"

"Proper cunning," said the Pilgrim.

The old man held his hands with the palms upwards and shook his head. He glanced at the fox who replied with a shrug.

"Guile nor sly nor skillful deceit are not your given trades?" said the old man.

"Secret knowledge," said the indignant Pilgrim.

The ovens were done stewing. The old man took the first and placed it on the ground before his guest, the Pilgrim. The second was given to the fox. He took the last.

He gave them each a wooden spoon fashioned of hazel.

They conversed on pleasantries and idle speculation of England's foray on the Continent of the coming Great War.

They had finished supper.

"Do you not worry what will be found by ascending on steps which lead to barrens and waste?"

"No," replied the Pilgrim sated. "Steps are steps. This flavor I have not tasted before this supper."

"Blackthorn leaves," said the old man as he stood and whistled softly.

"A fine last supper you've had," said the Pilgrim with hideous menace; and, with that: he fell fast asleep.

Nine wood sprites entered from the woods: Black Trunk, Knife Teeth and Black Tangle took spoons; and, six younger sprites laboured two apiece with the ovens as directed by Old Halfbond.

"What will Archimago de Goule wakened find?" asked the young Woman.

"He shall wake in Madness and forgetfulness kept of his Life," said the old Man. "The blackthorn leaves are of curses and dark secrets. The hazel wood spoon is of wisdom. He was cursed; because he was given all wisdom—Knowledge—of dark secrets he coveted so terrifying none, but few know of."

"Do you know these secrets?" asked the young Woman.

"Yes," the old Man laughing said. "You do as well."

"We were not cursed."

"We do not covet dark wisdom," he replied: "We know it and know of it but not by greed do we seek it."

The young woman gestured at the green flames and that fire was doused. All the woods were silent and still.

"It was a charming tale," said Cunning John Wren as they began following the departed sprites. "Shall I recite it for you?"

"Please," said Gwendoline.

†

They were arrived and had been taken to the library of Crooked Meg's castle.

Themis la Grise with Fille, Marcelle, Gwen as she now preferred her name, and Félix were peering at the incomparable works on the shelves.

Caroline d'Eirene, Mary la Toute-Douée, Theresa Aurélia de Phaenna, Oana la Verte, and Lady Constance were idly conversing on Fate.

Anne Felkin and Shiretoko-hantō Miyabiyaka were reestablishing their friendship in a spirited conversation while ignoring all of the others.

C. L. Nolan and Louis-Aldonse Milot were comparing notes in explanation of their proposed agency to Javelle. Merry Jules was silent in overwhelming wonder as he sat between them.

"Does one view what is seen when peering through a glass such as this?" said Hooke as he stared from the windows with their single large panes over the Sea.

Milot viewed through the window from where he sat. He rose and went to the window minutely examining the glass pane; and, pronounced: "In this case, one does not because of the inferior workmanship of the glass itself. It has many imperfections."

"These panes—I believe—were made in 1703," replied Hooke.

"Archaïc processes," said Milot. The others were situated as they were but were listening attentively to the discourse.

"I do enjoy peering through old glass," said Hooke as he turned; "These are wondrous when delicate rains fall especially with the imperfections rendered during archaïc processes. Imperfections in things and archaïc processes should be shunned, Monsieur Milot?"

†

"Mesdames. Mademoiselles. Maestros," said la Grise interrupting as their hôtesse entered and all turned to greet her: "I present Megan la Fae." La Grise introduced them singly those Megan la Fae had not met; and, la Fae did speak individually with each.

"Are you Morgan le Fey, too?" asked Félix timidly.

"Wildly amusing," replied la Fae, "it is that we are two different sorts given with similar names. We are regularly confused with the other which does offer such delights of mischief for us. We are particularly acquainted." Megan la Fae acknowledged those others in attendance by name. She gestured for them to sit; and, they did. "Meg will do."

"For me to adequately answer your questions of the inexplicable lingering fear rising from what seems without Reason or Logic, I must first explain Resveries," began Hooke. "However, I promised Mademoiselle de Vienne I would reply to her third query when we were at Sea; we are; and, so I shall."

Zoë had entered accompanied by de Vienne. The gentlemen stood. Zoë sat as then Milot and Nolan sat and Hooke remained standing offering de Vienne his chair.

"For those who may not know, l'Invalide—who is properly known by l'Éminence malus—has been spoken of these several months passed. L'Émissaire maléfique has not entered conversation whereas the Messenger has been spoken; they are the same." He faced de Vienne. "Your query replied: Elysion pyr."

She thanked him.

"Fey pass beyond places during Resveries; Man does dream.

"The various definitions of the word – I prefer Droom – dream – since composed – by ancient lands – includes several quite interesting: ecstasy; frenzy; to deceive, injure, damage; delusion, spectre, apparition; and deception, deceit, illusion.

"The lands of Dream are imaginary. The Deities of dreams were invented as was Time by necessity. One enters the realm of Hypnos and may pass in the lands of Morpheus and Phantasos and Phobetor but that is an illusion set by those who could not conceive of any other reason for dreams."

"Do shadows exist in dreams?" asked Félix.

"They do but are seldom seen," replied Hooke smiling. "Have you ever seen shadows in dreams? Have you ever seen your face reflected on a glass? or, seen your hands in dreams?"

Fille, Gwen and Elfriede de Vienne could not remember ever seeing shadows in dreams; Marcelle and Félix were silent.

"That dreams are prophetic," continued Hooke, "or divinations may be had was a conceit invented by Man because they lack comprehension."

"They are given to be symbols, ciphers, omens, prophecies; or, archetypes as Doctor Jung will say."

"Do spiritualists enter dreams?" asked Fille. "They say they do when summoning spirits."

"They do say that, don't they," said Hooke. "They lie. Spiritualisme is summoning them from 'there' whereas Somnambulisme is visiting them 'there.'"

He looked at Fille who nodded.

"La Langue française was precise," continued Hooke and smiled when Lady Constance interrupted, saying: "Oh?"

"The French word *rêverie* derived from 'rêver' which was once related to the phrase 'to wander,' *esver*. Rêver has since become 'to dream.' Though, M. de Montaigne wrote that 'a rêverie was psychic activity not subject to attention.'"

"What did de Montaigne intend when he wrote that?" asked la Grise.

"He did not wish others to unduly seek passage in *rêverie* as he had done where he engaged in various scenes of those definitions I've stated."

"Resveries?" asked Theresa Aurélia de Phaenna.

"Old French defined *resver* as 'to consider,' 'to reflect,' and 'to be delirious.' Resver is presently considered an archaïc spelling of rêver, 'to dream'; further, resver is considered to be from esver – 'to wander' – reexvado which it is based on the word *evado*, from the Latin."

Hooke stopped speaking. He strode across the library until he had gone to the opposite wall where a familiar work was seen. He ran the forefinger of his left hand down the gilt-lettered spine. "A wondrous work." He faced Meg. "May I?"

She nodded.

He withdrew the folio. "The Clouds." He ran his fingers over the embossed leather cover.

"Evado may be defined—amoungst others—in context as 'I escape,' 'I flee,' and 'I ascend.' Or, 'I pass beyond.'"

"My definition—Then—of the word resverie—in the state of Hypnos—is 'the act of passing beyond Pâle to wander.'"

"Why do you use Hypnos?" asked de Vienne.

"Hypnos—sleep—is a known state whereas Morpheus and his kin ain't," said Hooke as he looked up from the work.

"Pâle?" asked Marcelle.

"Extant—Chronos—Locus," replied Hooke in an offhanded manner as he returned *The Clouds* and viewed the spines of the hand-written and printed works in her library. Les Mademoiselles of which de Vienne was now included and Milot l'Encyclopédiste with C. L. Nolan were bewildered rendered. Nolan and Milot withdrew their notebooks.

"How does *that* concern *these* Night-Terrors?" asked Marcelle intrigued. "And, do they feel shadows?"

"*Steganographia*," said Hooke. "*De praestigiis daemonum. Pseudomonarchia Daemonum.* The five volumes of *Clavicula Salomonis Regis.* All of them are here!" He paused. "Reality—Chronos—Locus bind each and every aspect of all things in Nature even as Reality, Chronos, and Locus are wont to change as things in Nature—by Fates—ever change."

Marcelle looked at la Grise who shook her head and winked. Those newly engaged with Hooke were stunned silent by his demeanor. He selected one of the volumes. He opened it and began quietly laughing as he gently riffed through the pages.

"And, No. Night Horrors would not know if your shadow touched them. Night-Terrors stand at the foot of your bed where you cannot cast shadows."

Nolan and Milot disappointedly replaced their notebooks in their pockets. Fille, Gwen and de Vienne were baffled for what had been asked by Félix and Marcelle.

"Well?" said Meg amused.

"*Ars Goetia* which does seem to have been signed by the Seventy Two Demons."

"All of them have stayed in my home," said Meg; "Mister Nolan has visited on occasion."

Hooke replaced the tome and, after selecting a second work, was reading pages as he walked about the room. Some viewed Hooke; some viewed Meg and Zoë and la Grise in turn; Zoë and la Grise exchanged a glance and laughed: decorum had flown.

Meg turned to where Louis-Aldonse Milot l'Encyclopédiste was seated with disbelieving countenance.

"Monsieur Louis-Aldonse Milot l'Encyclopédiste," said Meg, "Mister Hooke informs me that these things are of interest to you." She gestured over her library.

"Yes, Madame," Milot l'Encyclopédiste stuttered.

"If Mister Nolan could," said Meg, "perhaps he would show them to you."

"Monsieur Hooke," began Oana la Verte but Hooke replied: "They you wish to know are those affected, too. They exist in Nature; the Laws of Physics are by Nature: all are affected."

"Oh," said Oana la Verte.

Milot l'Encyclopédiste peered across the room to Nolan who nodded. They each eagerly rose.

"Gentlemen, if you will," said Meg: "Later."

They sat themselves disappointed and perplexed.

"Mister Hooke?" Meg said.

"Madame," replied Hooke facing her. "I've heard tell," said Hooke as he turned and looked at la Grise who nodded smiling, "of your library but have not in this place been in all these years while attending séances and galas and salons in thy home. Thy marginalia's exquisite. Thy annotations are resounding; but your corrections are sublime works of Logic and Reason which invariably caused fits unto the authors." Meg smiled nodding remembering those fits. "If I may, I should like to be invited to your library for reading thy writings in these pieces."

"'Tis so done," replied Meg laughing. "My daughter has written in them, too. She will assist when you should come."

"Your daughter!" interjected Nolan in grand surprise.

Meg gestured to Anne still seated happily on a backbench conversing with Miyabiyaka on yōkai, bakemono and obake who were taking Holidays in Hookland.

"I led a large group of kasa-obake on a tour of the towns," whispered Anne; "It was delightful."

"Görres's Mystik in five volumes, the abbé Aubert's History and theory of religious symbolism, another Edifying miscellany, anonymous; a Treatise of bells by Jean-Baptiste Thiers, curate of Champrond and Vibraye; a ponderous tome by an architect named Blavignac; a smaller work entitled Essay on the symbolism of bells by a parish priest of Poitiers; a Notice by the abbé Baraud; then a whole series of brochures, with covers of grey paper, bearing no titles. Pluquet's Dictionary of heresies," said Hooke. "Durtal's library has these, No?"

"I did not know Anne was your daughter. How many other children do you have?" exclaimed Nolan.

"Des Esseintes and he often visited before Jean's notoriety befell them," replied Meg disinterested.

"More than ye shall know, Mister Nolan," said Meg as she turned to Hooke. "Sir?"

"Night Horrors, Marcelle, lie in the zone *between* the realms of Hypnos and Resverie," said Hooke as he returned that volume to it's place.

"It's been rumoured Huysmans would accompany them on odd occasions," whispered Nolan to Milot.

"I myself have heard that rumour, too," said Meg, "Monsieur Milot."

Nolan flushed.

"Madame," said Hooke addressing Megan la Fae, "perhaps, if you would, speak of imps consumed by Satan's flames."

"That's unexpected," replied Meg laughing.

†

"Odd ages ago," began Megan la Fae and said:

The Faery's Tale

It began in Saint Sæthryth's Woods. The Flesh of the Church of the Holy began in 1709 during the Great Frost after a small group of believers who believed in the foretelling of a spectacular cataclysm pontificated by an obscure fellow whose chosen name was King Abraham in the place he named Machpelah being denounced by Soule Sleepers. They were factional pure believers of the body as sacred from which a soul or spirit would not emerge after mortality. Hence, *In Ecclesiae ipsius carne Spiritus sancti.*

They believed words from their Good Book as read by Good King Abraham.

✝

"I do not know those words," said Megan la Fae.

"If I may," said Hooke; Megan la Fae smiled nodding. "'So he said: let Us make Man to Our image and likeness: and let him have dominion over every creeping creature that moveth upon the earth; and, God created Man unto his own image: to the image of God he created him: male and female he created them; and, God blessed them, saying: increase and multiply, and fill the earth, and subdue it, and rule over all living creatures that move upon the earth.'"

✝

Megan la Fae thanked him and continued.

✝

Over years, those inhabitants grew, by familial couplings, until the town was filled with generations of fell characters for they had increased and multiplied—men, women and children—seeking dominion over all creatures as was so ordained by words in their books. All erraunts, vagrants and persons from different climes were considered foul evil beings who could only be subdued by dominion or, as they believed, Death. Some would pass roads far from the village without incident; others were murdered: women were burned at the stake for being witches, men were hung, and children were slaughtered by pitchfork and hammers. It was murders they committed on the highways and lanes that garnered watchmen's alarms. Very secretive. Very evil. Then there came the occurrences when they'd steal sheep and pigs and horses from nearby folk. The murders and thefts which were done few at first grew more frequent as it seems their madness developed erasing all senses. At some point they ceased being Human. It was unknown when they did so; perhaps, not until evidences were discovered of cannibalism. It was on Mid-Summer's Night in the year without Summer, 1816. The good folk in the area were found unconscious or wandering with no recollection of what happened or where they had been or were in the woods; they were unharmed. The flames originated from the southeast of Hook that was agreed by all but 'twas not deduced if they had come from Barrowcross or any near place. Indeed! it could not be said if they came from beneath the ground or descent was made by an object flying falling in it's orbit from the clouds in Æther: they came. They were a single wave of flames which grew to thirty or fifty feet in height spreading in an opened fan shape. The flames had different colours witnesses said: black with frothing scarlet foam; crimson and black intermingled; blue with black; orange and black. All with black but different colors. It was several miles from Hook they were seen as a few inches high and ebbing returning from whence they came. The village was gone. All structures, all things; all was gone excepting for the stones used for house building; they had melted. They searched all of the woods for the villagers and they were soon found. Some were cast up in the eaves of the woods wedged amoungst the branches; some were found miles away laying in meadows and field; a few were found stuck against walls and fences. All were charred of flesh and muscle. It was never published how many of these creatures were found. Two-hundred were mentioned during those early days after the fire yet more were found for many, many years. Attics, cellars, cesspits. Barrows, abandoned crofts, chimneys. The last - Presumably - was found at the bottom of a well in 1893. Nigh three-hundred creatures were found it has been noted. The woods and lands were untouched by the flame. It was later said that all the bodies appeared in those places as if tidal-flood waters had carried them with massive force. The flames were so hot they melted stone. Yet not so fiery when they charred and were so cool they harmed neither Innocents nor Nature. All was returned unto Nature.

✝

Megan la Fae concluded her tale.

"I myself could see light of the fire against the dark of the sky from my isle. There was naught of malice nor evil sensed; nor benevolence or rectitude. They simply were.

"They said the village, was cursed by a witch who was being burned for her sins. That it was cursed may be; that it was destroyed by Witch is improbable as John Wren has said. It was never known on maps and signposts were never erected, so no official papers needed to be changed removing all knowledge of place. Saint Sæthryth's Woods was removed from all written works and maps. The county knew; they still know. They do not speak of it.

"The lights seen were attributed to sinister mageia sent from Barrowcross; though, there are tales of greater wonders at play on that night."

"It is interesting, that religious fervor begat all this," said Themis la Grise with grim bitterness, "with a good book."

"Of what image then was their deity?" said Lady Constance.

✝

"They – Night Horrors – are Ex nihilo. They come from the realm of Chaos." He turned and spoke directly to Lady Constance. "That, Lady Constance, is the sôle reason you have been unable evermore to see them."

"I thank thee, Sir," said Lady Constance, "for what none before could say to me." He bowed from his shoulders.

"They may follow one into a resverie but sleep – Hypnos – is of a different time and of a different place. They were very much like life from the Scyphozoa," continued Hooke;

"Later, as things do, they attained the lucidity of Knowledge and so are become like Octopus vulgaris; they're highly intelligent.

"Malevolence is taught and learned; some have learned. Malevolences seep; dark oblivion soon absorbs them."

"Dark oblivion absorbs?" asked Fille.

"William Cowper."

"Who are they? These Night-Terrors... Horrors," asked Marcelle.

"They are without shape though they can take the shape of others by corpse used as their own as Fille with Shiretoko-hantō Miyabiyaka would attest. The Titan."

Fille nodded staring in amazements.

"Malevolences are Night Horrors!" uttered Miyabiyaka la Sorcière brune gasping.

"They are in that shape weakened by encasement and Sky-light," said Hooke. "'Twas child's play; but unencased at Night thee would not be here with us on this pleasant day. They all were once neither good nor fell. It was Ages before, they thought of Man as Titans did, who not had ever seen one from Humanity: it reached down to retrieve one from Humanity and with forefinger and thumb fracturing all of it as it caught that Frailty. They are things once lurking attracted by sense who did follow from curiosity: Virtue or Vice, Strength or Fear. They follow because Modern Age confuses the senses of all things. They once did take those they found intriguing from curiosity: they no longer.

"They can be the dark in that place one visits having taken passage through the realm of Rêverie, watching. None may see it but the one who *dreams*, colloquially speaking. As was done with you, Mademoiselle de Vienne. It was watching. None others could see it. Perhaps, it was sensed by some, but that sense would have been fleeting."

"These are not Nightmares," said Marcelle as increasing dread filled her.

"Most perceptive," said Hooke. "No. A Nightmare may be exited escaping. Night-Terrors may be exited. If one should be taken by this *Dark*, it is not to be escaped. There are those who lie in coma because they choose to reside in resverie a little longer. There are those who choose to stay residing in resverie; and, so— that coma shall cease by Death.

However, if one is taken by this Dark, they shall cease in resverie as well as on this sphære but reside in the Dark—far from Death—in the zone between Resverie and Hypnos."

"Meaning?" said Meg who felt that dread risen in the room.

"My misuse of Cowper's line," said Hooke: "'Dark oblivion absorbs them all.' They have not gone to their Great Reward nor in their Resverie stayed but ceased. By boojum taken."

Fille would speak but was interrupted by Hooke foreboding: "No! Not Purgatory! Not Paradise! Kingdom Come nor Hades, Limbo, Elysium or any other locus named in all of the languages of different tomes! All of those one may take exit: Dark oblivion keeps all."

The room was chilled by an unseen fog as the late afternoon azure sky reflected the waves of the Sea.

"Those kept in l'Hôpital de la Divinité Bienveillante — from Marcelle's tale — are no different. What remains alarming is that they are kept. Kept! They rage. Their wraths are not directed at all Humanity but for those they sense are gaolers in amoungst Humanity until—Eventually—all on Terre are thought to be gaolers; and, so they too shall become hateful, malevolent; and, Humanity—Then—will undergo their wrath.

"Those who have learned Man's Seven Vices are few. Those who have learned malevolence are increasing; but that lacks gravity.

"They haven't name but are known as l'Obscurité dans l'Ombre de la Rêverie. Or, commonly— Malevolences. They are not all."

"Why are they coming in dreams — Resveries — if a person is not sleeping?" asked Marcelle alarmed.

"These Modern hours. They are their senses diminishing much as Humanity shall lose their Psyche's senses of Nature. That which was no longer is.

"Du reste, they do not come in dreams, Marcelle. Does not Humanity believe dreams are théâtre tales fomented by Psyche: ecstasy, frenzy, deception, delusion, spectre, apparition? They are deemed by them illusion. No?"

"They are not illusions!" screamed Marcelle.

"No, Marcelle," Hooke softly said, "they are not."

Meg rose hurriedly and went sitting on the arm of the large chair: she began brushing Marcelle's hair with her hand as Marcelle sobbing rested her head in Meg's lap.

"Théâtre tales they may be but *dreams* are not illusion."

He went and stood before de Vienne.

"When you were found were you in Hypnos or Resverie?"

"I don't know," answered de Vienne defensively.

"Resverie."

"You have been," said Zoe sadly accusing Hooke; he nodded as he viewed Marcelle.

"What is this to which you refer?" said Meg apprehensive.

"They are progressing, learning," replied Hooke as he sat in the corner chair. "They are now able to exit that zone of Chaos which harbours them. They'll eventually pass beyond Hypnos their advent during wakened hours. Balance ceased."

"Sir?"

"That darkness felt on the steps guarded by the Warden was lurking in the Hypnos of that place."

†

Hercule was exiting from le buffet de la Gare de Lyon when a waiter arrived presenting a telegraph message to him. Hercule read:

> Elfriede Marie-Thérèse de Vienne missing.
> She has for several days after your immediate
> departing Hookland and is to be presumed
> and believed she was kidnapped by villains
> of d'Aquitaine because we have received
> two fingers from her left hand and her
> nose.
> News follows.

He walked outside and, after wandering, was come to sit on the steps in le parc de Saint-Cloud for hours.

†

"The Flesh of the Church of the Holy," said Hooke, "in Saint Sæthryth's Woods, constructed it's village in a place of Hypnos; and, there within those woods, in that place of Hypnos, Malevolences appeared in 1806 and thereafter kept watch while malevolence, like mists floating across the lands escaped from that place, was infecting those of the Flesh of the Church of the Holy.

"The Believers had fallen into Madness by themselves: it was the nearness of the putrefaction from the Horrors which accelerated their loss of Reason."

"The flames consumed *everything* kept by those woods," said Themis.

Hooke nodded.

"Night Horrors advance; Malevolences lurking wait."

†

Hercule roused himself from his stupor. He heaving sighed as he began walking.

†

"We could have died!" shrieked Fille standing as she faced Hooke, trembling. "You would have let us die!"

Hooke sat impassive as he watched her. All were standing in clamorous discussion with each other except Marcelle who remained seated and silent.

"All of us!"

"He does not interfere thy thoughts. He shall not impel thine acts," said Zoë. "He does not deceive nor trick. It is for you alone to decide what you will do. His influence exceeds your knowledge; and, imagination. He shall not interfere with what you will."

Hooke withdrew several small envelopes from his coat pocket as he stood at the window watching the sky. He looked at them shuffling with his left hand. He gazed at la Grise who was watching Zoë speak. He replaced them.

"He commanded thee wait on the second step. Did that not seem an instruction you should not ascend beyond the steps? None inquired after his reason. Did you not think it queer your guide would stand at the bottom away from those steps? and those wee gentlemen would not come within one-hundred paces of those steps?"

"It wasn't dark. It wasn't Night. We could have gone on to that glade!" said Fille who had turned facing Zoë.

"Odd," said Hooke.

"Sir?" asked Zoë.

"Madame la Fae," said Hooke, "do Wyverns have four wings?"

"I haven't yet seen one with four wings," said la Fae; "but that isn't to say, according to the Good Doctor Pabst, they do not exist."

"Sleight of hand," said Hooke as he ran his fingers across the glass of the window. "The imperfections in this ancient glass cause a simple illusion: a sleight of view. How often it must occur when one cannot see with clarity because of a small imperfection of Perception that which is before them." He turned from the window. "It's gone."

"They come often," said la Fae who was smiling at Themis who nodded in reply.

"I think not," replied Hooke as he watched Fille. "Counsel was given. Reason and Logic were at play caused by Sense; but lacking knowledge." He looked at Marcelle. Marcelle turned and would speak with him; but Hooke frowned imperceptibly so that the others would not see, shaking his head. Marcelle shivered. "Knowledge was found."

"You knew we would not go!" said Gwen. "Lady Constance told you."

Hooke as he sat stared at Gwen who quickly sat herself and he briefly considered her before he turned his gaze to Lady Constance.

"I did not," Lady Constance solemnly said. "He has but asked me once. Only once. He wished to know if it would be raining on the full Moon in the month of Décembre in the year of 1809. 'Yes' was my answer."

La Grise surprised at Lady Constance's words quickly turned to face Hooke who was watching Marcelle.

"It was a test!" said de Vienne.

Hooke slowly turned his gaze and pierced de Vienne with his eyes: she could not move.

"There — aren't — tests!" said Hooke graven. "Are there, Gwen?" Gwen stared at him in disbelief. "Do you believe a test which ends with Death absolute should ever be applied? to schoolgirls! If that be so, you would have deceased long before ever meeting Madam." Elfriede de Vienne remembered that unfortunate event from childhood, gasped and was trembling.

Fille beseeched la Grise. "Did you know it was there?"

"No," said la Grise. "I did sense præsens, but it was none I had experienced before and it was shrouded by all from those who remain in that glade from all those centuries before."

"Would you have stopped us?"

"I would have," interrupted Marcelle as she stood from Meg's comforting.

Hooke abruptly stood for what he had been waiting did occur. "Highness? A word, if you would," he said. "Gentlemen." He gestured with the forefinger of his left hand at Nolan, Milot and Jules as he held the door of the library with his right. Javelle rose and bowed before Megan la Fae and Zoë. The gentlemen followed la Grise into the hallway.

"Ma'am," Hooke said nodding to Zoë and departed closing the door after himself.

"What?" said Lady Constance.

"A moment," replied Meg who smiled slightly at Zoë who too was slightly smiling.

They waited several minutes until la Grise did enter by herself.

"They have gone?" said Lady Constance.

"They've gone and send their regrets for not being able to stay the Night as planned," said la Grise to Zoë and Meg who were smiling slightly still. "Mister Hooke shall be speaking, while he and Monsieur Javelle are wherry rowing Messieurs Nolan, Milot and Jules, tales of Dark and Pâle, and their probable drowning by the King-Under-the-Sea inviting them to a game of croquet on the lawns of the glade beside the Lake in the Woods of Oceanus beneath the Sea.

"Messieurs Nolan and Milot are happily content with their notebooks, writing. Jean-Marie Jules sits wide-eyed."

La Grise went to Fille, Marcelle, Gwen, Félix, and de Vienne; and, gave them a small envelope on which their names were written in a drunken script sort of way.

"You may read them but he requests you do not exchange them until that hour comes as you may divine them."

They read: Marcelle comforted, smiled; Gwen was laughing; Félix frowned until after a small while she understood his words and gleefully sat; de Vienne went teary with tentative happiness; and Fille, who was hesitant but after the others had read his words to them, did read her's and, sighing, exhaled deeply as self-uncertainty withered.

They exchanged glances but were helpless.

"Lady Constance?" asked Fille.

"Such impertinence!" She peered at each of them for an interminable length of time. "Be still!" Their nervous movements were arrested.

Megan la Fae went to Zoë and whispered: "He has departed from them?"

"Yes," said Zoë.

"On the twentieth day in the month of Mars in the year of 1924," pronounced Her Ladyship. "All shall set the appointed hour after the final one them all divines."

"Eleven years!" said Felix.

"Thank you, Lady Constance," said Marcelle who stood and did curtsy. And, the others then did offer their gratitude.

Lady Constance smiled.

Hercule frowned. He stopped. He was being followed by thirty-seven small Gentlemen with lime-tinged hair. They continued walking around and formed a circle about him.

"Sirs?"

"Sir," said one after which each of the Gentlemen spoke. Hercule did turn to face each as they spoke:

"We"

"were"

"requested"

"that"

"you"

"should"

"know"

"all"

"is"

"well"

"for"

"she"

"is"

"with"

"Majesty"

"since"

"you"

"parted"

"and"

"we"

"are"

"engaged"

"by"

"Her"

"Highness"

"Caroline"

"in"

"your"

"service"

"until"

"comes"

"the"

"hour"

"as"

"it"

"is"

"n't."

Hercule stood silent staring at the horizon of the West; and, after an untold length of time, he closed his eyes and bowed from his waist with his right hand on his breast.

They bowed, too.

†

"What if we read each others's now?" said Fille.

"Eleven years is a very long time to wait," said Félix.

"You will not understand their true meanings," replied la Grise; "Each was written specifically for whom it was given; however, on that full Moon, a number will appear on the paper: arrange them; and, read them, as the arranged papers give the true meaning which will be seen by you, after all understand their own because all five are of a single pièce."

"Eleven years is still a very long time," said Félix; "What if one of us should die?"

"That is for them—or, you—to decide if, in that hour of your death, it is an acceptable hour to die. If one wishes to die, they will; if one does not, they won't," said la Grise. She continued as she turned towards Marcelle. "Or, if you had listened as Marcelle did listen, you would know the answer Marcelle knows."

They turned towards Marcelle.

"'All shall set the appointed hour after the final one does divine them all,'" said Marcelle who stared through the window at the Night sky. "Lady Constance said 'All' so none will die. Eleven years is a measurement of hours invented by Humanity." She looked at la Grise. "I shall wait."

†

"To Past returning," replied Javelle.

"I do not understand," said Milot.

"You have been in Parcul Târgului?" asked Javelle.

"Yes," said Milot but Nolan shook his head.

"What year did you believe it was when you visited?" asked Javelle.

"Ten years old. Twenty years old."

"It was 1883," began Hooke. "The arcades are created in the Modern Day of scenes of days once were: Modern Day persons enter viewing an archaïc tableau or play representing a thing of the Past; and, after, they exit on to the avenue they were strolling in the year they exist—it is Present; Fée and les Métis humains enter and *may* exit on to the avenue in the year of the setting in that Arcade—it is Past.

"That realm where Life is kept of the darkest dark in Fantasias for those fantasias are colloquially termed dreams when, in actuality, they are memories of the Past and of the Future.

"All places by end of the Great War shall be as they were. It is not that the Past is returning to this place of Humanity but Fée returning, after having visited, to their own realm.

"Humanity goes to it's future; Fée keeps it's Past."

†

"Does he still terrify you?" said la Grise as they were exiting from the library of Megan la Fae.

"I no longer know what to think," said de Vienne. "Or, believe."

†

It was Night.

†

C. L. Nolan, Louis-Aldonse Milot and Merry Jules the Cartographist were strolling in an aimless direction in the west of the Woods of Barrowcross after Hooke and Javelle went.

"Why isn't Devil's Scar a station?" asked Milot.

"I inquired of that once," replied Nolan; "Themis Grey-Witch informed me the county of Hookland – The Devil's Scar – was considered but not chosen: the house next to St. Nicholas church in Chiswick was selected due to it's proximity to London; but that did seem an odd choice to me because Hookland has always been a most popular tour with Citizens-fée. She explained it is the most popular place and because of it's grandeur – I don't know what she meant by that – it is the final destination for those taking Holiday in England."

"Reasonable," said Milot.

†

Chloris Delilas Sasa-zamani and Paul Jérôme de Loudun were seated at the Tent Revival on the fourth Thursday watching moving pictures entertainments for Enlightenment as the Lilac Witch was escorting de Loudun from Vese after visiting the arcades in that cité before they would continue visiting all of the arcades on the High Road.

†

"The Impostor came when the First Revolution began," said de Vienne.

"No. Do not assign significance to what they — Titus, d'Aquitaine, l'Émissaire maleficent, l'Éminence malus — did in an era of Humanity.

"It is similar to the notion that witchcraft was discovered by the Inquisition. Witchcraft existed far before. Those murdered by Inquisition were hapless folk. Witches cannot be murdered, No? Inquisition brought to the Masses views of Fey. All miracles were deemed Satanic excepting those in sanction by Church.

"The Law of 22 was writ by d'Aquitaine and his conspirators — Duc de Blangis, l'Évêque de Blangis, Président de Curval and Durcet le Banquier — against Fey and those deemed the Vulgars of Humanity, by this Aristocracy, inferior by birth, station, colour or unfortunate circumstances, and—Therefore—would and are to be extinction given. They exist in form in this age as Ordo Novi Templi until taking future contemporary titles.

"All things Fey are ending."

"La Belle Époque is ending," said de Vienne.

"Yes."

"Krakatoa?" said Zoë.

"'Tis rumoured Titus and Verge," said Merle, "wanted 1883 would begin a thirty-year coda for it's thirteen centuries ending in 1913 memorable."

"The Great War?" said de Vienne.

"It is coming."

"This Great War, the Grand Mortality where we all shall die?"

"Do you remember my saying 'Chaos is Nature and Nature resides in Chaos. All things which reside in Chaos are unceasingly ebbed by Chronos: all things decay.'"

"Yes," said de Vienne.

"The First Great War shall be fought by the alliances and ententes of Humanity.

"La Grande Flétrissure – The Great Withering – began in the Third Age - the Age of Steam: it was the First Industrial Revolution from 1760 until ending in 1840 where all things in Nature had undergone an acceleration of decay caused by Man's déprédation; and, so it was that their perdition began.

"The Fourth Age is the Age of Cupidity. La Grande Flétrissure continues.

"It is a play performed with but prelude and coda.

"They opine this second age of Industry from beginning in 1870 shall cease in 1914. It does but shall continue as Humanity continues inventions in the arts of Science, Medicine and War. The Third Industrial Revolution begins this year next. It shall be followed by a Fourth and a Fifth; and each shall there remain in the Age of the Great Withering.

"Humanity's acts of vengeance and rage are repeating themselves, but this Modernity exceeds all previous in an accelerated manner caused by Knowledge and Industry.

"Nature and Chronos are balances eternal in the revenant-states of Existence."

"You cannot you stop this Grande Mortalité?" interrupted de Vienne.

"I cannot," replied Merle.

"If Hercule were about to be murdered by l'Invalide would you let him die?"

He looked at her but made no reply.

"I am unable," said Zoë in reply to de Vienne's imploring stare.

"All will die!"

They viewed her but did not speak; de Vienne was sobbing.

"What of la Grande Mortalité have you heard in rumours said?" asked Merle.

"Fey are leaving because we all will die from Plague," said de Vienne.

Zoe sighed sadly.

"La Grande Mortalité is of importance to you but it does not affect you," began Merle as he waved de Vienne silent who would in her sobbing speak. "Humanity remains oblivious.

"Some have left. Some are leaving. Some will be leaving during the Great War. Others later. Some will remain as you shall do but less frequently visiting stay. Some will stay.

"Remember well: a purpose may be known but the end-game is seldom as expected; and—Often—the consequential results are greater than first believed. Terribly greater. It is a plague. Future proceeds; Past continues. That future entailed by Humanity does not. Humanity goes to it's future; Fey keep Past.

"Existence is kept by Essentiae unseen. Nature and Chronos are eternal in the revenant-states of Existence: Chaos. Chronos decays, Nature succors.

"They are no longer balanced — are Nature and Chronos — in this setting on this sphære. Humanity has accelerated the decay of that which in Nature succors them.

"The First-Citizens were not in that divine arcade of a garden: they have visited; those that wish returning are. It is the final act in this play of Humanity. La Grande Mortalité 'tis irreparably engaged in these fifty years to come.

"It is the Dégénérescence over centuries which shall continue unabated until all remaining — by the Laws of Physics — in Nature adjusting — shall be their consequences all caused by Man's abandonment of their place in

Nature: air and sand, lightning and fire. Les déserts infernaux— their consequences.

"They played their parts; and, so do exit dying: la Grande Mortalité is the death of Humanity."

✝

The Night Watch went escorting Zoë with his lantern as she would be visiting the Library of the Catacombs beneath the river Wey when they came upon urchins stealing coal fallen from carts and small pieces remaining around the chutes.

"What's this!" cried the Night Watch.

"We're not doing nothing not legals law like," replied an urchin.

"Scrounging coal?"

"It's not just any old king's coal," said an urchin.

"It's Welsh coal!" said another as she offered the Night Watch their tin pail who selected a fragment; and, sniffed it. "Indeed!" He placed it in his mouth savoring it. "Ah, I haven't had one of these shinys since my youth."

They offered him a large piece; he graciously accepted. "Ma'am?" said the urchin as he offered holding their pail for Zoë to choose her shiny. She graciously declined.

"Well done!" cheerfully said the Night Watch: "Carry on!"

The urchins they continued on with their searching while chewing on their shinys.

The Night Watch went whistling nibbling his piece of coal as he was escorting Zoë with his lantern.

"Small charities abound," said Zoë.

✝

The sky was with clouds but few set from Earth half-height to the sky suspended in flight at heights before the dark of the vault of Chaos.

Fille d'Achéron, Marcelle, Gwen, Félix Trique, Caroline d'Eirene, Mary la Toute-Douée, Snježana de Pasithea, Shiretoko-hantō Miyabiyaka and Zoë were at la gare de Perrache that would take them to the North to Cabillonum—Chalon-sur-Saône—where they would be visiting the Necromantia and Witchcraft arcades.

†

10

𝕸𝖆𝖈𝖔𝖓

Reformation: France, 1913 – L'Ancien Regime are returned by the Agents of the four Alchemic Virtues: Wisdom, Benevolence, Guidance and Grace from which Congresses, Parliaments, Presidents, Kings and Leagues and Courts are covenant with the conformity of the intellect and things of Reason and Logic.

Capricornids were departing, Cygnids and Perseids were all come attending for the Ghost Festival on the fifteenth day of the Lunar month and the appearance of the Lady of the Dead during the thirty days of festive celebrations in honour of her.

✝

Zoë had arrived in Mâcon, a small cité in le duché de Bourgogne which was formed during the French Revolution as of March 4, 1790.

✝

Merle was seated on the pavement of the Boulevard du Nord at a bistro having read his papers. He was holding a deck of cards. He was turning one of the cards between his index and middle fingers.

"I was given these by an odd gentleman. Very droll these. They are Tarot cards with colour gravures of tableaux from *les Malheurs de la Vertu* and bent corners for symbolic cheating during cardplay; or, Bassette; or, they are quaint cartes-de-visite. I haven't decided."

"Or, each," Zoë offered standing at his table.

"Yes," replied Merle, absently: "Or, each."

He tossed the card across the boulevard until it was lost in the park. "I had hoped for that monument." Merle was humorously perturbed. "I have struck it several instances this morning."

"And, that memorial might be?" asked Zoë.

"Another cénotaphe for lost and forgotten persons that will be wreathed on Remembrance Day," Merle idly replied.

He placed the cards in his coat pocket. "I've read my papers." He shuffled his papers. "But there was one piece from the States that confounded me." He peered through the pages until he found that piece. It was an advertisement. "What is a continental breakfast?" He held the page for Zoe to read as he pointed at the line of text. "Travel Continental Europe by Rail. Continental breakfasts provided."

"All continents are continental," Zoë offered smiling with amusement at Merle.

"Precisely!" Merle exclaimed. "I would like a continental breakfast from Shanghai but – seated here - I have none."

"And, your papers?" said Zoë.

"All contes d'horreur," Merle replied as he gestured at the newspapers. "These are histories: military affairs, the monarchie en Amérique, disposition of the militaries in state, the Bandits anarchistes, financiers, banks, industrialists, hostile manifestations, diplomatic actions, social movements, armaments, fatal quotients, systematic falsifications, colonies and protectorates; and, nécrologies.

"Industrialists rule continents; statesmen, states. Incuriously, those who failed to be industrialists become their simpering dupes: statesmen.

"All in affectation of grandeur and splendour are these turgid reenactments by the imbecilic faithful flaunting their stupidity."

He stood.

"His Eminence has returned; and, because novelty wanes: 'tis done."

Zoë laughed grandly.

"May I?" she asked. He smiled. He withdrew the cards from his pocket and presented them to her: she did slide her fingertip along the fanned remaining cards of the deck thrice before selecting one. "Rabelais? or, Sade?"

He smiled at her.

She gracefully sent with her fore and middle fingers the card across the boulevard: it wafted falling on to the base of the cénotaphe. Merle set the cards on the table.

"Rabelais."

"Then let us go."

They did.

†

"Those hours betwixt," said Merle as they went, "the prodigious Procession of meteors on the ninth and full Moon of 21 Vendredi in Février were in wondrous Lunacy wreathed all haunting with the spheres of Mysteries and Truth for the light of her face fell and as is her wont she laughed: All lunatics parled— bards and nereides, dryads and nymphs encharmed spoke in melodious voices of Tales slumber'd, of Histories golden, of Passions, of Sorrows, of Glory, of Death: tranced Mortals whom no god pities stood, still with prayers of fear."

†

Fille d'Achéron, Marcelle, Gwendoline, Félix Trique, Caroline d'Eirene, Aglaea d'Olive, Mary la Toute-Douée, Snježana de Pasithea, Shiretoko-hantō Miyabiyaka and Zoë were exiting the train from la gare de Perrache that had taken them to the North: Cabillonum–Chalon-sur-Saône–where they would be visiting the Necromantia and Witchcraft arcades.

†

They were standing on the height of the tor in a tumultuous scarlet sea beneath the waxing moon with it's sepulchral satellite in orbit.

†

"The Lunatic stands in grace and so standing in guileless cotillion with Nature becomes exultantly content," said Merle as Zoë stood beside him. "And–Thus–what was begun in 1900 passed has become but fin-de-siècle – Thirteen Year Century."

Merle laughed.

†

The Observatory de l'Éclipse de Lune was set on the farthest end of the Grand Canyon.

Merle paused and gestured to the West at the two radiances spied in the Night sky faintly seen before they brightly shown.

"We stand on the Palisades at the confluence of the Seas in silences in the diluculo of Dark and Lumière. Wisdom, Benevolence, Guidance and Grace are come returning in the splendour of Nature: the magnificence of Chaos," said Zoë. "Shall we adjourn to the *l'Odéon pneumatique* for are we not too lunatics in the guileless cotillion of content?"

Merle smiled.

They turned from their view over the Grand Canyon du Verdon; and, they continued.

"We are."

†

Themis and Hooke were strolling into Mâcon from having crossed le pont Saint Laurent in the light from l'Aube peering; it was deserted.

Odysseus was following far behind.

"Did you enjoy your holiday in the county of Hookland?" asked Themis.

Hooke laughed.

"Did you?"

"I did," said Hooke. "All of the locus, and all of the evils of Man and Fey, and all the citizenry of Fey on the Continent are representatively compressed into that single county; and, by Old John Wren offering himself as Guide touristique, les Mademoiselles shall be kept engaged for months."

"This came for you," said Themis as she presented him with an envelope.

Hooke paused and began reading the letter. He turned slightly away from Themis. 'Dear Mister Hooke, we the undersigned do hereby wish...'

Suddenly Hooke turned, alarmed.

An Explosion.

Themis was rendered unconscious. Odysseus had run to her and was dragging Themis very delicately by her neck from the burning structures on to the deserted rue.

A pistol was fired.

Odysseus was wounded but continued as he could moving Themis from the flames until he collapsed.

"Reynaerd," said Hooke as he turned to face the assailant. "Alsea." It was a soldier holding his rusted pistol that no longer would shoot. He was accompanied by several other soldiers of his company with their rifles aimed at Odysseus; they could not be fired for they too were rusting.

"Why?" said Hooke.

"I saved her life by killing it," said the soldier. "You should thank me."

They were startled by a pâle radiance and then a second radiance of pâle appearing and vanishing in moments before them as the flames ceased were doused by violently grown icicles and frost as ash: all things in that place were covered with frost and ice.

The frost-bound soldier shivering aimed his pistol at this side. He pulled the trigger; and, fell.

"Thank you," said Hooke departing.

†

Zoë was standing beside the bed as Reynaerd appeared with Themis in his arms and laid her on the bed. He took exit as she was begun being tended by her court of sylphides.

†

Professeur-Maître Huillard was standing staring at Hercule who swaying as on a ship-deck at sea stood in the vestibule as they had stared at each other silently for several long minutes.

"You're late," said le Professeur Huillard finally.

"I walked."

"Oh?"

"It was a lovely day in Paris, so I went a-promenading with my thoughts as company," replied Hercule pleasantly.

"Paris?" said le Professeur Huillard with grand disbelief. "You went walking – Here? – to your room – in Lyon – from Paris?"

"Yes."

"You slept?"

"I believe so," said Hercule resolutely; "Yes, I believe so, so my sojourn would be since I've been strolling in a state of the dream of la Géante luciferous; and, therefore, must be sleepwalking, so still I sleep." He thought; and, said pleased: "Yes."

Le Professeur Huillard stood dumbfounded.

Hercule zigzagging strode towards his room. "I shall lay me abed so I may wake."

Professeur-Maître Huillard watched Hercule wander into his room and close his door; he heard bedsprings.

"Odd fellow," said le Professeur Huillard.

✝

Fille d'Achéron, Marcelle, Gwendoline, Félix Trique, Caroline d'Eirene, Aglaea d'Olive, Mary la Toute-Douée, Snježana de Pasithea and Shiretoko-hantō Miyabiyaka went as did all past and present les Treize had ceased their endeavors by voyaging to Corvusweald where Themis lay.

✝

Merle was standing before the King of the Ghôles who stood with all his court filled raging against the fall of his Consul.

"He shall come," said Merle. "All he'll then thee tell thy rage to keep against they thou doth loathe for 'tis come what was wished in all these centuries o'er."

Tenebris King-Ghôle smiled grimly. He slowly raised his hand and all was silence. He spoke softly.

✝

Hooke returned hours after.

✝

He went to the rooms where Themis was resting; and, entered. Themis was bed-sitting. She wore a simple nightshirt of white batiste.

Zoë, Morgause la Fey and three of les Mademoiselles were there remaining after the parade of well-wishers had ended.

The Ladies of the House would exit when he entered. "Madeleine," said Hooke to the Lady's Maid who then stood silent and still; "Pernette," said Hooke to the Chambermaid who then stood silent and still; and, said Hooke who turned to where the Laundry Maid stood in the corner with clutched linens: "Marceline." He was frowning his charming expression of frustrated exasperation. "These are the rooms of and expressly kept for Mademoiselle la Grise—They are not mine—whom I am certain said to you may stay."

Hooke peered at Themis; she nodded: the Ladies of the House smiled broadly and delightfully continued with their engagements.

"Le Docteur Pabst declared me fit but wished me to stay abed for several days. I'm well," said Themis. "Your thoughtfulness."

He smiled crookedly.

"His thoughtfulness?" said Morgause.

"He did something and blocked the explosion from doing me greater harm than simply being rendered senseless," said Themis. "And, bloody bruised."

Morgause looked at him.

"An embankment of air," replied Hooke to her stare.

"Titus?" said Zoë.

"No."

"Odysseus's with Alsea," said Félix hesitantly. "He's getting better." Hooke did turn to her and smiled; she was calmed.

"It was an act not against Themis but me," said Hooke as he smiled sadly at Themis: "L'Invalide. Titus knows he'd withering cease if he ever meets her because she could sense him: he was informed of her audience with Tenebris King." Themis stared. "They have not found all." He sighed. "After I came following Alsea and Reynaerd, I waited until all was made well before I went and searched for him; and, then did find him. We spoke. I left.

"I took audience with the Ghôle King where all things in this l'affaire Grise were forthrightly explained. His rage remains unquelled; he understands the circumstances for which he must wait l'Invalide his final intrigue made. He makes other retributions."

"You killed him," said Marcelle.

"I have been graciously requested his Life to spare if he ever should appear violence against me. I have done so."

"Then?" asked Themis.

"L'Invalide was made Unfortunate," said Hooke. "I did as you since you showed intentional cleverness in the wounding of a leg." Themis laughed. "I did — However — inform him if he should attempt that feat against you or others, I would present him to those in the farthest realms of Oblivion, with an understanding all his memories and thoughts would be kept intact."

"What happened?" said Fille.

"A fellow's left leg was only withered but yet limping by Mademoiselle la Grise who may tell you her story one day about her seventeen-years old endeavor." He looked at Themis. "L'Invalide hobbles."

"Are you not bound by Gentleman's Agreement?" asked Zoë.

"I should be, Ma'am," said Hooke as he stared from the window at the clusters of light and dark grey clouds in the faint pale blue sky over the sea.

"Oh?" said Themis.

"If I hear he has caused harm, his body will be given to the Dark Elves as an articulated marionette; his spirit in a carboy would be shown to those who asked in keeping with my vow to not take his Life: his Life I'd give the Horrors.

"My afterscript."

Fille, Marcelle and Félix shuddering marvelled for now they did clearly perceive that which they were bound on voyage.

"These things you do!" laughed Morgause. "Duality."

He genuinely but weakly smiled as he stared from the window.

†

The Second Balkan War ended.

†

Zoë was ferried on the Saône until she came to the commune of la Truchère in the province of la Bresse.

Zoë went on the earthen lane. She came to five children who were standing outside of their cottage speaking Gaulois.

The mother and, by inference, the father had been declared witches under the Law of Suspects which brought the Escouade for the Suppression of Conjuration to their home: members of the Conjuration Escouade were standing on the dirt lane; members were speaking with neighbors.

"Are you a witch?" asked the youngest boy.

"Why?"

"They're looking for witches," said the oldest boy.

"No. I am acquainted with them."

One of the escouade went inside. He returned with an officious fellow. They eavesdropped.

"Good witches?" asked the oldest girl.

"All."

"How do you know who is good or bad?" asked the middle daughter.

"You don't. Not all good witches are pretty and not all pretty witches are good."

"I was told bad witches spit," said the youngest daughter.

"No. The Queen of the Witches spits and she is good. Do you spit?"

"No," said the youngest daughter as she shook her head. She stared at Zoë and smiling nodded in secrets.

"Do you say your prayers?" asked the oldest boy.

"I have none."

"Do you pray?" asked the officious fellow.

"I have no prayers. So, if I have no prayers learned under the duress of invented contrition, how should I pray?"

"She speaks Gaulois. Does not pray. Consorts with witches. She is a witch," said one of the escouade who were now all standing close to her.

"Mademoiselle," began the officious fellow, "by articles presented in *Un Acte contre de Conjuration, de Sorcellerie et le Traitement du Mal causé par les perversités du diable*, signed 1604, you are hereby arrested and are to be punished with death for..."

"I weary this," said Zoë as she sadly looked at him.

He fainted. Those outside of the cottage or speaking with neighbors lolled their heads before shaking them; and, falling. All in other places fell, too.

There was a crash from inside of a body falling breaking furniture.

"He's swooned!"

They were without memory of the purpose of the Escouade for the Suppression of Conjuration. They were without memory of *Un Acte contre de Conjuration, de Sorcellerie et le Traitement du Mal causé par les perversités du diable*, signed 1604. All who knew or all who throughout the lands of Terre had heard of the Conjuration Escouade were without memory of it; and, even though all of the structures and documents and signage of the Escouade remained, none knew.

"What happened?" asked the father as he stepped from the cottage and viewed the fallen bodies strewn.

"Vapours," replied Zoë. "I was looking for Jean-Baptiste-Tempérance Rule."

"Maurice, please show her."

"Thank you."

†

Hooke was seated in the cabinet adjacent the chamber of Themis la Grise. He was lounging reclined in a comfortable chair with his legs extended on an ottoman, staring at the white plastered ceiling of fifteen feet in height.

He was greeted by a sleepy Themis. She was wearing a nightshirt of blue-grey silk which fell below her knees; and, an unbuttoned dark blue redingote à la Hussar. She was barefoot.

They went to the garden where Alsea had arranged a bower for Odysseus whom they would visit in that moment of Dusk.

Odysseus was sleeping; but he opened his eyes when they entered. Themis went to him. He lifted his head and spoke. She turned to Hooke who tapped the end of his nose with the tip of his forefinger. She her nose did touch on his: Odysseus closed his eyes as he fell back asleep.

"That?" said Hooke pointing to a large tray littered with bones.

"Oie à la mûre," said Alsea. "He doesn't like any other sort with goose."

"He doesn't, does he?" said Themis, "Venaison à la mûre is his preferred repast when he stays with me."

"Blackberries?" mused Alsea as she and Themis turned to Hooke who flung his arms to his sides gesturing his innocence.

"Small charities," said Themis.

†

"Nature and Chaos do not decay," said Hooke. "Cycles are set by clockworks; clockworks are set by the majesty of Nature."

†

"We were expecting the Conjuration Squadron," said Jean-Baptiste-Tempérance Rule after Zoë, Madame Rule and himself were comfortably seated in the front room.

"They shall not come," said Zoë; "All have mastered their lessons of Fainting in Coils."

"There are many who do what we do. They're on all the world in all places where they each have a different group of féeries and nymphs they help. We are very cautious and secretive about what we do because of the authorities. Sadly, it was only this year we learned of the work performed by Docteurs Pabst and Guise."

"Les Docteurs Guise and Pabst have spoken highly of you," said Zoë.

"We thank you for your introduction. We speak by telephone. We have visited l'Hôpital Coulmier. We have instructed those we know they should be engaged; they offer safety while we can only offer comfort."

Monsieur et Madame Rule spoke at length about their individual endeavors over the years and how they met each wandering lost in the woods of la Forêt de Trois Fontaines.

"We have done all we could," said Madame Rule in conclusion. "We wish we could have done more."

"It is a great charity you have done," said Zoë. "The Elders are thankful. I have been asked what needs you would desire settled?"

"There is nothing we desire settled."

"Do you have pen and paper; and, a glass of water?"

Monsieur Rule bought a glass of water; Madame Rule brought the pen and paper.

"If you could, would you bring a handful of soil from your garden?"

Zoë wrote a single line. She requested Madame Rule sprinkle the soil on the paper. Zoë blotted the water with the soil on the paper.

"If you should wish to take exit, set this in the chimney on a fire of wood collected from the floor of the forest. This composed with water and earth consumed by fire set aloft by air shall make it's way to the Sylphide Elders; and, so will come."

"Things and times are changing," said Madame Rule sadly.

"We feel it," said Monsieur Rule sadly.

"Yes, things have changed," replied Zoë. "It is an unrelenting mélancolie barely perceptible by which they exit.

That mélancolie is not that they do make exit but from the state all has become that they must take exit."

†

"It was not unexpected," said Hooke.

"No," said Hieronymus-Baleberithe-Seere ad-Din al-Jinn. "They did not expect your arrival this soon. Their plot has been hurried but is still expected to use the Jubilee-Nephilim manœuvre of 543 and so shall we as was suggested."

"Hera will be displeased," said Hooke apathetically.

"The palace?"

"The théâtre beneath," said Hooke. "The Senatus. The fogs of umbrage set over that place by Serpents when you stood at the gates of the city-state of the kingdom of the Ninth shall be settled by Dark: Shadow and Shade from the Princeps Senatus they all shall emerge rising and descending all in their Darkness behind the fortified walls of the city-state allowing the palace to be an isle raised isolated in that Sea. They find no importance with thy doings. Do not engage them for by their acts the citadel shall fall."

†

Claude Maximilien Bassompierre and Themis la Grise had been walking in Ashcourt for they had by Chance encountered each other while Bassompierre was strolling wandering lost on his way to speak with Merle who was residing somewhere in the cité and la Grise, since she was on her way to speak with Zoë who, as it happened, was with Merle, offered herself as guide.

"Delighted," said Bassompierre after la Grise offered to escort him to that residence.

They had been apprehended by two assailants dressed in ministerial garb; they wore black kerchiefs over their faces: one held la Grise with a gun pointed at her head as the other was threatening Bassompierre with two pistols.

"We'll take that life of your's," said the first assassin.

"Mademoiselle la Grise," said Bassompierre. "It would please me, if would allow me my Chivalry, as payment for your generosities even though it is meager for your kindnesses, knowing that you could well do it yourself without interference from myself."

She acceded.

"That would be acceptable but Mademoiselle must leave," replied Bassompierre.

"She's witness," said the second assassin. "She's next."

"She has not seen your faces." Bassompierre sighed heavily in his disappointment. "Very unpleasant." He rummaged through his pockets; and, as he collected coins sorting them, he walked to the first assassin, turned and went counting aloud ten paces from him. La Grise and the two assassins were startled into silent observation.

"Payment?" sneered the first Assailant.

"Aye," Bassompierre replied; "but no."

He took the crown and holding with his middle finger behind it, he aimed along the length of his extended arm and one eye closed, flicked the coin at the Assailant.

The assassin toppled.

"Minister Truguet?" asked Bassompierre courteously as he tumbled a second crown across his fingers and, as he watched the coin, found himself surprised at the act. The Minister Truguet turned and fled. "I haven't forgotten this. Remarkable."

La Grise looked at the fellow who was staring wide-eyed at the sky; blood was seeping from the back of his head. His skull was fractured; his neck was broken.

"He's dead," replied Bassompierre conversationally as he retrieved his coin. "That is the late Claude the Minister of Intelligence-in-a-Booth." He pointed to the cuckold pin on the corpse's lapel. "Taberd's influence. Minister Truguet, too. I had so hoped they had greater wits to keep their beliefs; they didn't." He paused in thought. "I cannot.... Ah! It was in the Cabinet of Obscurities. Ten paces from the busts of previous Lord-Chancellors of that place. Coins were sôle missiles for use. Damage was voted. Toppling won. I toppled often. Busts were repaired." He reminisced. "Mister d'Anville was continually my single opponent in those bouts as he had a rather large iron manilla which he should have triumphed eternally but he had broken his arm which had not been splinted well as a child so his trajectories were—Unfortunately—often askew.

"Shall we continue?" asked Bassompierre pleasantly as he offered his arm.

"Him?" asked la Grise amused yet incredulous.

He pointed behind her. The Mortality Brigade was near arriving.

"Unfortunate end," he said as they did walk arm-in-arm. "Ah, well." He laughed. "There was one gentleman who triumphed against all of us. Most remarkable. He arrived unexpectedly—as he often would—but on that day he arrived whilst we were at a game of Topples. He was welcomed for participation in spite of his having not ever known of this joust; and, after some thought he did indeed accept the wager but first had to obtain a *proper* coin which required a short excursion after which he would be returning in the late afternoon. He returned. He was carrying what we thought to be a discus but on inspection it was a coin. A large coin. A very large centime.

"He explained—as he removed his coat and unbuttoned his waistcoat and rolled his shirt sleeves—he had gone to the residence of Pantagruel for a proper coin since he was unfamiliar in the sport and we were much practiced. Needlessly. He toppled each and every one of those remaining busts in such a manner that there are none survived except for pieces and dust. It *was* a discus!" He laughed. "We heartily paid his wager; odd though it was but—Still—he said he had not had his supper. Interestingly, I did not meet him again until during the fête on l'Île Barbe. He distinguishes himself as a charming fellow."

"What was the wager?"

"I cannot recall," replied Bassompierre: "He should be asked by you. He'll remember."

"This charming fellow?"

"William Hooke. Delightfully exceptional fellow."

Themis la Grise startled did laugh; and, said: "I shall."

✝

Mary la Toute-Douée, Elfriede de Vienne, Antoinette Vaïsse, Françoise-Aurore Marivaux, Aglaea d'Olive and Anne Felkin were attending an afternoon Tea Party in the manse of Dame Hades who was speaking of Opéra, Théâtre, and Grand Guignol diplomacy in all of the affairs of state.

✝

Zoë and Merle were attending the opening performance of all the one-thousand five hundred and sixty films of Georges Méliès at the Théâtre Robert-Houdin in Paris.

They were standing behind a family visiting from Bertaèyn.

Monsieur Epimetheus Bythos de Paimpont and his wife Tethys had brought their three children to the théâtre; it was the final adventure of their day-outing in Paris at the request of their oldest son, Aeolus.

"This place smells funny," said the middle child Fionnguala as she stood at the entrance.

"Jupiter Hephaestus!" cried Madame de Paimpont to the youngest boy who had picked up a smouldering cigar from the pavement and was smoking it.

Monsieur de Paimpont was having difficulty with his selecting of the proper coins he had emptied from his coin purse on to the counter: francs, centimes, sous, and coins from les Vénètes were mixed.

"I cannot remember the proper coins," whispered Monsieur de Paimpont to his wife.

"If you would allow me," said Zoë; Madame discretely nodded and Zoë did slide with her fingertips the proper coins across the counter to the attendant.

They thanked her; and, entered.

"A Théâtre Méliès must be enjoyed by all," said Zoë over her shoulder as she paid for their billets.

Merle bowed from his shoulders, smiling.

†

Themis and Hooke were seated at the edge of the river above Anmon no taki after having strolled amoungst the beeches of the forest of Shirakami-Sanchi.

"Pantagruel's centime?"

"You were with Mademoiselle Hinojosa attending a Conseil de Préservation in Chichén Itzá for that continent," replied Hooke ruefully, "when all les Treize were in conseils on the four continents."

"Thy wager?"

"If I had lost, I would have had to wash seventeen years of spoilt dishes and cutlery; the little mentioned Thirteenth Labour of Hercules." She winced. "Fortunately, as I did not do so, I collected my spoils of Nabeyaki udon from Hakodate, one saveloy from Brighton and two iced cherry lime rickeys from Penelope's in Shreveport."

"Seventeen years?"

"Thirty years ago, their scullery volunteers mutinied after being informed they were obliged to wash tureens and bowls and cups," replied Hooke. "I had my supper with it's delightful libation in the garden of Bassompierre. We conversed on Venus."

They did view all below them in silence until Themis said: "I now know whom I should thank waiting after my return." She looked at him with fond wistfulness. "Thy gift was delightful."

✝

Zoë stood at the edge of the cimetière of Temple de la Raison et le culte de l'Être Suprême of la Cathédrale Saint-Vincent and listened to the eulogy spoken by a Reformation Statesman about the tragic story of a soldier who had lost his leg for which the soldier was reprimanded and dishonoured discharged for the negligence causing him loss of his leg: they spent one full year searching for that missing leg; untold monies were spent because every clue was followed: every suspect was arrested and interrogated until the leg - Finally - was found in Nantes and brought to the cité of Mâcon after which it was presented and pinned with an Insigne des blesses patriotiques for it's ultimate sacrifice with l'Armée du Rhin.

The leg was given full military burial.

Zoë went with an inarticulated sadness.

✝

The Lord Jean d'Aquitaine was standing in the shadows of l'Arc de Triomphe du Carrousel. He was furiously impatient waiting.

Hooke strolled to him amused at the choice Lord Jean d'Aquitaine had set for this rendez-vous.

"I summoned him!" wailed Lord Jean d'Aquitaine.

Hooke smiled.

"Where is he!"

"He has taken to reading all the years of the life of Krazy Kat, in his study."

D'Aquitaine argued his superiority over Merle concluding with his demand that he should have been given jurisdiction over the order of Chaos.

"Thy character lacks Wisdom, Benevolence, Guidance and Grace," replied Hooke; "Thy intelligence has been made malformed by Vanity, Avarice and arrogant Jealousy. Thy pretentions were ended when thy plots began."

Hiolle with his brigade were standing at the ready a few paces behind. They waited.

†

D'Aquitaine continued his arguments over Merle.

He paused.

"Where have you taken me?" said d'Aquitaine with faltering disdain.

They were standing at the obelisk on the Palisades.

"Minister d'Aquitaine," said Hooke. "Thou canst not murder which thee fears."

"Why then you?"

"An axis of Sphæres aligns with this stone. That axis has been corrected.

"You wished Lord-King of all things in Nature and that which lies beyond Reason that are beyond the vault of sky beyond the Dark where all that is known lies.

"You were admonished about things lurking and things unknown, were you not?

"You have stood here on many an occasion yet have not solved the riddle of the Obelisk. You continue. You wanted to be told the answer so you could progress against Humanity and Fey; Humanity and Fey art thee. Thy hatred from that division has driven you as Lunacy."

D'Aquitaine would have interrupted but Hooke gestured slight with the fingers of his left hand: d'Aquitaine was silenced.

"Over centuries you have sought an answer to this stele and none were found since none exist. 'Tis but an obelisk. Not lighthouse; not beacon; not helter-skelter. An obelisk forged from molten volcanic stone; and, scrieved while it was cooling." He stood before it. "It is a signpost which you have believed to be mark of the end of a chersonese."

Hooke passed his hand over the obelisk. "The glyphs and runes are of a map." The glyphs and runes shown like light reflected from a calmed ocean but d'Aquitaine could not see them.

D'Aquitaine could move.

"We do not stand on chersonese. That which you seek beyond there lies. It has always been there waiting." He pointed to the great bridge of stone arches set over the Ocean of Dark. "There is no riddle to solve to take that voyage." He turned and did face d'Aquitaine.

D'Aquitaine was still. He slowly shook his head; his eyes were wide. His countenance was of Horror, Terror, and slowly surfacing was Greed; and, Fear.

He tilted his head down and rubbed his forehead with the sleeve of his coat.

D'Aquitaine looked up.

They were standing in a titanic chamber with a silvered-glass on the far wall and an oculus of iris diaphragm behind them; and, suspended betwixt from the walls by iron flying buttresses was a gravitational lens. "Where have you taken me?" said d'Aquitaine with risen dread.

"Chambre noire," said Hooke. "Thy wish do."

D'Aquitaine closed his eyes; and, thought his wish.

"There," said Hooked pointing to the darkened glass as the aperture was slowly opening.

Lord d'Aquitaine looked; and, he convulsed; and, he mouthed words which were not heard. His eyes were become opalescent.

Passers-by stared at the body of d'Aquitaine where he had fallen unconscious with fits of grand mal seizures with his blood seeping from his eyes as they sojourned in the late of Night.

"Catatonia automatique," said Hiolle.

Hooked watched as d'Aquitaine was placed in a Navy ambulance and driven away.

"The Lake at Saint-Lazare," said Hiolle, "as you requested."

"All for this to rule as Lord," said Hooke as he viewed those of Man passing-by. He bowed from his shoulders at Hiolle before he strolled away with the passing masses.

"For this."

†

"La simplicité—Parfois—se cache sous les apparences complexes; il est parfois la simplicité qui est apparente, et qui dissimule des réalités extrêmement complexes," replied Merle. "*La Science et l'Hypothèse* from the chapter Hypothèses en Physique."

†

Hooke was walking by three Unfortunates seated on the steps.

"Sir! Sir!" beckoned la femme pieuse.

"Madame?" said Hooke as he went to where she sat.

"Who is the better? Shakespeare? or, Molière?" asked la femme grincheuse.

"Their stories are equally good. Molière has greater detail of character whereas Shakespeare has greater allusions. They are not comparable. Molière and Aristophanes—I think—would be a better comparison for discussion."

"Mercy!" said la femme pieuse as the Voluntary for the Masses Brigade had arrived.

"Cease!" demanded le Connétable of the Voluntary Brigade as he approached Hooke.

"Yes?" said Hooke.

"It must cease!"

"Why?" asked Hooke slowly.

"Church and libraries are hypocrites," said le Connétable. "They are demeaning and disparaging these delusional Citizens-Unfortunates."

"Why?" asked Hooke slowly.

"They are known to tithe money! They are destitute!"

"They would be destitute even after accepting charity," said Hooke.

"They are filling coffers of thieves and hypocrites," said le Connétable. "It denigrates them!"

"They believe they are contributing to the sacred element of faith: Charity." Hooke viewed them. "Pardon," asked Hooke: "Does alms asking for this library–la Bibliothèque Lamartine–denigrate you?"

"No," they replied; and to which l'homme maussade said: "I keep mine."

Le Banquier

"Mercy and Death have come!" screamed le Banquier as he watched the Gentlewoman dressed in grey gaily strolling towards them as he approached the steps. All activity ceased. Le Connétable and the Voluntary Brigade peered scouring all along the avenue. The Unfortunates tittered. "You've been detained!" said Themis arriving. "I was sent for you."

The Citizens-Unfortunates began laughing.

"He mocks you!" said le Banquier abashed in fury.

"This is far too pleasant for me not to remain," said Hooke.

"I must ask you," said la Grise to le Banquier: "Witch's Mercy?"

"No," said la femme grincheuse. "He is a good man. There are, of course, some that do mock folk as like us but he does not."

Le Banquier faced her but he could not regard her countenance of withering amusement.

"He helps others who are more unfortunate than us," said la femme pieuse.

"What!"

"Sick and Infirmed mostly."

"He is saintly?" asked le Banquier.

Themis glanced at le Banquier. "Entertaining, too."

"Oh, no. He drinks," said la femme pieuse. "He is kindly generous."

Hooke smiled.

"He's a shepherd of the cloth after all."

They laughed.

"Who are you talking about!" demanded le Banquier.

"Curé Fiacre," said l'homme maussade, "of course."

"I do remember that time," said la femme grincheuse, "when drunk as he was he gave such a rousing rendition of *Dies Irae*, it was all I could do was tap my feet."

"He cannot drink," offered la femme pieuse to Hooke. "Two small cups are his limit."

"He becomes impassioned," said la femme grincheuse; "Then he drinks his third."

They began telling each other the Priest's best sermons.

"Your coins are better kept by me!" said le Banquier furious.

"They are gullible!" yelled le Connétable.

"Gullibility when taken for truths," said Themis, "and used in acts of Kindness and Charity is not a sin."

Hooke smiled. He took from his waistcoat pocket six coins. Le Banquier covetously stared; and, le Connétable stood with his mouth agape overflowing filled with flustered words. Hooke gave la femme pieuse, la femme grincheuse and l'homme maussade each two fifty-franc Napoleons.

"You should place them in the collection box," said la femme pieuse as she would return his coins.

"I give you alms as you would have; and, so— it is for you to decide what you will," said Hooke politely.

She stood and dropped one coin into the collection box.

La femme grincheuse thanked him grumpily.

"Deceitful!" cried l'homme maussade. "No one uses gold coins!" He threw them in the street where the coins fell at the feet of the Voluntary for the Masses Brigade. A fellow retrieved the coins and said peering upwards "Thank you" before he and the brigade retreating ran fast away followed by le Connétable of the Voluntary Brigade.

Le Banquier requested Charity; Hooke ignored him.

"They that are content in Life should be allowed to be so," said Hooke.

Le Banquier threatened Hooke; Hooke ignored him.

"'Je dormirais mieux avec un cannibale ivre qu'un banquier sobre,'" said la femme grincheuse.

L'homme maussade attempted stealing the coins of la femme grincheuse. Hooke finger-flicked a centime at the head of l'homme maussade; he unconscious toppled.

"Saints alive!" exclaimed la femme pieuse.

Hooke smiling broadly turned to la femme grincheuse; and, said: "Yes?"

Le Banquier stared at the coin; he stared at Hooke; he wet his lower lip with his tongue.

"*Moby-Dick; ou, le Cachalot*," answered la femme grincheuse.

Curé Fiacre stepped from the Bibliothèque and emptied a basin of water on to le Banquier.

Le Banquier fled screaming.

"There are those - as you seem to know - that are charlatans of Piety who care not for these people as penitents but for their tithes. Obversely, most care little for those sorts but are happy for the opportunity to give charity which may gain them Kingdom Come entry," said Curé Fiacre. "And, then there are those who give charity sôlely for the continuance of Knowledge."

"They are few in number."

The Priest nodded before saying: "I assist as I may in this place of Knowledge and Learning."

"*Moby Dick?*" said Hooke to la femme grincheuse who then pointed at the Priest.

"Piety comes from all places," remarked the Priest; "doesn't it."

"Holy water?" asked la Grise.

"Mop."

Hooke bowed from his shoulders. He offered Themis his arm which she took; and, they went.

†

"Did he see Order?" asked Zoë.

"No. He viewed in reflection the allée leading to the entrance where the Sea which lay beyond is seen."

"Coeus," said Zoë.

Themis did not know.

"An arcade of amusement by Coeus," said Hooke. "It is on the Palisades. We should go." He paused. "Hera's Wall, too." He turned to face Zoë. "The Mortality Brigade has taken him to the sepulchral lake in St. Lazare."

"It would be an irony if it were not you involved," said Zoë. Hooke bowed from his shoulders.

"He has finished?" asked Themis.

"No," said Hooke. "He's one last act of vengeance."

"To view this amusement takes purity of heart?" said Themis.

"No. Purity of heart is a fancy from folktales which seems only to be from those kept virginal or deified with a wealth of Virtue. 'Tis far scarcer," said Hooke smiling: "Contentment."

"Before you go," said Zoë: "Krazy Kat?"

"I sent them addressed l'Hôtel Parthénon by post; they arrived early," replied Hooke. "Did you enjoy them?"

"Very much," said Zoë.

"Crazy Cat?" said Themis.

"An American cartoon, set in the lands of the Cohonino, printed in newspapers of the time. Sunday editions are color-illustrated," said Hooke. "I too have them; but it may take us a lengthy while to read all of them."

"If it is to be a lengthy while," said Themis, "we should read them encamped in a garden by the Sea."

He laughed.

"Yes?"

"We should then find them on our return waiting in the garden."

"Reynaerd?"

He nodded.

✝

Zoë was speaking with the Gardener. He was kneeling tending his garden in the shadow of the beech over his cabane at the mid-afternoon.

"Spirit dreaming," said Zoë in reply.

"Yes, it was," said Joseph le Vieux as he raised himself. "May I tell my story to you, Cher Madame?"

"Please," she replied.

Zoë sat on the stone wall of his small property. He stood before her leaning against the large Fagus sylvatica tortuosa as the right leg of his trousers would be errantly fluttered by zephyrs from the Saône.

"Odd ages ago," began Joseph le Vieux and said:

The Bûcheron Tale

Le Fusilier had volunteered in his thirtieth year because of a fervent patriotism for France. He fought in 16 Août 1870 la bataille de Mars-la-Tour with l'Armée du Rhin. He fought in all of the remaining battles until la bataille d'Héricourt was lost on the 17th Janvier in 1871; and, so was ended la Guerre de 1870.

It was hopeless. They retreated and would take their march to Suisse waiting for the requisite formalities of remonstrances and capitulation. The snow was treacherous. The Fusilier broke his leg after they had entered Suisse wandering into the forest of Doubs.

They felt safe but his leg would only make things worse for the others because they believed Prussian cavalry were following them. It had been splinted as best they could but he could walk no farther. He would stay; they would go. He used his rifle as a crutch and found a large tree to sit beneath because Night was soon falling. It was snowing. He fell asleep. He did not sleep long because he was dreaming he smelled smoke from a campfire. He saw a light in the forest. It was a campfire. He cried out and it was doused. He saw shiny eyes. They came. He raised his rifle from where he sat. They were cats. He lowered his rifle and laid it beside him.

The cats were sitting in a row. 'I shall likely be taken by Death before morning,' said le Fusilier. He removed his leather knapsack. 'I would appreciate you joining me in supper.' He shared what was remaining of his food with those cats of the forest. He spoke to them on war, on patriotism, on the failures and folies of gouvernements. He told them he regretted les Corps législatif having declared war. He told them he regretted le Gouvernement de la Défense nationale continuing it. 'I do not regret my station as a fusilier; but patriotism cannot win battles,' said le Fusilier. The meal ended. The cats went back to their fire in the clearing. 'I am sorry for our madness,' he said to the forest. The Ghost of the forest watched him as it stood across from him in the woods with delicately falling snow. Le Fusilier was sad as he sat there and watched them. He fell asleep.

He woke in a hôpital in Suisse. His leg below the knee was missing; it had been amputated. He was told it was healing before he was found by the soldiers of Suisse. They told him he was found sleeping soundly by the rivière Doubs. He had been taken by soldiers and interned with the others who had fled across the border. They were released after all was done by means of remonstrances and capitulation with the Guerre de 1870.

He returned to his regiment in Besançon, where on his return, there was some fuss about his missing leg. He was dishonourably discharged for negligence. He went home.

He was not but six months in Mâcon before he left for Morez. After that night in the forest with the ghost and cats, he was enchanted by the woods. He found a forester's cottage far enough away from the town that none would come but close enough for him to venture with his wares from the forest. He wandered to that place of the forest for firewood. He only gathered dead wood fallen on the carpet of the forest. He brought small things as offers to keep the woodland folk from harming him and particularly to feed the birds who did lead him.

It was on one dusk, when he was resting beside the chimney with it's bright fire, returning from the town of Morez after taking his branches and sticks to there, a shape appeared at his window. He stared. He rushed as well he could out into the silent night; she had fled. It was the ghost from the forest of Doubs. Several nights later she returned. She did not flee. They stood several paces from each other. 'The cabane has been unused,' said the Spirit. 'I was curious who would be living in this such a far place from those in the valle. I was curious who was so gracious. Yesternight, I watched you sleep but your face was to the wall and I could not see it.' She faded with the night.

It was on the next morning, when he went into the silent woods and saw her waiting on the lane of the trees. He followed her as they spoke of things. She was of Spirits yet she had the warmth of body. We did do this often walking in the woods at all hours of light and dark.

It was on one afternoon, as he was gathering branches and sticks from the carpet of the forest, she came to him. 'Would not a hatchet help you?' she asked. 'I do not know on which trees I would use one; I cannot harm them,' he replied. 'The birds you have befriended would gladly help you,' she said, 'in repayment for your kindness.' They strolled in silence as he thought. 'I must think, Cher Madame,' he said; and, she replied: 'Then let us not further speak of this for now; I will ask you again on the morrow.' All was silent. They continued conversing as he gathered his wares until dark was appearing. She faded.

On the next day, she was waiting with a golden axe. 'Would this suit thee?' she said as she offered him the axe. 'I haven't need,' he replied. She let it fall as they went into the woods.

On the next day, she was waiting with a silver axe. 'Would this suit thee?' she said as she offered him the axe. 'I haven't need,' he replied. She let it fall as they went into the woods.

On the next day, she was waiting with a simple hatchet of steel with a handle of ash. 'Would this suit thee?' she said as she offered him the axe. He nodded. She handed it to him and, as they went, she explained which branches were dead on the trees; and, what to say to the trees in permission for taking of their withered branches. Birds followed them in the silence. He found the axe with the ash handle on the table but he could not remember ever having it.

It was on one night, le Bûcheron woke from his sleep. The Spirit of the Woods was laying beside him on his bed.

'Am I dreaming?' said le Bûcheron.

'No,' said the Spirit as she lay beside him. 'These dreams are mine.'

They had done this for many years until he no longer saw her for her dreams had come to an end.

He stayed a few years but it was lonely. He followed le rivière Doubs river northwards with faint hope of seeing her again; he did not but he did enjoy the path on which he went with his sadness. He eventually reached the Saône confluence of the Doubs and the Saône in the Bresse plain and returned to Mâcon where he beheld he could no longer live so close to others.

He hadn't seen her for more than many years. Then one night he saw her face in a dream looking at him.

He remembered waking on many a morning and the room was oftener colder than the other rooms. Colder than outside. He doesn't remember anything of the nights except visiting with her. But there, on the half of the bed in which he didn't sleep, that half was warmth irradiant.

He knows her face. He hears her voice. He sees her gown. He sees her smile.

He shall, possibly, one day venture up the river and follow le Doubs to it's end.

†

Joseph le Vieux had concluded his tale.

"I hope le Bûcheron is able to follow le rivière Doubs to where his rêverie does lead him, Monsieur Joseph le Vieux," said Zoë.

She bowed from her shoulders; and, she did leave as he returned to his garden.

†

Marcelle had been led by Reynaerd to Hooke who was seated on a sofa in le Salon des Mers.

"Those were done by John Martin," said Hooke as he gestured to those spectacles painted on the vaulted ceiling.

"You didn't abandon us," said Marcelle, "when you left us on the isle of Megan la Fae."

"I did," replied Hooke smiling as he gestured Marcelle to sit beside him.

"Didn't." She shook her head frowning. "If you had, I would not have been welcomed by all I've met here."

Hooke offered her the book he was reading, *De Mysteriis Aegyptiorum, Chaldaeorum, Assyriorum* Venice 1497, which she accepted. "Have you read this? It was written by Iamblichus."

"No," said Marcelle without looking at the work.

"It's interesting."

"What magie do you do?" asked Marcelle who was becoming agitated. "Goétie? or Théurgie?"

"I don't," said Hooke. "Magie is expressed to be spells. Spells are embellishments, alchemical mutations, mechanical transfigurations—All those sorts—on Nature.

"Charms, beguilements, alchemic ingredients, and words spoken from obscure texts are employed which alter that on which a spell is made; conjuration and incantation are identical in process.

"All laws of Nature are found in the Sciences. I do not alter Nature. I merely engage those laws."

"How do you use Nature?"

"That's the sleight-of-hand, isn't it?"

She nodded vacantly.

"Themis Grey-Witch," said Hooke.

Marcelle dropped the book, gasping.

He retrieved it.

"It is to be waiting nineteen years hence thirty-six."

He smiled. "We shall see."

"Intrigues," mused Marcelle.

"Of a sort," replied Hooke. "There are no coincidences, only Chance. No?"

"We all read your cartes in eleven years and I succeed Mademoiselle la Grise in nineteen."

"Possibly."

"Has anyone else asked?"

"No. They will in their own time. I imagine Félix or Fille shall soon be arriving when they are shown this place."

"Why her!"

Hooke cast a look of disbelief at Marcelle who shrugged but slightly smiled. "She remains bound by three stations but relinquishes her title as Themis Grey-Witch."

"I can't be her," said Marcelle.

"No, you cannot. That is not possible for anyone to do. You have taken rise of a discernement similar to that which was had by Mademoiselle la Grise in her youngest years. It is of arcane things." He smiled at his thought and saying as if to himself, "She is les Treize incarnate."

"Pardon?" said Marcelle.

"What is le Baiser de la fée?"

"It's a spider's bite, isn't it."

"Did you ever not hear that in the realm of Fey there are three sorts: benevolent, malicious, and those benevolent who lack not of mischief."

She nodded.

"A benevolent Fey would not because they are benevolent; a malicious Fey would not because it would give those bitten an avenue to being of Fey. A Fey of mischief is capable but voluminous unlikely. Who in the realm of Féerie would want to be the pestering of all three proper fairy sorts?"

She did not know.

"Piskies. It is spiders; but piskies enchanted them long, long ago and they take them to whomsoever they wish to have be bit either because that person is half-Fey or not half-Fey: it is their whimsy. However, on those rare miscalculations in their plots, they have selected those who are Fey."

"Mother and Father were Féerie which is why I am!"

"No. Your great-great-great-great-maternal Grandfather was and your great-great-great-great-great maternal Grandmother was half Fey. Your great-great-paternal Grandmother was wholly Fey. Heredity is such a marvellous thing."

"I don't understand."

"Quiescence." She quizzically looked at him. "Dormancy."

"Oh."

"There was found none other of Mademoiselle la Grise over this Belle Époque," continued Hooke. "We waited. Suddenly, Marcelle appeared. We were curious." He grandly smiling stared at her. "*Very* curious. How was Child Marcelle not been known to us before her mysterious appearance? It was le Docteur Guise who found le Baiser de la fée on that day he came to visit your aunt and uncle. It was Hiolle the captain of the Mortality Brigade and Javelle the Scribe of History who traced your lineage. We waited but we knew it was the most mysterious Marcelle to be."

"Do the piskies know this?"

"They have no care for what they do," said Hooke. "They would not remember you if you should by Chance wish to thank them."

"What should Child Marcelle do?" said Marcelle smiling.

"All which Marcelle ever has done," said Hooke. "Acuity and curiosity simply for the sake of learning are rarely found."

"What if Marcelle refuses?"

"You're incapable. Besides, you've already accepted your Fate," said Hooke. "Do you not remember—It was those months ago—wandering with Her Majesty and Félix watching Shadow and Shade in Saint-Étienne and Lyon?"

She shook her head; but slowly remembered. "You again!" said Marcelle with joyful laughter.

"And, afterwards Majesty took you two to the coffee-house—*l'Odéon pneumatique*—in the quartier Perrache where you and Félix agreed that you each had found meaning for all those things you had thus endured in Life."

"How did she know of that place!" exclaimed Marcelle. "I would not think she'd attend those places like that."

"We've often gone there after she was shown," said Hooke; "and, because she enjoys them, she does. So, you do see, that all that's done has been concluded."

"It would be better if you said Marcelle accepted her luck," said Marcelle; and, after thought she asked: "Does she know?"

Hooke set his elbow on the back of the sofa and placed his cheek resting on the palm of his hand. He stared at her slowly shaking his head. "Who brought you?"

"Oh," she replied quietly.

"She waits for us on the terrace," said Hooke as he rose. "Luncheon?"

†

"You, sir, are an idiot," said Hooke without humor.

King Vinea did vehemently protest.

"Of course, she could," said Hooke. "It would be as a simple wave of her hand she could hide the Sun from view."

"No mere witch has that power," declared King Vinea. "I am of the few able to hide things from sight."

"She is no mere Fey," replied Hooke as he watched Themis la Grise. "And, Yes— she does have that power in that she may if she chooses rearrange clouds and Sun be hid. It's been writ you are cleverest and most dangerous of all recorded in *Lemegeton*; yet thou still disappoint me. Mayhap—one day—she shall expose thee. Thou an idiot steadfastly remain."

"Impossible! I shall prove it." King Vinea began stomping to where la Grise stood; his steps were arrested: Hooke held King Vinea by the collars of his shirt and coat, lifting him from the ground.

"Sorcerers and Demons of State know things. The Grey Queen knows more mischief than they," said Hooke. "Do you suppose there is but a single method for Sun hiding? There are three. She will happily accept your challenge. She will—after hiding Sun from you—take her exit laughing gaily and think no more of you hid in darkness eternal."

"Earth would be in darkness! She could never do that because it is against the compact of les Treize which forbids it."

Hooke set the King on his feet.

"Earth wouldn't," said Hooke as he turned taking his leave. "It isn't written anywhere."

"Impossible!" King Vinea bellowing shrieked.

"She'll blind you."

†

Caroline d'Eirene, Mary la Toute-Douée, Theresa Aurélia de Phaenna, Aglaea d'Olive and Zoë were walking along rue Sigorgne.

They passed several Artistes en plein air. They, from la Société du Romantisme, were seated and standing with their box easels before an ancient weathered wall of l'Hôtel Senecé in delicate decay embellished with lichen and moss from which they were painting majestic scenes of Nature.

"Seascapes," Zoë mused as they went.

†

They had visited for hours in the library south of Acheron Quay. It was darkening as Old John Wren and Gwen were walking from Persephone's Gate.

"You do not laugh," commented Old Wren.

"Am I to do so?" asked Gwen.

"No," said Wren; "but it may benefit you if you did laugh where you have not otherwise so done."

"When did I do that?" asked Gwen.

"When we first stepped into the Library."

"Do you laugh?"

"Yes. Of something delightful, joyous or merry my laughter is expressed in a smile."

"Why would I do those?" she asked with her studious frown.

"Nature delighted sighs," replied Wren. "Nature merry laughs. Nature joyful thunders."

"I've heard one-hundred thirty years of the Thirteen Witches's colours change," said Gwen after they had a few miles walked. "Change?"

"Yes," said Wren. "All sorceresses and sorcerers change. You were once Tochi no akaru-sa who then became Gwendoline, and recently Gwen. You see, you have changed yet you still remain Tochi no akaru-sa and ever-after will."

"Who will I become?"

"That is for you to wait and see. All are similar yet each has a particularity which none other has. Fille d'Achéron, Félix Trique and Marcelle will return soon. They may see."

"What is mine?"

"It is that which you have but do not believe; it is that which you are but cannot conceive," replied Wren merry smiling.

"You aren't telling me, are you?"

He shook his head.

She sighed frustrated.

They went in silence until after a length of miles she with delight did sigh. Old Wren nodded as he viewed all before them.

She smiled.

†

Hooke was guiding the three members of the Illapses Agency, Ltd.—C. L. Nolan, Louis-Aldonse Milot and Jean-Marie Jules—through the city of Prague in the kingdom of Bohême.

The Lamp-Lighters were illuminating the coal-gas lamps and the few electric lamps requiring their handles be turned on the boulevard. Those whose houses faced the boulevard continued lighting their lanterns and lamps as was done for centuries.

"Where are we?" asked Milot.

"Prague," answered Hooke. "We are going to the old quartier of Závist, presently known as Zbraslav, to the oppidum where therein lies one who would speak with you for the benefit of your Agency.

"Would you care to solve a Thought puzzle while we take our way to that locus?"

"A Logic puzzle, you mean," said Nolan.

"I haven't been in this quarter," said Jules. "Very different."

"Thought," said Hooke.

They agreed.

"If a fellow goes to le Marchand de tabac and purchases a bright red box of matches which he places in the side pocket of his coat where his handkerchief is kept, and later uses that handkerchief for his dribbling nose as he walks soon returning to his apartment where he performs small insignificant tasks including setting his coat over the back of his chair before he selects his favorite pipe after which he goes to his coat but cannot find his box of matches causing him inspection of all the pockets of his coat, and all the pockets of his trousers, and all the places in his satchel but cannot find his box of matches necessitating he peer around the kitchen amoungst those things he took from his satchel placing them in their proper place but cannot find that box which causes him to peer about the rooms but still cannot see it and then recalls he used his handkerchief on his nose while walking home from le Marchand de tabac and so resigns himself that the box was lost on the street when he retrieved his handkerchief thus realising his needing to return to le Marchand de tabac and purchase another box of matches reminding himself to be more careful in the future as he dons his coat and takes his hat and then goes into the kitchen where he had left his glasses only to see that bright red box of matches prominently standing on the white enamel stove and thereupon he laughing says 'Thank you' as he takes it."

"Yes?"

"Would that red box of matches have appeared, if that fellow instead of his self-reproach for forgetfulness, had cursed himself against the Fates of all the High Heavens for their merciless cruelty? when it was at first not found."

†

Zoë was seated on a banc de fidèle set on a hill overlooking the valley Grésivaudan.

Zoë at first heard the sounds faintly but, as it was approaching, she understood those sounds: it was music of a metal instrument.

Hercule appeared playing a lamellophone. He was smiling. He was bobbing his head metronome-like keeping cadence as he walked. He strode to her and, when he reached her and he stopped walking and playing, he bowed.

"Your attendance's requested," said le Troubadour silencieux.

"Thy instrument?" asked Zoë.

"A Mbira dzavadzimu," said Hercule. "Elfriede Marie-Thérèse de Vienne gave it to me. She said I should have something because I no longer was speaking whilst walking so she gave me this kalimba, and she also gave me a sanza, a kisanji, a likembe, and a kongoma. I did not much like the kouxian included by she. Thumb pianos are best." He thought. "Does Liszt play them?"

"Perhaps not."

He noticed; and, said: "You are sat on a Fidelity Bench."

"Oh?"

"Those are for churches."

"That grand significance is not mine. It is a bench. Simply, a bench," said Zoë as she was turned to face Hercule but after returning her gaze to the valley, said: "It is a magnificent view, is it not?"

"They can do that?"

"What? Monsieur Troubadour silencieux," she replied as she thus did watch Hercule.

"Benches brought from churches."

"This particular seat was not in a church. The significance is measured by the person who uses it. So, even were it taken from cathédrale or parish, it would remain a bench for me. But, Yes— they can be taken from churches."

"Nothing happens?"

"No," replied Zoë kindly. "'Nothing happens,' as you would say, even if one in a cathédrale sets oneself on it."

Hercule thought. "Cathédrales?"

"Nothing happens," Zoe replied with a gentle smile. "Significance is given by those who attend them. All structures are buildings made; however, there exist many structured marvells whose beauty is wondrous. Did not Maître al-Jinn show you the Shah Cheragh mosque?"

Hercule nodded. "It was beauteous."

"After your exit, did you bring with you some significance of that most revered structure?"

"It's magnificence and beauty."

Hercule turned and stared at the Grésivaudan.

"If you would," asked Zoë, "would you consider seating yourself beside me on this bench? and take your pleasure in this splendour."

"May I?"

"Of course."

He did so.

"It is a magnificent beauteous wonder we view," said Hercule after sitting silently for an hour.

They sat watching Night's rise from the West.

†

"This place is strange for me," said Nolan having been silent for several miles. "It hasn't Genius loci."

Hooke paused. "Gentlemen?" He looked at Milot and Jules.

They concurred.

"Odd," said Jules. "I was unaware until you mentioned it."

"I as well," said Milot. "The Sense of Spirits is missing."

They worried.

"Man's progress has swept away all sense of the Antiquities.

"Romanticism made attempts with written texts and art that all things lost should be returned even should none have existed previously: enchanting places were invented. Modern Age suffocates with Humanity's delusional beliefs," said Hooke. "Parochialism is truly an annoying vice of Man."

They agreed but, with furtive glances amoungst themselves, were uncertain if they had been included in that statement.

"What are these isolated enchanted places Man finds so enchanting?" asked Hooke.

They named places from Europe and in the different realms of the other continents.

"Are they sacred?" said Hooke, "in that they are not sanctified as holy."

They thought.

"Some are."

They named the few sacred places they knew.

"Have you ever been to them and entered?"

Nolan and Milot replied they had not. They turned to Jules who was silent until replying "A few," but would speak no further of those adventures.

"Have you ever been to a place thought sacred?"

They did not know.

"And, those which aren't? Why are they enchanted?"

"Avallon is enchanted purportedly being the actual Avalon of Arthurian legends," said Nolan; "but it is not considered sacred."

"That kingdom of Obéron and Titania in Shakespeare," noted Jules.

"All Myths," replied Milot, "have sacred places of deities. Man supplicates in those places. Common folk of Fey dwell in those places."

"True," said Nolan. "I've yet to see faeries tithe for passage." He thought. "Nor places enchanted."

They continuing discussed Hooke's second question but could find no logical conclusion other than it was a concept invoked by Man for things Man had dismissed as superstition and legend even though superstition is commonly based on the truth of Myths and legends which grew from a small inexplicable event in Man's History.

"Sacred loci are always enchanted by Spirit but no enchanted places are sacred," replied Hooke.

"Yes?"

"Then could not those seeking invented enchanting places be under a spell of nothing more than an invented nostalgia for things never seen but existing? which were written in later centuries formed from lore and legends and Myth.

"Sacred loci were held to be sacred by those who lived there passing that belief in all of the following-after lineages.

"Enchanted places, it so seems, were not held as sacred by those bedwelling but a common place in everyday Life: places enchanting had no grand significance for them what kept there."

"So, for Fey there isn't an enchanted place," said Nolan.

"There are enchanted places," said Hooke. "Fey merely do not consider them so; Humanity does.

"If one were to stand in the realms of Myth, what would one sense in that Reality?"

"Myth," said Milot. Nolan shook his head as he formed his thoughts on a realisation. "Fey," said Nolan as he turned and faced Milot. "It would encompass all things. Loci aren't isolated."

Milot and Jules assented.

"We are not in an enchanted place; we are in a place of those enchanting," said Hooke as he began strolling gesturing in the direction of their destination. "Shall we?"

"How would a small inexplicable event in the history of Fey be noted in Man's?" asked Milot.

"That we leave for different hours, Monsieur Milot," said Hooke, "if you gentlemen have not solved that riddle before then."

They continued.

†

Themis was seated in the secluded room of Persephone at the fashionable restaurant—La Varenne—with it's haute cuisine of eleven courses and service à la russe at the request of Persephone for a private audience with her in High Tartarus.

Persephone spoke on many subjects: André le Nôtre was enlarging the gardens in the manner he had performed at Versailles and Hrafnwæld in Hades; the rising indignities of Kingdom Come; the flourishing malaise she has felt since leaving Clermont; the importance of demure comportments by femmes for remembering their feminine station in Feminity even though not all did seem to know of that importance; the Territoires in a composed and temperate state; Hades involved in all sorts of intrigues and plots; Hades stating spies were everywhere and none should be trusted; insufferable house staff; she watching grandchildren.

Persephone concluded when coffee and digestifs were served.

†

Hooke, Nolan, Milot, and Jules were passing a newsstand. Hooke went to the stand viewing the papers while those three waited. Hooke selected a paper; he paid. He read a few articles on the front page as they continued walking before he handed it to Jules, saying: "I've always liked this paper."

Jules stumbled. He pointed at the headline. Nolan and Milot clustered beside him: they as if by Medusa's stare stood.

BISMARCK NEGOTIATES LEAGUE OF THE THREE EMPERORS

†

Milot l'Encyclopédiste and Merle were walking on rue Mercière in Lyon.

"Heinrich Cornelius Agrippa conducted his séances with the Society of l'Agla on this rue," offered Merle since Milot was in the depths of his thoughts after hearing Merle speak.

"My works are different."

"It is expected."

"Why?"

"Those with whom you spoke were scholars" said Merle: "Adept but ignorant. You have read the identical works they have read. Your perception and perspective were different than those of the scholars. You are not different for you have always been the same.

"You have found that which you sought. You were thought prodigy in childhood; but none ever told of you because of the lingering fears that prodigies were insane. You suspected then; you suspect still."

"Métis humain."

"Yes. It was at Hooke's salon you understood," said Merle. "While the others were invited because of their curiosity or fears, you were invited by him because you wished to know."

"*My* introduction of myself to you was not by Chance," said Milot.

"No."

"You said it was *your* wish at the Card Games," said Milot hesitating. "What was thy wish?"

"Again, you have suspicions but would like to know."

Milot nodded.

"After his leave taking, you are to be in the stead of Consul-Amanuensis Javelle who has been epitomising all of these ever changing mythologies in the annals of Myth; but you shall do so in the manner you deuced Spheres and Choirs— Myths."

Milot smiled.

†

Hooke and Fille d'Achéron were seated at the table in the middle of the long hall playing a game of chess.

"Yes," replied Hooke.

"I'm an oracle!"

"What will be my move, Mademoiselle l'Oracle?"

Fille pondered on the pieces.

"Queen takes bishop."

Hooke moved his knight.

"I would have taken the bishop."

"You do know Lady Constance does things other than telling fortunes with her hours."

"What things?"

"She has staved Night Horrors. She has brought better living conditions to those in the lower quartiers of Hades. She has spoken with all in all places; but her grandest exploit was the allowing of a lost traveller entrance after papers were misplaced, personally escorting them through Hera's Gate to the realm of Tranquility."

"I didn't know!" said Fille as she moved her knight.

"Her withering gaze has been known setting Malebranche and Seraph fleeing."

"Why does Shiretoko-hantō Miyabiyaka watch over me?"

"Miyabiyaka la Brune watches over you because Gwen has become the apprentice of John Wren le Sage since Theresa Aurélia de Phaenna who originally watched over you was asked to watch over Marcelle since Mademoiselle la Grise has other engagements requiring her guidance; and, because Lady Constance doesn't.

"What did you do as one of the Hesperides in the lands of Asphodel?" said Hooke as he took a pawn.

"I tended to those in need who after drinking from the Lethe still had fragments of innate knowledge. I found lost travellers escorting them to where they should have gone," said Fille as she took his rook with her bishop.

"What did you do as one of the Hesperides at the farthest edge of Hades in Limbus?" said Hooke as he took her bishop with his queen.

"I tended the trees; I tended the woods. I tended Hera's orchard in the West but I - Mostly - spoke with those old and ancient in residence there," said Fille as she retreated her second bishop.

"What did you do as one of the Hesperides in the fields of Elysium?"

"I served libations."

"Which did you prefer?" said Hooke as he castled.

"Asphodel was interesting but I did not like it. Elysium was dull. Limbus was wondrous except for Hera and Athene." She lowered her voice in whispering. "They bicker constantly. I'd say terribly vindictive. And, sullen. Petulant, too. Hera constantly plotting revenge on the nymphs for the original sin of the earlier ones seduced and raped by her consort; Athene was always causing uproars destroying everything around her for the slightest or imagined slight.

"I miss conversing with those old, ancient men."

"About?"

"Science, philosophy, magic, religions. Everything really. I like Rhetoric. It was difficult at first. I have been getting better at discourse," said Fille as she moved her knight.

"Who did you prefer?"

"Demontheses, Isocrates, Isaeus, Plutarch, Aristarchus and Cicero."

"Do you know who those fellows are?" said Hooke as he moved his queen.

She shook her head as she moved her queen. "Check."

"They are those who conceived Rhetoric," said Hooke as he moved his bishop endangering her queen.

"So, what—Exactly—is my compact?" said Fille as she moved a pawn defending her queen.

"Keeping deities from interference by Suzerainty with petulant vengeance, sulking tantrums and general mayhem led by their pompous arrogance of station towards those of Fey," replied Hooke as he moved his rook taking the knight. "Check."

She accidently knocked pieces over, startled by the magnitude of her compact, and sent them flying off of the board.

"We've drawn," said Hook standing. "Let us go this way." He began walking the length of the hall to the West with Fille hurrying to take her gait beside him. "Did you happen to ever spy Lady Constance when she was speaking in Hades?"

"Yes," she replied very slowly peering at Hooke with the gravest of suspicions.

Hooke turning his head to his left smiled at her.

"No!" She shook her head vehemently. She ceased walking. "I can't do that. I am incapable. Not them! Not any of them like them! I'm not like Lady Constance! No!"

"Very true; but one fine afternoon you shall," said Hooke as he paused. "Did you not once have a few words with Hera in High Tartarus on your way home?"

"How do you know these things!"

"Messengers," said Hooke with unconcerned nonchalance. "Ravens and crows. And, all sorts of fauna. And, le Marechal. And, nymphs. Les Treize. Al-Jinn. Most everyone." He resumed walking.

"You have all them as spies!" said Fille as she hurriedly reached his side.

"No," said Hooke. "I am told things others believe I do not already know. Hera was pleased you accepted her decree, yet it was only afterwards she realised you did not accept her decree; she was furious. Lady Constance spoke with her: she acquiesced to the words spoken by Lady Constance. Your father was informed afterwards by Persephone. It was the first time he laughed before her or anyone else. It was Silas Verge who was told by

Persephone who told me when we were in Lyon. So, Lady Constance may not watch over you but she has yet to withspeak the words you've said to others.

"And, Lady Constance has told Demontheses, Quintilianus, Cicero, Plutarch, Isocrates, Aristarchus and Isaeus of your progress; they're pleased. They all between them have wagers on who shall attempt cursing you into a tree or river or lake."

"I don't want to be cursed into a tree or river or lake! Nothing!"

"Do not worry that. There are many who can undo curses. It would be an honour; but I do believe a curse would in fact be reflected on to whosoever should invoke it."

"You?"

"Themis Witch-Queen."

Hooke was holding open the door which led to the two-storey atrium with it's iron works and glass roof.

"Keeping deities from interfering with Humanity?"

"If it pleases you."

✝

Hooke and Marquis Marchosias were sitting in the library of Corvusweald. The letter Hooke had been given by Themis la Grise was signed: Les Mademoiselles.

✝

Marquis Marchosias was reading the questions each of them wrote and would write Hooke's reply.

✝

"Mademoiselle Marcelle," said Marquis Marchosias: "If 'Dark oblivion shall absorb them all' do they not exist in this Reality?"

"Night Horrors?" said Marquis Marchosias.

"All les Exemplars have stayed them."

"You?"

"They fled."

"Simple sense," said Marquis Marchosias.

"They cease in this Existence. They cannot return—Reincarnate—they without memory. They only know that place. They are akin to them in the Meadows of North Asphodel after having from the river Lethe drunk."

Marquis Marchosias pondered.

"That was my reply for Mademoiselle Marcelle."

"Ah," said Marquis Marchosias.

He wrote.

†

"Mademoiselle Félix," said Marquis Marchosias: "Sacred prostitutes were suffragettes?"

"It was demonstrative theurgic ritual conceived by the Patriarchs for the benefit of Demeter, Cybele, Gaea, Damona, Nantosuelta and all of the other deities of fertility. That is one of many pendulous Contes d'Homme." Hooke went entering his library. He returned several minutes later. "Please send this," said Hooke handing Marquis Marchosias a pamphlet:

LYSISTRATA

"Do you never send tragedies?" said Marquis Marchosias.

"Why?" said Hooke. "Why send a tragic tale when all of these wights are confined by tragedy in Life? Comedy and satire acknowledge tragedy." Hooke smiled. "That opéra-tragique passage ye've been humming so grandly so?"

"*When I was a lad,*" replied Marquis Marchosias. "Her Majesty sits tragedies."

"She does," said Hooke, "because she cannot comprehend them. They defy her Logic because they haven't Reason.

"It was less arduous for her to watch *Macbeth* or *Andromache, Hamlet*; or *Oresteia, Antigone*; and those tragedies written in all of the Modern Ages for faint intellection of them rather than witness all of Terre: they are distillations of Modern Ages undemanding for her the continuance of that mode of observation."

"Mademoiselle d'Achéron," said Marquis Marchosias: "Why do you do the things you do?"

"For furtherance of the four Alchemic Virtues."

"That's all?" asked a surprised Marquis Marchosias.

"How many possible different acts may be performed for each of the four as well as the various combinations of those Virtues as well as the various numerous combinations of those Virtues with the subsets of lesser Virtues relative and implied by those four Virtues?" replied Hooke.

"Wickedness!" shouted Marquis Marchosias after his thought of numbering them collapsed. "They, I wager, must learn them by their own sleuthing."

Hooke nodded.

"Mademoiselle de Vienne," said Marquis Marchosias: "Is innate knowledge the same for all of us? We know things similarly and other things we have not thought."

"Innate knowledge, by observation, is distinguished as three given sets: Simple; Curiosity; and, Memento.

"Simple is Logic, Reason and Perception; and, the faculty of tracing the effects of those simplicities to their causes.

"Curiosity is delicate inquisitiveness with the ability to conceive or envision what one wants to know and in so doing does so.

"Memento is that which would have been known in previous states of Existence and, are of such great significance, they are, consciously, albeit vaguely remembered, in a present state; remembrances of another or loci are most common.

"The measure of each within is variable: Perception is the reason why you each think different things differently."

†

"Mademoiselle Gwen," said Marquis Marchosias: "Witches Hierarchy?"

"Hierarchy is established by capabilities alone: the Queen is one of les Exemplars whose abilities are greater than those of all thirteen; les Exemplars, or simply les Treize as they are informally known, are highest of the Elementals, are Sages Exemplar; Sages; Sorceresses and Sorcerers; Witches and Shamans; Alchemists who are practitioners of High Alchemy; Apprentices; Novitiates."

"High Alchemy?" said Marquis Marchosias.

"Low Alchemy, Alchemy and High Alchemy. Alchemy you know. Low Alchemy you've seen performed where the dupe performs conjuration but things happen horribly yet humorous in effect; Low Alchemy is performed by them what do not know they've been duped by al-Jinn and his students at the Solomonărie. High Alchemy are those same works from al-Jinn but read knowingly: they are cyfred."

"How so?"

"They must be submerged in water to be read."

"Clever," said Marquis Marchosias. "Do you not wish to include the Witches Peculiarity?"

"I should," said Hooke: "An edict—whose original title would translate as *Edict of the Philosophies of Governance of Practitioners of the Magies of Theurgy and Goety*—was issued during nascent days of the Iron Age. It is the editio princeps. It is presently referred to as *Principia Theurgia* because it sets forth les Treize have aegis over those juvenile deities from Antiquity who would perform with witchcraft interventions of malice and mayhem in the affairs of Man; and, by being so, all ill-tempered deities despise and harbour loathing of all who are or were one of les Treize."

Marquis Marchosias continued writing. He read, "Note:— Les Treize are far more dangerous and clever than those malcontent imbeciles so noted in the contes of History."

"Thy name," said Hooke; Marquis Marchosias his signature made.

†

Marquis Marchosias read from the three additional letters.

†

"Louis-Aldonse Milot," said Marquis Marchosias: "How many kingdoms exist in the Sphæres?"

"On this planet Terre in this region of Eves in Chaos—or, Nature, as you prefer—lie four départements deemed which in actuality are Sphæres: Limbus, Hades, Nubilus and Scopulus; Limbus, Hades and Nubilus are the empires of Fey whereas Scopulus is the territory of Man wherein each has four continents: the twenty four continents have kingdoms, duchies, provinces, protectorates, principalities, colonies, sultanates, emirates, city-states and territories in constant flux of waxing and failing; further, the empires are in confluence with the others: those three confluent lands—Hades and Limbus, Limbus and Nubilus, Nubilus and Hades—beget different kingdoms, provinces and autonomous territories in constant flux of waning and rising."

"Why do you not simply tell him?" said Marquis Marchosias but immediately raised his hand with index finger pointing up. "Wait. Do you have something of his?" Hooke laughed. He pointed to the letter Marchosias was holding. "Ah." Marquis Marchosias began drawing circles, signs and sigils on the letter and, after placing it on the carpet, spoke words in an ancient tongue.

Louis-Aldonse Milot appeared standing on the letter; he was dressed in his pyjamas and dressing gown. He was polishing his glass eye with his pocket handkerchief.

"Good Evening," said Marquis Marchosias cordially as he gestured for Milot to sit beside him on the sofa which Milot did in his state of disconcerted shock.

"We were replying your question 'How many kingdoms exist in the Sphæres' when le Marquis thought it best you should be here to listen," said Hooke. "Come."

Milot replaced his glass eye.

His Garçon de cuisine, his Pâtissière and five of his seventeen Apprentices entered with dishes suitable for a very late supper. His Garçon de cuisine and his Pâtissière selected things and presented the plates, cutlery and serviette to Milot who took them stunned. Hooke thanked them. They exited. "Marquis?" Hooke and le Marquis served themselves returning to find Milot still holding his plates, cutlery and serviette in the air; Hooke gently lowered the hands of Milot. "Please."

They dined until Milot awakened. Le Marquis offered Milot his letter, who after reading it, said "This is the conjuration scheme?"

"Very good!" replied Marchosias. "Summonings are less intrusive; the recipient is allowed to dress properly. Conjurations are one of the reasons Fey are in a terrible humour when conjurated. Please never do that."

"I shall not!" replied Milot as he swallowed his forkful of duck with black cherry marmalade. "On one of those instances I spoke with Monseigneur he said I should ask you about the fourth sphère of Fey that doesn't have place. How does a Sphære exist if it doesn't have place?"

"Did he?" said Hooke with a small laugh. "It has no place because it does not exist in the realm of Chronos. You visited one."

Milot startled. "This is of those mysteries Monseigneur wanted me to learn."

"Somewhat," said Hooke; "But it is one of those mysteries you will learn which shall make objects and things you find much easier to comprehend. The effects of Nature exist in the realm of Chronos; Nature does not. The effects of Chaos exist in the realm of Chronos; Chaos does not. The effects of Nature exist in the realm of Dark; Dark does not. This place of Mystery exists in those three but does not. Locorum obscurorum." Milot would speak: Hooke gestured— Milot was silent. "One day."

"Or, an evening when you are properly dressed," offered le Marquis.

"Have you read Μαθηματικὴ Σύνταξις?"

"Terribly," said Milot.

"The Almagest has been poorly translated. Those who have done so did not read it properly."

"Cryptic."

"Yes," said Hooke; "You should improve your Greek before continuing with your questions of Sphæres. *Prodromus dissertationum cosmographicarum, continens mysterium cosmographicum, de admirabili proportione orbium coelestium, de que causis coelorum numeri, magnitudinis, motuumque periodicorum genuinis & proprijs, demonstratum, per quinque regularia corpora geometrica?*"

"Yes," said Milot.

"You should read it again. Ask Félix to show you."

Milot looked at his watch. "Gracious! Constance is waiting for me!"

"I could send someone," offered Hooke.

"Yes. That would be good."

"Someone?" said Hooke as he opened the door. Enceladus came to him. "Monsieur Milot has an urgent matter."

"Indeed. Constance - my cat - is waiting for me to let her in for the night."

"That's a difficulty," said Enceladus. Hooke laughing, nodded. Enceladus took exit. Milot was confused.

"He's mostly raven. Cats do not take kindly of them."

"I could go," offered le Marquis. Hooke gestured. "This letter was written at your place of residence?"

"Yes? My study."

"Excellent," said le Marquis. He vanished.

"What happened?" asked Milot in an amused manner.

"He conjurated himself to the room in which you wrote the letter."

"Oh?"

"An article made—like writing—or used for a length of years—a pillow—in your residence is infused albeit very faint with that spirit of Place," said Hooke. "Let us continue."

"Le Marquis?"

"It may be a while. He likes cats."

"Sense of Place?" Hooke smiled. "If this place of Mystery does not exist in Chronos, are there others? Do they decay?"

"They do not decay," said Hooke; "There are others."

"Sacred trees die."

"Do they?" said Hooke; "They can be drowned in flames; they can be murdered; but do they die of old age?"

Hooke went to the coffee press: he offered Milot coffee who declined.

"All places exist in the Past, you must remember. Sacred places - Nemessos, as example - do still remain as they once were though cannot be seen as that in this Present-Day; nevertheless, those places remain sacred regardless of name."

Hooke sat.

"Sacred places are not Locorum obscurorum. Sacred places are obscured by the spirits of that place: Genius loci, Genii loci or Genius locorum."

"Nemessos?"

"Murder," said Hooke as the library was beset with subdued darkening.

Le Marquis returned.

"A most charming Causeuse she is," said le Marquis pleasantly as he appeared. He was immediately concerned with the changed demeanor of Hooke. "Sir?"

"It passes," said Hooke.

Le Marquis frowned sternly at Milot who confused gestured his ignorance.

"We continue," said Hooke. "If one takes Dante's Commedia—La Divina Commedia dell'arte—for simplistic illustration of the three Sphæres commonly thought to be, l'Inferno may be entered from la Terra; l'Inferno, il Purgatorio; il Purgatorio, il Paradiso.

"L'Inferno is excluded as Sphære because - as defined by Dante - one must enter Hades through Acheron on the surface of la Terra before voyaging in Ascension.

"If that be so, la Terra is situated precisely where Ptolemy surmised: he was not writing purely astronomically but metaphorically as well.

"Ptolemy wrote of Sphæres incased in Sphæres—Hollow Worlds—which again allows for Dante's ascension from Hades to Purgatory to Kingdom Come with Kingdom Come being the outermost sphere, if it were an ascension.

"That supposition would then allow Dante and Ptolemy to have accurately observed and written of three spheres. Limbus excluded since Dante preferred having it set in Hades.

"However, because Dante wrote he entered Hades by a river set on Earth and then did proceed down the back of Lucifer does that not signify that Hades is the outermost world and, that by his descending, all illustrations of his journey, after exiting Hades, should be rotated so as to show he was descending ventured upside down relative to the center of that sphere of Hades. Dante would believe he was ascending when he was, in actuality, venturing down."

"That's why!" exclaimed le Marquis pointing at the gravures of the illustrations by Doré.

Hooke smiled.

"True that Dante's descending in l'Enfer was Grand Guignol stage direction for dramatic effect when all ascensions are leading Dante to Glory," said le Marquis.

"However," continued Hooke, "as delightful as that theory may be, there was no Ascension or descending; but rather traversing on a horizon: Hades, Purgatory and Kingdom Come being equal are simply destinations. The gates of Passage are where they are. Dante would have found passage in the depths of those spheres.

"Unfortunately, there is not a Sphære given with the name of Purgatory."

"Everyone knows that!"

"I didn't," protested Milot.

"Dante believed Purgatory would be best suited for his contes de fées to be a Sphære rather than a kingdom in Hades; Limbo and Elysium were made punitive."

"True."

"Even so, those despicable beliefs that one in Purgatory who was neither great nor evil should stay benevolent in that place yet know they are not in Kingdom Come. Those in Purgatory would have the same lives they had on Orbis terrae with an hourly reminder as they saw through the gates their Kingdom Come they would never reach forever in the Great Hereafter."

"Insidious!" said Milot.

"Why do you bother!" said le Marquis

"La Divina Commedia dell'arte," said Hooke: "Purgatory is a Customs-House. Asphodel is the lands of Asylum at the end of the culs-de-sac. Elysium is a kingdom set in the confluence of the sphæres of Hades and of Limbus."

"Kingdom Come?"

"Holy Superstitio; holy Religio," said Hooke. "*Allgemeine Naturgeschichte und Theorie des Himmels* by Kant you have read; this reminder of his thoughts: 'In the universal silence of nature and in the calm of the senses the immortal spirit's hidden faculty of knowledge speaks an ineffable language and gives undeveloped concepts, which are indeed felt, but do not let themselves be described.'

"*Cosmologia Dives* shall describe undeveloped concepts of Sphæres."

†

Those three continued their colloquy of various subjects Milot was keen to understand; and, when their very late supper was finally done, Milot wished to be returned to his home.

Le Marquis did so.

✝

"Mister C. L. Nolan," said Marquis Marchosias: "What if, by Chance, one were able to enter, whether by conjuration or invocationis, an enchanted place, would that person, if they wish, be able to return from that place of Spirit?"

"The hours in which spirits stay are not those you keep. They can but, as Jean l'Ancien has often advised, those who visit are seldom given want to leave because, when found on their own recognizance, that place has attracted the person by memory or perceived sacrosanct intent by Syren's allure as much as that person yearned for it. Reciprocating attraction. It is often ill-performed; it is often dangerous.

"What purpose?

"If one were to enter so as to take residence, that would be understandable; but to enter an enchanted place with curiosity is no different than entering one's W.C. Novelty? Investigation? Sleuthing? Lark?

"Bethink thee twice before acting on that Syren's voice."

✝

"Jean-Marie Jules," said Marquis Marchosias: "What significance do cardinal points have in the maps of Faeries?"

"There are none more than what ye've previously deduced. It is the lines formed by the edges of the shadows on the compass with elevated cardinal points which should be investigated."

"Why do you tell him these things?"

"I'm fond of him. He is universally shunned yet has found forgotten passages and sacred sites for years. Truly monumental given his affliction."

"What affliction would that be?"

"He's Fée humaine."

✝

Themis la Grise went idle and leisurely walking on the avenue. Her corsage was lilac satin; her silk-stockings were mauve; and, her skirts were velvet of sea-green color. She wore grey opera-pumps.

She was standing on the ridge of Manaslu as the ice once silver was changed to gold by the alchemy of Nature.

✝

Hooke and Félix were at playing a game of pétanque at the furthest end of the great lawn. Snježana de Pasithea la Sorcière bleu had gone visiting with Alsea.

Félix rolled her boxwood boule close to the cochonnet.

"Do you know why your father printed those works of arcane knowledge?

Hooke lobbed his boule.

"Monsieur Tatillon's request?"

They inspected. Félix had two points.

"We tied!" exclaimed Félix.

✝

A dark figure was approaching from the house.

✝

Hooke tossed the cochonnet. Félix rolled her boule. Three large birds who had arrived were circling far over the lawn.

"Your father and he were the publishers," said Hooke as he tossed the cochonnet. "That was kept secret. Those works were collected by him and translated by your mother. Your father was the printer. He printed them for you to read which you have been doing. You may wish to ask her when next she visits of their history."

"I will." She waited. Félix was mesmered watching them in flight in the depths of the skies. "When do you tell me my fortune?"

"Our final mène," said Hooke ignoring her question as he lobbed his boule.

Félix was flustered by his seeming indifference.

La Madame Gamayun took his first boule and laughed returning to the sky.

"It took it!"

"It was la Madame Gamayun who took it," said Hooke. "Hela la Sirin is of dark feathers and Navjaci la Alkonost is of the light feathers. They're come visiting Ocythoe in the Woods." He laughed. "Unexpectedly."

"She took it!"

"It's fair play."

†

The dark figure was approaching from the house.

†

"Snježana de Pasithea la Sorcière bleu."

"Because blue is my favourite colour?"

Hooke stared at her who was smiling grandly: "No."

Hela la Sirin plummeted and took the second boule of Félix as it was rolling and laughed returning to the sky.

"She took mine!"

"Yes?"

"I can choose who I would represent when I am la Sorcière bleu?" said Félix with faint composure.

"No."

"Why?"

"All are bestowed with Wisdom, Benevolence, Guidance and Grace."

"I am those!" interrupted Félix.

Hooke, who was holding his boule with his right hand, extended his left hand to the left of him where she stood, with his thumb and forefinger an inch apart, as he was staring at the cochonnet.

"Guidance?" said Félix after consideration.

"Teaching."

Hela la Sirin took his second boule and smiling nodded before leisurely flying off to the Woods.

"All who know the practices of Goëtia are similar, yet they each have a marvellous trait distinguishing them from others that is, to wit, la Sorcière bleu and thee have slight in common so you are not replacing her - since that is what les Mademoiselles are deducing—Erroneously—of this - merely things are changed. There is always a balance of mysteria regardless of colours unless—Of course—one happens to be from an ancient lineage then that colour would be deferentially their's."

"Ancient?"

"All Grey-Witches have been of a single lineage," replied Hooke. "Those tomes you've been reading are very different, aren't they? Logic, Reason, Sense, Perception."

"Grace?" interrupted Félix.

"Themis la Grise," said Hooke, "may explain it to you."

†

The dark figure was approaching from the house.

†

Navjaci la Alkonost took the second boule of Félix returning to the sky.

"All true believers shall break their eggs at the convenient end?"

"Before nine in the morning, it's large end first. After dark: small end first," said Félix.

"Between nine in the morning and before dark?"

"Who does that!" she said with her young-age face of contempt.

"Vatican Hill?"

"It is a hillside on the west bank of the Tiber River in Rome. Hill of the Vates."

"Do you know how argent exhalations of Æther collected by projection are made useable in medicaments?"

"A retort of half-formed glass set on an iron pan over roiled water from the Sea taken, during the Midwinter night, in a copper ladle with a tin-lined bowl having seven holes, collected in a bottle with a curved pouring pipe of cobalt glass."

"Sorbet?" said Hooke as turned to face Félix and tossed, from over his shoulder, his final boule high in the air.

Madame Gamayun took his final boule and smiling nodded before she went flying off to the Woods.

She stared amazed as Madame Gamayun descended with her ill-got spoils into the Woods beside the Sea.

"You've bested me," said Hooke.

"This can't be!" protested Félix. "They stole them."

"House Rules," said Hooke calmly as he spooned his ice. "All things of this realm are in play."

"Your House Rules," said Félix.

Hooke smiled.

"Lightning?" said Félix.

"Especially," said Hooke.

Félix thought to reply; but she remembered their conversation on Shadows and Shades: she weakly smiled. She was suddenly made aware of a downdraught over her. She meekly peered, peeking; Navjaci la Alkonost was stationary suspended a few feet above them by the slow beating of her wings.

"If you would, she should like your boule," whispered Hooke.

Félix mechanically tossed her final boule towards Navjaci la Alkonost who deftly caught it with her beak and smiling nodded at Félix before flying off to the Woods.

"Sorbet!" declared Félix collecting her wits.

Hooke pointed to the gentleman who was standing behind her with an etched glass tray with silver raised galleries. He held the tray and removed the silver dome cover: one sterling spoon with one glass cup filled of sorbet for her; Hooke had his.

Hela la Sirin returned. She landed and went to where the first boule of Félix had remained and took it.

She took her spoon; and, she took her cup of sorbet: it was lime.

"How do you know this is my favourite!" said Félix vividly accusing him.

Hooke to the first footman—de Sérifontaine—turned. "Do you know who knows how we know this is mademoiselle's favourite?"

"We were informed Mademoiselle Trique favoured this during an en plein air repast in the parc de Montjuzet; and, while strolling with Mademoiselle de Pasithea in the cathédrale city of Weychester; and, when visiting Madame la Fae on her isle; and, when lodging with Mademoiselle la Grise at her home in Hookland; and, while seated in the coffeehouse *l'Odéon pneumatique* with Her Majesty; and, during His Majesty's Salon where the kitchen was requested for fifth helpings; and, every Thursday after supper at her aunt's and uncle's house," said de Sérifontaine. Hooke nodded. He went.

"A mystery."

"Oh," she quietly replied. "That?"

"Grapefruit."

She shuddered.

"All those tomes," said Hooke as he began strolling returning to the house, "of Logic, Reason, Sense, Perception they are until read by submergence in a flat-bottomed vessel of rainwater which you've done for years yet not once thought 'twas odd." He had a spoonful of his sorbet.

"That's why!"

"No," said Hooke as he handed his cup of sorbet to Hela la Sirin who had been patiently waiting as she went strolling beside them. "But it suffices."

Hela la Sirin returned to the woods. Félix stared at Madame la Sirin and she stared at Hooke and she silently went beside him.

†

Themis had taken the three members of the Illapses Agency, Ltd. to the Century House standing on the embankment of the River Thames.

It was of Palladian architecture of gargantuan magnitude of breadth, depth and height designed by Inigo Jones. It was a massive but unassuming granite structure with it's Doric columns. It was set on the stylobate at the end of one-hundred and thirty limestone steps.

They stood on the grand staircase and watched: vehicles arrived; wights strode up the staircase; wights strolled down the street and up the steps to enter the House; several very different wights did arrive: a géant, a fellow with a squid on the top of his head, a fellow with stag antlers emerging from his head, a merman struggling using crutches ascending the steps, a fellow with the body of a serpent and a humanly head, and several goblins.

They were confounded by those appearances but more so was that the populace on the street did not react.

She continued walking up the steps.

"What is this place?" asked Milot.

"Gentlemen's house," said Themis.

"Haven't you ever wished to enter?" asked Jules.

"How droll." She laughed. "Women are not allowed. Never but once did a Femme enter into that sanctum and she did so with a fox! Such scandalous effrontery was blasphemous! Numerous members resigned after that fateful incident. Those who allowed such wanton mutiny of the rules were discharged."

"Who attends?" asked Nolan.

"All sorts. They are few who are not such as Pantaloons, Mountebanks or Guilers. Let us enter."

†

"Your engagement with Dame Hades was an introduction in the bureaucracies of State," said Zoë. "Aide-de-camp, Chargée d'affaires, Ambassadress: all for the acquaintedness of Congresses, Parliaments, Presidents, Kings and Leagues and Courts of Prædictas Fatales. The ministry changes. It returns to being a congress from all of the nations. Your station shall be above that of Minister-Cardinalis Taberd, but it shall not be that duty."

"I have heard of him," replied Elfriede de Vienne. "We never met."

"You shan't. Minister-Cardinalis Taberd was taken ill and shall not return. Chancellor-Ambassadress de Vienne has not need in meeting him."

"When?"

"Whenever you wish," said Zoë: "There is still the matter of ministers returning and finding suitable replacements for those expectedly deceased. Though, it is known the War of Indignations, which is simply the Second War of Revelation, shall before full Moon next begin."

"What am I to do?"

"You are to be the sôle agent of the Congress in all matters extraordinary which would require involvement by the public and represent those petitions made by the public of the congress; surrogate to each. And, prevention of Suzerainty which shall appear, as it forever does, between greater over lesser states and nations; Fille d'Achéron and you are both responsible for that objective.

"There are ministers enough who will assist you with details of this Indignant war, if you should wish to begin in this recently formed rôle."

"How am I ever to do that!"

"That is for you to decide, my dear. I imagine it will be nothing more or less than what you have done with Persephone excepting you are tasked with greater responsibility with Divorum—Fey—than Man.

"You will interact with those remaining but nothing more. Here and there you'll be until that hour when you decide there is nothing more to do for the state of Terre.

"The Ministry returns to the shadows in that locus of Reality."

"Withering," said de Vienne.

"Aye," said Zoë. "This poisoning is the final Acte begun during the Plague Years."

"The Industrial Age?"

"No. The Industrial Age was the institution of cause but it was the foregoing Acte — The Plague Years — where clockworks were set for their abandonment of the beliefs of Fey and thus as well assuring the doom of Scopulus."

"Plagues have occurred in every century."

"Those are the plagues of Nature," said Zoë. *The Plague Years*, when spoke by Fey, are those years of exploratory conquest, under letters patent signed by monarchies of the Republic of Venice, Portugal, Castile, Duchy of Courland and Semigallia, England, France, Spain, Sweden, Denmark, Norway, Germany, Prussia: Western Europe.

"They brought their European diseases of body with them; but it was not those diseases which left colonial places in a ruinous condition destitute and deprived of the beliefs of the Ancients.

"The thirteen British colonies demonstratively succeeding.

"The Plague Years forebode all of the things to come sending plagues with their European diseases of their superiority, of their righteousness, of the mind: the Age of Discovery."

†

Merle was reclined in a Morris chair; his legs on an ottoman of similar design. Hooke was laying on an Art Nouveau couch with his feet on the armrest. They had been speaking of all things transpired and those which would come to pass.

"Al-Jinn?" said Merle.

"He shall be my guest when that congress is summoned," said Hooke. "I wish to make amends for the discourtesy of his never having been formally introduced to the Ghost-Lords."

"He knows?" said Merle.

"He has been invited for picnicking at the palace," said Hooke, "on a day of significance as yet unknown to me. He accepted."

"All's soon aright," said Merle. "Her Majesty?"

"She fares well," said Hooke.

"Thee?"

"Resurgam. Thou?"

"Ad Profundis."

"After?"

"Sojourning with Her Majesty on Traces until departing from the Barbary Coast to see if one travels backwards in time as the Bridge-Keeper did say. Thee?"

"Ad amor aeternam."

"Et lux in tenebris lucet et tenebrae eam non conprehenderunt."

Their dwindling conversation slowly recessed further until they sat reposed in the stillness of the vast plain of Cassiope in the province of Zhįʼii-tsintah in the kingdom of Sæ Sgàilean.

†

Elfriede de Vienne was walking in Nevers and turned entering a cul-de-sac. Malebranches and fell men appeared.

"No!" Hooke said as he appeared and placed a hand on her shoulder as she would approach them in defiance. "Thy hands have not bloodied: they shall not now nor ever. I have given an unspoken oath for Honour that your protection I would keep: I do so now. Come!"

And they departing vanished in the Dark as Hercule did appear.

†

They had entered into the antechamber but, as there were none to greet her, they began walking to the Great Hall.

"Madame! Madame! Madame! Women are not permitted," bellowed a wizened Vice-Footman who ran hurriedly after her. Themis paused; and said as he approached her: "I was unaware."

The Vice-Footman panting nodded appreciatively; he gestured Themis to follow him. Themis smiled as she continued into the great room.

Furors occurred.

Le Directeur with numerous members of staff approached as their raucous protestations had been heard heralding their long advance across the Hall. "Mesdames are unpermissable!" le Directeur declared.

"My name was set as a member," replied Themis.

"Unlikely," retorted le Directeur.

Proteus had looked up from reading and, on seeing it was Themis, wandered over to the place where she and her guests were standing.

"Please," said Themis as she walked towards the front desk.

"Irregular," said le Directeur grimacing. "Name?"

"Themis la Grise."

All of those stood by le Directeur and all those encircling Themis blanched; those close to her stepped backwards several feet from her.

Le Directeur read the members tome. "Irregular." He shuddered.

"Who authorised this?" demanded le Director.

The Desk-Clerk ran his finger from her name in the ledger to the sigil at the end of the line.

Le Director gasped with grimaces.

He faced Themis. He smiled a very painful grimaced face. "Identity papers."

"I have none"

The Desk-Clerk whispered while le Director read the entry of her membership.

"No admittance!" exclaimed le Director triumphantly. "We cannot prove your identity."

"She is who she says," said Proteus from the back of that ensemble.

She turned. "Proteus, I am surprised you would be in attendance, but it is a pleasure." He bowed.

"She may be any sort of common impersonator," said the Vice-Director.

"Ah, well," said Proteus with a mischievous grin.

"Perhaps," she replied to the Vice-Director as she stared at him unblinking, "I may signify my station by setting alight the hair, or" — She waited as Ares passed-by. — "toupees, of all Gentlemen and fellows within this place which means those on the upper and lower stories, too."

"You wouldn't dare!"

"My pardon," interrupted Nolan nervously: "She doesn't dare; she does. I have seen her set afire ships of pirates in the Strait of Malacca."

"She wouldn't!"

C. L. Nolan groaned.

She did did Themis la Grise an elegant rising J-like flourish with her left hand slightly above the head of the director: his hair was afire. The flames jumped frolicking from head tumbling scampering on to head of all those members and guests and staff in that structure who then ran screaming and shrieking, bellowing and roaring except for those who delighted in the effect. Ares, Jupiter and those others with toupees threw them on the floor and danced stomping them.

The three members of the Illapses Agency, Ltd. were whispering. Jules stepped forward. "We determinedly thank you for escorting us when Mister Hooke suddenly unexpected could no longer introduce us to this establishment." He paused. "And, not setting our hair alight."

"My pleasure," said Themis. She turned. "Proteus, I should like to introduce you to the three members of the Illapses Agency, Ltd., Hookland."

"Charming place," said Proteus.

They strolled into the Great Hall.

✝

Hercule with his dagger drew a large ensō in the air above him. The unclosed ensō was of all the hues of the Prusse in the sky. The air grew silvery flecked with points of light as the dagger he then balanced the point of the blade on the palm of his hand stayed stationary in the air after withdrawing his hand.

Light began in rivulets seeping from eyes and mouths and ears until it became like flames engulfing their heads; the demons and men screamed hideously before their voices were mere echoes heard from a distance. The blood seeping from the headless standing bodies formed a pond as tar of Shadows rose from the floor: the silvery air and stationary points of light were dissipated by the rising shapes of ghôles.

The dagger slowly descended radiating small ripples of the tiles until it was vanished beneath the floor.

"Sirs," said Hercule as ghôles rose.

Javelle appeared followed moments after by Hiolle: they surveyed the scene as the ghôles engulfed remains and went then returning to the darkness of Dark.

"Count de Plessis," said Hercule.

Javelle did nod. Hiolle stood in anger.

The shrieking screams were farther in the distance but echoing still.

Hercule departed.

✝

C. L. Nolan, Louis-Aldonse Milot and Jean-Marie Jules were introduced. Proteus offered Themis his chair which she accepted.

"It is a rarity that fellows of your persuasion and station are guests," said Iapetus.

"They are not guests," replied Themis. "Mister Hooke has done so."

"As it is we have Themis la Juste as a member," said Proteus.

"We are members?" said Nolan.

"Yes. Though, they did not ask about that, did they?" said Themis.

Nereus and Paean who dispelled with extinguishing fires entered into the conversation after Iapetus refused to have his burning head extinguished.

"What of Humanity?" said Paean.

"Fata divus," said Themis.

"Mister Nolan," said Nereus, "are we to understand Spiritualism in this Age is not Spiritualism?"

C. L. Nolan spoke mainly for them. Milot interjected; Jules viewed all of the marvells in that salle.

"So, yes. Modern Age has replaced devils and demons and Fey with ghosts; and, Mysticism," said Nolan in conclusion.

"Ghosts?" said Iapetus incredulously.

"Haven't you followed this Age of Victoria?" laughed Paean. "Very sterile. Ghosts are the perfect representation of the Other World for them. They are white and pale. Purity; and, languishing."

"It is the Edwardian era, my dear sir," said Proteus.

"Nevertheless, the ancient works of Occult, Spirit and Esoteric have existed since before Aristotle but were not popular until the Victorian age had it's *Spirits*."

They continued conversing.

†

Ningishzida had been intrigued watching Jules as Jules went strolling with his right-hand trailing on the walls and occasionally facing across the floor counting steps before smiling. Ningishzida introduced himself to Jules after speaking with Themis who explained the extraordinary practice of Jean-Marie Jules; Poseidon concurred. They wandered off in conversation of secret places Jules had found as well as the places that had not yet been found by him.

†

Themis was playing Jeu de tarot with Poseidon and Aglibol who were losing.

✝

Hooke and Elfriede de Vienne were standing beside la Lys in Merville. They were surrounded by the thirty-seven small Gentlemen.

She stared confused and angry at Hooke. He very slowly shook his head frowning and said sternly: "He does not wish you to remember him as what he does to protect you. Thou art confused as should be; but thy anger 'tis selfish. Speak with Hercule not by the anger of thoughts you hold towards me."

"Hercule!" said de Vienne. Her thoughts were muddled and embarrassed was she at Hooke's words.

"Wait until he comes," said Hooke as he disappeared walking in the shadows.

✝

Themis was playing Jeu de tarot with Poseidon and Aglibol who were losing.

King Vinea approached within ten feet of their game, declaring: "Hecate is my queen!"

The salle went quiet with murmurs of reproach as well as encouragement. Poseidon and Aglibol would stand to defend her honour but she shook her head. She stood.

"My honour remains unbesmirched by thy simple act as Gentlemen, Gentlemen," she said smiling. She turned to face King Vinea. "Sir?"

"Witches are not allowed amoungst Deities and Kings even should they be Queens." She unblinking watched him. "There are many here unamused by your parlour trick." She unblinking watched him. "Go thither!" She tilted her head. "Thou art smote!" King Vinea gestured with the palms of his hands of his rigid arms at Themis who did not move. All were astounded: she was unharmed.

Laughter and boisterous clapping was heard from the foyer.

Hieronymus-Baleberithe-Seere ad-Din al-Jinn entered.

"Themis Grey-Witch!" bellowed al-Jinn.

"Maître al-Jinn, what a pleasant surprise," said Themis.

"Idiots!" bellowed al-Jinn to the small coterie of King Vinea. "He needs assistance." He peered around the salle. "And, those who are dismissive of having a Femme extraordinaire in this hallowed house, for your own safety, should follow."

He went to King Vinea who was standing Medusa-stricken, picked him up by his throat, and hurled him at that small coterie. They dragged King Vinea from the House; and, fled.

"Sirs," said Themis to Poseidon and Aglibol, "I shall have thirty coconut cream pies sent to your rooms by afternoon tomorrow. I forfeit." And, with that, she and al-Jinn went taking a turn around the Great Hall.

"Why are you here?" asked Themis.

"I've never been. I volunteered. Hecate heard her name spoken by Vinea, whom she detests, was come beseeching me and wanted you to know she is not to be included in his villainies."

"All these coincidences! What is happening?"

"Never mind that, lassie," said al-Jinn delighted. "We have things in need of intrigues."

"Lassie?" said Themis gaily. "You've not called me that since then."

"'Tis certainty."

Elfriede de Vienne was standing on le quai Courbet beside la Lys in Merville. She was surrounded by thirty-seven small Gentlemen.

Hercule arrived.

"My dear sir," said de Vienne, "I must thank you for your chivalry."

He nodded abstractly as he stared at her until she graciously replied: "I'm unharmed." He smiled faintly.

"Monsieur Hooke brought me here and now you have come," said de Vienne. "All these mysteries." Suddenly, she remembered her vision vividly of the Wonder Box having displayed of Hercule and her strolling beside a river. She shivered.

"Why here?" said de Vienne composing herself.

"I was here." Hercule peered about. "It's not like metropolises but this quietude has a nice place." He nodded. "I liked it."

They began strolling on the bank of la Lys.

"I know I am being rude to ask but was not able when we sat together but are you Hercule Némésis I've heard about?"

He shook his head. "Hercule."

"Your familial name."

"Hercule. Only that."

She was confused.

"I was abandoned. Nuns raised me. I was sent away—Seven—because I was acting in behaviors scarily frightful for the others and nuns. The bishop thought me possessed by Devil. I was sent away."

"Where?"

"Everywhere," replied Hercule. "Adventures. I met Maître Hieronymus-Baleberithe-Seere ad-Din al-Jinn in Marseille. We journeyed everywhere. He took me as apprentice until—in a Spring—one day—he introduced me to Professeur-Maître Jacques-François Huillard who he thought I could be of service since my apprenticeship had concluded many of those years before I met Professeur-Maître."

"How long were you with Maître al-Jinn?"

Hercule shook his head with narrowed eyes and his mouth pursed.

"How long have you been with Professeur-Maître Huillard?"

Hercule shrugged.

She peered at him.

"I unremember things," said Hercule. "There are things I do I do not know when I could them do I do. Those seem familiar."

"Under-Orderlies?" asked de Vienne. "You spoke of them in anger once when you were speaking thoughts of yourself."

"The Grand Blessé-Invalide," mused Hercule remembering; and, replied: "My gratitude. I remember! I was angry because I could not remember the Asylum of Saint-Lazare of Reason but you have remembered for me." He thought. "I do vague remember service of the Under-Orderlies at the Asylum Saint-Lazare. They were Under-Orderlies performing Under-Orderly methods of things orderly. I remember their Delicates method."

"That is?" said de Vienne amused

Hercule unbuttoned his trousers; he let them fall to his ankles. Hercule was wearing a voluminous number of lace and silk delicates of all colours.

She stared at his delicates. She pointed. "Those?"

"Delicates," replied Hercule conversationally: "Les Fleurs — from gardens in London, Kuching, Lyon and Zone-Saint-Cloud and Hambourg; and, Shanghai — gave them."

Elfriede de Vienne abruptly departed. The thirty-seven Gentlemen faced Hercule. He gestured. "Discreetly." They followed her slowly strolling in a single column.

Hercule was curious about her departure but shrugged and buttoned his trousers; and, went continuing on their stroll along on the bank of la Lys.

†

Themis la Grise, al-Jinn and the three members of the Illapses Agency, Ltd. were continued walking on the embankment of the Thames.

"I did nothing," said Themis.

"No?" said al-Jinn.

"Subrupio," said Themis; and, to the disbelieving glance of al-Jinn, replied: "Proteus, Iapetus and - I believe - Naberius, who was standing in the foyer, were the Knights of the Realm. Medusa's stare, Oasele prometeic and Visul Nyx were sent; but I could not tell who did which because they went simultaneously." She laughed "It would have been Şarpe internalis by me."

"Serpent internal?" asked Nolan.

"Aye, what may that be?" said al-Jinn merrily. "I showed you Şarpe, but you've made a difference."

"The serpent would exit his mouth, coiling upwards beginning with the legs; and, while doing so, would be enlarging to normal size beginning with it's head until the mouth was large enough to consume him beginning with his head while it's tail was uncoiling from his body. I'd imagine that afterwards it was intending on strolling from this place down to the Thames and go."

Al-Jinn was delighted. The three members of the Illapses Agency, Ltd., who were well acquainted with Magie rituelle and lesser charms and spells, were again reminded of their station.

"Ningishzida is an interesting deity, isn't he," said Jules to Themis.

"We have twice spoken," said Themis. "Sir?"

"Ma'am," began Nolan hesitantly. "How does one perform Şarpe internalis if not by some form of Chrysopoeia?"

"He is interesting," replied al-Jinn; "She is interesting. I believe he found you præstigiously more interesting. Did he ask King Purson to speak with you and, when you did, he refused to answer your query of a secret place you wish to find?"

"The enchantment requests a spirit of a serpent, which may be near-by, to enter the encasement of the object. The spirit is bound by pseudo-homunculus: the spirit has a carapace which transforms into it's previous encasement."

"How did you know?" asked Jules.

"Resurrection-of-sorts," offered Milot.

"No," replied Themis with a mild vexatious tone. "Le Turc mécanique."

"I watched them when I entered," said al-Jinn; "They were in argument about you. Purson knows of hidden things, and treasures, and secret things; divine things; a place kept secret. Things you seek."

"Purson was an odd fellow," said Jules; "He kept staring at me as we spoke. A surprised expression."

"What secret place?" asked Nolan and Milot simultaneously.

"Shall we sit?" said al-Jinn gesturing to a bench. Themis sat and, when the Illapses did not accept his invitation, al-Jinn sat beside her.

"Titkos Hely," said Jules smiling and amused at Nolan and Milot. "That's the name I was first told when I spoke with an Antiquaire in Magyarország. 'Secret Place.' It was in 1781 I first heard rumoured whisperings about a place-that-wasn't where a treasure unbelievable was to be found. Though, none knew what that treasure was. I went in search of the 'The Place that Wasn't' simply to find it. In treasures I have no interest." He sighed profoundly. "I—Eventually—found it after fruitless searches yet I did not come to it." He looked at each who were nodding in encouragement.

"Odd ages ago," began Jean-Marie Jules and said:

The Cartographe's Tale

It began after visiting l'Exposition Universelle in 1878.

I had not forgotten about that secret place, but I had ceased following rumours after having done so for ninety three years. There were Chance incidents, after my abandonment, over the next four years which made me rethink those years; I discovered I was making inappropriate inquiries. It was at l'Exposition Universelle I met an antiquaire who knew me that I could not recall ever having met. We spoke. I was informed it was needed for me to return to the last city I visited if ever I should wish continuing. It was there I was instructed to visit an individual from the Swiss Confederacy, before it fell to invasion by the l'Armée Révolutionnaire française in 1798, who would be waiting for me in the shadows of the castle Vaduz.

I traveled to Vaduz.

He stood in the shadows. He wore black robes with the cowl covering his face which I did not see because he was staring down over the ville. His hands clasped at his waist were bone white. I did not recognize his accent though he was speaking a Germanic language albeit oddly familiar. He said he was from an order of Chevaliers errants.

He informed me the map I had obtained in Hambourg was intentionally in error. He asked me if I still carried salt from Lunéville Saltworks; I did.

I showed him that map.

He pointed to Valentschina. He pointed to Türtsch. He informed me the gate was not directly aligned with Türtsch but six degrees North of it where I would find a shrine to which I would offer the Lunéville salt.

I went from Vaduz and went to the commune of Valentschina in Austria. I went six degrees North of Türtsch. I found the shrine. I made my offering. I turned from the shrine. The chevalier errant was standing behind me. I thought, at first, it was the same chevalier from the castle but when he spoke his accent was different. He kept his head bowed. He led.

We retraced my steps until we came to a clearing that was not there before, where, at the opposite side of the clearing, was a stone wall with a grille; beyond the grille was a dark forest. The chevalier spoke softly. The gate opened. He bid me farewell.

I entered the forest. It did not seem long before I stepped from the eaves of the forest.

The light was nothing but long twilights. It seemed in those moments during the long twilights the rolling hills were swells of the sea.

It was a stone cottage.

All about was hills. All of the small hills led on an incline to a larger hill on which the stone cottage sat. It was a great ocean where swells were lulled set in acts of rising and falling on which one could walk. The house without a path set in the rolling hills of grasses was—Perhaps—three leagues from where I stood at the edge of the woods; there was not path nor lane; and, shade and light never changed in that place; but smoke was ever rising from the chimney.

I was ill-prepared.

I measured it with thumb and index: it was about two inches. It was always about two inches. I used my glasses, but the cottage was always about two inches; I tested by sight by viewing the trees which were found to be magnified as would be expected, except there. My sextant mysterious did not function. I walked for hours across the fields yet the house was never closer. I walked for hours more until by my time-piece it was after midnight and still the house was never closer. I slept for hours. I continued my journey from the previous hours for hours across the fields but the house was still not ever closer. I changed course. I turned to what I believed was Northwest because my compass, on entering that land, only pointed North, and, after midnight where shade and light never changed, I slept. I was no further West than I was closer to that house. I changed and turned South and marched towards the forest I could then see.

The clockworks of the Sky were once again in movement when I entered the woods. I was returned to the lane from Valentschina I had walked three days earlier.

†

Jean-Marie Jules had concluded his tale.

"It was not three days later," said al-Jinn.

"No," said Jules. "Three years."

"What significance do you place on being informed of the Swiss Confederacy?" asked Nolan.

"I cannot find significance. L'Armée Révolutionnaire française in 1798 neither," said Jules.

"Does it have a name? This place?" asked Milot of al-Jinn.

"Yes," said al-Jinn.

They waited expectantly until Milot said: "It cannot be spoken."

"No," said al-Jinn. "It cannot be spoken because it seemingly does not exist. 'The Place that Wasn't' is a fine guess by Monsieur Jules."

Themis had gone quiet during that conversation. "I know this place." Al-Jinn smiled. "My Mother told the Lore-Tales of it. They were tragedies. None ever crossed the clearing. Some heroically died in their attempts; some went Mad; some disappeared; few returned."

"Were names spoken?" asked an excited Jules.

"Yes; but, they were of a language long disguised," said Themis. "They were not the actual names but clever obfuscated variants.

"Obfuscare - 'I darken' from late Latin - is a horrifick curse to use. Those variants of the names themselves may be curses when spoken."

"What is the object they sought in that lore?" asked an intrigued Nolan.

"Other tales, as she I have read them all," said al-Jinn, "have it as the home of a great mysterious alchemist who may solve ills; a demiurge imprisoned; a beautiful goddess imprisoned; a goat, a lamp, a horse, a loom, a sword, a spear, a crown, an orb, a spindle. It is possible that any one of those would be found or several found at once. Or, none.

"It is an evil place. Those gentlemen may be fair, or they may be evil foul. No one knows since none have taken refuge in that cabane."

"Did any lore speak of where this clearing may be?" asked a thoughtful Jules.

"It is not the clearing you must care about!" said al-Jinn in his great stern voice: "Do not ever mention the cabane or clearing or forest beyond the gate; nothing you find beyond the gate is to be mentioned when seeking answers. It is the gate!

"All things seen may be in a different place than at first perceived. Remember!"

"That object is unknown," said Themis as she thought at length. "It is again shrouded in obfuscations. My favorite tale had the object be the original box of Pandore. The contents of the first box were not mentioned. I must remember." She paused while she thought with eyes closed. "There was mention in another tale about a vessel. I must remember." She opened her eyes. "They were not virtues but something else. It may have been an oblique reference to the box of Pandore.

"It is well documented that all High Gods younger are vindictive and vain."

Themis stood speaking to herself and, as she continued, she was in rising indignation.

"Cowardly.

"Arrogant.

"Personifications.

"Whining.

"The twenty-nine Vices en tout."

She paused.

"Aphrodite, Hermes, Athéna, Peithois were written to have given Pandore gifts so to form 'beautiful evil.'

"The Graces and the Horae would have done so guileless.

"Hesiod wrote 'the earth and sea are full of evils' after she opened the box. Those evils diseased all in the four kingdoms. All. It was *their* box. It was *their* evils!

"'Only Hope was left within her unbreakable house, she remained under the lip of the jar, and did not fly away. Pandore replaced the lid of the jar. This was the will of aegis-bearing Ζεύς the Cloudgatherer.'

"Elpis was not in the second box!

"Pandore 'All-giving.' Anesidora 'She who sends up gifts.' Pandore la Bénéfique. Pandore la Maléfique. Two boxes! I must find those tomes."

"Pithos," said Milot who finally could no longer his irked silence keep.

"If I choose to say 'box' instead of the proper word – *pithos* – please indulge me," said Themis la Grise coolly. Milot alarmed nodded in a fervent manner. "You shall read them with me."

"I..." would begin Milot with an apologetic tone but al-Jinn jerked him away from Themis who stood in a delicate slowly swirling vortex of snowflakes. "Ma'am," said al-Jinn holding Milot in the air by his collars.

"Ζεύς!" she exclaimed calmly. She placed her left hand over her mouth and nose as she thought. She breathed slower. The pavement was creaking as ice spread from where she stood.

"Flee," said al-Jinn as he gestured to Nolan and Jules as he released dropping Milot next to them who did not hesitate: they three fled.

"Maître al-Jinn," she began as that delicate slowly swirling vortex of snowflakes crept over walls and street with ice in the snow globe of her rage: "I've found myself a conundrum: eunuch; or, limace; or, syphilitic– are what I cannot decide is more appropriate for that pissy drunken letch. Sir? Which do you believe is most appropriate?"

"Cyclus patientes is most appropriate," said al-Jinn laughing.

"So it is," she said. She closed her eyes for many minutes. She smiled. "Retribuo."

"Seven," said al-Jinn after she concluded.

She opened her eyes shining.

"Retribuo," said al-Jinn proudly.

"You taught me."

He offered his arm and she took his arm in her's as they would go in search of the fled and missing Illapses Agency.

✝

Fille d'Achéron, Elfriede de Vienne, Marcelle, Tochi no akaru-sa, Félix Trique, Caroline d'Eirene, Madame Gallardo, Mary la Toute-Douée, Dame Hinojosa, Aglaea d'Olive and Zoë had gone by ferry northwards on the Saône from Mâcon. They began their sojourning to le Morvand from Chalon-sur-Saône.

✝

"Ningishzida said something," said Jules. "I believe he was asking Purson a question which I should ask someone. I believe this because Purson refused to reply to my question but did reply to a very similar question asked by Ningishzida. I've yet to know."

"What did Purson reply?" asked Themis.

"'One cannot arrive at the cottage by treading with legs of two on land but by those of the Æther must be done yet none with wings may fly' was his answer," said Jules. "I cannot make out what it means."

"What ever it is you intend, keep exceedingly cautious," said al-Jinn. "It is an evil place even if those Guides are not.

"I believe it to be a beautiful sleeping goddess; and, those who would rescue her, they must be virtuous, virginal, and worthy of posing in printed advertisements for gentlemen's fashions."

"Assiette de mode?" She smiled at him.

"The Sleepy Beauty Goddess would not want an ogre to have triumphed over Evil to then save her with his kiss. Contes de fées never lie."

"How tall is he?"

"Three foot."

"That's fine. How many teeth does he have?"

"He has all."

"That's favorable."

"Does he play Tarot?"

"One of the finest players ever known."

"That's done. I would be pleased."

Milot, Nolan and Jules smiled weakly.

They laughed.

†

They entered Maroviduenno that which was formed as a promontory of the dark large aspect of woods extending northwards into the Jurassic sea.

They stood on le Mont Beuvray near the site of Bibracte.

†

Themis la Grise and the three members of Illapses Agency, Ltd. were strolling on their way to a place commended by Nolan in Soersditch.

Hieronymus-Baleberithe-Seere ad-Din al-Jinn had left them in Whitechapel wandering to the Old Street station before he would take the Northern Black Line to Highgate.

"There is a tome of three-hundred and thirty seven volumes you should read if you wish more to know of the Fey, *Les Curiosités*," said Themis. "It is a collection of illustrations and text in minutiae of all Fey known."

"Why are so many women in the higher stations of Life?" asked Nolan. "The Moeræ are Clotho, Nona the Ninth, Lachesis, Decima the Tenth, Atropos, and Morta; the Horæ are Thalatte, Flora, Auxesia, Hegemone, and, Carpho; and the Charites have Aglaea, Euphrosyne, Thalia, Cleta, Auxo, Peitho, Phaenna, Pasithea, Charis, Antheia, Eudaimonia, Paidia, Pandaisia, Eupheme, Philophrosyne, Eucleia, Euthenia and Pannychis. The Muses!"

"Fey are of these three sphæres; these three sphæres are of Nature," replied Themis: "Nature is Matriarchal."

†

Marcelle was standing in her room at l'Hôpital Coulmier while Alcyoneus the Messenger waited for her reply for that which he had presented her with a folded page of delicate rice paper written:

The low viscosity entrails-type darkness had flowed effusive from the glass and the depth of dark was reflected on the obsidian become effluvia that had the chamber filled; the dark lantern had been positioned Cyclopean light burned eternal of entrance wooden steps corrupted by Age that led into the ever darkened lands beyond the glass purloined, waiting for one who would not be returned; on the mantle a single silver sterling candlestick strangled by the wire wound on a carte which was printed,

An Invitation of Logic and Sense from the Cheshire Cat

She opened it. It was blank. She smiled and went to the casement turning it so the blank side was pressed against the glass exposing it to the Sky-light, read:

> *If the pendulum of the mind alternates between sense and nonsense, and if in all chaos there is a cosmos and in all disorder a secret order where strangers used to gather together at the cinema and sit together in the dark, like Ancient Greeks participating in the mysteries, dreaming coming to consciousness without pain,*

are we set in Madness?

Marcelle made her reply. Alcyoneus the Messenger bowed; and, went.

†

Zoë, Themis la Grise and Morgan le Fay with Acionnae de Tronçais, who had come for an audience with Zoë, were standing on the pavement after having had a light repast when numerous English-speaking tourists beleaguered arrived with maps in hand.

"Ma'amzelles?" said their self-elected guide who to them spoke the name of the establishment they were seeking.

Zoë astounded with amusement pointed to the sign above them,

La Brasserie des renards heureux

"Mercy." They entered the brasserie.

"The brassière of the happy vixens?" Zoë mused.

"Veneration and glorification of the Holy brassière would be novel," noted Acionnae de Tronçais.

"A glass-cased reliquary would be needed," added Morgan le Fay.

"Pilgrimages," said Dame Hinojosa.

"Citizens-femme could show their's as they all are to be fashioned from the relic and are Holy, too," said Caroline d'Eirene.

"How many vixens should there be?" asked Marcelle.

"Thirteen," said Zoë.

They laughed.

"Lady Constance would never," said Acionnae de Tronçais still in high laughter.

"No," said Themis. "I will ask her. She does believe not any like her. We will prove her wrong, if we invite her to participant in this Holy endeavor. She was not always as you see her. She'll oblige."

"She'll protest," said Zoë; "She will not—However—blush."

†

"Mneme happily sends her regards and wishes this play of your design cease before others are made inconsequential in the scheme of things," said Hermes approaching them, "as demanded by Athene; and, after thy reflections are made end, do come visit." He peered leery at Themis.

"Hermes," said Themis: "Walk with us."

Hermes disconsolately viewed Zoë, Themis la Grise, Morgan le Fay, Acionnae de Tronçais, Fille d'Achéron, Elfriede de Vienne, Marcelle, Tochi no akaru-sa, Félix Trique, Caroline d'Eirene, Madame Gallardo, Mary la Toute-Douée, Dame Hinojosa and Aglaea d'Olive: all smiling. He did most reluctantly.

"Why do not Apollon or Dionysos or Minos come?" asked Morgan le Fay.

"They are made inconsolable," said Hermes, "with laughter. Perseús would but is unable due to his walking about the palace holding his screaming head he himself severed in the manner he did with the Gorgon Medusa's."

"Hera?" asked Zoë.

"She has taken to her rooms due to the flames having removed her hair and eyebrows; and because she cannot speak after having been changed into a peacock.

"Artemis cannot speak because she was turned to stone after the flames were extinguished by her attendants.

"Athene, who speaks, flayed herself of skin to make her cloak after the flames were extinguished."

Zoë laughed smiling at Themis.

"Rememorari - 'I remember' - was made a curse of reflection," said Themis. They looked at her with feelings of amazement.

"No other?" inquired Morgan le Fay still looking at Themis.

"No," said Hermes. "None dare approach."

"Hermes," said Themis, "please relate I shall honour the gracious request of Mneme and, while I'm there, I should very much like to speak with you about that involvement of your's with fair Pandore."

Hermes bowed; and, he departing fled.

"These things you do," said Morgan le Fay.

†

They entered the civitas of the Aedui. They wandered singly and in pairs in the commune.

†

Dame Hinojosa made her farewells and went on the road that, after passing through the Arroux gate and over the river, to the West towards Lutetia, the valley of the Loire, and Cenabum for in that place was a bridge crossing the Loire on to Autricum, for she would visit those two places—Cenabum and Autricum—where all the great Druids, Shamans and Sages would assemble at the end of the year in the one of those villes.

†

Autun was known as a place of Rhetoric. Fille d'Achéron, Elfriede de Vienne and Zoë went to the théâtre.

Themis la Grise and Morgan le Fay departed from them as the others went on the road that went to Autun.

Caroline d'Eirene, Madame Gallardo and Mary la Toute-Douée went viewing the shops and galleries in le passage couvert de la Halle.

Marcelle, Tochi no akaru-sa and Félix Trique went to the hamlet of Couhard and walked in the shadows of la Pyramide, porteur de légendes.

Acionnae de Tronçais and Aglaea d'Olive went to la Génetoye visiting the cella of tour de la Grenetoie.

All met at the appointed hour in the shadows of la cathédrale Saint-Lazare d'Autun before continuing on to Château-Chinon.

Félix was standing in her room at l'Hôpital Coulmier while Chthonius the Messenger waited for her reply for that which he had presented her with a folded page of delicate rice paper written:

The low viscosity entrails-type darkness had flowed effusive from the glass and the depth of dark was reflected on the obsidian become effluvia that had the chamber filled; the dark lantern had been positioned Cyclopean light burned eternal of entrance wooden steps corrupted by Age that led into the ever darkened lands beyond the glass purloined, waiting for one who would not be returned; on the mantle a single silver sterling candlestick strangled by the wire wound on a carte which was printed,

An Invitation of Logic and Sense from the Cheshire Cat

She opened it. It was blank. She smiled and went to the gas-jet lamp on the wall turning it so the blank side was held aloft towards that lamp, read:

> *If the pendulum of the mind alternates between sense and nonsense, and if in all chaos there is a cosmos and in all disorder a secret order where strangers used to gather together at the cinema and sit together in the dark, like Ancient Greeks participating in the mysteries, dreaming coming to consciousness without pain,*
>
> *are we set in Madness?*

Félix made her reply. Chthonius the Messenger bowed; and, went.

†

Fille was standing in her room at l'Hôpital Coulmier while Enceladus the Messenger waited for her reply for that which he had presented her with a folded page of delicate rice paper written:

The low viscosity entrails-type darkness had flowed effusive from the glass and the depth of dark was reflected on the obsidian become effluvia that had the chamber filled; the dark lantern had been positioned Cyclopean light burned eternal of entrance wooden steps corrupted by Age that led into the ever darkened lands beyond the glass purloined, waiting for one who would not be returned; on the mantle a single silver sterling candlestick strangled by the wire wound on a carte which was printed,

An Invitation of Logic and Sense from the Cheshire Cat

She opened it. It was blank. She was perplexed. She looked at that page from different angles and distances; she looked at the page reflected in the mirror; she set it in the basin filled with water; she held pressed on the window of the casement bleached with Sky-light.

Enceladus the Messenger discreetly coughed with his fisted hand covering his mouth. She turned her head and would step from the window removing the page from the glass but he furiously shook his head: he stared at the page. She looked at the page; she looked at him; she looked at the page. She slowly turned her head towards him and, tilting her head towards the window with her eyes peering at the page, nodded at the page. He nodded an emphatic single nod.

She smiled and turned the page so the blank side was then pressed against the glass, reading:

> If the pendulum of the mind alternates between sense and nonsense, and if in all chaos there is a cosmos and in all disorder a secret order where strangers used to gather together at the cinema and sit together in the dark, like Ancient Greeks participating in the mysteries, dreaming coming to consciousness without pain,
>
> are we set in Madness?

Fille made her reply. Enceladus the Messenger smiling bowed; and, went.

†

They did wander in Château-Chinon.

†

Caroline d'Eirene, Madame Gallardo and Mary la Toute-Douée made their farewells as they would stay.

†

Elfriede de Vienne was standing in the front room of her apartment while Mimas the Messenger waited for her reply for that which he had presented her with a folded page of delicate rice paper and she read what Marcelle and Félix and Fille had read.

She opened it. It was blank. She was perplexed. She did what Fille had done.

Mimas the Messenger discreetly coughed. They did perform that silent pas-de-deux the Messenger Enceladus and Fille had done; excepting the illumination being from the electric lamp on her table.

Elfriede made her reply. Mimas the Messenger smiling bowed; and, went.

†

Hooke was standing leaning against the barnacle-encrusted base of the obelisk of Comte de Gabalis at the carrefour of les Quatre Éléments in le Grand Parc de Lorraine.

"Sir?" said Hercule.

"Hercule," replied Hooke.

"You know me?" said Hercule taken aback by Hooke's greeting.

"Most assuredly."

Hercule bowed.

"Please."

"Sir?"

"I prefer this," Hooke said as he extended his hand; Hercule much surprised shook Hooke's hand.

"I've told ye knowests the most obscurest secrets of things, O Wise Master of all Arcana arcane, for I have a great imperative matter to ask of thine great and all encompassed knowledge."

He stated in lengthy soliloquy he followed steps but was lost at the dark seaside and was then compelled to seek him whom that would know.

"How did you know I would know?"

"Maîtresse Fey-Queen."

"Ah." Hercule thought. "Why are you?"

"I was waiting."

Hercule nodded.

"There is one you seek but cannot find him where he would be."

Hercule nodded.

"It is a lengthy stroll."

"I must."

"Then let's," said Hooke as he began strolling on the allée ombragée which led North. They did walk into the shadows and were soon walking on the Palisades until they were come to the eaves of the Murmuring Woods of Miseries.

"Necropolises of all things given are interesting in that they are filled with the Hope which was not given," said Hooke.

"Necropolises?" said Hercule. "I know Metropolises."

"Similar."

Hercule peered his squinty eyed stare at Hooke as they went; Hooke smiled.

"It was here I went lost," said Hercule when they were arrived at that place. "Very strange."

"The winds have changed and fogs are raised. If thee had taken several paces in that direction" – He gestured with the index and middle fingers of his left hand. – "you would have met him."

"Ah," said Hercule. He thought. "These are the Woods of Miseries aligned in a row facing Dark." Hooke nodded. "These are the hamadryads from the Woods of Miseries in the place of King Hades."

"They stand eternally facing Dark when even as set in Hades," offered Hooke; "and, from other places."

"Rêverie," said Hercule nodding. "Place." Hercule remembered his urgency. "Sir!" said a determined Hercule.

"Hercule," said Hooke as he turned to face him.

"I must inform you of an intrigue I have uncovered mere moments ago. I must have satisfaction.

"The paramour of Elfriede Marie-Thérèse de Vienne caused an unforgivable trespass on her after she said he reminds her of you. I met him. He was an evil malodorous fellow. He leers when speaking. His speaking is simpering malignancies. His malignancies are treachery."

"Le Grand Blessé-Invalide," said Hooke.

"Aye," said Hercule.

"Why do you wish with him to duel?" said Hooke.

"Her Honour. It was he who begat the villainous act of malebranches and fell men."

"No," said Hooke.

Hercule was puzzled and heartbroken, furious and dismayed.

"She was not in any danger when Count Jean de Plessis made his visits," offered Hooke.

Hercule frowned with an unbelieving stare.

"You were protecting her by simply visiting with her," said Hooke: "She had wearied of his visits because you did thee continue thine, Monsieur Hercule. The ambuscade was plotted by Count de Plessis fearing what she may say; or, more dangerous, what you may have told her about le Grand Blessé-Invalide." Hooke held his hand at a slight angle requesting Hercule not protest. "All we knew ye spoke naught of him." Hercule nodded. "She was seldom unaccompanied by others. She was ever unforgotten."

Hercule disbelieving frowned. Hooke with a countenance of his disbelief stared at him until he understood, saying: "It was you!" Hooke nodded. "Why were you there?"

Hooke smiled staring.

"Night Watch."

"Night Watch," said Hooke.

"Summons!"

"You had wished it," said Hooke.

Hercule thought before remembering it was a silent wish he thought; he smiled.

"His appearance shall be ended by an other," said Hooke; "and, it shall stand in these Woods."

"Why?"

"Honour," said Hooke, "*Her* Honour may have been paramount for thee but you did prevent her *herself* from greatest grievous harms by coming to her in your act of Chivalry."

"Oh." He bowed. "I shall continue as I will my visits."

Hooke nodded.

"This way," said Hercule as he would have went but Hooke interrupted: "I believe this way would be best."

Hercule peered in either direction. He shrugged. He went walking side-by-side with Hooke as they conversed on Jabberwocks, Boojums and Snarks.

†

They went through the hamlet of Saint-Martin-de-la-Mer on their passage to Quarré-les-Tombes.

†

Aglaea d'Olive made her farewells for she would continue northwards to Troyes.

†

C. L. Nolan was standing on the high street in Ashcourt while Pallas the Messenger waited for his reply for that which he had presented him with a folded page of delicate rice paper.

Nolan opened it. He went to a gas-jet street lamp on the high street and read what was written after the page was turned to it's blank side as he held it up to the lamp.

He made his reply. Pallas the Messenger bowed; and, went.

†

Alcaeus bloody and bruised lay at the bottom of the steps; his right arm was broken by his fall. Reynaerd stood straightening his jacket and waistcoat at the entrance of the house.

"His Lordship still remains away. I shall, yet again, say - My fourth - Mademoiselle la Grise is still not within; and, No— you shall not enter this house, believing I have lied, in search of Mademoiselle la Grise unless you are—Miraculously—invited by her."

†

They entered Quarré-les-Tombes. They were met by Admiral Paul-Pierre-Clément Duplessis standing beside his dirigeable which would return them to Mâcon.

†

Acionnae de Tronçais made her farewells as she would continue to Avallon.

†

"How slow life is, how violent Hope is," said Guillaume Apollinaire as he was seated on a bench beside the pond of Saint Cloud with Merle. "Without poets, without artists, men would soon weary of nature's monotony," said Apollinaire. "The sublime idea men have of the universe would collapse with dizzying speed. The order which we find in nature, and which is only an effect of art, would at once vanish. Everything would break up in chaos. There would be no seasons, no civilization, no thought, no humanity; even life would give way, and the impotent void would reign everywhere.

"Then those who see things with this Orphic vision see things as they are."

"Thank you again for—Most graciously—allowing me to read the manuscript of Alcools," said Merle:

> L'angoisse de l'amour te serre le gosier
> Comme si tu ne devais jamais plus être aimé
> Si tu vivais dans l'ancien temps tu entrerais dans un monastère
> Vous avez honte quand vous vous surprenez à dire une prière
> Tu te moques de toi et comme le feu de l'Enfer ton rire pétille
> Les étincelles de ton rire dorent le fond de ta vie
> C'est un tableau pendu dans un sombre musée
> Et quelquefois tu vas le regarder de près

is an sublime divinity of Life."

"I was lost," he replied: "Time pressed me and I did not want to sleep under the stars. Then curiosity prevailed and, fumbling along the wall, I went in order to explore the cave of sorcery. I went on. At last, I had the courage to look backward: the ghosts of my days."

"As Baudelaire wrote," said Merle: "'It was created with rage and patience.'"

He nodded

"Perhaps," said Merle, "yet your work shall be censored by Church and State while delightfully confounding the Masses as did the works of Sade, of Baudelaire, and of Mallarmé."

He laughed.

"I sing the joy of wandering and the pleasure of the wanderer's death."

✝

"In that epoch," said Merle as he stood at the obélisque in Père Lachaise, "balance was made: Baudelaire's grotesques on depravity and sin and decadence; Mallarmé on love and sorrow and life; Guillaume Apollinaire on farce, frailties and le fabuleux."

✝

Milot l'Encyclopédiste was standing in his study while Porphyrion the Messenger waited for his reply for that which he had presented him with a folded page of delicate rice paper. He read.

He opened it. It was blank. He was perplexed. He did what they before had done.

Porphyrion the Messenger discreetly coughed. They did perform that silent pas-de-deux what they those others before had done; excepting the illumination was from his fireplace.

L'Encyclopédiste made his reply.

The Messenger Porphyrion smiling bowed; and, went.

†

Hooke and Hercule were walking in a very narrow allée in the shadows of the Palisades until that path was laid of stone and the allée was slowly become a vaulted passage of weathered red brick.

They leagues continued.

Hooke withdrew his dagger as they approached a door of indiscernible design.

"That!" exclaimed Hercule remembering.

"Yes," said Hooke, "'tis mine."

Hooke held the dagger in the palm of his hand. They passed through the door.

They went in silence until Hercule boldly stood. "Sir!" Hooke paused and turned. "I insist." Hercule bowed; and, bowing said: "My thanks I give for your generosity lending me that key."

"Thy days of knight-errantry are ended."

"I did not seek quixotic adventures," said Hercule.

"No, you did not," replied Hooke; "You did—However—do acts of chivalry when adventures in need did find you. All these years passed; and, all those forgotten."

They exited from the Night Chambers. The door of the antechamber was gone. Those words carved by Merle on the door were now engraved above the archway though none had seen it made so.

Hercule was walking slowly in thought; Hooke's gait slowed.

They astonished all who saw them in the Ministry those who were gradually returning from their Holidays in seclusion.

They had come to the statue of the Ancient in the vacant rotunda.

Hooke offered it to the statue which extended it's arm and took the blade, with its hand, so that only the pommel shown. The arm was raised on to it's bosom.

"It dropped it," said Hercule with a questioning stare at the statue.

"All those years ago," said Hooke.

They exited and waited at the kerb for a taxi.

†

Jules le Cartographe was seated in his tub interrupted with his bath while Polybotes the Messenger waited for his reply.

They did as before was done; excepting the illumination being from the tapers on a candelabra.

Le Cartographe made his reply. The Messenger Porphyrion smiling bowed; and, went.

†

Fille d'Achéron, Elfriede de Vienne, Marcelle, Tochi no akaru-sa, Félix Trique and Zoë were seated in the gondola as they were being escorted to the commune of Nuits.

†

They visited the temple of Cybèle.

†

"Man perceives itself to live in the Present," said Elfriede. "Still, doesn't one reside already in the Future as well as reside in the Past.

"So perhaps the Present is merely observing one's Life as it passes from the future into the past as if one's Life were being presented in a cinema where they are the sôle person in attendance; also as actor in a Théâtre du Grand Guignol play.

"And, if all as of Chance exists, may not those acts of Chance happen in the Future as well? Chance may occur in the Present but chances are it has already occurred and you are merely viewing it."

They stunned gazed at her. "How do you say such things?" said Fille.

"I don't know. I haven't been able before when I was not with their Majesties, Monseigneur or Lord Hooke."

†

They were requested to follow by a small Gentleman; and, they followed him and went below in the Mithraeum.

The small Gentlemen had prepared a late supper. Several were dressed in typical waiter fashion serving plates and bowls with knives and spoons. They served wine.

"Dear sirs," said Zoë, "you are offering this our most delicious supper with bowls."

They held aloft the knives and spoons.

Zoë nodded.

†

"The Lady in Orange has given us to give to you this given to her by His Eminence."

†

They boarded.

†

The airship was aloft. They viewed all in the Night below as they sojourning for days would return to the commune of Mâcon.

Fille d'Achéron, Elfriede de Vienne, Marcelle, Tochi no akaru-sa, Félix Trique and Zoë were marvelling at the land unfurling beneath them supping their peach parfait shaved-ice cones.

†

Themis and Hooke were walking to la gare monumentale de Mâcon; he was carrying a basket with bottles. There would be few at la Jungle of the station during this hour after l'Aube.

Amélie, Clément, Jean le Grand, Paul le Matelot and le Duc Napoleon were seated. They stood when Themis approached with Hooke following after.

Two members of Ligue de Tempérance were standing near-by in recitation.

"They are not without sin."

"No, they are not without sin," replied Themis: "They are without Hope."

"Caused by sin!"

"Yes. The sins of others who keep them in this perpetual state of beggary. They wish to be oblivious to their pain. They wish to forget. They wish to be forgotten."

Themis took a bottle giving it to Amélie. She did give one each to Clément, Jean le Grand, Paul le Matelot and le Duc Napoleon who set them on the grass. They thanked her. They sat.

Hooke set the sixth bottle on the grass.

Amélie shared her's.

"If they continue this behaviour they will all die."

"Yes?" said Themis.

"Self-murder."

"They know," replied Themis. "They have not lost their will to live. It is Lethe they seek."

"Lethe?"

"Lethe translates as 'oblivion', 'forgetfulness', or 'concealment.' They wish for Oblivion."

"They can be saved!"

"They cannot. It is too late for they who have over countless years been continuously made grievous and their Hope destitute."

"You coddle them."

"Coddle? No. I succor them as I may."

"Murderess!"

"That is as may be."

Themis and Hooke left them seated on the grass at the furthest edge of the station while the two members of Ligue de Tempérance standing near-by continued in recitation of their religious tracts on sin.

✝

Zoë and Merle were strolling la Haute Voie romaine. She with her parasol.

✝

Thoas the Messenger had given and departed after having presented Themis with a folded page of delicate rice paper. She laughing crumpled it tossing it into the flames descending down the chimney.

> *If the pendulum of the mind alternates between sense and nonsense, and if in all chaos there is a cosmos and in all disorder a secret order where strangers used to gather together at the cinema and sit together in the dark, like Ancient Greeks participating in the mysteries, dreaming coming to consciousness without pain,*
>
> *are we set in Madness, Mademoiselle?*

were heard spoken by Hooke.

"Lunacy," she replied.

†

It was an auspicious evening. The fireflies arrived early but would flourish during the full Moon in the presence of the Ghost Festival, Hachigatsu Bon, and the festival in honour of the Lady of the Dead on that evening.

Madame Gallardo who was once the Blue Witch who chose the shade of indigo had sent invitations for the third Anniversary of his death, Simon.

All of the present members of Les Treize were in attendance as were several members from the Past: Dame Hinojosa was once the Cardinal Red Witch; Françoise-Pélagie Fayère de Marly, the Yellow Witch; Marie-Giselle Wreath, the Brown Witch; Françoise-Marguerite Foules, the Pink Witch; Béatrice Étiennette Milot, the Lavender Witch; Shaman Yuhuan of Kucha, the Lilac Witch; and, Yemoja the Shaman, the Cyan Blue Witch; Guenevere de Sens, the Green Witch; and, Megan la Fae and Morgan le Fay who were once Grey Witches. They were attending with their Patroness, Morgause la Fey who was standing beside Zoë.

Odysseus and Archimedes le Noir sat on either side of the small obelisk with megalithic designs.

Hooke and Merle stood away from the gathering with Marcelle, Fille, Félix and Gwen were standing beside Hooke who was less frightening to them than Merle.

"Who was Simon?"

"Simon is Madame Gallardo's familiar," said Hooke. "Simon is a familiar who cannot be been seen by others. All departed familiars have an act of remembrance like fireflies arriving; they're all different."

"They've ceased but are not gone."

"Like Simon," said Gwen. Hooke smiled tilting his head and nodded.

"Why three Season-sets?" asked Fille.

"It is three cyclic actes before to reach where one wishes to be," said Hooke.

"Why isn't this done during the full Moon?" asked Marcelle.

"This is the morning of the e'en before full Moon, No?" Merle continued: "This ceremony begins the succession on the eve and wanes after second night following has become l'Aube. There shall be a second ceremony of smaller attendance at the full Moon risen followed by a single attendant on the third night waning. Rising, dwelling and departing as a single breath. It is well and good that most delve during the height of the Moon. But all three nights are overwhelming in comparison. Ponderously overwhelming."

"First acte, second acte, third acte," said Fille.

"There are some things," said Hooke, "done after full Moon when the effect of it—as it is the same as Solstice and Equinox—has changed things."

"They change things?" asked Marcelle.

"Always," said Merle. "Tomorrow more so. It is the Ghost Festival."

"Ghosts are spirits," said Hooke.

They were thoughtful until eventually Gwen did ask, "That stone?"

"It is an obelisk fashioned from menhir."

"What are they?"

"Menhirs are three formae," said Hooke: "a gravestone; a sarcophagus of stone; or, one who was enchanted as stone."

"They hew megalithic columns for use in a fashion of those found in Nature," said Merle as he viewed the hand-holding circle speaking whispers as colours shone with a veiled and tremulous light wavering faintly seen.

"Why all of the colours?" asked Félix.

"Your studies do not include Newton?" replied Merle.

She shook her head.

"We shall correct that," said Merle. "All those colours form white."

"I was told white was purity," said Marcelle.

"We shall correct that for all your studies," said Merle. "Purity does not come from a single source as seen before you."

"Black light?" asked Gwen.

"That light is the colour of the Absolute," replied Hooke.

"Shouldn't they be standing in a ring around the gravestone?" asked Fille.

"Why?" said Hooke.

"Circles and rings enclose enchantment castings and conjurations," answered Fille.

"He's not ceased," said Hooke. "That stone has nought significance therefore it isn't necessary for what they do. Circulus and ring are strengthful for enchantments cast and for conjurations or protection when an object or thing is focused in the center; but they are also beneficial for communing when many are in attendance of the circulus.

"All simple geometric shapes are employed.

"Though, if you look closely Majesty stands South and Morgause la Fey stands North: they the ring align.

"A single line tethered on each end shall, with the object or thing set at midpoint, often be employed for similar effect."

"Why?" said Marcelle.

They were concluded. Marcelle's question was forgotten as the honoured Guests approached the long table set on the lawn.

Supper was set on the long table on the lawn. Odysseus and Archimedes le Noir remaining at their places were served poke; Simon had a plate of sushi set for him at his place between them.

Madame Gallardo was offered regrets from those the other Elder Shamans and sorceresses invited who could not attend. They conversed on all things of the Modern Age and it's coming War.

"Why are we here?" asked Marcelle.

"History lesson," said la Grise.

"Observation," said Madame Gallardo.

"Reflection," said Lady Constance.

"Family!" said Fille firmly. All who heard smiled or laughed softly or nodded sagely at her reply.

"She certainly is as you said, Themis," said Yuhuan with a keen stare at Fille which rendered Fille unpleasantly ill-at-ease.

"We were accepted many years ago," said Gwen.

"Le docteur Guise!" exclaimed Marcelle; "He's been saying such very odd things since I went there."

"A conspiracy of the highest order," said Zoë.

Merle laughed. Zoë bowed from her shoulders.

"Everyone knows," said Gwen.

"Very few know, my dear," said Morgause la Fey; "and, we do hope none others are informed of this knowledge."

They nodded somberly.

"Why are they here?" whispered Fille pointing at Hooke and Merle.

"They were invited," said Zoë.

"Come," said Madame Gallardo as she rose from the table. "Our Bon Odori waits."

"Sir!" said Marcelle as she went to Merle as the others went further on to the lawn. He turned and smiled. "Marcelle?"

"I have been told you know all of the obscure and secret things that are in all places, O Wise Master of all Arcana arcane," said Marcelle.

"Monsieur Hercule?" said Merle.

She nodded.

"Pray, Mademoiselle Marcelle, what would you ask of me?"

"Le Docteur Guise has said many things to me. Some I knew; some I did not know; some confused me; but one dumbfounded me." Merle smiled; and, she continued. "He told me of several guests who late at Night when they've fallen asleep in their comfortable chairs with their hearing trumpet in their ears, one can hear their thoughts."

"Thoughts may be heard; or, they may be sensed," said Merle. "You have *known* what someone had were their thoughts you sensed. Or, surmised. Thoughts may be heard as Monsieur Hercule is oft wont to do when walking."

"Yes," said Marcelle. "When he speaks his thoughts I can hear him. He escorted us to the Museum speaking his thoughts while we walked."

Merle nodded.

"Those — speaking thoughts and sensing thoughts — are extremes. Le Docteur Guise is correct. There are some whose thoughts are heard when they retain their hearing trumpet in an ear for all which may be heard. Those guests have thoughts they hear in their heads, No?"

She nodded.

"So, if they hear their thoughts, another may hear their thoughts, too."

"Do they" — She gestured to the others in attendance. — "hear my thoughts?"

"No," said Merle smiling gently. "Thy thoughts are thine own until thou wishes them known."

"Do you?" she asked hesitantly with great apprehension.

"No," said Merle laughing. "I do not."

She sighed deeply. She would have effused her thanks but he interrupted her. "They wait for us," said Merle as he gestured to the others who were patiently waiting.

†

They all did dance.

†

The ceremony had ended. All those remaining were seated on the lawn telling tales of adventures for hours after.

Les Mademoiselles were seated by themselves conspired with conversation about the letters Hooke had sent.

†

Themis and Hooke were walking the lane leading their horses by the reins after having ridden over the lands suffused by the light of the full Moon.

"I still find it odd your brick library missing," said Themis.

✝

Marcelle, Félix, Elfriede, Fille and Gwen were standing beneath the full Moon waxing brilliance over Barrowcross in the county of Hookland. They were engaged in an alchemic process Félix remembered from reading for the apparitioning of Spirits of place.

It succeeded.

They could very clearly see the spirits of the sacred glade summoned by them; the spirits were not seen in darkened greys as all had informed them. They were very confused and alarmed as a creeping fear was rising in them.

They saw beyond the glade that the world was of the Dark.

They did not make spirits visible: they themselves were taken to the time of the spirits of being in that place. They were amoungst them; they were now the shadows of that glade.

They watched as a darkened form approached and stood at the edge of the glade. It laughed quietly at the unattended fires and tools of Alchemy. It continued walking towards them entering that locus they were. It was Old Wren.

"That's ye done for this evening, Ladies," he said as he gestured for them to exit.

"You're looking well, Mister Wren," said one of the spirits.

They gladly did.

"As are you, Mister Willows," said Wren.

Old Wren was by Mister Willows, who did make an earnest petition, and stayed continuing in their long-held argument of which was most efficacious in the kingdom: the Proclamation for the Discouragement of Vice of 1787 or the Proclamation for the Encouragement of Piety and Virtue, and for the Preventing and Punishing of Vice, Profaneness and Immorality of 1787 when performed by the Society for the Suppression of Vice in 1802.

✝

Hercule was walking with the head of the ghoul under his arm as they went to find it's body. The head of the ghoul had been an entertaining informative fixture at the house in Hookland of Themis la Grise.

Hercule made his gratitude known for the words the ghoul had spoken during their previous conversing on Life on the need for fortitude in the face of insurmountable Femininity.

†

The three members of the Illapses Agency, Ltd. — C. L. Nolan, Louis-Aldonse Milot and Jean-Marie Jules — were seated in their closet as the full Moon was waxing.

A departed messenger had presented them with an invitation:

> You are requested your attendance
> at an Amusement lasting one-fifty years.
> Persephone's Gate.
> Marron, Fructidor— Morning.
> Carriage waiting.

$$\text{-}\hat{H}_3\text{-}$$

"That's his sigil," said Jules.
"We daren't refuse," said Milot.
"Most irregular," said Nolan.
They would go.

†

The Alchemy camp was gone. Wren had watched it be taken as he spoke with Mister Willows. There stood in the grey glade a single radiant silhouette watching them. He smiled. He went and returned to Mister Willows leading the Shade by her hand.

"Mister James Bartholomew Willows," said Wren, "Miss Tochi no akaru-sa."

"Sir," said Gwen to Mister Willows.

"Miss Tochi no akaru-sa," replied Mister Willows; "Willows."

"Mister Willows," said Wren, "do you suppose we could saunter for a length, whiling hours, as full Moon wanes this night, while we continue speech of wiles and mores, and vice and virtue with Miss Tochi no akaru-sa?"

"Delighted!"

Wren and Willows turned to Tochi no akaru-sa who did smile.

They strolled.

✝

Le Maréchal d'Empire, Hieronymus-Baleberithe-Seere ad-Din al-Jinn, Samael, and Orphiel were sat in the cabinet of Hades as the full Moon was waxing: they were come to agreement that the Great War of the Three Kingdoms should be allowed to occur.

"Her Majesty so obliges us," replied al-Jinn and said smiling: "I was informed Shades shall in their way serve this cause but not our alliance."

✝

Tochi no akaru-sa was standing in the meadow with Willows and Wren while Damysus the Messenger waited for her reply for that which he had presented her with a folded page of delicate rice paper written. All three read it:

The low viscosity entrails-type darkness had flowed effusive from the glass and the depth of dark was reflected on the obsidian become effluvia that had the chamber filled; the dark lantern had been positioned Cyclopean light burned eternal of entrance wooden steps corrupted by Age that led into the ever darkened lands beyond the glass purloined, waiting for one who would not be returned; on the mantle a single silver sterling candlestick strangled by the wire wound on a carte which was printed,

She opened it. It was blank.

"May I?" Wren said to Damysus who grandly gestured he do so and said, "Of course, Sir." Wren thanked him. Tochi no akaru-sa gave the page to Wren who turning it so the blank side was held aloft towards the full Moon setting, read:

> If the pendulum of the mind alternates between sense and nonsense, and if in all chaos there is a cosmos and in all disorder a secret order where strangers used to gather together at the cinema and sit together in the dark, like Ancient Greeks participating in the mysteries, dreaming coming to consciousness without pain,
>
> are we set in Madness?

"Full Moon magic," said Tochi no akaru-sa.

"No," replied Wren offering the page to her which she accepted. "This is a simple ruse from Antiquity: alembicus water, Witch's pen, an enchantment, a charm. Those who do not know fret for years and hours over attempting a blank page to read."

"That's marvellous," said Willows. She smiled.

She made her reply. The Messenger Damysus bowed; and, went.

Willows, Wren and Tochi no akaru-sa continued on their way.

Morgause la Fey and Virge were laying on the blanket of disposed leaves on the grass beneath the full Moon waxing brilliance at the west end of the garden on their estate in the woods of le duché de Luxembourg; she was lounging on the incline of the meadow as he did lay with his head on her lap. She was retelling her story of leading Merlin Ambrosius astray in the labyrinth far below Skara Brae in search of la Bête glatissantea after he had concluded his retelling of his episode cheating at dice during the Card Salon on l'Île Barbe including a part forgotten of how le Maréchal accused him of sleight-of-hand when he had not done so who then challenged him to a knife-throwing duel where whosoever was scratched by the edge of the blade but not pierced for whosoever was scratched first lost. 'There'll be none of your magie,' he said and I replied 'I shall not my magie use.' Le Maréchal went first and so he raised his hand over his shoulder but his hand went trembling numb whereupon he loosed his knife which fell did causing that he nicked his shoulder; and so he was the first to be scratched. 'I defeat you,' I proclaimed; and, when he protested, I did speak: 'It was not mine; Morgause's was.' 'Bastard!' he cried merrily. 'Hercule cheats magnificently but Virge cheats cleverest of all. Beware them!'"

"I taught you that!" said Morgause interrupting with her laughter.

"Yes, my dear," said Virge smiling, "thy magie is ever working in the ways of Mystery."

†

King Vinea was speaking with les Enragés in a place deep below the surface of the snow dunes hid from view of the full Moon waxing over Nubilus.

†

Themis and Hooke with eyes closed were laying in the bower of Odysseus when Félix, Marcelle and Fille came running to them for those three wanted Hooke to explain what happened during the Alchemy ritual; but, he declined: "Some other time."

"Lay with us," offered Themis, "and close your eyes, listening."

Marcelle, Félix and Fille laid beside them and closed their eyes.

Those six in the bower were listening to the winds in the trees which were heard as the waves of oceans fell and returned on beaches of sand as full Moon waned.

†

Monsieur et Madame Louis-Aimé-Honoré Pilare had come to visit their daughter — Elfriede — by invitation from Zoë. They were in the territoire de Crêches-sur-Saône strolling on the High Road beneath the full Moon rising after the troops aligned against Napoleon had damaged and fled the commune.

"I don't know what it is I'm doing," lamented Elfriede. "I don't know why I was asked."

"Madame asked," said Pilare as he gestured to Zoë. "I assented."

"I do assent," said Madame Pilare. "I'm sorry I said those things. I'm happy now."

"If thee would my excuse accept," said Zoë who then did exit.

They continued their conversation, strolling.

†

Merle with his hands in his trouser pockets was standing beside Zoë who was seated on the rocks above the Sea of Fog as the full Moon waned.

†

It was in that hour Sky-light was first seen as it begun creeping over the East.

Hooke, Marquis Marchosias and les Mademoiselles were standing on the steps of the entrance to l'Hôpital Coulmier. Guise stood at the open doors.

"This, Mademoiselles, is thy final lesson," said Hooke, "of Place and Spirit and Sanctus because each of you have not shown an aptitude for understanding the dangerousness, significance nor importance of them."

A dark shape was walking up the allée.

"Why is he here?" asked Félix.

It was a three-headed dragon approaching.

"I telephoned him last evening. I asked he meet me here at nine," said Marchosias; "He comes early when suspicious."

"Marchosias," said Buné, Great Duke of Hell.

"Buné," replied Marchosias.

"You wish to trap me, the Great Duke of Hell Buné?" said Buné.

"No. As I mentioned, when I telephoned, it is a wager. The wager being I informed Mister Hooke you could walk up the steps of this place and enter."

"Why are they?" said Buné.

"Witnesses, Buné le Duc," said Hooke, "who none standing will interfere with you."

Duke Buné walked to the steps. He suspicious looked at all who waited on him. He tentatively stepped on to the first step. He peered. He stepped on the second step: he disappeared.

Les Mademoiselles would have spoken but Hooke said: "Wait." They did as minutes they passed.

Duke Buné appeared at the lowest step striding off the staircase.

"There. It's empty."

"Yes, it's in disrepair," said Guise. "We are waiting."

Hooke paid his wager. "Much obliged, Sir." Marchosias paid Duke Buné his share of the wager and off they went to find amusements.

"Duke Buné entered the hospital when it existed in 1649," said Guise. "It was ruins. He was shown it. He wasn't taken anywhere; nothing happened to him. All things enter sacred places: some are shown that which is sacred; others, that which places were or become. He knew the passage to return; if he had been one of those who had not known that way, he could not have returned."

"That Directeur?" asked Marcelle.

"That is a sacred place victoriously infected by Malevolence and le Directeur Mortuorum," said Hooke. "The spirits are imprisoned. They cannot do what was seen with Duke Buné. They can—However—summon."

"You came because of them?" said Marcelle softly.

"Yes," he replied.

"Barrows?" asked Tochi no akaru-sa.

"John Wren le Sage or Themis Witch-Queen are who you need ask," replied Hooke; "Barrows may be malevolent even when they are of a Sacred place." He stared at them and, did Hooke graven in demeanor and tone continue: "It comes to this: if you have need of rest..." — "Or, hiding," interjected Guise. — "or hiding, find a simple place — of which are vastly common — Thanks are given — and the spirit—or, spirits—of it shall keep thou succored from harm; if you find a sacred place from Malevolence, and are perceived in need by thy fright-filled thoughts, that place shall summon one to come to you when Ritus thou observe; if you find a sacred place, and are perceived in need by they as messenger of Benevolence, they shall aid thee in ways beyond thine comprehension because Benevolence tends Benevolence."

"Of the four Alchemic Virtues, Benevolence is the simplest to learn and practise yet a greater strength of Cause than those remaining three.

"If thee wish continuing visits localities of Sanctus — sacred places — on larks trespassing in Ages past — taken without thanks given for their benevolent acceptance — and lack the knowledge for returning, I shall think of you quite often in that Age remaining.

"That abhorrent behaviour 'tis expected but not from those who are said to know 'Honour keeps Honour' yet thee thus have failed to observe in consistence that which is greater."

He faced Guise. "Docteur Guise." Hooke departed.

They stood very still long after he had gone. "Come, let us go inside," said Docteur Guise. They silently turned with expressions ashen pale from sadness and worry following le Docteur. "'Benevolence tends Benevolence.'"

†

Hooke, Hiolle, Javelle and Milot were standing in a bed chamber.

The room had been locked from the inside. His servants heard screams. They finally broke down the door to see his body being punctured bleeding; and, then:— it stopped.

Minister-Cardinalis Taberd was murdered: his mouth had single wounds; his throat was slashed being swung wavering from side to side; his eyes were repeatedly stabbed with each stroke increased in a hysteria of violence as evidenced by bone and blade fragments.

"There are none need be informed," said Hooke. "All knew this was to be occurring as soon as he returned to the brutality of edge and point, he wished once gone: his barbarity finally escaped. Those who would others destroy are all eventually consumed by their hatred. Their burning destroys others; it will destroy them. Still, they blame others.

"He shall not ever know what he has here done. All but innate knowledge was taken. His hatred succored."

Hooke left while those three continued with their work.

"Whose resverie?" mused Milot.

✝

Themis, Milot and Jules, who had requested was accepted to be allowed to attend, were reading the Lore-Tale tomes.

Morgause la Fey did so, too.

✝

Zoë went on the lane which lead to the zone of the city. She walked on the planked path leading to the waxworks arcade.

Le Musée des Litanies de Satan

She stood next to the ticket-booth reading,

L'ENFER

A Grimoire macabre of Woes
set over all Civilized Creation

by
the Devils of

SATAN

————————

Les étonnants spectacles in peep-chambers

—————

Claude-Théodulf-Gérard Noailles, Proprietor

————

†

Zoë spoke with the ticket-attendant who allowed her entrance into the théâtre of stationary Hours.

Zoë entered.

†

The Museum Impresario Claude-Théodulf-Gérard Noailles stood tall. He had a large walrus mustache attached to his long rouflaquettes. His hair was scraggy on the sides and back but bald on his crown except for one short tuft above his forehead.

He wore a dark blue tailcoat, a starched white shirt, white tie, white waistcoat, black pantaloons and black shoes with striped stockings.

"I have visited this museum before but, as it was mentioned by an acquaintance, at Musée Grévin in Paris, that you have new cabinets and tableaus, I thought to visit," said Zoë.

"Infidels!" The Museum Impresario Claude-Théodulf-Gérard Noailles mumbled before composing himself and asking: "When did you come, Madame?"

"At opening."

"Years ago. All exhibits will be new." Claude-Théodulf-Gérard Noailles gestured for Zoë to proceed first.

"Charles Baudelaire le Dandy dressed so?"

"I have no knowledge," replied Claude-Théodulf-Gérard Noailles adjusting the sleeves of his shirt.

Zoë walked across the lacquered floor stepping on the three darker squares. He was confused. He mumbled about it never not working. He stepped on to the first square: it was a panel that fell one foot down; and, he fell. He stepped on the second panel: it fell; and, he fell. And, the third panel fell as he stepped on to it falling.

They descended the steps.

"The descended works are kept safe from Summer," said the Impresario Noailles.

They entered into the Musée.

✝

The tableaux cabinets were displayed in large stalls along the walls of the long salle. Wood and wrought iron railings kept visitors at a distance.

The first cabinet was titled,

MIRACLES

The cell in which Fanny painted.

Coffin Births.

A row of trees where women were naked and each was fettered to a tree by an iron collar fixed by a short chain fastened to the tree.

The tableau of Leda and the Swan.

Io naked transforming to be the white heifer.

Danae imprisoned in a tall brass tower with a single richly adorned chamber with no doors or windows was sleeping naked while golden rain falls though the skylight.

Harmonia becoming serpent.

"That is her wedding day necklace," said the Impresario Noailles gesturing to a necklace on a maroon satin cushion in a glass case.

Another stall had more women in torture.

Another and another.

And others.

The second cabinet was titled,

WITCHCRAFT – HERESY – IDOLATRY

One stall had a display of a nude cast in gold. Beside her was a naked woman with her foot in an iron boot into which a gent is pouring molten gold. Another woman fastened to a rough wood table was having her clothes stripped from her body. All punished for offences against the Holy Office of the Inquisition.

Beautiful witches naked burning at stakes.

Beautiful witches naked drowning.

Beautiful witches naked hung.

Another stall had more women in torture.

Another and another.

And others.

"You take delight in display of femmes in melodramatic distress by torture," said Zoë.

"No. The public demands."

"And, men in distress?"

"Of course," said the Impresario Noailles. He lead Zoë to a different area. More women under torture and one man was seen. "Witches and their instigator from Loudoun. We did have a projected tableau of Aphrodite's origins showing Uranus castrating Cronos and she was born from the foam of the sea. Royal patronage caused it's removal from Versailles."

"You indulge them."

"I offer them fancies."

"You have pale white women."

He was puzzled.

"Those of different skin or countenance of different peoples in your display-tableaux are missing."

"They do of course have barbaric histories but they are less interesting. They lack intelligence."

"As women do as attested by these tableaux."

He shrugged.

The third display was titled,

SURGERY AGAINST MADNESS

The fourth cabinet was titled,

SCÈNES MERVEILLEUSES

The fifth cabinet was titled,

SCÈNES VERTUEUSES

The sixth cabinet was titled,

VÉNUS SACRIFICE

The seventh cabinet was titled,

SATAN'S SUNDAY SUPPER

The cabinet was hidden by a red velvet curtain.

"A conflagration," said the Impresario Noailles.

"Oh?"

"Yes. One of the gas jets had broke and when lit, all the room was filled with flames."

"Blood?"

"No!"

"And, that one?" said Zoë. "L'Issue?"

†

The final cabinet had thirteen figures. It was a large and darkened chamber that smelt of fœtid decay. They were tall with red and black flesh of leprous design. They had arms; they had tentacles as arms; they had bodies of serpents. Their eyes seemed to be watching but they were stood as waxen statues. All their mouths were sewn.

"They looked scary in the dark until I saw none – None! - had pointed beards; they cannot be devils unless they have pointed beards." He sighed. "My customers find them amusing."

"Perhaps, they are demons from the lands of l'Archaïque."

"Demons are mythical inventions invented by the Church. This Modern Age does not condone demons. It has been written so."

Zoë remained quizzical. "Perhaps, it is because they have seldom been seen."

He produced a pamphlet from beneath his coat. "Les démons sont fausses!"

"May I read your pamphlet?"

He handed it to her.

"Devils are condoned by the Modern Age?"

"They are known."

"And, demons?"

"All demons must register with the Minister of Intelligence in his spherical booth in the rotunda upon entry into the country. None are registered. Therefore, none have been seen. Therefore, none exist."

"Devils have registered?"

"Nonsense. They are already known."

"This passage states demons may take the shape of man or animal."

"Precisely! Demons may take the shape of man *or* animal. These are neither: they are each! Trickery. Thus, they cannot be demons!"

"If demons are false, if no registrations have been made with the Minister of Intelligence and since these do not have pointed beards, what may they be?"

"Injustice!"

"If thou wouldst," said Zoë: "all intrigues and plots are ended and thee art abandoned by those deceased or fled until Death at leisure shall find them as you as well if you wish to as statues stay. I've a proposal for which that curse could cease by single thought of thy congeniality."

Claude-Théodulf-Gérard Noailles was flustered and confused.

Zoë returned the pamphlet; and, smiled.

Zoë took her leave from the Impresario and from the museum she did exit.

†

Zoë was strolling la Haute Voie romaine.

†

Hooke seated on the veranda viewing the lands in the East had received an invitation.

"Should we follow him?" said Reynaerd.

"No," said Hooke frowning with his thoughts. "It does not return to from where it came but to where it shall meet it's Death."

"Wary?"

Hooke nodded.

"Damysus. Mimas. If you please."

The Messengers appeared. He spoke to them individually: Damysus departed; Mimas stood waiting.

"We shall be found at Lugosdunon if we are escaped."

"We shall attend immediately," said Reynaerd.

Hooke and Mimas were grimly silent as they took their exit.

†

Zoë and Merle were standing at the edge of Cabillonum. They faced each other: he held her left hand with his right hand as he bowed from his shoulders as she did him a courtesy in kind. She gracefully turned and strolling went on la Haute Voie romaine as she would take her way to the south of the département of l'Yonne.

†

Merle had remained standing on the High Road at the edge of the Grand Canyon du Verdon until the radiance of Lumière pâle was faded from view.

Merle was descended in the valley.

†

Zoë was strolling on la Haute Voie romaine.

†

Zoë was seated at a carrefour on la Haute Voie romaine where she was listening to a gentleman who was found standing on the crux of the roads. She waited Hooke's coming.

"It is a rage. I've never had one. It's a rage of helplessness. It's sadness; sublime sadness. My grief rages. It's Melancholy I cannot explain. It seems like a sorrow for all things. I'm angry. I don't know why. It's everything. I should be able to find wonderful things when I look but there they are and all I feel is the tragedy of it all. All at once it is everything. All my emotions are weeping. My throat is tightened. I hear them. They're screaming. I have been wandering I don't how long. I want to cry but I can't. It's been months since I've been like this. My grief drowns me. I cannot cry! My tears will not fall for them. My breaths are not my own for I cannot breathe. My dreams are melancholic and are anger. I stand there staring at all things around me and my eyes are teary yet I cannot cry. My dreams have never expressed my emotions. My Sense has abandoned me! I cannot continue; I cannot go back. I sit here where you find me. I cannot stay here. I cannot think. My screams are everywhere. I cannot escape. It's a rage of hopelessness. That things have come to this! This! They take their pleasure infecting Joyful things with Death. Death and lies against all things good. All things joyous. All good things. All things we once had. All things we once believed. It's is Death-in-Life. A walking sepulchre; my ghost has escaped but not I. The tears I cannot let fall are blinding me. I don't want to sleep; there isn't comforting. I would forfeit my life to sleep in madness if my madness were simply an illusion of things once were. I drown but cannot die. My screams are heard but never pass my lips. I cannot die. I cannot live. I hear my screams of rage and hopelessness. I cannot die."

He collapsed.

✝

He went departing.

✝

Zoë was standing at the carrefour on la Haute Voie romaine as Hooke held in his arms the body of the Gentleman who had collapsed from his grief.

"Zhį'ii-tsintah," said Hooke.

Zoë touched his cheek but Hooke stepped away from her.

"You rebuke me," said Zoë puzzled.

"No, Ma'am," said Hooke; and, then said softly, "No." He smiled sadly. "My rage has been staunched by thine graciousness but I do not wish it made gone. I wish to keep it as breathing relic of his suffering and pain."

She too sadly smiled.

✝

Zoë was sadly strolling on la Haute Voie romaine.

✝

She by a shrine was come: on the road-shrine on a post of polished ebony: the shrine on the post of thirteen feet height was Régence and delicately carved of polished ebony where slept the skeletal-carriage of a corvus articus. And, on the post, was nailed an affiche for the Théâtre de l'Opéra des Ténèbraes du Paradis which was presenting *Les Vinaigre Séries* by Edouard Gorie, Floréal, 1842.

And, over that affiche, was a small affiche nailed:

Observations written after observations o'er

†

Zoë was strolling la Haute Voie romaine.

†

She by a shrine was come: on the road-shrine on a post of polished ebony: the shrine on the post of thirteen feet height was Régence and delicately carved of polished ebony where slept the skeletal-carriage of a corvus articus. And, on the post, was nailed an affiche for the Théâtre de l'Opéra des Ténèbraes du Paradis which was presenting *Les Tombeaux Séries* by Edouard Gorie, Floréal, 1842.

And, over that affiche, was a small affiche nailed:

Of Buffoons and Burlesques

†

She by a shrine was come: on the road-shrine on a post of polished ebony: the shrine on the post of thirteen feet height was Régence and delicately carved of polished ebony where slept the skeletal-carriage of a corvus articus. And, on the post, was nailed an affiche for the Théâtre de l'Opéra des Ténèbraes du Paradis which was presenting *Les Tombeaux Séries* by Edouard Gorie, Floréal, 1842.

And, over that affiche, was a small affiche nailed:

Of Curiosities and Marvells

✝

Zoë was thoughtfully walking on la Haute Voie romaine.

✝

Themis la Grise was standing in her mother's garden; she held the invitation Hooke had given her to read.

She wore a simple high-necked day dress of silks in sea-green grey colours with a dark grey collar and cuffs; her jacket was unbuttoned showing her white chemise. She wore light grey gloves. She was barefoot.

He stood silent inhaling all of the fragrances of the garden to be found standing beside her.

"Thou art filled with rages and grief," said Themis as she viewed him standing there with his eyes closed.

"Toutatis was succumbed by his rage, his sorrow, his grief," replied Hooke as he breathed slowly.

"It is a trap," said Themis after viewing him at length.

"Would you care to join me?" he asked opening his eyes kindly smiling at her.

"Yes."

✝

Zoë was walking on la Haute Voie romaine.

†

She by a shrine was come: on the road-shrine on a post of polished ebony: the shrine on the post of thirteen feet height was Régence and delicately carved of polished ebony where slept the skeletal-carriage of a corvus articus. And, on the post, was nailed an affiche for the Théâtre de l'Opéra des Ténèbraes du Paradis which was presenting *Les Tombeaux Séries* by Edouard Gorie, Floréal, 1842.

And, over that affiche, was a small affiche nailed:

Of Reason and Logic

†

She by a shrine was come: on the road-shrine on a post of polished ebony: the shrine on the post of thirteen feet height was Régence and delicately carved of polished ebony where slept the skeletal-carriage of a corvus articus. And, on the post, was nailed an affiche for the Théâtre de l'Opéra des Ténèbraes du Paradis which was presenting *Les Tombeaux Séries* by Edouard Gorie, Floréal, 1842.

And, over that affiche, was a small affiche nailed:

on Chaos

†

Themis la Grise and Hooke stood on the grounds of Oppidum Ubiorum in Cologne in le duchié de Lotharingie. A large raven was in flight circling them.

"Do you know where this takes us?" said Themis.

"I believe so," said Hooke. "Gentlemen."

Seven large ravens appeared.

"Allow none but he thou knowest coming."

They bowed.

†

The large raven flying over the oppidum flew away after Hooke and Themis entered the passage.

†

Zoë was walking on la Haute Voie romaine.

†

Jean Lafayette-Lafitte le Sonneur was standing in the middle of the road staring at his opera glove provided by the Illapses Company, Ltd. He looked from his glove as Zoë was nearing.

"Madame!" said Jean Lafayette-Lafitte le Sonneur: "You walk by yourself on the Roman High Road."

"Yes?"

"Why?"

"It is expeditious. It follows the avenues of passage set in the land of Gaule. High Roads have no significance regardless of their given name; they are avenues. Simply, avenues."

"I see," said Lafayette-Lafitte le Sonneur. "Where is la Perle de la Mer Noire?"

Zoë pointed.

"I was given this with this glove," said le Sonneur; "Do you know what it could mean?"

Of Illusions and Ideals
on the ill-kept incunabula of Idylls

"No."

He was perturbed.

"Madame," said le Sonneur. He went in the direction Zoë had pointed.

Zoë her promenade did continue.

Zoë was concluding speaking with the demons from the arcade, Les Litanies de Satan.

"Thou knowest Mister Hooke." They shuffled and mumbled and groaned. "He shall give thee coins you are to give the Impresario Claude-Théodulf-Gérard Noailles for his collection and, if he should refuse, you may return with him to Mister Hooke on thy way to the parc keeping those gold pieces for thy own. And, if thou be quick, a grand amusement waits for thee at home."

They bowed; and, joyfully fled.

Zoë was strolling la Haute Voie romaine.

They were standing on a massive staircase in a chamber of pale grey stone filling the width of the chamber beneath a ceiling not more than fifty feet above them. At the top of the staircase were two great doors; at the bottom of the staircase was a pool of clear water. Runes, sigils and glyphs were engraved on walls and ceiling. The room was not dark nor was it lightened; it was as if in a grey fog.

†

Zoë was seated on a Fidelity Bench set beneath in the shade of an sacred ancient beech as Hercule was begun his tale.

"Odd ages ago," began Hercule and said:

The Knife Sharpener

La Vieille Femme lived in le commune founded in 1793 with the name of Beauvais-l'Isle-Barbe. The Knife Sharpener traveled once a week over le pont de l'Île Barbe to visit with her and to sharpen her scissors to be the edges of a razor. She spoke with him but seldom directly.

'I know not what the curse may be, and so I weaveth steadily, and little other care hath bothered me, she years ago did say to me,' the Knife Sharpener once remarked to me. 'Her cræft was wondrous.'

The Knife Sharpener offered his services for inexpensive prices but worked at a slow pace due to the unparalleled level of his expertise.

The Knife Sharpener had a shop in le quartier of Saint-Rambert-l'Île-Barbe. He visited those who could not come. He had done this for years.

A new company – L'Excellence Cie. – was established in le quartier de Vaise: 'Excellent service at lowest prices. Faster.' It would collect the items and return to the workplace where staff would perform the tasks of repair.

L'Excellence Cie. began sending a tricycle sharpener with grindstone to the places across the Saône.

The Knife Sharpener pushed his cart. He used flat stones.

The tricycle sharpener of l'Excellence Cie. was replaced by a courier who took the items back to the workplace where staff would perform the tasks of repair.

Citizens began sending their items to the new company; visitors kept increasingly visiting their shop. Citizens who did traffic with him—The Knife Sharpener—was slowly dwindling.

The Knife Sharpener still visited the few who preferred him as well as la Vieille Femme who lived on l'Île Barbe.

He closed his shop but continued pushing his cart to those who wished his service in le quartier of Saint-Rambert-l'Île-Barbe.

It was only a few years before l'Excellence Cie. changed for the worse. It cost more in payment for less good work performed at a slovenly pace.

Citizens went to the adresse of the shop of the Knife Sharpener instead but found an antiquarian.

They accosted him in the streets and rues.

He declined their apologies; he declined their regrets; he disbelieved their contrition and remorse.

They followed him to his house.

He declined their apologies; he declined their regrets; he disbelieved them. He had no sympathy for their plight.

The Knife Sharpener still visited the few who preferred him as well as la Vieille Femme who lived on l'Île Barbe.

Some became angry at him for the predicament in which he kept them; they vandalized his tools. He repaired them; and, he continued.

They became angrier at him for the predicament in which he kept them; they vandalized his tools and cart. He repaired them; and, he continued.

They became vengeful at him for the predicament in which he kept them; they vandalized his tools and cart and house. He repaired them; and, he continued.

His home was burning on that night when la Vieille Femme stood in the lane which she had not ever done once before. She poked her finger in the flames; her finger was set with small flames dancing. She whispered to the flames. The flames exploded spiraling and like fireflies flew off over in every direction. She went home.

He—The Knife Sharpener—and those he helped repaired his home; he continued.

Those involved were wounded in an unusual fashion because what ever they used or touched was burned: if they held a match, thumb and finger; if they held a torch, hand and arm; if they kicked a bucket of petrol, foot and leg. But that was not what was unusual. It was that the wounds healed shriveled and black and those appendages could not be amputated ever after.

The Knife Sharpener still visits the few who he prefers as well as la Vieille Femme who still lives on l'Île Barbe.

†

Hercule had concluded his tale.

"Dost this tale have a moral, Maître Hercule?"

"One should never cross with anger witch or demon they have never met but — Especially — one should never cross one who you do not know," said Hercule after thought.

"Thank you," said Zoë; "but you must go for you are needed. We shall, one day, speak in a different place."

Hercule bowed.

✝

Zoë was strolling on la Haute Voie romaine.

✝

Jean Lafayette-Lafitte le Polisseur de bottes was standing in the middle of the road staring at his opera glove provided by the Illapses Company, Ltd. He looked from his glove as Zoë was nearing.

"Madame!" said Jean Lafayette-Lafitte le Polisseur de bottes: "You walk by yourself on the High Road but have no parasol."

"Yes?"

"Why?"

"My parasol was given Brighde to shade her from the full Moons when she strolls the tides of Solstice."

"I see," said le Polisseur de bottes. "Where is Odesa?"

Zoë pointed.

"I was given this with this glove," said le Polisseur; "Do you know what it could mean?"

> Illusory incandescences
> are illuminating Ideals found in thoughts
> of far forgotten intrigues

"No."

He was perturbed.

"Madame," said le Polisseur. He went in the direction Zoë had pointed.

Zoë was amused.

✝

Zoë was strolling la Haute Voie romaine.

✝

Hooke and Themis were standing in the middle of the chamber. Themis went to the side wall at the West and gently let the fingers of her right-hand wander over the engraved tattoos on the stone. Hooke strolled down the steps to see what was below in the pool of clear water; he went back towards the two great iron doors but stopped. He peered at the ceiling; he smiled.

"Hercule," said Hooke.

"Sir?"

"Félix," said Themis. She arrived holding hands with Marcelle.

"We're under water," said Marcelle.

Those three wondered at those words she spoke.

"Hercule, what is this place?"

He peered about. He went to each wall and ran his forefinger along runes and glyphs following paths he saw where no others but Hooke could see. He peered again at the ceiling.

"Puzzle."

"Thank you," said Hooke. "Félix, what can you understand in those signs?"

She read them. "I cannot." Themis looked at her. "I can't!" replied Félix miffed. "It's gibberish. The sigils, glyphs and runes are not in any form or sentences. They don't read from the left nor from the right nor from the top to the bottom from the left or right and not even from the bottom. They're only characters! Word fragments. There are not any words on the walls. Not any. Nothing. None! I don't know what half of the sigils are! I don't know what half of the glyphs are! There is'n't any sense to them! Runes with glyphs!

Sigils with glyphs! That's another thing! The glyphs are from everywhere! Every place everywhere! They're scattered all over! *Everything's every*where!" She paused. She deeply inhaled but slowly exhaled through her mouth; and calmly said, "That's why."

"Thank you," said Hooke. "Marcelle, since you are here, what lies beneath and above?"

Marcelle stepped towards the pool; she paused. She went several steps up from where the others stood. "Ocean's salt-spray," said Marcelle in a reverie. "Night Horrors!" She violently shook her head to wake. "They're different!"

"Yes," said Hooke with his eyes closed in contemplation. He looked at Marcelle. "Thank you."

"Where are we?" asked Félix.

"We are leagues beneath le Palais des Vertus de l'Hiver éternel in Nubilus."

"Have you been here before?" Themis asked Hooke.

"No," said Hooke amused. "We have Night Horrors below waiting if we should go that way." He pointed. "We have Night Horrors waiting above if we should go that way." He pointed. "Hercule, how would you solve this puzzle?"

Hercule gestured to the walls and ceiling. "The patterns of words I cannot read are formed peculiarly in mathematical progressions. I - I believe - would take a single æon to plot them. But some are clustered around different single engravings. Everywhere. I do not know which begins."

"We shall not begin," said Hooke. "Félix, does the character 'water' or a derivation of the character for water appear in those markings?"

"Yes."

"Stone?"

"No."

"Light?"

"Yes."

"Does anything possibly sensible appear before after above or below the character for water?"

She read the words; she pointed at a place: "Ocean rising. Ocean Tide ocean rising. There are only a few others that I can see through this fog with different sensible combined words." She continued reading. "'Light' seems to have seven possibly sensible words: illume, dark, portentous, waves, particles, spectral, dampening." She read further. "Nope. 'Light' has thirty-one - seven - thirteen - three - seventeen - nine possible usable characters." She moaned. "'Light' has different and same words in combinations; 'coruscate' in different forms is written is several places. 'Light' has many instances." She pointed to a different place. "Here." She pointed higher on the wall — "Here" — and walked along the wall reading and pointing in all directions. Hooke mischievous smiled to Themis who tilted her head slightly to him with her eyebrows raised. Félix would continue in her exuberance but Hooke said, "What would happen if you touched that character for light? and, illuminated it."

She looked perplexedly confused at Hooke.

"Pardon." Hercule went over. He awkwardly gestured Marcelle to follow. He touched the mark Félix had indicted as light with his finger. He recited: "Haec - lux - in - eo - revelatur." He peered at Marcelle and Félix who nodded appreciatively delighted.

"It's writing all the words in proper orders!" shouted Félix with astonished giddy delight.

The runes of light were lit in a path which led over the four walls and ceiling. The sensible words followed and then all of the remaining runes and glyphs were illuminated. It shown as an elaborate curlicue design.

The chamber was well lit causing the greyness to be dispersed.

"You could solve that," said Themis.

"Eventually. Hercule and Félix were able to deduce this place faster than I. However, since Marcelle fortunately unexpectedly arrived, she more importantly noticed the gravest of two flaws in this puzzle: I could not sense the Night Horrors."

"Nor I," said Themis.

"I couldn't until I felt the ocean's Winter spray," said Marcelle. She smiled. "Oh."

Félix agreed.

Hercule shrugged.

"Two flaws?"

"She noted that light was missing."

"What do you intend to do?" asked Themis.

"We descend."

Themis blankly gazed at him; the others were startled.

"Hercule, if you would, please escort Félix and Marcelle back," instructed Hooke.

Hercule looked at them; they shook their heads. "We would prefer to remain," said Hercule. Hooke glanced at Félix and Marcelle who silently insisted.

"How do we descend?" asked Marcelle.

"By Zone cardinalis," said Hooke after he stared at le Trio diabolique for several very long minutes. "Le Trio diabolique."

"Sir," said Hercule. "May I?" Hooke bowed from his shoulders. Hercule he smiled and went counting paces from one side of the chamber to the other. "One-hundred ten and three." Hercule took three paces on the single step. He was pleased.

"The doors are thirty-three feet in height," said Hooke; "It is the size used for doors taken in grand ceremonial places; therefore, the steps lead to a landing identical to the doors with an opening identical to the height of the passage beneath the pool."

Hercule nodded appreciatively.

Marcelle and Félix sat themselves on the steps.

Hercule counting paces ambled went from the wall. "Fifty and six." He stood. "Here."

"Marcelle, would you please stand where Hercule is standing," said Hooke; she rose and went standing where Hercule stood.

Hercule thought. He went to the landing and counting paced from steps to the recessed doors. He walked down the staircase counting his paces until he stood at the pool; he thoughtfully counted, with his head bobbing, the steps in the pool. "Seven-hundred sixty and one." He turned and stood as he silently counted the steps ascending. He nodded. Hercule strode to a step. "Here." He pointed to the doors. "Three-hundred and eighty." He pointed to the pool. "Three-hundred eighty and one."

"Félix, would you please stand where Hercule is standing," said Hooke; she rose and went standing where Hercule stood.

"Seven-hundred sixty and one?" asked Félix.

"Length of this chamber," replied Hooke as he watched Hercule.

Hercule went to the place where Félix and Marcelle would be aligned at the crux. "This."

"What?"

"Zone cardinalis," replied Hooke. He gestured in the four Cardinal directions beginning with West.

Hooke had Themis stand one step above, while he stood one step below, from the step Hercule indicated.

"If I may," said Hooke, "have you turn facing East extending your left hand towards the door parallel with the steps while I do the same towards the pool facing West. If you would," Hooke continued as he extended his right hand; she clasped his hand. Their clasped hands were held over the Zone cardinalis of the chamber.

"Where shall we stand?" asked Marcelle with exhilarated apprehension.

"Where'er thee wish," said Hooke.

"What are we to do?" asked Themis.

Those three exchanged glances shrugging and remained where they stood.

"Magnétismes," said Hooke.

She laughed.

"Why do you stand like that?" asked Félix.

"We address the four Cardinal directions by facing one and indicating another. Absolutes, balance and equivalence strengthen confluence in effects," said Themis as all air became charged and pale fluctuations of light were seen fluttering about them.

The room was filled with the faintness of their light. Their light in turn became fused with the light from the chamber. The engravings on the surfaces of the chamber grew with intensity.

They waited.

The doors burst open from howling winds carrying the Night Horrors with them; the pool rose in a water spout carrying Night Horrors with it: the Horrors were treacherously wounded by the light bending from the staircase, walls and ceiling; air and water collided directly overhead of where Hooke and Themis were standing forming a funnel sending the Horrors against the ceiling where the light-charged water from the pool drowned them, and the light-charged air pressing them beneath the water broke the Horrors against the ceiling.

The intensity from Hooke shown brightest growing; Themis was gradually engulfed in that light until together they were shinning brighter than the Spirit-light. They were no longer seen: they fading ghost-like had disappeared.

The intensity of that light in the chamber grew far greater in it's immenseness; the engravings were melting deeper into the surfaces. All things of that structure of the vast keep were made translucent.

That maëlstrom of light where Hooke and Themis had stood continued for a length of time unknown.

Suddenly, the storm of raging wind and water ceased; the light was subdued: the Horrors were gone.

They – Themis and Hooke – appeared standing but Hooke was holding her tightly.

Marcelle and Félix would have belaboured them with questions about their disappearance but did not: Hooke was darkly staring at them.

"Sir," said Hercule after a great length of silence passed while Themis and Hooke stood embraced in radiance which was slowly diminishing.

Hooke was staring at Themis who nodding smiled weakly: they stepped apart.

"We formed a horseshoe," said Hooke. "The Essentiae combined was greater than from two single entities. The surfaces of the chamber were themselves the third Essentiae and became conductive. The three affluent sources were rendered more intense by confluence. Light was magnetised drawing wind and water which could carry the Horrors because Horrors are the corporeal form of a greater terror. That tremulous light which you may have seen ignited greater illumination from the chamber; it was not brighter but that intensity was shown beyond measure. That confluence of air, water, stone and light destroyed them."

"The Spirit of this chamber aided us," said Themis thoughtfully.

They—Marcelle, Félix and Hercule—each furtively looked at their hands and arms.

"You felt delicate sensations; but are not harmed."

"They will return?" said Hercule as he peered at the ceiling.

"They've ceased Existence."

"By light?"

"No." He thought. "It was la Lumière archaïque: Dark. For the moment think of it as Light augmented."

"By you?" said Marcelle. Hooke ignored her being kept in his thoughts as he led them down the steps. Marcelle turned to Themis appearing grave who nodded whispering, "Yes."

"You both saved us," said Félix.

"It was far greater tragedy we delayed for an unknown length of years," said Themis.

"Why is it far greater tragic things happen always with you?" said Marcelle.

"Why a horseshoe?" asked Félix. "Why not a circle?"

"Phénomène magique," replied Themis.

Hooke paused. He shook himself from his reverie. He slowly turned his head to view Themis. "Witch's curse."

"They do!" she replied smiling.

Hooke with the index finger of his right hand drew a ring of fire in the air. "Like this?" He blew on the flames: a smoke ring. Themis gestured and sent a smaller smoke ring hurtling through Hooke's ring marauding it. He began laughing; and, then sighed. "I saunter." He set his hands in his trouser pockets, sauntering.

Marcelle and Félix paused on the steps and turning faced the centre of the chamber; they did curtsies. Hercule bowed. They continued following.

"Why down?" asked Marcelle.

"Curiosity," replied Themis.

"Why curiosity?" asked Félix.

"Learning," replied Hercule.

"Thomas Aquinas opposed curiosity over studiosity because curiosity he considered a vice, studiosity a virtue," said Félix.

"He does," replied Hooke; "We've disagreed on a great many subjects; that being one."

✝

Merle was strolling across the bridge set over the Ocean of Dark.

✝

The runes were illuminating before them and were diminished after several feet behind them.

"It's following us," said Marcelle.

"It's leading Hercule because Hercule was the one who requested it."

"What do you think happened beyond the door?" asked Themis.

"I'm clueless. They know and so they would not come down; or, they do not know but since they cannot account for what occurred above, they dare not come; or, they have not come down from above believing work was done believing none could have escaped their diabolical snare."

"Sir," said Hercule, "how did you know we were beneath Palace of Fidelity of the Four Kingdoms of the Laws?"

"The glyphs, sigils and a number of the runes used in that chamber are found in Elder cabinet-celles I have been when visiting the Palace of Fidelity. I believe that that chamber was once for Penance where one would remain until solving the puzzle."

"A number of the runes?"

"Esoteric runes — I know some by happenstance but ignore them in the main because they are inferior — are literal translations into a Present-Day vernacular."

"I use them," interjected Félix.

"That—Eventually—shall be corrected for all les Mademoiselles," said Themis.

"What do you use, then?"

"L'Archaïque," said Hooke. "Old before Antiquity. Mademoiselle la Grise and Maestro Hercule do."

Hercule peered squinky-eyed at Hooke.

"How do you learn it?"

"You and Félix have learned those you have been reading but inflections when speaking are missing," said Themis. "And, you've been reading some as they were written in secrecy: those are intentionally weak. They're often backwards. Or, cryptic."

"Underwater!"

"Or," continued Themis, "underwater with the appropriate key for reading words in an order of—Say—every third for six lines followed by every ninth word for three lines followed by every twenty-seventh word for five lines followed by that single line following; and—Then—repeating the sequence. Thrice. Read the next three pages fully; and—Then—repeating the sequence until the final page is reached wherein you are—Cryptically—asked to remove—Say—every thirteenth word before you have learned that which was to be known."

"That would be simple to write down," said Félix.

"Does'n't," said Hercule. "Words you write, from those books, with any instrument, on any surface, disappear. Memory. They are things only to be read or listened are learned." They looked at him to which he said in reply with an emphatic nod: "Yes."

"One is taught things from everyone," said la Grise. "Maître Hercule has given you valuable lessons during this our enlightening adventure." Hercule paled. "I did not know until I did know I did it."

"Perhaps not; but you have—Nevertheless—given them incomparable lessons, Maître Hercule," said Hooke. "Chivalrous."

He blushed.

"Why are we going down?"

"I know what is higher. I do not believe water filled this passage before our puzzle was given. Hercule? What order did the wall engravings spread?"

"Evenly. They filled the wall of the entrance and the wall of this passage at an identical moment before filling the sides and ceiling."

"Why?"

He thought. "Progress. The wall filled first the entrance would be getting closer to returning; the exit in similarity was done."

"A gracious gesture," said Themis.

"True; but; they also made it a simple task of taking simple exit from that place of Penance if one should wish."

"What!" exclaimed Marcelle.

"There is neither door nor grille at the bottom of the staircase."

"Oh," said Marcelle.

"Are we going to Hell?" asked Félix.

"Hopefully."

†

Zoë was strolling la Haute Voie romaine.

†

Jean Lafayette-Lafitte le Fabricant de capot was approaching staring at his opera glove provided by the Illapses Company, Ltd. He looked from his glove as he was Zoë nearing.

"Madame!" said Jean Lafayette-Lafitte le Fabricant de capot: "You sit by yourself with a Magpie on the High Road but have no goggles for riding in your palanquin."

"Yes?"

"Why?"

"I have no palanquin."

"I see," said le Fabricant de capot. "Where is Odesa?"

Zoë pointed.

The Magpie stood and went to le Fabricant de capot. "Papers," said the Magpie as it thrusted a wax-sealed envelope at le Fabricant de capot. It returned and sat.

"I was given this," said le Fabricant; "Do you know what it could mean?"

> Of Lilith gone strolling on the lanes
> with lilting tiger lilies for Lucifer

"No," replied Zoë.

He was perturbed.

"Madame," said le Fabricant. He went in the direction Zoë had pointed.

Zoë was amused.

†

Zoë was strolling la Haute Voie romaine.

†

Hooke paused and viewed Themis as she watched him. Le Trio diabolique continued slowly counting their paces. He stared. Themis closed her eyes slowly and open them as she smiled her pleasant Winter smile. Hooke nodded. They continued.

"Have you ever been to Hades?" asked Themis when they had reached them.

"By accident," replied Hercule. "I saw it was not the forest I was walking and turned around in traces following my way before I entered the woods I was continuing walked."

"Maître Hercule has given guidance in abundance with lessons enough for a sennight," said Themis. "Still he does yet another."

He smiled faintly.

They were nearing an iron door their exit.

"Guards?"

"Likely," replied Hooke; "Unsuspected guards."

"What do we...."

Hooke made a small dismissive gesture with the fingers of his left hand.

A twenty-foot-wide hole did open from the violence caused by the explosion of compressed invisible flames.

He looked at the bodies of soldiers emblazoned with a king's colors strewn about the courtyard. He looked at the ruin of the structures and of citizens from where the blast did go against the palace of that place. They were standing in the citadel of President Glasya-Labolas. He shook his head as he led his sight upwards to the white tower of the citadel: opaque red flames wreathed in helical fashion rotating rising on the tower of the palace until the tower collapsed: the flames soaring continued higher until they were gone from sight.

Dust and debris descended over all things. Small fires were set. The soldiers and citizens approaching ceased all movement. It was silent. All of the citadel had become silent.

Hooke ignoring them went back to the tunnel. He placed his hand on a wall and the stone was changed becoming Volvic molten lava tens of meters thick which expanding filled that passage from le Palais des Vertus. He turned facing the soldiers as the molten mass crept slowly from the passage.

"Safe passage?" said Hooke.

The soldiers parted. All of the soldiers and all of the citizens watched in silence, for the arrival of Hooke had spread throughout the citadel, as those five went the avenues and lanes to the main gate which had been lowered for them.

"How did you do that?" asked Félix.

"Methane gas," replied Hooke as he peered across the plains.

"The laws of Nature."

"Mm-hmm," Hooke replied with his mouth closed.

They had not waited long before they saw a small cavalry was riding hard towards them from over the grasslands. They wore the colours of le Maréchal.

The horsemen arrived.

"Sir?" said the Captain as he dismounted.

Hercule looked at his pocket-watch. It had stopped. He wound it; it remained so.

"Captain Bon Amens, if you may, could we impose on you for the use of two horses so that we may accompany you leading us to le Maréchal?"

Hooke took Hercule aside and whispered while Hercule stood immensely attentive before saying "Kerepakupai Meru." Hooke nodded.

"Honos. Athos." They dismounted holding the reins for Themis and Hooke who thanked them.

"Guard them," said the Captain. The company remained as those three went across the plains.

One of the cavaliers drew near.

"Hercule?"

Hercule squinted with his right eye closed looking at the gent. He thought. "Hlæja the Tall," said Hercule. "Welcome."

"Where have you come?"

"Nubilus," replied Hercule conversationally before he fell silent with his thoughts. "The Palace of Fidelity."

The company was stunned silent staring at the tableau of Hercule standing with two young girls while in the background the whole of the citadel was burning.

"Damaged," he nodding said to himself.

†

Zoë was strolling la Haute Voie romaine.

Jean Lafayette-Lafitte l'Avocat was standing in the middle of the road staring at his opera glove provided by the Illapses Company, Ltd. He looked from his glove as Zoë was nearing.

"Madame!" said Jean Lafayette-Lafitte l'Avocat: "You walk by yourself on the High Road though you do not have Passe-port à l'intérieur."

"Yes?"

"Why?"

"I prefer the billets for a grand Ombre spectacle."

"I see," said l'Avocat. "Where is Sevastopol?"

Zoë pointed.

"I was given this by a Pie with a satchel," said l'Avocat; "Do you know what it could mean?"

Of Syrens and Silences on the shores
of sultry seas

"No."

He was perturbed.

"Madame," said l'Avocat. He went in the direction Zoë had pointed.

Zoë was amused.

Zoë was strolling la Haute Voie romaine.

Le Maréchal d'Empire with several of his Maréchaux de camp stood watching smoke rise from the citadel of President Glasya-Labolas. Captain Bon Amens stood discretely to the side.

Hooke had explained all of which had transpired.

"Night Horrors," mused le Maréchal d'Empire.

"Two riddles of l'Hôpital de la Divinité Bienveillante have been solved," said Hooke: "how the Night Horrors were given corporeal form; and, by whom. Le Directeur Mortuorum has been suspected but now 'tis known."

"What do you intend to do about him?" asked le Maréchal.

"I was hoping you would spread rumours of our adventure mentioning him by name," said Hooke, "and, the exploits—of whatever you care to relate or grandiosely invent—concerning Marcelle's and Félix's part in it. We wait the arrival of Marcelle la Grise. I wish to know who follows." He turned to Themis. "We lack knowledge of a piece hidden missing from their board. Something is not right." She did worrisome nod and would ask of him an explanation later.

"Pleasure," said le Maréchal.

"That passage from the chamber of Penance?" asked one of the Maréchaux de camp. "Before it was sealed by les Enragés, where did it originally lead?"

"I do not nor could I surmise where it originally did lead. It could have been banishment as simple as Hades or Limbo. Or, some place more sinister. I do not believe, from watching the lightened engravings spread across the surfaces of the chamber, half-made — or, half completed — penance was acceptable. The engravings may have altered due to the magnitude of the sin or sins. Or, if Indulgences altered penance. I cannot guess where it first led.

"I wager Oblivion."

"You requested safe passage?" ask Maréchal de camp Bahimouth the Grim.

"Yes. Safe passage I them offered."

"Are there more tunnels?" asked Maréchal de camp Baphometis the Stout.

"I believe not. Regardless, all of the Horrors in that palais were destroyed."

"Oh," said Themis.

"The chamber *was* one of Penance," replied Hooke as he turned to face her. "I was certain when the chamber itself intensified. It was a fourth element in our need; we - you and I - were a second and third element for it's need. When the doors opened, I sensed other Horrors. Did you?"

"Something unknown was all," said Themis. She thought. "I remember." She looked at Hooke. "What did you mean by agreeing with Marcelle that they were different?"

"They were all half-formed Horrors."

All movement and speech ceased.

"*Please elucidate,*" said le Maréchal slowly.

"Malevolences not fully formed into their corporeal state of Horror," replied Hooke: "Whether they are simple abnormalities, or a new stage of their progression, I cannot say." He faced Themis. "We'll see."

"The chamber?"

"The chamber—It raged—after sensing those Horrors near-by and those beyond in the tower and palace of that once sacred place, and sent through the walls of the structure la Lumière archaïque with an increasing intensity due to more of the structure—long dormant Spirits of place were awakened with unfathomed rage in other chambers and vaults—being involved: they became one. It was then we too were become part of the ever-increasing cycle of it's rage until it ceased when those Horrors were decayed unto particles by all of the Spirits of that place."

"That!" exclaimed Themis. "That is what happened! We became part of that single Spirit." She thought. "We were a single Spirit!"

"Yes."

"Équivalence spiritualis!"

"Yes."

"That's what you do!" she said as she collapsed on to a chair, sobbing.

"Yes," Hooke replied softly as he went to her stooped bending on one knee before her. He took her hands in his.

"The Spirits kept us together and returned us," she said in a small voice as if speaking to herself.

"Yes."

"They knew."

"Yes."

She kissed his hand.

They did not move until le Maréchal ceremoniously dropped a glass of water shattering on the floor. Le Maréchal and the generals, when Themis collapsed, turned their backs to them studiously studying a map of the continent hastily pinned on the wall by the Captain.

Themis and Hooke stood.

"My apologies, Bonhommes," said Themis.

Le Maréchal went and offered her his handkerchief which she accepted. Those others in that room were speechless.

"All of the Spirit-Ghosts ye've woken," said le Maréchal as he stood with his nose inches from Hooke's, "abetted by our Themis Witch-Queen, who has now become benevolently known by those Spirits, have returned as a single Spirit in that place?"

Hooke nodded.

"Oblivion as Spirit!" said le Maréchal. "Équivalence spiritualis!"

Hooke nodded.

"That sets it," said le Maréchal. "Ivos!" His aide-de-camp entered from the hallway. It was Bill from the Flying Squad. Le Maréchal withdrew coins and counting took twenty gold pieces jangling them in the direction of Ivos who smiling accepted them.

"Scariest?"

"Bastard!" proclaimed le Maréchal grandly laughing as he Hooke embraced. They hugged.

"What did you do to the flames?" said Themis one eye closed squinting at Hooke.

"Barber's pole."

"These cartes de visite are waxing more poetic with thy insults," said le Maréchal.

"Her influence."

A servientis—Hob yr Anwybodus—entered with a note he presented to a Maréchaux de camp. He took exit.

"You are demanded at Court by Her Majesty Queen Persephone," said Maréchal de camp Baphometis the Ugly.

"Captain? May we continue use of the steeds? We shall send them to your men at the citadel after we reach the palace."

"Of course."

"It was stated great urgency was needed," said Maréchal de camp Baphometis the Ugly.

"We shall with all the imperative haste that can be mustered comply."

"She will be pleased."

✝

Zoë was strolling la Haute Voie romaine.

✝

Jean Lafayette-Lafitte le Courtier was standing in the middle of the road staring at his opera glove provided by the Illapses Company, Ltd. He looked from his glove as Zoë was nearing.

"Madame!" said Jean Lafayette-Lafitte le Courtier: "You walk by yourself with no chevalier."

"Yes?"

"Why?"

"They have no Cartes de participation au cortège."

"I see," said le Courtier. "Where is Constanța?"

Zoë pointed.

"I was given this on the middle of the lane," said le Courtier; "Do you know what it could mean?"

> Stoïc Syrens on the Strand
> singing their Songes
> with musical accompaniment
> by a chamber symphony band

"No."

He was perturbed.

"Madame," said le Courtier. He went in the direction Zoë had pointed.

Zoë was amused.

†

Zoë was strolling la Haute Voie romaine.

†

Zoë was come to a path which led from the High Road down to the riverside where Oana la Verte, Hélène Eunomia la Jaune, Shpresa la Rose, Theresa Aurélia de Phaenna, Dilys d'Euphrosyne la Cramoisie, Shiretoko-hantō Miyabiyaka and Chloris Delilas Sasa-zamani were waiting. The lime-tinged Gents had prepared a late luncheon. Several were dressed in typical waiter fashion.

After picnicking was finished and farewells were made, they all did fly off on their besoms.

Zoë returned to la Haute Voie romaine.

†

"Eleven courses?" said Hooke as they rode at a leisurely pace.

"I tasted most of them; they were delicious. I ate little," said Themis. "She has a hearty appetite, but she ate less than I."

Hooke laughed.

"How did Captain Bon Amens know of our whereabouts so soon?"

"Damysus was sent to la Maréchal as a courtesy for whatever was to befall. I knew we were summoned to Nubilus because of the scent from their messenger; I suspected—I suspected but did not know—another from Hades was involved." Themis frowned. "King Vinea is the principle who engages directly with les Enragés.

"Mimas followed us to Cologne and was sent to al-Jinn requesting his destruction of that passage we entered and informing him not to enter himself after us."

"What isn't right?" asked Themis with grim seriousness.

"If we acknowledge that their logic was sound, that I was to be imprisoned for a great length of Chronos passing, it was for a specific reason; I cannot deduce that reason. Something else is at play that we've yet to know. That is troublesome."

"What do we do?"

"We wait."

Zoë was strolling la Haute Voie romaine.

†

Jean Lafayette-Lafitte le Marqueur de billard was standing in the middle of the road staring at his opera glove provided by the Illapses Company, Ltd. He looked from his glove as Zoë was nearing.

"Madame!" said Jean Lafayette-Lafitte le Marqueur de billard: "You walk by yourself on the High Road but have no jongleur."

"Yes?"

"Why?"

"Chansons de geste of the folk of Fey are missing."

"I see," said le Marqueur de billard. "Where is Odesa?"

Zoë pointed.

"I was given this by a Highwayman chased by a Jackdaw," said le Marqueur; "Do you know what it could mean?"

She was sleeping on the seashore
in shades of the steles of Selene

"No."

He was perturbed.

"Madame," said le Marqueur. He went in the direction Zoë had pointed.

Zoë was amused.

†

Zoë was strolling la Haute Voie romaine.

†

Porphyrion the Messenger was waiting for them.

Themis spoke to the horses thanking them and wishing them safe return to those who waited for them. They galloped away.

He whispered in the ear of Hooke for a length. Hooke thanked him, stood, and disappointed shook his head.

Themis stood silent.

"The first carriage arriving for les Trois bienveillants was impostors who failed Hercule's question with an incorrect counter reply. They were apprehended but took poison.

"They were safely taken by the second."

"Whose?"

"Colours unknown."

✝

Jean Lafayette-Lafitte le Banquier was standing in the middle of the road staring at his opera glove provided by the Illapses Company, Ltd. He looked from his glove as Zoë was nearing.

"Madame!" said Jean Lafayette-Lafitte le Banquier: "You walk by yourself on the High Road yet you have no troubadour to accompany you."

"Yes?"

"Why?"

"Le Troubadour silencieux is with his Lady fair."

"I see," said le Banquier. "Where is Euxinograd?"

Zoë pointed.

"I was given this," said le Banquier; "Do you know what it could mean?"

Of Venus and Vicissitudes
on the verge of vernal days

"No."

He was perturbed.

"Madame," said le Banquier. He went in the direction Zoë had pointed.

Zoë was sad.

✝

Zoë was strolling la Haute Voie romaine.

†

They were announced and did through the attending nobles, courtiers and camarilla go to the daïs where under a baldachin Hades and Persephone sat on their thrones.

Persephone was vindictively pleased.

The court was standing in silent waiting.

Hooke bowed from his shoulders. Themis nodded.

"What have you done?" asked Hades.

Hooke related all that which did occur. He concluded that le Maréchal was waiting for a command from Hades before inspecting the citadel for the traitor Glasya-Labolas who in all likelihood had fled.

"Why was Mademoiselle d'Achéron not summoned?" asked Persephone.

"Félix was more appropriate, Highness," said Hooke; "Hercule was of necessity. Marcelle was come by Chance."

"Why was your young consort taken and not one older with Elder knowledge?" demanded Persephone.

Hooke turned his head slightly towards Themis. She shrugged.

"Why would you of All require assistance?" continued Persephone.

"Hours passing," replied Hooke as he faced Persephone. "The happenstances in le Palais fidelis would affect with malice each of the kingdoms which I could not allow. I did not have the luxury for a few years of amusement indulging myself solving that puzzle: assistance should always be welcomed when council is of goodly benefit, should it not? Highness."

"What then!"

"If you have no other concerns, may my guide and myself depart from thy kingdom," said Hooke, who was ignoring Persephone, to Hades.

"How dare you!" screamed Persephone standing throwing her fan at him; but it fell far short of it's mark. Persephone stared at Themis who was attentively watching Hades and Hooke.

"If you would be so kind," said Hades, "before your guide takes you from us, please reply to Her Majesty's question."

"Your Highness," said Hooke bowing from his shoulders to Hades. He turned to Persephone. "Madame." He nodded. "I do not betray my vow in memoria Spiritus sancti de deorum antiquitatis for anyone; therefore, I give preference to none. I would have asked my young consort – Themis Queen – to accompany me into the pool where the Horrors lurked and, if she did, we would have created a chasm between there and here destroying all of the kingdom of Glasya-Labolas and quite possibly that which lies beyond for many leagues since we would have not had that chamber encasing light augmented, for remember, Madame, we still had that single Spirit-Ghost in aid."

"I would have," said Themis. "*Highness.*"

"How were those three not destroyed yet all of the kingdom of Hades would be!"

"The chamber–that Spirit–kept encased that Dark," said Hooke; "Transparence for they."

"You could have done that for the populace of Hades's," said Persephone. "Why didn't you!"

"They are'n't my subjects," replied Hooke: "No."

"I banish thee," screamed Persephone as she stood from her throne shaking from her fury.

"I accept thy banishment from this kingdom to be fulfilled on the second full Moon during which I depart from all the lands under the rule of His Majesty, Hades," said Hooke impassively. "However, until then, I shall keep a lengthy visit in coming days."

She gestured as if to curse Hooke. Hades rolled his eyes; and, groaning sighed.

"Choose wisely, Madame. For it may be by thine own hand thy sovereign's made widower."

"You wouldn't dare," she replied with practiced haughtiness.

"Inmurus," said Hooke as he stared unblinking at her; he waited until she was made confident nothing did happen before he said: "Specere." All then did see, by the delicate swirling of coruscations from pin-prick lights, her encased by Hooke in a large sphere: Transparence.

Persephone was beside herself apoplectic in her fit of screaming at Hooke. Specere faded. She was hurriedly attended by her camarilla, her ladies-in-waiting, and those femmes de la cour of high station. Her voice went shrill. Persephone was stunned surprisingly; she clutched her throat. Her voice then ascended higher and highest before she went hoarse; then, silent.

Guards of the Court were quietly entering.

Hades looked at him shaking his head slowly and smiled with his eyes. He gestured for him to approach. Hooke leaned down so that Hades could whisper. Hooke whispered. Finally, Hades gestured for him to return; Hooke did.

"Be gone."

They nodded solemnly.

Hades rose and went from the Court of the Thrones. All of the Guards of the Court had quietly entered and slowly began pressing towards Themis and Hooke.

Hooke was walking with his eyes closed, shaking his head. Themis wrapped her right arm around his left arm as they went walking; he opened his eyes; and, smiled.

Themis flung her left arm behind her spreading her fingers rigidly sending with muted violence all in the court flying tumbling through the air against walls and ceilings and the balconies of the arcades high above the tiles. Persephone was allowed by Themis to be, in Transparence, remaining seated.

They took exit.

✝

Zoë was strolling la Haute Voie romaine.

✝

Jean Lafayette-Lafitte le Boucher was standing in the middle of the road staring at his opera glove provided by the Illapses Company, Ltd. He looked from his glove as Zoë was nearing.

"Madame!" said Jean Lafayette-Lafitte le Boucher: "You walk on the High Road but your shadow has flown."

"Yes?"

"Why?"

"They do that in dreams."

"I see," said le Boucher. "Where is Odesa?"

Zoë pointed.

"I was given this," said le Boucher; "Do you know what it could mean?"

> Venus as vixen in virtuous guise
> set sail on a steamship
> o'er vague-setting skies

"No."

He was perturbed.

"Madame," said le Boucher. He went in the direction Zoë had pointed.

Zoë was amused.

†

"That was charming," said Themis.

"I did appreciate your two earliest sleights of hand," said Hooke.

"I did, too," replied Themis. "The second one I thought necessary." He stood bemused. "Félix. She found it on the back pages of an illustrated magazine's advertisements under practical amusements; she ordered it. Where're we off to now?"

Hooke pointed to the carriage driving up the boulevard to the palace.

"Hades whispered his gratitude for the demise of the Horrors and for the exposure of Glasya-Labolas. He also mentioned that since Her Majesty and Queen Fey no longer take her on adventures she has grown profligate."

"She's jealous?" said Themis. She thought until remembering: "Afternoon Tea!"

✝

Zoë was strolling la Haute Voie romaine.

✝

Jean Lafayette-Lafitte le Castor was standing in the middle of the road staring at his opera glove provided by the Illapses Company, Ltd. He looked from his glove as Zoë was nearing.

"Madame!" said Jean Lafayette-Lafitte le Castor. "You walk on the High Road merrily."

"Yes?"

"Why?"

"It is joyful."

"I see," said le Castor. "Where is Moldova?"

Zoë pointed.

"I was given this," said le Castor. "Do you know what it could mean?"

Venus as vampyr in vitreous guise
set sail on an airship o'er Prusse-setting skies

"No."

He was perturbed.

"Madame," said le Castor. He went in the direction Zoë had pointed.

Zoë was sedate.

Themis and Hooke were on the Palisades. Hooke was leaning on one side and Themis was sitting on the side facing the Sea against the phare of the Ocean.

"You wished to know if it would be raining on the full Moon in the month of Décembre in the year of 1809."

"You had once mentioned your fondness for rain. It was to rain on that day albeit a Winter's rain but it wasn't snowing nor sleet. Simply raining."

"I was not cold," she remembered fondly. "It was full Moon against the skies of Winter Solstice. That was your reason for waiting to ask me."

He smiled.

They viewed all before them silently with their thoughts.

"Lady Constance no longer believes what she once did about you; you are grown much too mysterious for her in her eyes: she wares thee. Thy Fate she was never able to see and it has been over this century mine has faded from her."

"I did not know."

"One-hundred and four years it has been yet never waiting."

"Clotho, Nona the Ninth, Lachesis, Decima the Tenth, Madame l'Implacable, and Morta; Thalatte, Flora, Auxesia, Hegemone, and, Carpho; Aglaea, Euphrosyne, Thalia, Cleta, Auxo, Peitho, Phaenna, Pasithea, Charis, Antheia, Eudaimonia, Paidia, Pandaisia, Eupheme, Philophrosyne, Eucleia, Euthenia and Pannychis."

"Yes."

He took her hand and bowing kissed it.

†

Zoë was strolling la Haute Voie romaine.

†

Jean Lafayette-Lafitte le Boulanger was standing in the middle of the road staring at his opera glove provided by the Illapses Company, Ltd. He looked from his glove as Zoë was nearing.

"Madame!" said Jean Lafayette-Lafitte le Boulanger: "You walk on the High Road in solitary solitude."

"Yes?"

"Why?"

"I'm never alone."

"I see," said le Boulanger. "Where is Odesa?"

Zoë pointed.

"I was given this with this glove," said le Boulanger. "Do you know what it could mean?"

> Venus as Virtue in voluptuous guise
> set flight o'er the Moon-setting skies

"No."

He was perturbed.

"Madame," said le Boulanger. He went in the direction Zoë had pointed.

Zoë was content.

†

Zoë and Themis Fey-Queen were walking hand-in-hand; they laughed like anything to see the clockwork pageantry of Chaos engaged with it's marvells over all the somnambulant cursèd land: "If this were only seen by all," they said, "it 'twould be grand!"

11

Bucarest

Interlude: France, 1913 – The advent of the Congress for the Reformation was embraced by all of the Stewards of Fey except for those from Orbis paradisiacus who were betrayed, by their hubris exposed, in the plots of Horror and Terror waged in the three kingdoms of Fey.

The existence of Orbis terrae does not signify that Man exists and so Man remains in the contes des Fey as Myth.

†

The illuminations from the streams of the Night sky passing were set shining through the clouds over the realm of Avallon.

†

Marcelle and Félix were standing at the steps of the great house—Lugosdunon—in the county of Lucidusmons.

Charon had driven them. "All other matters of deities and imps will wait," he said finding them standing lost on the quay amoungst all the turmoil of that place during the arrival hour.

They had gone from the Acheron Quay and then turning to the East they drove in the shadow of the arête—The Knife of Hydros—passing the Sea of Redemption, a vast lake extended from beneath the range of mountains, for a taxing length of leagues, until they went winding up the zig-zag drive to the house, set on a high eminence formed against the mountain, from which one could see Hera's Wall.

They thanked him.

He smiled.

"My daughter wanders with Lady Constance. She would appreciate your company for however long you and she are able to stay. May I inform her—Discreetly—you are in this place?"

"O! Please do!"

He gestured. They went up the grand staircase while he waited below.

†

Mikhail, Orphiel and Hieronymus-Baleberithe-Seere ad-Din al-Jinn were walking with Zoë as she went on the High Road.

†

They rang the bell. The door was opened by the Housekeeper. She waved to Charon who then went.

They handed her a letter. "His Lordship."

"If you would, I should summon Mister Reynaerd in this matter." She left with their letter. The door stood opened.

They waited.

"It's the same as his house by the Sea," said Marcelle. "The gargoyles are still staring." Félix with great trepidation took a few steps entering the entrance hall. "It is." She immediately went out from the hall for a figure was coming from the shadows. They tried acting nonchalant but failed.

"Les Mademoiselles inséparables," said a familiar voice. They would descend the staircase and flee down the zig-zag lane but was heard: "Please don't."

They stood where they were.

"I have conferred with my adviser," said Hooke as he passed them and sat on the topmost step. "They concur." He gestured with the hand holding their letter for them to sit beside him.

They did.

"Why do we sit here?" asked Félix.

"Messenger," replied Hooke.

✝

Portul Pădurilor—Harbour of the Forests—is a commune established in the fifth of the lessening centuries. It was within walking distance from Bucarest.

Parcul Târgului—the Park of the Fair—a few miles from the Harbour was constructed on the oppidum in early Modern Ages as arcades, amusements and magasins were added throughout all those centuries of Modernity.

✝

"Something's different but I cannot think what," said Félix.

"I have bouts of weightlessness but do not act differently," said Marcelle. "I don't know what is different. I feel differently."

"What's happened to us?" said they.

"Do you know—Truly know—what Spirits of Locis sacris are? Spirit originates from the Latin 'spiritus' which is from 'spiro' as in 'I breathe, I respire; I live.' They are Spirits so they are not ghosts." He looked at Marcelle. "Yes. Ghosts breathe but they do so in their own place in the hours which they are." He stared across the grass plains. "Spirits breathe in all time because the sacred place in which they are is not in the currents of Chronos.

"A Spirit of a place is thought an illusion which cannot be sensed yet it can be imagined; or, it is thought as of Ghost that can be sensed." He peered at Marcelle who nodded. He peered at Félix who nodded. He smiled.

"When one first visits a place of Sanctus, things happen. Benevolence is exchanged no matter how small or great it is tendered by those two Spirits: thou and they."

"This cannot be!" said Marcelle as she began crying softly.

"What am I missing?" asked Félix with tears welling because Marcelle was crying.

"Themis has spoken with Jean le Sage who believes you are not yet prepared but he acquiesces to the thoughts of circumstance she laid before him.

"Les Inséparables-in-Waiting."

†

Mikhail, Orphiel and Hieronymus-Baleberithe-Seere ad-Din al-Jinn were walking with Zoë as she entered in the commune of Belena.

They came to the courtyard of l'Hôtel-Dieu de Beaune. It was orderly populated with Unfortunates who had come seeking Charity: the elderly, the disabled and the sick; the orphans, the women about to give birth and the destitute; families, individuals and those abandoned; and, those dying.

"They must have done something," said the middle-aged wife. The middle-aged husband nodded, saying: "I do not understand why the hospice helps these sorts: they give nothing to us but they help those undeserving."

"This class of people always expects free services, don't they," the wife replied.

"Yes, my dear, they do," replied the husband with disappointment. "It's so disappointing."

"Why do they persist?" said Orphiel.

"They obviate questions of responsibility," said Mikhail.

"They obviate responsibility," replied al-Jinn.

"What should they do, Madame et Monsieur Quincey?" asked Zoë as they went to those two.

"They should pray for Hope," said Monsieur Quincey.

"They have," said Zoë.

"Then they should be happy," said Madame Quincey.

"Why?" asked al-Jinn.

"Hope shall come when least expected," replied Madame Quincey.

"And, if that beneficence has not come in all these years passed?" asked Mikhail.

"They should pray more often," said Monsieur Quincey. "And not drink. Definitely not drink. Prayers by those who drink are not heard. It is drink which keeps them from Grace."

"You are pious?" asked Mikhail.

"Yes. We attend every Sunday."

"High Mass on Christmas Day."

"You know Psalms and Scriptures," said Orphiel.

"Of course."

"Yet nothing in those passages arises in defense when these acts are done for Unfortunates? Weak? or, Poor? Old? or, Frail?" said Mikhail; "Where is mercy?"

"Charity?" said Orphiel.

"We pray Mercy for them. That is our blessed Charity since we cannot save all of them."

"When do you give this Charity of Mercy?"

"When we can."

"You cannot assist individuals during your blessed day?"

"It isn't possible when there are so very many of them. Prayers and thoughts for all."

"That," said Orphiel.

"Shall you pray for Hope when this sphære Infernal turns?" asked Zoë.

"No."

"Why?" said al-Jinn.

"We are blessed. We will be saved. His decree," said Monsieur Quincey.

"He would never allow that," said Madame Quincey.

Mikhail closed his eyes sighing greatly. Orphiel stood silent.

"Them?" said al-Jinn gesturing over the courtyard.

"They cannot be saved. It is the life they chose."

"They cannot be saved?" asked Orphiel.

"No. They cannot be saved because of the things they've done in this life they chose."

"They ignored our guidance and prayers. They drink."

Orphiel gestured with his right hand: the couple collapsed.

"Sir?" asked Zoë.

"They shall wake," said Orphiel as they began walking away from the couple. "He is blind; she is mute. They shall wake and be taken into that Hôtel-Dieu of Charity. They are blessed and shall wait for that Hope which shall come when least expected."

"I cannot comprehend these creatures," said Mikhail. "I have tried. I simply cannot understand them."

"The æquity of Lies; the inégalité of Life," said al-Jinn.

"Who then is worse?" asked Zoë: "The sorts who delusion themselves with blamelessness and offer nothing for those less fortunate suffering? or, those who openly proclaim their hatred of Unfortunates and Impoverished?"

"They are in equal measure vile," said Orphiel, "deserving abhorrence."

They continued.

†

Hercule had taken residence in Parcul Târgului where he lived in a gentleman's caravan. He was standing on the steps for he had received a package. He peered closer and close at the adresse sent: he nodded with a frowning expression, sagely; and, entered closing the door of his home.

†

Hermes arrived on his motorcycle as Themis stepped from the entrance hall walking down the steps to him. He handed her a small elongated parcel.

"Majesty," Hermes said bowing before riding off.

"Majesty?" said Félix as Themis returned up the staircase.

"It's one of my names."

They waited.

"Themis Fey-Queen."

They were flustered.

"Do you what you like," she said laughing. "I care not. Curtsey or don't; bow or don't; prostrate yourselves or don't. However, do not ever correct me my use of the word *box* when speaking of Pandore." She turned to Hooke who was staring across the grass plains. "Sir?"

"Aye," Hooke said as he rose and followed Themis as they went into the house. Félix and Marcelle would have sat on the steps for the length of the evening; but Hooke said gesturing from the entrance: "Mesdames?" They astounded went.

✝

Les Taurides du Sud were arriving.

✝

Bezaliel had joined Mikhail, Orphiel and Hieronymus-Baleberithe-Seere ad-Din al-Jinn walking with Zoë.

"Fallen?" mused Bezaliel. "Fallen then come to be 'Those who are awake' by fabulistes of those books of Myth, who inserted that bit of burlesque, from the apostolic meanderings of Man, hiding their divine frailty in Nature and jealousy of Fey, for Culte-followers who would take solace reveling in their stupidity against all things not of their Ignorance."

"Fallen?" laughed al-Jinn.

"We were on Holiday in Hell," replied Bezaliel. "Hades we'd been before."

✝

Parcul Târgului—the Park of the Fair—was surrounded by a wrought iron fence set in a foundation of red bricks and Portland cement standing fifteen feet in height. All could see the expanse of the amusements; the Ferris Wheel and the Icarus balloon with it's gondola rising on the hour were the easiest to spy.

Amusements Spectaculaires were visited by payment of a single carolus at the gates of the entrance of the parc.

†

The Hansom cab, from the Station, arrived at the entrance of the Park of the Fair.

Elfriede Marie-Thérèse de Vienne exited. She thanked Albert Talloires the driver and brushed Voltaire as he stood harnessed to the carriage; Voltaire stamped his feet.

She had not yet seen Parcul Târgului with its amusements, arcades and Salles d'exposition of the ever later Modern Ages.

She was amazed; and, delighted with all she could see.

"Mademoiselle de Vienne," said Henry de Saint-Cyr the Turnstile-Keeper allowing her to pass forgoing the price of admission. She was far too engaged by the sights to notice he knew her name.

She paused at the arcade.

Autochthones and Wights

Toute Connaissance ment jusqu'à ce qu'elle soit a trouvé

It was lit by candles. The figures were seen and the shadows were seen through the two large glass plate windows but all were embraced in the dark and silences of the Night. The figures were waltzing.

She stood at the end of the main boulevard enthralled and did not notice the gentleman who had left his platform from which he had been speaking as Barker approached her.

"Mademoiselle de Vienne," said Sénateur-Maire Jacques-François Huillard: "We welcome you!"

She turned her head startled from her rêverie.

"Professeur-Maître Huillard?"

"He's gone," replied Huillard with feigned mourning as he led her on the boulevard. "It is Huillard le Maire after Bassompierre and myself decided I would be Sénateur-Maire and he would be ambassador since I had travelled world over but he had not. He is quite pleased being 'The Great Bassompierre.'"

"All things in the Harbour and Parc are from 1883 with a few from 1913," said Elfriede.

"It was decided by each kingdom 1913 would be the last Modern Age," said Huillard le Sénateur-Maire. "Though, cités and communes are set having completed in 1883 while 1913 is beneficial for goods and wares. This parc, with arcades specific for their localities, may be seen in locations on each of the continents of Terre and Fey. I have toured them guided by the Great Bassompierre; all're marvellous."

They had come to the first carrefour. Huillard le Sénateur-Maire stood in the center causing all traffic to cease as he pointed down the avenue to the North.

"Three avenues and left. It will be on your right side," said Huillard le Sénateur-Maire with his right arm extended and gesturing his fingers bent downwards. "Go."

She went three avenues and then left on rue du Chauve-Souris-d'Argent. She strolled admiring the structures of shops stacked as vitrines.

She read the boards of Edgar Gélis with the letter-pressed panels of advertisements over his shoulders as he went by her. The panels stated:

La Sainte Vénus Mutoscope Arcade

A
Delightful – DISTINGUISHED – Delirious
Absolutely Unequaled
ARCADE
It relieves Distresses from Mental and Physickal Exhaustions
&
'tis warranted to be indispensable
Sensational Display
at Every Individuals Performance
of

She heard familiar music approaching: a kalimba played.

He was smiling. He was bobbing his head metronome-like keeping cadence as he walked in the center street amoungst the traffic. He strode to her and, when he reached her and he stopped walking and playing: he bowed.

She would speak with him but before she could, he unfastened his trousers and let them fall to his ankles: he was wearing the pair of her delicates that had been fashioned into culottes for him; and, no others.

She smiled.

Hercule replaced his trousers and offered her escorting of all the Parcul Târgului to see.

They went.

†

They were seated in the cabinet of Hooke.

†

Themis unwrapped the package laid on her knees: it was two wands useless and malformed. Themis waved her hand over them; they transformed.

Themis explained that wands were to be used when beginning because, later after knowledge and confidence were sufficient, the wand would no longer perform as it should and so would transfer mote-particles of it's Spirit of all things – water, moonlight, earth, fire, air, the Spirit of the great Alchemist, the Spirit of the Woods and Spirits who once did use the wand – to them.

"A filament of glass made from sands found in the Valle de la Luna heated with bellows of air from Tengri Tagh tempered in the ocean of Venus reflecting the Sea of Tranquility when it brightly shines in the Winter..." said Themis who let Félix continue aloud instead of mouthing the words, "over which this filament shall be taken to an oak tree in the sacred glade in the forest beside River Saüs allowed to grow one-hundred years thirteen encasing this filament before it shall fall unattended to the terra and shall be let lay three years ere to be taken from the Grace of the Spirit of the Woods by the Alchemist who shall engrave..." She hesitated to which Themis replied, "Thorn." "By the Alchemist who shall engrave with a stipule from the highest branches of the Vachellia xanthophloea tree light from the full Moon kept in a silver bowl words of the blessing of the Ancients."

"Spirits," said Marcelle in a hushed voice.

"Geist-Kings," said Hooke. He went to the arm of the couch and sat himself. "You first were infused by a mote-part from that single Spirit and then all of the other Spirits in that place who entered the chamber; those individual Spirits infused you as you did so with them.

"An Équivalence spiritualis."

"That is the reason each of you feel different because you are become different," said Themis as she went and set the wands on a shelf of illuminated manuscripts. "Hercule, too."

Marcelle thought. She began trembling. "It wasn't just the chamber, was it?" She stared at Félix who covered her mouth from shrieking with each of her hands.

They turned in unison to stare at Themis who stared at them with merry wide eyes. They very slowly turned to Hooke who, with a very slight smile, was very slowly shaking his head.

Félix and Marcelle stared at each other.

Marcelle crying slid from the couch on to the floor, Félix laid her head on the arm of the couch in a state of somnolent stupor, sobbing.

Themis gestured to Hooke. "They took that well," she said as they took their exit from those two.

†

"Why do you continue requesting their reason? You already know," said Orphiel as they went.

"Progress," replied al-Jinn. "Their Modern Age reasoning has changed over the centuries. Western countries establishing inconvenience. The belief of inconvenience is now innate. Words changed; excuses have a subtlety of disdain. A purity of Life now exists wherein they cannot cotton to the idea one dying should spoil that purity; elders, infirmed, Unfortunates are sent to die elsewhere. They may not consciously believe a child born with hindrances is the work of demons and Satan; but they treat it as such in that it was not born in the image of their deity.

"Dying things are not in the image of their deity."

"Earth dying poisoned caused by them causes Unfortunates dying poisoned by them on Terre by their deity," said Mikhail. "How on Earth do they know what that image is?"

"Oh, but they do," said Orphiel. "It is a character with pale skin living in the north of the continent of Africa during their Age of Iron."

"Menglöð and Svipdagr are from Oea on the Barbary Coast," offered Bezaliel, "aren't they."

Zoë pursed her lips from smiling as she went with them as they their discoursing did continue.

†

Sénateur-Maire Jacques-François Huillard and the burgesses from the Magistracy were treading the rue which led to the arcade. It was a hectare in the woods of smaller arcades for all subjects invested with Natural Magick. The weathered wood signboard stated,

Magia Naturalis

Twenty arcades

1 Of the Causes of Wonderful things

2 Of the Generation of Animals

3 Of the Production of new Plants

4 Of increasing Household-Stuff

5 Of changing Metals

6 Of counterfeiting Gold

7 Of the Wonders of the Load-Stone

8 Of strange Cures

9 Of Beautifying Women

10 Of Distillation

11 Of Perfuming

12 Of Artificial Fires

13 Of Tempering Steel

14 Of Cookery

15 Of Fishing, Fowling, Hunting &c

16 Of Invisible Writing

17 Of Strange Glasses

18 Of Statick Experiments

19 Of Pneumatick Experiments

20 Of the Chaos

Where are set forth
All the Riches and Delights
of the
NATURAL SCIENCES

Knowledge abides

Sénateur-Maire Huillard and the burgesses from the Magistracy were inspecting the newly obtained objects of 1913 Modern design delivered to the arcades of Household-Stuff and Cookery.

They wandered.

†

Themis, Marcelle and Félix had met Fille at the bouchon Richelieu on rue Thanatos in the Vieux Aïdes arrondissement of High Cocyte.

Marcelle and Félix conspiratorially spoke of their wands; Themis had instructed them to be discrete about such things.

"Those two wands were made by the great Alchemist. Any one of renown can create a wand of lesser majesty but since it is a great length of years, they are generally passed to the next witch."

"What if we lose them?" said Marcelle.

"I hope for your sakes that never happens," said Themis with a pleasant face but a cold and forbidding tone.

They sat upright.

"What if it's stolen?" asked Fille.

"That cannot happen. Those who would steal a wand are made hollow homunculus as soon as they hold it: their spirit is destroyed by the wand. That is the Obfuscare curse. They do not know they have ceased to exist."

"The War of Indignity?" asked Fille. "I seldom see Father these days so I haven't been able to ask him."

"It is referred to as the War of Indignity," said Themis, "because it has been caused by Limbus which begins the new year in the month of Sanctuary—Arah Nisanu—which begins in the Spring whereas Hades's celebrations of the new year begin with Samonios at the beginning of Summer while Kingdom Come does their celebrating on the day with dark Moon before the Winter Solstice as the beginning of a new year.

"They required reason."

"Big-Enders; Small-Enders," said Félix.

"It's orderly," said Fille.

"Proper," said Themis: "The Three Kingdoms signed the Treaty of Lyon, 1913. Or, commonly– the Revanchists Treaty."

The serveur arrived.

†

Mikhail, Orphiel, Bezaliel and Hieronymus-Baleberithe-Seere ad-Din al-Jinn were walking with Zoë as they were continued strolling rues in the commune of Belena.

The aged gentleman–Auguste Haffreingue–was walking on the lane ahead of Mikhail, Orphiel and Hieronymus-Baleberithe-Seere ad-Din al-Jinn walking with Zoë.

He paused and shivered. He collapsed in convulsive fits of a seizure but was of beatific countenance.

Mikhail and Orphiel hurried to assist him standing; and, after his composure he regained, he accompanied them as they leisurely continued on their walk.

"They happen infrequently. Eidetic visions of one most dear appear; and, I collapse. They are - Though - appearing oftener than before but I do not protest them nor wish them gone for I do believe I shall no longer be dearly departed from her I do so long in her company to be.

"A gentleman wearing a beaver hat in Saint-Étienne told me I should visit Côte d'Opale. That's where I go."

Zoë smiled.

Auguste Haffreingue spoke of single butterflies – Aporia crataegi – approaching coming from places unknown remaining stationary near him before flying away.

"What did they want?" he asked sadly.

Mikhail nor Orphiel nor Bezaliel could an explanation offer.

Auguste Haffreingue spoke of a cockroach in the kitchen which he could not murder with his newspaper; it disappeared beneath the stove. He went to the W.C. and noticed a small dark shape ascending the wall behind him: it was the cockroach which stood on the wall at the level of his eyes. He tried hitting it with his hand but it scurried disappearing beneath the bureau. He later approached the bureau and the cockroach scurried and stood on the carpet waiting: the cockroach was staring at his face. He said he looked at it and, after he had stepped on the cockroach, felt confused remorse. He kept it there by the basin.

"What did it want?" he asked sadly.

Mikhail nor Orphiel nor Bezaliel could an explanation offer.

Auguste Haffreingue spoke of a crow who landed on the railing of his balcony staring in through the open doors as he sat in his front room. He stood and approached the balcony, but the crow would fly away each instance he would approach the balcony when the crow would land on the railing of his balcony.

"What did it want?" he asked sadly.

Mikhail nor Orphiel nor Bezaliel could an explanation offer.

Auguste Haffreingue spoke of a cat with four kittens. One was aloof but pestered by flies. He thought it was much like himself when young. The next day that kitten remained by itself while the other three with their mother were numerous paces away from it. It lay; seldom raising it's head while the others were wandering in the yard. It was not aloof with independence: it was dying covered with flies. The next day the kitten was at a distance from where it had been laying on that day he knew it was dying: it was laying on it's side in a repose of contentedness for it had died. The mother and kittens were not seen again.

"Why did this need to happen?"

Mikhail nor Orphiel nor Bezaliel could an explanation offer.

Auguste Haffreingue spoke of a single butterfly approaching with orange and black markings flying passed his balcony in the coldest days of Winter.

"Why was it there?" he asked sadly.

Mikhail nor Orphiel nor Bezaliel could not explanation offer.

Auguste Haffreingue thanked them for graciously listening and ascended the steps to the station of la via Agrippa de l'Océan where he would wait for the stage coach to Boulogne-sur-Mer.

Mikhail, Orphiel, Bezaliel and Hieronymus-Baleberithe-Seere ad-Din al-Jinn continued strolling rues in the commune of Belena with Zoë.

†

Hooke, Marcelle and Félix were seated in his library. He was reading their letter.

"Constitutus?"

"Elfriede helped," Marcelle replied.

"For reply to your query of particularités, you should ask those you'll become." He faced Félix. "Snježana de Pasithea." He faced Marcelle who nodded.

They were seated on the couch; he was seated in a chair opposite them. They were fidgety playing with their wands.

He stood. He set their letter on the type case. He went to them gesturing for their wands. He took them. He wandered about the room searching; he hummed. He opened drawers; he peered in various cabinets. He found a piano-roll box. He placed the piano-roll back in the vitrine; he placed a wand in the box.

"What are you doing?" asked Félix concerned; he ignored her.

"What are you humming?" asked Marcelle.

"La fille aux cheveux de lin."

Hooke withdrew a Thoth papyrus scroll from a faded velvet pouch. He read a few lines before haphazardly placing it on a shelf. He placed the second wand in the pouch.

He gave Marcelle the velvet pouch; he gave Félix the box.

"You're not homunculus," said Félix.

Hooke turned his head slightly to the left shut his right eye and stared squinky eyed at them.

He gestured.

They withdrew the wands from their scabbards.

They were puzzled.

"It feels different."

"You're not humonculi," said Hooke.

They sourly glared at him.

"They are different because they aren't ours?" said Marcelle.

"Indeed," said Hooke. "An Équivalence spiritualis."

They exchanged wands.

"How did you know?"

"May I?" he asked with each hand palm side up extended.

They gave him their wands.

Hooke twirled the wands so that the base of each was seen with glyphs of silver. "These glyphs?"

Félix peered very close. "This is 'Laguz,' water." She thought. "That... I don't know."

"That is Japanese; it is the 'Moon' character. Laguz is the character for water. Lagu–Sea–in Gaulish is 'mor' which is found Morgause which a different spelling of Morgan or Morgen and all of the others translated as sea-born.

"Where were you born?"

"Vannes."

"When did you learn to swim?"

She went wide-eyed.

"Ocean."

He gazed at Marcelle who was remembering all of her childhood and a comment once said by Themis. "Themis, too, is sea-born. Her name is judiciously different as her father wished yet–Regardless–she was imbued by something thou and she both do share."

Marcelle shuddered from happiness revealing itself.

"What!" exclaimed Félix. Marcelle turned to face her but she could not speak.

"They were each during full Moon born."

They both stared at Hooke.

"It seems—by Chance—you've each coincidentally things in common caused by singularités with those whose wands were given thee as well as those happenstances by Her Majesty." He stood. "I'll be in the garden, if you should wake before darkness."

They nodded absently; he smiled.

He took exit.

†

Hercule was conversing his newly established position with Sénateur-Maire Jacques-François Huillard.

"Chivalry?" said Sénateur-Maire Huillard.

"Temperament."

†

Themis was strolling with Fata Muirgen le Gaulois – her grandmother – and her great-grandmother, Mori-gena. They went in the great parc of Zhį'ii-tsintah.

"Filia Félicite has mine," said Fata Muirgen le Gaulois, "and Filia Marcelle has her's."

"I have no words," said Mori-gena.

"And, to believe this lies beyond his monumental garden in honour of your mother's garden," said Muirgen le Gaulois.

"It is there," Themis said as she pointed to the house they were approaching, Sidhech'įįdiilucidus.

"You have been there before?" said Muirgen le Gaulois because great-grandmother Mori-gena was returned to her silent wonder of the parc.

"I was for a day once," replied Themis. "He invited me before he departed last."

"This is where you were! A day! My child, you were gone for a year!" said Muirgen le Gaulois. "Disappeared you did!"

"Ghosts, my Love?" said Mori-gena with an impish grin as she viewed all that was before her.

"Sæfgryndes."

"You knew and told no one!" accused Muirgen le Gaulois.

"I was not asked by you daughter nor did you ask your father, dear," Mori-gena said with a sly wink to Themis. "Third remains."

"Then?" replied Themis to Mori-gena who looked at her with merry eyes. "You are not intending to tell us are you, Granny Morgue?"

Granny Morgue very slowly shook her head.

Those two began laughing; and, Muirgen le Gaulois, who would preferred to have remained perturbed, smiled.

✝

C. L. Nolan was revising his manuscript *The Arthurian Wonders; or, On the influences of Theurgy and Goëtia in the beliefs of Fairy in the Other Lands* after Javelle le Chronologiste had lent him *Li Tournoiemenz Anticrit* by Huon de Méry, Raoul de Houdenc's *Le Songe d'enfer* and other works pertaining to the forest of Brecheliant.

✝

Jules le Cartographe was standing in the chamber, after having moved his four-post bed from over the carpet which required the tacks at the edges removed before rolling the carpet so he could unscrew the floorboards exposing the door that was opened with a simple charm, riffling loose pages of incunabula kept in Emperor folios.

Jules le Cartographe shuddered for he had found what he sought.

✝

Milot l'Historien was reading the works Javelle le Chronologiste had given him to safeguard.

†

Hercule and Elfriede passed an arcade on the allée des Dames.

The Garden of Dementia

The arcade was large in width and depth and height. The roof was vaulted of a wrought iron structure with glass panes. The arcade's façade was large glass panes set in the woodwork carved of Art Nouveau designs.

Entrance   3 c

Souvenir pamphlet   23 c

Stereoscopic cards   17 c

Appearing in the clothes as a Humour
and photographed

27 fr. 13 c

Three ash trees were growing in the walled courtyard garden. A stone block wall with steps to a large wooden door was set in the rear; and, a scene of the city and sky behind the stone block wall was a painted backdrop curtain hung from the batten.

There were nine persons who represented the characters in the 1857 lithograph by Armand Gautier in the walled garden of the Hospice de la Salpêtrière. They were personifications of the Nine Simple Temperaments: Charity, Temperance, Courage, Justice, Honour, Mindfulness, Mercy, Sublimity, and Sérénité.

The persons were seldom all nine Humours in the garden: they would exit and enter but for Sérénité who would be led by two orderlies dressed in white as they would in an appropriate manner of their Humour until all nine were on stage speaking recitations in cacophony; and, they then would take their place assigned pose in silence. Sublimity was spectral in appearance standing on the wall.

All would recitations make but for Sérénité. Sublimity was heard speaking from afar in a sedate voice of tones.

The persons were actual patients of the Titania Convalescences but not of the same dementia; they were paid wages for their performance. The patients often wanted to be Sérénité who were paid albeit less but they were allowed to travel from the hôpital by horse-drawn omnibus. The performers changed every eleven days.

Visitors in the arcade would stand on the carpeted boards between the glass of the façade and the garden sand; and, so be viewed by passers-by on the pavement.

The photographs were made by Autochrome Lumière cameras for stereoscopic cards. Nobles and Wealthy did delight in posing and circulating cards with others who had done so, too; commoners often would pose in the character of their own dementia.

Mikhail, Orphiel and Hieronymus-Baleberithe-Seere ad-Din al-Jinn were continued strolling rues in the commune of Belena with Zoë for Bezaliel had left them to visit Devona in her subterranean spring of the river Douix in the canton of Châtillon-sur-Seine.

†

Odo Bayeux and Vera Petrova-Stratiev were dressed in dressing gowns with blue and white pin-stripes over their clothes.

The Goblin and the Dwarf were each reading one of the pamphlets—*Morbus Olymphe, or, An Admonition against Theurgy of Celestes misbefallen by Venial Promiscuity*—they had purchased from him as he spoke. They had previously purchased *On the Advent* from Vera.

Marcelle and Félix and Fille - who arrived later - were standing behind the Goblin and the Dwarf with the Great Bassompierre standing behind them.

Odo Bayeux was concluding with the summary that failure by Theurgy must be attributed to the conscious knowledge given by deities wherein he spoke of passages and lines writ by Saint Augustine in *De civitate Dei contra paganos*, particularly, Theurgy being an art effecting evil as well as good both with the gods and men but the argument of Celestes refusing obtrusion with Man, thereby requiring the demons's assistance to secure the friendship of the gods since demons are immune from contagious diseases, is made false due to the satires with the character Apeilon Protagoras by Philemonus, who was immediately recognised to be Apollo, master of medicine and healing, ill-health and deadly plague, for there it was the common theme of curing those of the Highest Station, known by their nymphomania and satyriasis, of Lues venerea from their exploits, by Apeilon Protagoras.

Le Docteur Antoine-Augustin Guise arrived.

"In short, it was Man who wished intermediation of demons with gods," concluded Odo Bayeux.

The Goblin and the Dwarf who had been standing for two and one-quarter hours listening to him speak peered up from their reading; and, nodded.

"Docteur Guise," said Odo Bayeux. "It was a lovely day. These two personages encouraged me."

Vera and Odo Bayeux collected their pamphlets as Docteur Guise took the box on which they had been arranged.

Marcelle and Félix were delighted to see him. They introduced Fille to Docteur Guise, Vera and Odo.

"We shall all come visiting soon," said Guise.

"Thank you, gentlemen," said Docteur Guise as they passed by the Goblin and the Dwarf.

They bowed.

Vera and Odo went to the waiting horse-drawn omnibus which was nearly full with passengers waving to Félix and Marcelle.

Guise and Bassompierre spoke heartily in whispers. Guise gestured at Marcelle, Félix and Fille. Bassompierre grandly smiling said "Mademoiselles" as he parted from them.

Vera and Odo went to the open upper deck; le Docteur Guise stood at the bottom of the curved steps.

Marcelle and Félix and Fille watched as the omnibus departed.

"It seems so very long ago," whispered Marcelle.

✝

Titus was walking with his cane.

Hooke was seated on the stone wall of the oppidum viewing the plateau of Gergovie.

"I preferred Merdogne," said Titus as he stepped to where Hooke sat. "How did you know?"

"I was informed." Hooke gestured to the half circle of nine large ravens who landed from flying standing behind him.

Titus threw his cane at them: Hooke caught it as he stood standing thirteen feet tall; and, he lifted Titus by the hair of his pompadour with his left hand. He gave the cane to one of the ravens.

"What in God's name are you doing!"

Hooke stared with disbelief.

"It's what they say," wheezed Titus; "They don't even know the name of their deity."

"Why?" said Hooke and lifted him higher.

Titus would have begun his simpering burlesque, but Hooke lifted him higher until Titus could be looked in the eyes.

"I'll say!"

Hooke set him on the ground. Titus fussed with his hair while speaking.

"This was not agreed to because it was never entered in the Argument of Sanctity."

"And?"

"Your concordance was made with King Ghôle; he broke it! He did! It wasn't me!"

"And?"

"I thought it would be amusing. My prior entertainment being concluded."

"And?"

"There's nothing you can do because it was in accordance with what was written by you. And, since it wasn't written, I was entitled to do it."

Titus's head wobbled on his shoulders for his neck had been fractured by Hooke.

"What!"

"It wasn't written." Hooke held Titus's glass eyes in his left hand and placed them in the pocket of his waistcoat.

"What!"

"You are still free Will able to voyage unhindered by others."

"I keep my sense of sight."

"True. Spirits and shadows in fog."

"I suppose you'll murder me now since that wasn't written, too."

"No," said Hooke pleasantly with a sinister tone.

"I don't like that tone in your voice."

Titus was crowned with an aureole. Titus began screaming. He shook his head except the halo was aligned with his spine: it did not move. He dared not touch it.

Sylphes and imps and all manner of small faeries appeared.

"I did—in light of these your most recent afflictions—engage guardians for you." They flew about Titus; and, they danced about him in grand circles as if he were a maypole albeit a cursing, stumbling, and flailing maypole. All were laughing as they pinched and poked, pricked and nipped him. "They shall attend you most graciously since you were most grievously engaged with the foulest of amusements against them."

"Bastard! My cane!"

A sylphide hit his head with his walking-stick which caused it wobbling to and fro.

"It's there."

"Bastard!" shrieked Titus while waving his hands over his head.

Hooke began walking from Titus who, between his screams, cursed Hooke.

"They'll come!"

"I think not," replied Hooke as he paused and turned staring in the far distance; he smiled. "I believe those two would prefer your incapacitation and infirmity rather than remaining maltreated henchmen in thy service. They'll flourish." He pointed in the direction of Nemessos. "However, there does come one for you."

The Fée were become silent with fright.

"He comes as friend," said Hooke to them.

"Who comes!"

It was the ghôle Titus had abandoned.

It embraced Titus from behind with his good arm and hand.

"How is this! It's deceased!"

"La Sorcière qui garde les Bois murmurant des Misères," said Hooke. The Fée were silent and less frighted after hearing that name. "We spoke. It was her request and I did my curse unmake; he lost a forearm but not Life. It was she who went on behalf of all to speak with le Roi des Goules." The Fée murmured excitedly. "Her compassion; her solace."

"Interfering!"

"No," replied Hooke calmly. "If you recall, no witch was asked to sign that proclamation; they were deemed incapable. What they do of their own accord does not interfere with thee. Thy amusement continues. Deaths await."

Titus began curses and incomprehensible entreaties of compassion and forgiveness.

"Highness – Mesdames – Messieurs." They quieted and faced Hooke; the King clasped Titus's mouth rendering him silent and nearly unable to breathe.

"La Sorcière made one second request which was that this fellow's eyes were to be returned if His Highness came; he has done so.

"I give this eye to the Fée to place where ever they wish for him to find and when thus it shall be returned. I give this eye to the Fée to hold until His Highness wishes to take it; His Highness is to be given welcome by all of Fey."

The King Ghôle spoke.

"He wishes me tell thee the Lady of Good Counsel – la Sorcière de la lumière noire – did parlay an Entente-cordiale of Faerie and Ghôle for which he by his life offered has astipulated; and, that he shall this day take the eye to be placed in the kingdom of Ghôle where it may be found on the nights whence full Spring Moon waxes.

"He further states by her Ho'oponopono has been written in the Book of Rule."

The King Ghôle released Titus gasping. The King Ghôle was given an eye which twitched in his hand: he bowed low; and, departed returning to the forest Nemessos.

"Who is la Sorcière murmurant des Misère?" said Titus as he raised himself on one elbow. "I do fraign this sorceress would know!"

"She is of those you believed beneath thy station to learn or know," replied Hooke. "And, after this amusement, she is one you should hope never by Chance do meet."

"What has she ever done worthy of my condescension," said Titus weakly contemptuous sneering.

"Did you not first meet Asmodeus when he was a fine fellow fit in common form?" Titus squinted in his apprehension; and, nodded. "Did you not wonder his appearance changed? after he did engage your plot of setting fire unto all of the settlements of the Sylvan folk in Abonabrogilos."

"I thought it was you!" exclaimed Titus shivering.

"Asmodeus met her by Chance thrice with airs of peacock arrogance after malignancies against Fey were made; and, after third Chance done, he seldom—These days—departs his hôtel particulier on the far bank of the lake of Cocytus and sits his chambers with the terror of she who may one day visiting come.

"'Twas Olympe who so recently rose her ire," replied Hooke as he departed and the Fée were escorting Titus in a game of Blind Man's Bluff.

"This domnizelle?"

Hooke was heard to say from leagues afar, "The Grey Queen."

"O God!" whimpered Titus.

✝

Elfriede and Huillard le Sénateur-Maire were wandering about the parc as he was introducing her to the shop-keepers and the proprietors of the magasins and arcades.

They were standing at a table of books on the pavement of a bookshop, Iliso Elilambileyo.

"*The Rise and Fall of Savægyne through the Ages or, Tales and stories so impossible to believe yet accurately set before the Masses for their elucidation of the Demented Savages of Myth recently discovered in Otherworldly Places,*" said Elfriede holding an elephant-sized tome of one-hundred seventy and three pages with one-hundred thirty and three tipped-in color plates and an unknown number of en-page engravings. "This is N° 77 of two-hundred and thirteen volumes."

"It is the Folklore of Man," said Huillard. "Monsieur Milot continues with a different series from that series writ by Monsieur Javelle."

"Do folk read these?"

"My dear Madame Virago Antepenultime, there are many, many, many who have never visited Terre. And, even more who've not gone beyond their county borders. Perhaps, they have not read particularly that series; however, there are voluminous numbers of them published from which they can select.

"For them, it is all folklore."

✝

Themis was standing with Félix and Marcelle watching the preparations for battle at Hera's Gate with other sightseers arrived by motorbuses from all near-by counties.

Apaté, Cacus and Dionysus with numerous mænads dancing in religious Extase walked towards them in triumphant pomp.

"Why do you protect them with cheap bordello parlour tricks?" demanded Dionysus.

"I do not protect them," said Themis. "They know the proper ancient lines to speak but their spells themselves are dangerous."

"You fear their weakness will bring them Death."

"No," said Themis. "'Tis you who Death would greet; or, worse. It is done not to protect them but those who would do them harm."

Marcelle and Félix looked at each perplexed by disbelief.

"You lie!" screamed Dionysus.

"Marcelle, since you lag in charms and spells, I would like to illustrate for them the poorness of your enchantments." Marcelle nodded with severe apprehension. Themis gestured over Marcelle who was made radiant by the removal of the counter-spells placed on her. Themis turned to those attending. "She stands naked." Themis whispered: "Just clutch your skirts with your left hand to steady yourself and extend your right hand in the manner and form you wish."

Marcelle did.

Apaté and Dionysus gestured: light of different colours and widths and radiance was seen escaping their hands with curses sent towards Marcelle, Félix and Themis. Cacus blowing with his mouth sent fire flaming at Marcelle. The mænads went galloping on their hands and feet at them.

Fire of dragons, lightning of various shapes and colours, catherine-wheels of jet issued from Marcelle's hand in a ten foot wide torrent at those who would curse them increasing in diameter as it continued through the commune of Fidelis Rug. The spectacle of her spell was ended changed becoming sea-foam jets of flames coruscating thin lightning streaks of green were cast which went for leagues until dissipating.

The torrent of Marcelle's thirty foot wide enchantment passed through Apaté, Cacus, Dionysus and the numerous mænads leaping in religious Extase before passing through the camp of demon-musketeers before passing through the wall of Hera which then collapsed the battlement on to the arriving column of artillery of le Maréchal and went disappearing as a fifty foot wide enchantment over the dunes of Nubilus. All was devastation.

"That was drastic," said Themis conversationally, smiling. Themis replaced the counter-spells over Marcelle as she went to view the carnage invited by the Celestes. "This way," said Themis over her shoulder.

Marcelle and Félix followed.

"I saw everything," said Marcelle.

"A simple spell was of perception so you could see what was happening at a very slow pace."

The mænads were steaming flesh on skeletons.

"Apaté used Obfuscare; Cacus, Death by Fire; Dionysus, Death by One-Thousand Knives— his cruelty shown.

"Your's was magnificent; I haven't any idea what was done so I would care to see."

Dionysus was standing on a single long shriveled leg with one very small arm and one very long arm; his head was a small shrunken skull with an appropriately sized bull's horn on the left side. All of the body was charred muscle and flesh.

"Granny Morgue liked Minotaurus's horns and stork legs. My Mother preferred fire. Mine was that sea-foam and milky pale green. So, it was you who thought of what?"

"Disproportionate limbs. I don't know why?"

"That would leave the head by the Alchemist. That's charming!"

"Shouldn't we do something to help them?" asked Marcelle.

"Why?" asked Themis genuinely curious.

"Because I did this."

Ambulances were arriving. Nymphs were arriving. The Mortality Brigade would return the bodies and corpses of the Cælestialis to the Customs-House of Nubilus. The mænads deceased would be let lay; those wounded, tended.

"Yes, you did do this; but you were not the cause of it," said Themis. "You may not have noticed that it was we three they sought to murder." Marcelle roused herself. "You kept us safe." Themis laughed. "You saved us with a spell, that, by all intent, was a veritable comet created by drunken goblins and imps." Themis gestured to the arriving attendants. "They come."

"Thank you, Madame Scary," said Félix laughing which caused Marcelle to smile.

They went to Apaté and Cacus who were gravely wounded: they were unrecognisable. Those at the edge of the spell were affected by minor afflictions. They viewed the remaining. All felled were in various combinations of the spells cast by those spirits. Charred flesh was majority.

"How many?" asked Félix.

"I do not know. Le Maréchal may know after nécrologies are issued. Those deaths of the Cælestialis shall remain unknown."

One of the mænads not terribly wounded crawled over to Themis. "You must help."

"There is none to give. That enchantment was raw and yet to be tempered by her, thus lacking form, for which there is no cure: it was pure rage." She turned to Marcelle and Félix ignoring the pleas of the mænad. "You do not know rage; your wands do. It is your Will which shall temper these branches into the forms you want. Your Temperaments shall guide thy Will; thy Will shall forge thy spells."

Marcelle and Félix stood staring.

"What should we do?" said Themis as she went pleasantly strolling from the wreckage and mayhem made by the rages of Marcelle's wand.

There came no reply.

"Sitting for hours in the Oideion on the Quay?"

They frowned.

"Shave-ice from a box supported by the two front wheels of a tricycle peddled by the Bicycliste while rising above the third wheel on a curved bar a small gent will be seated beneath a small parasol playing a glockenspiel on the High Road in the county of Pyriphlegethon?"

They shook their heads.

"Ice-skating on Cocytus Lake?"

They shrugged.

"Sisters of Aphrodite House for Wayward Children?"

They winced.

"La Sirène menstruée in the quartier of Vieux Tartare?" They looked askance. "Majesty took you two to the coffee-house — *l'Odéon pneumatique* — in the quartier Perrache which, by her account, you enjoyed immensely. This is her second favourite."

"That!"

They began strolling.

"What was that green?" asked Marcelle. "It was different than the others I felt."

"It matched those stockings you wear," said Félix, "when you're the Grey Witch."

"Goblin-light," said Themis. "It's a long story." They entreated beseeching her with their eyes. "I shall tell you as we go," said Themis with her hands outstretched: Marcelle took her left hand and Félix took her right hand. "It's one of my favorite colours."

"Can I wear pink and grey?" asked Marcelle.

"We should talk," replied Themis.

"I told you," said Félix.

They went.

It was Marron in Fructidor, 1913.

Milot l'Historien, C. L. Nolan and Jules le Cartographe were standing at the gate of Persephone. They were accompanied by Tochi no akaru-sa who watched Old John Wren enter the shadows of the woods.

They waited.

New pastries were set on steps and stoops of those who believed the visitations of Heng'e during the full Moon would bring them gifts.

†

"So, it begins," said Hooke.

†

New pastries set on steps and stoops were collected by féeries and imps who would take them to the Lady on the Moon selecting her favorites as les Treize present and past and soon-to-be performed charms on those places deserving.

The pastries declined were given amoungst the old and young.

†

Tochi no akaru-sa, Nolan, Milot and Jules were taken by de Sérifontaine to Lugosdunon. Tochi no akaru-sa was warmly greeted by Marcelle and Félix.

Reynaerd was waiting.

†

Nolan and Milot were entertaining Marcelle, Félix and Tochi no akaru-sa with tales and woes.

†

Jules le Cartographe was seated in salle of Antiquités in the library of Hooke.

†

Mikhail, Orphiel and Hieronymus-Baleberithe-Seere ad-Din al-Jinn were concluded strolling rues in the commune of Belena with Zoë. They had traveled one league from the cité. They stood viewing the façade of a tall structure not unlike a firebox and mantelpiece in a Rococo design lit by gas-jet lamps.

Al-Asturlab

Hermes al-Magest was leaning against the wall lost in thought when they arrived.

"Why do you use as your workshop title *The-One-That-Catches-The-Celestial Objects?*" said al-Jinn.

"I have wanted to converse with one," replied Hermes al-Magest.

"Angels?" asked Zoë.

"No. Selene." He thought. "Achlys. I'd like to talk with Achlys. Dark before Chaos existed. Why could not Chaos exist before Dark shined?"

He led them inside.

He had an equatorium, a triquetrum, a rubul mujayyab, a shakkāzīya, and an almucantar quadrant. A very large frame quadrant was the back wall of his atelier.

"Aether, Nyx, Uranus, Hemera, Asteria and Astraeus," mused Hermes al-Magest, "would be, too."

"How would you know?" said Mikhail. "Do you know their faces? or, appearances?"

"No."

"You may have met them in dreams," said Orphiel; "Have you considered that possibility?"

"I have. I have dreams of persons whose faces I cannot see. They have spoken. I'm not certain. I wrote my dreams. It is as you say: I do not know them so I may have met them. They may have been. Things they spoke were of grave designs. Very mysterious."

"You continue?" said Zoë.

"Yes. It is a journey, my dreams, where I would hope to find that Celeste; but if I do not, I shall have taken a miraculous journey."

"Learning in itself is a meaning, perhaps?"

"I believe so," he replied. "Mostly that voyage. It is when one comes to their end they are disappointed. Seldom so when on a journey."

They continued.

†

"The Lord shall be attending soon," announced Reynaerd to them after their late supper had been taken. "Her Highness the Queen is waiting in the garden."

Marcelle and Félix led Tochi no akaru-sa, Nolan, Milot and Jules to the garden. They were greeted.

"My dear," said Themis to Tochi no akaru-sa who ran to Themis hugging her.

"Jean le Sage wanted me to be with them. 'When you will, I would like to continue our adventure,' said Jean le Sage. I bowed before him. He patted me on my head. 'Take care, Mademoiselle.'"

"Odysseus has been collecting Authorities and putti," said Hooke as he came to them, "as they would be spying on things they cannot see. He brought five wings of a seraph—His evening prey—during the festes of Chang'e. He, Marchosias, Nahum, Raesmius the wolf of Andras, Vapula, Ipos, Sabnacke and Barbas are as merry as Sin as they take expedition hunting these interlopers in Hades. Vapula caught a Power. Odysseus keeps lead by six heads."

"We have a question they would like to ask you, Sir," said Tochi no akaru-sa.

"Bonhommes?" said Hooke.

Nolan and Milot exchanged glances. Milot stood. "Sir," he said with his tone of formality, "we were met and graciously escorted by de Sérifontaine. We stood on the drive. This place we four saw in ruins. Yet we observed ghosts in movement throughout on the floors. We entered no ruins; there are no ghosts."

"You spied ruins with it's ghosts because you were not entered in the house," said Hooke. "Hence, you were not shown until after entered. Did you not spy—albeit briefly—ghosts wandering in ruins when arriving on the allée to the entrance of Corvuswæld?"

"I did but since it was Night, I believed myself haggard by mysteries and trepidation. Hallucinations."

"Those who have not entered my homes see ruin and Ghost. They are believed haunted. Misbehaving children are often brought to scare the wits from them after threats of sacrificing them to the ghosts. If they should stand where we are arranged, they would be amoungst ghosts."

They nodded.

"You did not notice, did you?" said Hooke as he smiled at Marcelle and Félix who shook their heads sharing glances.

"I was told you were to be told," said Tochi no akaru-sa: "'She has not need of their's but one she needs yet not her's.'"

Hooke smiled.

"Shall we walk?" he asked all assembled.

They went in the garden and continued until they had gone several miles coming to an ancient oak rising majestically in a clearing.

"That's Taranis!" said an excited Tochi no akaru-sa.

"No," Hooke said. "They are of the same lineage. Old Taranis is but a child to him."

"Does he have a name?" asked Tochi no akaru-sa.

"He does but it would be a day in saying it," said Hooke.

"How do you greet him?" said Félix.

"Smiling," said Hooke as he approached the oak and did speak. They spoke at length for the great oak spoke thoughtfully slow.

Hooke gestured to each in the semi-circle around the tree as he spoke of them. He spoke of Tochi no akaru-sa last explaining what Is e an spiorad beò ris an canar Iain an seanair ghlic requested; the tree laughed swaying it's branches surprised at hearing that name. The tree bent a large limb with a few suitable branches: Hooke cut one with his folding knife.

The tree spoke and Themis replied smiling; they conversed.

Hooke clasped his right hand over the branch and with his left hand pulled the branch through his clasped right hand. The branch was smouldering black shining.

"Fire," whispered Marcelle.

The ground erupted as a great root was extended from the earth wrapping itself around Tochi no akaru-sa. Hooke handed the still smouldering branch to her. "One not their's yet her's." She shuddered.

He smiled.

Tochi no akaru-sa held her wand with both of her hands and she bowed very low before the Elder Oak who reached down and held her shoulders with the tips of two branches. The branches and great root returned to their places.

She stood.

"Honoribus," said the Elder Oak.

She nodded.

Hooke thanked the Elder Oak who bowed graciously. They went returning to the house.

"What did you and the Great Oak say?" asked Marcelle.

Hooke gestured to Tochi no akaru-sa.

"They discussed us," said Tochi no akaru-sa blushing.

"What language was that? It sounded familiar yet not familiar," said Nolan.

"It should be," said Hooke. "It is a Gaulish language. Malebranchese is. Serpents speak a variant form of it when speaking with us. There are other Gaulish variants in Gaelic and Brythonic forms from ages before—for convenience sake—l'Âge du bronze of Man they and others speak still."

"Sir," said Nolan as he stopped walking. "Are we then to suppose that these languages spoken in these Sphæres are before Man appeared."

Hooke nodded.

"Équivalence," said Tochi no akaru-sa as she stared at her wand living still.

"Yes," said Themis.

†

Mikhail, Orphiel and Hieronymus-Baleberithe-Seere ad-Din al-Jinn were in colloquy as Zoë picked flowers from a garden.

"Of course," began al-Jinn, "they would have a clause of Superstitio for those who would seek divine knowledge in an effort learn the fundamental sorcery deities use.

"As to the improper use of that divine knowledge, Mortals who have not found divine knowledge invoke religious law in their self-proclaimed locus religiosus, which must be maintained to further the proprieties of divine honours, sacrifice and ritual by practice of proper, respectful performance of the rites of veneration whereas neglecting the religiones owed to the traditional gods was atheism causing Ira deorum when, in these days, negligence of respectful prosperity rites does anger those who are no longer venerated with the perpetual giving of tithes."

"Your tone infers it may not be sôlely religious deities you speak of," said Zoë as she handed al-Jinn her bouquet.

He smiled.

†

Hooke was staring at the members of the Illapses Agency, Ltd. They had stopped their return to the house after Jules with his elbow nudged Milot and nodded his head towards Hooke.

"Mademoiselles, if you would, I promised Monsieur Milot an explanation—which may be of some benefit to you—of an object."

Hooke, as he spoke, had drawn two large circles in the soil: they were overlapped. The circle on the right: he drew an 'N'; the circle on the left: he drew an 'H'. He drew a third circle overlapping those two: he scratched an 'L'.

He drew a smaller circle far below those three.

"Hades – Limbe – Nubilus," said Hooke. "These" – He touched the overlapping areas. – "are the confluences, the Territoires."

"Liminalities," said Nolan.

"If that's the word you choose to use," said Hooke.

"I thought Limbo was in Hades," said Jules.

"It is," replied Hooke; "Twice. However, as all are things with Man's understanding of things, that are poorly known, it's this: Limbe itself is not in Hades, since it is an orbis itself; but – Rather – the confluence of Limbe and Hades sets Limbe in Hades. The confluence was visited at the edge, yet never explored by Dante, during his tourist's vagabonding, with Virgil and Beatrice. Limbo is Sanctus. It is neither religiosus nor profane."

"These confluences?" said Jules.

"Confluences have no stable borders with those worlds. Confluences continuously ebb and flow in the flux of those who reside and depart." They each reacted in their own fashion. "The land of Limbo–in Hades–is entrance to a Parc de Distraction."

"Pugatoria is in Hades," said Milot.

"What?" replied Nolan.

Hooke nodded.

"The sôle aspect which escapes you is what these Sphæres are properly? I simplify: Hades, demons; Nubilus, deities; Limbus, féeries. Territoires are confluent with citizens of those places."

"Limbus is the kingdom of Fey," said Milot.

"No." Hooke viewed them each by turn. He drew a fourth larger circle around those three. "That is the kingdom of Fey."

They nodded.

"The fourth sphære in the kingdom of Fey?" asked Milot.

"Another one!" exclaimed Jules.

"Locorum obscurorum," said Hooke. "It is a sphære, but it is not a sphære." He thought. "It is a sphære yet not in the kingdom of Fey nor created from those confluences in the kingdom of Fey: it is the flooding wiellgespring of Fey that lies in the realm of Aiōn."

"What name does it have?" asked Jules.

"It has none." He peered at Jules. "No— it is not found on any map." He thought. "Atunuususulu. Use that."

They were confused.

"Much as you believed Hades was a small kingdom in a hollow Earth which was a sphere in a hollow Purgatory which was a sphere in a hollow Kingdom Come, things are not done so. Just because you could come from Hookland via the gate of Persephone and arrive here to my house does not mean you have left Hookland."

"What do you mean?" asked Tochi no akaru-sa.

"Reality, Time and Place are seldom what they seem. If this house is identical—as Mademoiselles Félix and Marcelle did so surmise—to the house in France it would mean the house in Limbe is identical to those in Hades and France and Nubilus; four houses identical yet in different realms. Where in Reality does this place exist?"

Jules who had been entranced in thought, startled at the words Hooke said, lept to his feet standing in great agitation. "A thousand pardons!" He ran excitedly. "I must find Reynaerd!"

Hooke smiled slightly and turning from them he went to Themis. He whispered.

"We must be off," said Themis.

They left.

"He's preoccupied, isn't he," said Nolan as they went returning to the house.

"All the worlds at War," said Tochi no akaru-sa; they were struck with amazement. "Master Wren informed me."

Nolan and Milot, by a hall boy, were shown their rooms while conversing on the odd behaviour of Jules.

Tochi no akaru-sa was led to her room by Marcelle and Félix discussing all which had happened since they were last together seen.

†

"Gentlemen," said Hooke.

His messengers appeared.

"Please inform him."

"Where might he be, Sir?"

"He's been with Her Majesty taking her promenade on the High Road. Belena, perhaps."

They departed.

†

The armies of Hades on their side of the wall had set torpedoes and bombs exploding Hera's Wall simultaneously when Titans, géants and angels led by Principalities set torpedoes and bombs on their side of the wall exploding. The fallen gate and the fallen sides of the mountains opened a mile-wide entrance.

A length of the top of the wall remained on the south side extending like a half-broken arch.

Themis and Hooke were standing in the midst of the battle. They were speaking with one of the Kings of Hell—Purson—who had explained what happened.

"Uercassiuellaunos has not come," said King Purson. "We cannot hold the gate for long."

"Hera's Wall is long. You are not accounting for it's length. It is not just here in Terra'irae but extends to Orbisalius in Limbe. While this skirmish occurs at this gate, another - similar to this - is being performed at the gate of that confluence.

"Uercassiuellaunos had two objectives: enter Nubilus south of the gate in Orbisalius and enter Nubilus north of this gate. Sapeurs have created a third gate in Orbisalius through which he advances following along the wall in Nubilus. He'll come ere long."

Räum, Duc Vual, Duc Gremory, Prince Seere and Bifröus le Comte had come. They peered at him suspiciously.

"Terra'irae is the name of the territory—Confluence—between Hades and Nubilus."

"It is not on our maps," said Duc Gremory.

Hooke smiled.

"No, it is not on your maps. Nevertheless, Gremory le Duc, Terra'irae has existed long before thee. That you do not know of a thing's existence does not imply it does not exist."

Purson and Bifröus waited calmly, intrigued by his genial composure as the others protested his ignorance of cartography and War.

"Sirs."

Thirty-nine small Gentlemen appeared with a large rolled carpet-like object on their shoulders.

They unrolled the map.

"Thank you," said Hooke. They bowed and went.

"This is one of three maps remaining. All others were destroyed after Hera's Wall was erected for reasons of Safety. Have you ever not wondered why some folk in this valley are pleasantly dispositioned yet display schizophrenic rage?

"Very few officials of State venture through and beyond the West Lands, if one goes proceeding to the North, one arrives in Limbe."

He looked at the assembled: none had gone to the North.

"Hera's Wall is long." He strolled on the map pointing with the pointed toe of his boot at the wall. "These broken lines are of the territories. There are three—

"Terra'irae is where we stand. It lies in the confluence of two city-states: one on the continent of Empurios in Hades and one on the continent of Virtus Major in Nubilus. It is the Ninth Circle. The Palace of Fidelity.

"Orbisalius, in the southeast region of the continent Soillsegnatae near the Duchy of Montmartre, is the name of the confluence of Limbe with Nubilus at the northwest of Virtus Major near the city-state of Speculae.

"Morpruia is the confluence in Limbe southwest in the province of Madlir and Hades northwest on the continent of Cælestia in the kingdom of Aquipendium.

"Hera's Wall was done so as to embank between the confluence of the two sphæres, Hades and Limbe. The gates allowed passage between the two orbium at the exact same places in each realm where resides the seats of Authority in the confluences with that found across the Sea of Winter.

"Limbe and Hades have not such seats of Authority in their confluence."

Themis strolled on to the map. "Here?" She pointed to an odd glyph on the map with the tip of her shoe.

"Odd," replied Hooke smiling. She took his arm as they went from the map. "Gentlemen, I bequeath thee that," said Hooke as he and Themis left.

"Jules?" said Themis to which Hooke he nodded.

†

Zoë was strolling with Mikhail and Orphiel; they were met by Izanami no mikoto as she was standing with a gentleman whose horse was wandering in the meadow.

Hieronymus-Baleberithe-Seere ad-Din al-Jinn had left them after a messenger requested his presence at the advent of Restoration.

The Traveling Apothecary

Constantin the Attic was waiting for a fellow who would be coming to where he waited for he had purchased his caravan. The caravan was a large cabinet. A small cabinet on four wooden stilts was set by the steps. No signs nor banners nor pennants were displayed. Constantin the Attic once preferred to wait on Black Lanes in the county of Hookland; but thought he would depart from Malevolences and Vile.

Izanami no mikoto introduced Constantin the Attic to them.

Constantin the Attic introduced them to his wares: he had printed spells and curses with disclaiming admonishments on the reverse; twigs and small branches of all the shrubs and trees; river and sea stones from the minor lakes and waterways guarded by Nymphs; water from Templar graves; waters from sacred springs; water from the stream at the Devil's Scar; water from the basilica cistern in Constantinople; glass phials of dew drops from the orange tree of Hera; wood splinters from the rowboats hung from beams of the vault of the church of St. Ellen-of-the-Tracks in Old Mump on the Islands in the Marsh; hair from a mummified jester's wand; ash from places that cannot be spoken; sand from the shores of lakes and deserts in the realms of Poseidon; leaves from the Mare-hag tree at Thornbane.

He had an apple from the Apple Altar, the half-ruined 200-year-old apple tree on the green at Maiden's Tye in the county of Hookland, which was said to offer divinatory fruit; salt from the Gis Estuary, Solomon's mines, and the tears of the Sirens who cry for their lost loves; individual Ojime beads of cinnabar or ivory or bone.

He had all things written in Περὶ ὕλης ἰατρικῆς.

Guenevere de Sens and Fanchon Frood arrived. Madam Frood was leading a bridled mare.

Izanami no mikoto, Mikhail, Orphiel and Zoë were unsurprised by their appearance.

"Mesdames," said Constantin the Attic welcoming them.

"Madam Frood," said Zoë.

"Fanchon Frood has now officially become Apothicairesse," said Guenevere de Sens; and, addressing Zoë said: "We discussed things."

Constantin the Attic was happy.

"Where do you go?" said Zoë.

"I shall go escorting Madam Frood as she would wish assisting as I may," said Constantin the Attic. "Bucarest, you said."

The captivated Fanchon Frood did nod.

†

The air was filled with the dust of War.

Themis coughed. She spat. The demons looked at her: amused, delighted.

"Thou spitten," said Bifröus.

"Dust," she annoyed replied.

"What of Limbus?" asked King Purson.

"Limbe does not have the modern technologies as Hades and Nubilus do," said Hooke. "They courageously—they haven't standing legions—made a cannon duel and took their retreat leaving the cannons behind.

"Nubivagae believe they espied cowardice. Limbi folk do feint. The forces of Nubilus are being drawn with their modern armaments further entering Limbe where those of Nature shall use the marvells of Nature."

"If they have not embraced modernity, how are they to do?" said Bifröus.

"Al-Jinn attends offering guidance. A guard of Zabaniyya are in the midst of their murderous assistance against those who unwelcomed would make to enter. Nature gives itself.

"Limbe victorious."

The kings nodded grim frowning.

†

The ostentatious coach was twenty-four feet long and twelve feet in height. It was built of gold. It was pulled by a team of eight white horses wearing black leather with golden bells harnesses driven postilion-ridden in four pairs. The coach was attended by four postilions, nine walking grooms, eleven footmen walking behind the coach, and four Paladins of the Guard of the Throne of Hera walking at the four corners of the coach carrying their long partisans of Hera's sigil. Two ornately dressed footmen walked beside the body of the coach with their appropriate hands on either door. The leading horses were Podargos, Lampon, Xanthos and Deinos with four common horses harnessed behind them.

All activity by the belligerents ceased.

"It still reminds me of a hearse," said Themis.

Hera stepped from her coach of State in the dust risen from her arrival.

"Themis," said Hera in her grand condescending manner.

"Hera," replied Themis as she held a honeysuckle-scented silk handkerchief against her mouth and nose.

Themis spat; Hera was appalled, "How dare you!"

"My apologies," said Themis. "It wasn't my reply, Madame." She gestured over the scene of carnage surrounding them. "I would never show disdain in your presence with such a trifling act as this."

Hera smiled gloating at the reply of Themis but soon frowned confused by the reply of Themis.

There was a massive explosion seen rising from the North.

"He comes," said Hooke to the King. "Another entrance. He brings King Beliel with half of his eighty legions of demons and fifty legions of spirits. The others stand at that new entrance."

Hera was stunned.

"What have you done!"

"It was during les Ides de Mars lièvre of this year we are and were agreed in Diplomacy," said Hooke. "I was simply requested as Observer."

"Why didn't you stop them!" screamed Hera.

"It is your wall," replied Themis as she pointed to the widening collapse caused by the belligerents. "My understanding is it was created as a physical manifestation of Hortus conclusus which none but few of the Celestes wanted."

"My gate!"

"*Gates.*"

A landau drawn by four-in-hand approached.

Lady Constance and Fille stepped from the carriage. Lady Constance was walking aided by a walking stick.

"Not her again," muttered Fille.

"This is not your favorite?" said Hera.

"No," replied Hooke.

"You lie."

"All les Exemplars past and future, present are my favorites," replied Hooke smiling at Fille.

"If you two would go, Fille and I would have a word with Madame," interrupted Lady Constance.

"We do not forgive. We shall remember this effrontery against our sanctity for all times. 'Mnemosyne collapses Cronus,'" hissed Hera.

"Walter Benjamin?" mused Themis. Hera raised her chin imperiously. "Chronos collapses Mnemosyne."

Hooke nodded.

Hera hissed.

"They have other grander things needful of their attention instead of this trifle," said Lady Constance as she locked her right arm with Hera's left arm escorting her from the gate. Fille walked on the left side of Lady Constance. "Please hold this for me, would you," said Lady Constance as she handed Fille her cane; "and do be careful with it, Dear. It's very old."

"I cannot believe this!" protested Hera gesturing over her shoulder to the rubble of that was once her gate and wall.

There were battalions of angels and thrones approaching from a league beyond the gate. The land collapsed falling in the gigantic hole appearing.

Hooke turned to Themis. "Goblins."

Themis and Hooke strolled from the battle.

Le Maréchal d'Empire rode at the head of the column of the legion with King Beliel at his side. His generals following in line leading the cavalry, velites, legionaries, musketeers, and artillery of Gribeauval guns and mortars.

"Uercassiuellaunos!" exclaimed a very happy King Purson.

"What news?" replied le Maréchal d'Empire as he and his staff with King Beliel stopped to speak with the King Purson while the column continued to the ruins of the gate.

"Lord Hooke he's taken with the Grey Witch," replied a hallebardier pointing his halberd in the direction they had gone.

"He gave us a map of the confluences in the territories," said King Purson. "I heard the rumours of Hades and Nubilus. I never knew."

"Very generous. Keep it well; and, hid: some will come seeking it due to those charts being pronounced heretical pipe-dreams. That pit?"

"He said 'twere goblins," said King Purson.

"That's unexpected. They hate them more than they despise us so we'll see how long it lasts." He turned his horse towards the Maréchals de camp. "Sound charge."

The heavy cavalry charged through the battle with le Maréchal d'Empire leading them with his great harpe flaming.

Guenevere de Sens, Izanami no mikoto, Mikhail, Orphiel and Zoë were waiting as Marquesse Shass had paused as he was amused by the hectographed pamphlets displayed on the table of a dolmen set beside the High Road. Theourgia, Sorcellerie, Nécromancie, l'Alchimie, Spiritualisme, Spiritisme, Mesmérisme, l'Ésotérisme, Hermétisme, l'Occultisme, l'Astrologie and Magie were represented; but it was those kept beneath the table he found of interest: he collected them. He purchased one of each: seamy dime novels of the lives of parishioners of l'Occultisme.

"These puerile works of decadence and torture from Alphonse-François Huysmans, as I was informed by Duke Vapula, were written by the alchemist Reginald de Sermisy of Dibben Terrace in Hookland," said Guenevere de Sens; and replied to Orphiel's expression: "Yes, I read them."

They continued walking as Marquesse Shass would begin reading aloud the tale of Madame Minerva and the Occultist.

"The previous volume ended with Madame Minerva hanging by a rope tied around her ankle over a pit of tar waiting for the arrival of Satan," said Marquesse Shass. "The heads of witnesses were on the floor in a circle around them. They are not dead and could speak when spoken to by others. They are annoyed at their predicament. Kleet le Magnétiseur was conjuring."

"Madame Minerva née Mary Merkley is a Trance-Medium who performed at Spiritualism by communication with spirits. She has come to France with her *Madame Minerva's Traveling Spirits Intercession Caravan* since her name is now known as a charlatan in the Colonies," said Zoë. "Miss Merkley was naked?"

"How else," replied Guenevere de Sens.

†

Hooke and Themis met Ogbunabali, Mictecacihuatl, Hel, Śmierć and King Yama as they were strolling returning to the gate.

"Karasuto'aruku!" said Hel delighted greeting Themis; and, said "Tsukinokaminarito'aruku" greeting Hooke with a formal tone.

"Hel!" exclaimed Themis surprised.

Hooke smiled.

Themis and Hooke welcomed all in turn.

"Why have you come?" asked Themis.

"This amusement cannot be ignored," replied Mictecacihuatl.

"Sojobo is in Limbe with his subjects doing what they may," began Ogbunabali; "He has them Hyakki Yagyo marching." He laughed. "It is a marvell to behold because you see others have joined those parades of one-hundred becoming ten-times longer with merrily marching marchers.

"Shinigami are joined with the legions of le Maréchal d'Empire. Onibi are frolicking in the lands. Jubokko have taken residence." He pointed: shade trees had grown tall in the territoire of Terra'irae. Atmospheric ghost lights were everywhere.

"Kitsune scurry and karasu'tengu fly protecting commune and village from invaders.

"Bakeneko are taking shapes of les Enragés."

"He is modest," said Śmierć. "The Japanese demons are whelming over the continents of Nubilus. Nurasushukujo with her Nureon'na sisters followed by chōchin'obake gone by way of Oceanus to the furthest lands: they are attacking ships at sea and marauding ports on the coast and up the largest rivers."

"Onibi are everywhere harassing all," said Hel.

"Hades and Limbe is grown quiet," continued Śmierć. "Those from Hades were repulsed. They have yet to decide further adventures.

"Limbe and Nubilus are active but Limbus is playing a defensive game of leading them further into the territory for ambushes and attacks from behind; Nubilus has squandered their advantage; but it is Nubilus and Hades which are the true belligerents in this war."

They continued speaking, as they stood oblivious of their surroundings, of what they had seen displayed on the four continents of those three sphæres.

†

They were walking up the steps carved on the mountain side to the battlement of the wall. It was several days after Hera's Gate had gone.

"This will be thought a fateful coincidence by Historians," said Themis. "Your doing?"

"No," replied Hooke. She laughed. "I was merely musing whilst visiting the plotters in either of their two kingdoms.

"All the plots of Caelestium and kings are exposed."

"How long?"

"Le Maréchal d'Empire, Hieronymus-Baleberithe-Seere ad-Din al-Jinn, Samael, and Orphiel anticipate a one-hundred years and fifty war; mutual Armistice; several numerous small battles in the autonomous territories until a single battle—the Battle of the Nebulous Plains or the Battle of the Seven Hills or the Battle of Victors or the Battle of the Long Valley—occurs wherein the monument column of Némésis is destroyed which triggers begins a second War — the Inescapable War — lasting thirty years. A thirteen-day war begins by the final revolutionaries of Kingdom Come.

"The Second Armistice is declared. Nubilus cannot continue.

"Grand casualties on each side. Wounded are nursed and healed. Hades and Limbus shall give them place and work; Nubilus offers all blessings of wonders but gives naught else.

"Those deceased are sent where they would. Most - Likely - shall take a Season in a Sphære they've not yet been or choose their favored."

"Hera's Wall would take five decades to repair. She refuses to pay for it. The wall is left as you see it is."

He viewed.

"Titus and l'Invalide wished anarchy but it doesn't come: this is a simple exorcism of bloodletting for battle in the eternal Serenity."

Hooke and Themis were standing on the battlement on the arch remaining from the fallen mountain side.

Authorities and Principalities led their legions against the armies of le Maréchal, King Beliel and King Purson. There was fighting along all the length of the wall.

He gestured to the North. "It's there." Themis wandered away looking at the views from the heights of the arête.

Hooke was watching across the landscape observing. He raised his head slightly observing the sky. He smiled.

Hermes arrived carrying his caduceus.

"Your Lordship," said Hermes fretful.

"Hermes Psuchopompos," replied Hooke. "Officialis?"

"I was dispatched 'Gabriel sur une béquille! Baise tout! Why in Hell is he here?'" Hermes nodded. "Persephone wants your head to be presented to her on a silver tray by Queen Themis, with her causing all manner of turmoil amoungst the children of the Lecherous One, who was graciously invited to speak with all of the deities residing in the majesty of Hades but has ignoring not replied so thus I was dispatched to inquire why Her Majesty the Queen was to be arriving here at this fête not attending the parabole cordiale with the deities she has maimed, ridiculed and besmirched by her acts against their generous patronage." He paused. "And, why you are not quailed by the wrath of the Court."

"Her Majesty arrived because she will be..." Hooke began in good humour but, as he was peering through the mâchicoulis, extended his left hand pausing their conversation.

A great archange rose from beneath against the Nubilus side of the wall.

"Orphiael," said Hooke pleasantly.

"Why come?" said Orphiael the Archange as it hovered above them with it's beating wings. "Thou wert condemned to exile after thy treacheries against l'Hallow majestueux were known."

"Visitor."

"Who will protect her who fouls divine law while you are away here? She who fouls her name!"

"I was informed the final oracle who could has long since ceased sense of her," said Hooke.

Orphiael was wide-eyed with astonishment.

Hooke with the forefinger of his left hand held at shoulder height pointed upwards.

A great shadow descended as the archange would peer upwards and swooping piercing armour caught with the talons of it's right claw the body of the archange before rising returning in the sky. Orphiael screamed in an agony it had never felt before.

Hooke turned to Hermes.

"Sight-seeing."

"What just happened?" Hermes stared open-mouthed.

"Orphiael was alerted on my having been arrived. Spies. Orphiael was flying close to the ground. The Serpent watched on high and followed curious as to the reason why an archange would be in that state of subterfuge. Orphiael arrived; the serpent pounced."

"Serpents loathe celestial beings."

The Shadow returned. It was Merle's Serpent.

"She and I shall be no more than tourists viewing from the hills these opening pleasantries of this noble war against Indignity."

The Serpent was hovering at the wall. The archange bellowing was pummeling the leg and body of the Serpent. The Serpent fractured the armour of the archange against the parapet: the wall crumbled.

Orphiael was stunned.

"Our vanguard," replied Hooke to the confusion of thoughts by Hermes. "Tell them what you will with truth or lies; they'll be rancorous regardless of what you say. Do you know the conte de fées of *The Great Flood in the Vale of Sorrows?*"

"Everyone knows it," said Hermes.

"Good. Say to them I threatened you bestowing that rage over all in this kingdom on whom deities be, excepting His Majesty. Say what ever you'd like." Themis returned. "Off ye go, lad." Hooke assisted her to sit on the Serpent's back; she sat with both her legs on the same side of the Serpent; she crossed her ankles. "I henceforth ignore all edictal summons to the court. I shall keep private audience with Hades; none other." He sat himself behind her.

"They still dislike me so." She in gaiety did laugh. "I'd forgotten. Is it because a femme who is queen fouls the name of a deity who also happens to be femme?"

The Serpent soared away flying to the North. Hermes stood watching until they were gone from sight.

"Merde!"

✝

Count Stolas and la Mujer Lechuza did meet those on the promenade with Zoë.

They wished to thank her for her kindness during le Grand Dérangement.

They were eloping intending to become benefactors for orphans in the city of Selwasithiche in the département of Gwydion, Orbisalius. The legions remaining with Count Stolas were accompanying them as the bridal procession.

They made their farewells.

✝

The Serpent flew to the palace.

Themis was assisted by Reynaerd as she stepped over the parapet on to the tower; Hooke jumped.

"Thank you," said Themis. The Serpent bowed in reply.

The surface of the turret was set with a large carpet and picnicking items. Sterling, porcelain, glass dome covered dishes, warming dishes. It was a very large presentation.

Several serveuses were waiting.

Hieronymus-Baleberithe-Seere ad-Din al-Jinn was already dining. He stood and offered Themis the bouquet of flowers given him; she took them.

The angel was bellowing and screaming.

The Serpent spoke.

"That would be cruel," said Hooke.

The Serpent with it's left claw tore off one of the wings of the archange Orphiael. It loosed the angel over the sea of Dark who attempted flying only to spiral faster into that sea as darkness reached for it and pulled it down.

The Serpent flew away laughing with the wing of the archange; a cacophony of cries was heard from afar.

"This tower once was identical with le phare d'Alexandrie. It thus appears as a gilded funerary monument without the crown or furnace," offered al-Jinn. "Hades and Limbe have the proper tower."

"Safety?" said Themis seated on the pillows on the carpet giddy from the spectacle of all things occurring as the war between Hades and Nubilus was continuing far below them.

Hooke raised his head staring; Themis did so, too.

Serpents from all places of the sphæres were gamboling circling and spiraling over the palace.

"Safety."

"Aži Dahāka, Zhulong and Seiryū visited earlier," said al-Jinn, "as emissaries and they offered regards and wishes that you and Aureoleis visit with them in Limbe after these expeditionary buffooneries are ended."

"We shall," said Hooke as he looked at Themis smiling.

"Tenebris King shall join you?" asked Reynaerd.

"He'll not," said Hooke. "He's below joyfully in high spirits laughing raging with his wrath."

They dined.

✝

Hades was standing in a corner of the room of Strategies listening in the Ministry of War to the generals and admirals speaking, arguing and imploring amoungst themselves.

Hermes rushed to Hades and whispered to Hades as Hades did crookedly smile.

"The Raven-Lord has gone sight-seeing," said Hades, "with Themis Queen abetted by the Serpent of le Monseigneur who was carrying the Archange Orphiael across the Waste in the direction of the palace. The Raven-Lord has a matter he takes to them; he aids our cause but shall not assist.

"The Ghôle King has ransom over the palace. The Ghôle King seeks his own vengeance against them; he aids our cause but shall not assist.

"The Raven-Lord has made it known he shall not indulge your demands nor entreaties. He departs from our lands one Moon hence. Le Maréchal has spoken with him who said he does not wish to interfere because if he did, and you should be victorious, it would be believed to be by his doing. He has no doubts of victory and so he wishes to remind: you shall be victors if you occasionally remember employment of strategy and tactics le Maréchal and al-Jinn composed after their involvement in the War of the Titans."

Hades began walking to the door with his hands in his trouser pockets; Hermes following.

"One last," said Hades pausing at the door. "Le Maréchal said that if any Treasons are done in the kingdoms of Hades, Tenebris Ghôle-King, at his Lordship's request, for which Tenebris agreed, shall take thee for work in the furnaces of Vulcan at the depths of the Goblins ne'er again to be seen.

"My heart-felt concurrence was given.

"Step lightly, bonhommes."

He left.

†

Their repast was ended.

†

"How do we return now that our vanguard has gone frolicking?" said Themis.

"The stairs," said Reynaerd as he held open the door in the tower.

She looked queerly at Hooke who replied: "Stairs."

"I know of their ruse but not when expected since al-Jinn is now a distinguished guest and Her Majesty comes with us," said Hooke. "Please, do what you like."

Reynaerd nodded.

They went down the stairs. Hooke led them through the empty halls. Themis was viewing; al-Jinn strode with silent merriment.

"Ursumael," said Hooke.

"Sir," said Ursumael.

"The Consuls?"

"They have come. They are furious but did thy bidding."

"All others?"

"There are few of us; but, there are many remaining who would defend the palace even against thee."

"Please leave this place taking les Tempéraments and those you wish gone with you," said Hooke.

"Thank you, Sir," said Ursumael. "Majesty." He smiled. "Ḡēnijssgoinneil."

"Ursumael the Staunch," replied al-Jinn pleasantly in kind.

They descended the steps.

"Where are we going?"

"Mithraeum," said Hooke as they descended. "This palace was constructed over the tower of it. We were before at the lowest level of the Mithraeum in that Penitents chamber."

They descended a magnificent staircase. The floor they reached was of stone.

"Mithraeum," said al-Jinn.

†

The solitary figure stood on the higher most dune of snow. It wore a great black cloak. The cowl was pulled low on it's face. It was leaning on a staff.

†

They came to the antechamber of the théâtre. The polychrome statue had the same body of that seen in place where Merle addressed the Lord-Chancellors; but the face was of a beautiful woman with jet-hair and a long grey beard. The pedestal was similar yet the words engraved were different.

It turned it's head when they entered.

"We are welcomed," said Themis. "She is different."

"They are different because three Mithraea exist," said Hooke. "This, the one in Hades, and the one in Limbe. Les Mémoriaux bienfaisants are of those lands."

"Les Tempéraments?" said Themis. "I do not remember these factions."

"Six," said al-Jinn, "are to be found in this parlement: Les Tempéraments are Arch-Lords from the Noble Houses. They are as should be as Ursumael the Staunch does illustrate.

"L'Asemblee are innocuous. They are the majority easily swayed. They are from the Noblesse. They are seen in the théâtre-boxes as common silent dignitaries.

"Les Noblesse d'épée are Life Peers who philosophically stand between l'Asemblee and les Tempéraments.

"Les Enragés are Arch-Lords of the Imperial House who destroy by their own whimsy and intrigues or those intrigues set by Les Pyracanthes who plot. Les Pyracanthes are Lords spiritual who prefer to be seated on the stage; les Enragés are sat in the front rows.

"Les Empiristes are Arch-Lords of the Imperial House, Lords spiritual and Counts-Palatine who profess their goal to be civilizing savages by the method of dominance from Colonialism and Imperialism."

✝

They entered.

✝

Mikhail, Orphiel, Erlik Khan, Izanami no mikoto and Ereshkigal were strolling with Zoë. Erlik Khan made a comment about pastries since he was unable to be given one from Chang'e.

"We should visit Mother Emanuel," said Orphiel.

They were soon walking in Charleston.

"The Church-Ladies," said Mikhail as they soon were able to see the table set on the pavement on the northside of Calhoun Street. "I strongly recommend the shimmering blueberry cobblers."

"Shimmering?" asked Erlik Khan.

"They mix blueberries with a syrup of plain soda water, cane sugar and pummeled blueberries," said Mikhail. "It is effervescent."

"My dear Ladies, I would like shimmering pies."

"How many would you like?" asked Sister-Lady Cornelia smiling as she already knew his reply.

"I wish all of them," said Mikhail.

The Church-Ladies laughed.

"You come irregularly but only for those and take all of only those," said Sister-Lady Cornelia. "We do have others, you know."

They assembled all of them. A portly imp with a crate strolled up the pavement. He collected the cobblers.

"I do know, Madame Cornelia, as you are kind enough to remind me on my visits," said Mikhail as he paid twenty dollars paper currency for pies he and the others would take; he refused the monies they would give him back. Mikhail thought. "Peach is delicious." He thought. "All are. However, your effervescent blueberries are spectacular. I cannot change."

"No plates? No forks? No spoons?" said Izanami no mikoto.

"You do have hands, don't you," replied Orphiel as he held one with a hand and began eating his shimmering blueberry cobbler.

"Why not all of them?" asked Zoë.

"Madame?" said Mikhail. "You shall sell these delightful pies by the end of the day, Yes?"

"Yes," replied Sister-Lady Victoria.

"One-hundred seemingly," said Mikhail after he counted the remaining pies.

"If you say so, sir," replied Sister-Lady Victoria.

"I could not conscience depriving those one-hundred of their happiness by these pies." The Church-Ladies laughed. "I kid you not," replied Mikhail laughing caused by their infectious laughter.

"You do so with those shimmering blueberry pies," noted Orphiel.

"Ah. That I do," said Mikhail. "Still, they can find happiness from other flavours."

"And, colours," said Ereshkigal who had selected a raspberry pie.

"Shall we adjourn sightseeing?" asked Orphiel.

"Thank you, dear Ladies, for this happy breakfast fare," said Zoë as she held her blueberry shimmering cobbler.

"Ladies," said Mikhail as he bowed before them. "Thank you."

They went.

The portly imp, following after, held the crate filled with pies on his shoulder with one hand and with his other hand he dined on a sweet potato pie.

†

The Théâtre-Hall was fashioned as an amphitheater set in an opera-house. It was filled with fragrant smoke. They stood on the stage.

"The Scholae Palatinae are missing," remarked al-Jinn. "Le Commission Extraordinaire des Onze are attending."

"They lurk," said Hooke.

Twenty-two small Ministers were aligned standing in a half-circle against the walls of the amphitheatre.

"Why does Baleberithe the Vile accompany you?" said Iphelael demanding stood from his place in the front.

"My Guest," said Hooke idly gazing at those individuals standing and seated in the théâtre.

"Her!"

"She is Queen," said Hooke as he strode to the side where were seated les Pyracanthes on the stage against the wall and gestured to one who stood fuming from it's regal chair taking that regal chair to the center of the stage setting it for Her Majesty. "Her sôle visit." She sat. Al-Jinn stood beside her with a hand resting on the back of the chair. Hooke went to the front of the stage.

Fury against and recognition of those two were made by les Perfidiosus.

"Emotions are instinctual precepts," said Hooke absently. "They have not evolved."

Hooke nodded to the Messenger-at-Arms.

The Bailiff began reading the names of those deceased from a Notice nécrologique. "Les Pyracanthes: Grand-Minister Nivard-Largillière, Lord-Chancellor de Vircy, Minister

Duseigneur, Lord-Chancellor Jean-Ignace Bouchon, High-Chancellor Cotgrave, Honourable Minister Gallande, Grand-Minister de Coligny, High-Chancellor Penthièvre, Arch-Chancellor Murat, Minister de Trie, Arch-Chancellor de Clermont, Arch-Chancellor Longueville..." He continued but after ten minutes he paused. "There are a great many pages. Do you wish me to pronounce all those deceased, Excellency?" said the Bailiff.

"Please," said Hooke.

The Bailiff nodded and continued. The assembled grew increasingly disquieted as Hooke stood patiently while for one hour while the Bailiff read the names of deceased les Pyracanthes, les Enragés, les Empiristes and those few from Noblesse d'épée and l'Asemblee who had been seduced with grandeur.

"There are no more?" asked Minister Claude-Eustache Toussaint.

"None," replied Hooke. "Those who did not return from the Ministry and l'Hallow gratiosum, l'Hallow benevolens, l'Hallow auspicium remain missing as their existence in this Sphære ceased for 'tis Oblivion what keeps them."

An uneasy pall fell.

"Le Sainte malveillance?" asked Minister Felimare.

"L'Émissaire malefique wanders. L'Éminence malus you have seen in his coffin-box. Le Sainte malveillance shall remain sundered."

"Omnes vita sancti!" was heard as murmurs, bellows and screams.

"How do you defend words of 'All life is sacred' yet you allow vile murders of Innocents caused by your collusion with neglect, abandonment and greed?" said Hooke politely; "Or, worse with acts disengaged from all sense of Morality against those for whom you sanctimoniously disdain regarding their simple lives so very far below from your stations of grandeur and wealth tithed from they." They were silent. "Bonhommes?"

Those of les Noblesse d'épée and l'Asemblee who had not conspired disappeared as if by the light of fluttering flames extinguished.

"All sacred things are kept so by the law of Divinities," was heard from the side of the stage.

"And, madness wherein no demons of mind exist in those that have come by the law of Divinities," replied Hooke laughing. "Merely, Extase."

The lime-plastered walls slowly erratically changed in the manner of disparate pools of water collecting.

"You interfere!"

"No, I do not engage interference with thy intrigues and plots," said Hooke. "Tempora labuntur."

"Hostis humani generis!" was screamed from the theatre-boxes.

"Res humanae has never been my concern, Chancellor Orphilus," said Hooke: "Res fata. Sic semper erat, et sic semper erit."

The walls were basalt.

"All seated in this Odeon know of it's existence though it has never been seen. For those who wish recitation of the words on these walls, it shall not be done. For those who wish through covetous fever to have knowledge given by the engravings on these walls, it shall not be done. For those who wish the assumption of the authority granted by those engraved words, it shall not be done. For those who wish to usurp through intrigues and plots of subversion the authority granted by this Basalt Proclamation, it shall not be done."

Hooke gestured broadly.

"My entente," he said. The walls displayed light with frost fog rising from the engravings of sigils and glyphs. "Nature and Chaos are balances eternal in the revenant-states of Existence. Existence 'tis from l'Abysse. Life kept on Sphæres." He gestured. Several lines shown darkly.

> Punitio non refertur primo per se in correctionem bonum eius qui punitur sed in bonum publicum ut alij terreantur, a malis committendis avocentur.

"It was written at thy request and so too shall thee be made.

"Thy play was staged; tale was told." He stared at the ribs of the ceiling. "Post tenebras lux: l'Obscurité des Ténèbres de la Lumière dans le Noir brillera et la lumière brille dans les Ténèbres et les brumes de l'Obscurité."

"Omnia mutantur," Themis pleasantly replied. Hooke turned and nodded in a formal manner; but, smiling.

"Did you once not hear," Hooke admonished as he viewed those in the théâtre: "'The purpose may be known but the end-game is seldom as expected; and—Often—the consequential results are greater than first believed. Terribly greater,' in this very Hall?" Les Tempéraments were comforted. "Thy plots and intrigues have succeeded and thee would not ever have been found were it not for thy putrescent sense of grandeur." He laughed. "The trap thou laid in that chamber set this end-game. Thy hand was shown: the imprisonment of Ghost-Lords; the engagement of Malevolences; the keeping and loosing of Night Horrors. All revealed — by Chance — in thy arrogance where was laid consequences terribly greater."

Two Pyracanthes and one of les Enragés vanished.

They remaining were fearful.

"No," said Hooke. "They flee: tenth or ninth or all circles none are to be sought; they exposed themselves with sly cowardice in the abandonment of these and shall again. We'll wait."

The Thirteen and Nine Ministers who had been standing against the back wall of the amphitheater bowed before they vanished briefly seen as great ravens.

"Thee may—by Resverie—come returned if thou knowest knowledge of it how to do." He pointed. "Those three lines." He went to the foot of the stage. "Ira Sacrum Resurgam."

They were terrified.

The High Arch-Lord of les Pyracanthes was quietly furious; the High Arch-Lord of les Enragés was pale from wroth; several others protested loudly. Some had returned to their original places; others had set themselves where they were standing. Some still stood. Some were sobbing. Most were dumbfounded.

"I do not engage thy malefic intrigues," said Hooke. "I engage *thee*."

Les Tempéraments in the théâtre-hall disappeared as if by the light of fluttering flames extinguished.

The mithraeum acted as before but with tempered rage. Those three ghost-like wavered but Themis and al-Jinn did not disappear. Those remaining—les Pyracanthes, les Empiristes, les Enragés and their conspirators—would move but were imprisoned in their pose; and, vanished.

Themis and al-Jinn exchanged glances. Themis rose from her chair.

Themis, Hooke and al-Jinn went wandering through the second salle, The Night Chamber.

"All of the *pious* members of l'Asemblee and Life Peers were removed from the amphitheatre being sent returned to their different residences," said Hooke. "Les Tempéraments in this théâtre-place were set on the dunes, as they requested, to view the spectacle soon-to-be. Spirits engaged with displacement of les Perfidiosus for they could not take bodily vengeance against them; they may return."

"They've gone where?" said al-Jinn amused.

"Hades."

"Eh," said Themis.

"'Tis unknown by all. There are three: Hades, Limbe and Nubilus. All three mithraeum are identical in structure; all three théâtres are identical; structures external being different. I was surprised by such a place as that chamber but it by being in one place it is in each of the three. Except." He smiled. "Those simple exits lead to two different places. Nubilus does lead to Oblivion: they exist in darkness for Eternity; Hades and Limbus lead to the bottom of the Lethe where those sent would return with naught but innate knowledge.

"I may never have know if it were not for them."

"You did not know about it!" said al-Jinn.

"No," said Hooke laughing: "Before Night Horrors entered, spirits were felt all throughout the palace by their residence in the tower. 'Twas kept from me."

"Thy pious nature," said Themis.

"A veritable Diogenes the Pilgrim," said al-Jinn.

"Except for the eyes," replied Themis. "Galeas?"

"Perceval," offered al-Jinn.

She nodded pleased.

"I thank thee," said Hooke. "I've often thought myself Alonso Quixano."

Al-Djinn bowed. Themis glanced at Hooke before pronouncing: "Similar eyes."

Hooke bowed.

She curtsied.

"Do they know where they lie?" said Themis.

"Some may recognise Lethe's fragrance; some may not. A great ignominie les Fées humaines is to be had," said al-Jinn. "Do they know the significance of this sardonic act?"

"They do," said Hooke.

✝

They entered a smaller chamber.

Flames of black erupted in the chamber ascending over the tower of the palace.

It was large: a single glass in a frame of black polished wood suspended in the air entwined by thorny stems and briar.

They entered the glass. Themis turned her head to see the chamber awash in flames of pale green; and, Light augmented.

The black flames had ascended on the tower and were entwined with the colours of the pale green flames and Light becoming aurorae encircling the phare and, in the Skylands of Hades and Nubilus risen, was seen by all in the territoire of Terra'irae.

The illuminations raced as rising tides all throughout the palace structure escaping: all fighting ceased.

The tide ebbed inches from the wall with it's watchtowers destroyed by Ghôle which was a length of leagues from the palace.

✝

Fissures opened in the dunes radiating from the palace. Darkness ascended.

†

Hooke, Themis, and al-Jinn were in the garden of his house, Lugosdunon. They watched.

†

And, then— a silent domed explosion of light was slowly voluminously raised from the structure destroying the tower and that la Lumière archaïque fell collapsing the aurorae imploding all of the palace.

The shockwave of that Light was felt for leagues and leagues.

The wall of the citadel disintegrated.

†

The phare of black flames was all that was found.

†

The dark figure watched.

†

Reynaerd came to Themis with a tall vase of cobalt blue glass filled with spring water from Châtillon-sur-Seine. She placed the flowers in the vase.

"Your cabinet, Ma'am," said Reynaerd.

†

Marcelle, Félix, Nolan, Milot, Fille and Tochi no akaru-sa rushed to the garden. They halted. They stared at the gargoyles.

"What happened?" asked Themis as she watched the waves of light extend over all of the lands in view.

"They're Watchers!" pronounced Marcelle.

"No," said Hooke.

"We were told you keep Watchers," said Milot.

"No," he replied. "One does not keep Watchers. Though, you have met them on occasions not by happenstance."

He smiled.

"My proclamation was induced by the wrath of the Ghost-Lords." He sighed deeply. "They allowed me the destruction of the palace for they could not assist in it's demise; but they would indulge me. Any who remained were of the plotters: they've ceased."

"You did that," said Themis.

"I did," said Hooke.

"Why not the palace?" asked al-Jinn.

"It was become sacred."

"Spirits?" asked al-Jinn.

"They are there. The palace was constructed after the phare was destroyed by them. The phare was sacred; the palace was vanity. The phare shall be rebuilt in years to come and they shall with it rise in the majesty of Nature."

"I was not invited picnicking for that," said al-Jinn keenly.

"They – All Ghost Lords – thou have long wished to see and wert accepted the moment you set foot on the tower. You were given safe passage in all of the realms they keep."

"Why?"

"My gratitude."

Al-Jinn raised his eyebrows.

"All things Gēnijssgoinneil has done."

Al-Jinn bowed from his shoulders with his head bent down.

"Monsieur Jules?" asked Themis.

"He sits in the Library," said Nolan.

"Goblin light?" asked al-Jinn.

"Her Majesty's influence."

†

The dark figure was greeted by Reynaerd at the door of the great house, Lugosdunon.

†

They heard Barbary organ sifflante exhalations from which was heard music from *La Mort de Tintagiles*.

Sénateur-Maire Huillard who was leading Elfriede and Hercule turned at the corner of the rue transversale. A small crowd was assembled. Caroline d'Eirene was standing to the side of the canvas. A very large painted curtain of canvas of a forest by Henri Julien Rousseau was the background scenery for the performance.

"Ladies and Gentlemen! Mailloche and Belette were found as displayed in this painting! during an expedition into that Dark Land of Death — Oviliswiændia — whose continent shall never be spoken! for, even in this Modern Age, we must keep divine knowledge from those lacking superstitions and so shall never be seen on maps!" They made their way and stood behind the Impresario who was speaking. "All my companions were murdered by Damned Things in the Darkness of Dark! It was by Fate that I alone escaped! Escaped! Alone!

"As an explorer of the arcane Truth, whether it be seen in a burlesque, a library, a pamphlet discarded on a bench in *l'Évanouissement Clavecin*, or in that most tell-tale form to learning things of the Great Unknown—Library—in intense admiration of it and it's Almighty Author, if at any time I have forgotten the boundary line that I ought not to have passed, and brought terror and horror or aggrieved bewilderments to those in their sanctuary of Ignorance, I implore His pardon; I have never wished to frighten others from that practice of Ignorance, and I would not do so with those amoungst you who are content with Ignorance, which alone leads to happiness here and hereafter; but, merely, offer passage to the unknown depths of learning and, if in any of my passages an immoral sentiment has been aimed at, I consent it should be ignored for it is only the bravest who should wish curiosity; yet I never recollect being actuated in my travels by such sentiment. That Knowledge, in it's fullness, amazement, exquisite albeit frightening realisations, may, by being portrayed in it's nakedness, awaken like nature in some degree an approach to passion, I must allow, but where no immoral sentiment is intended, I affirm that the simple undisguised truths are innocent; and, frightful."

The Impresario who was speaking was dressed in fancy dress à la Turque of 1750. He held a long leather strap on which was fastened a small monkey with wings on which was fastened a dodo.

"Mailloche and Belette shall continue our performance that not even Heads of State have seen!

"Be forewarned! Be prepared! Frightening truths abound for those who wish Curiosity's embrace!"

†

The dark figure was waiting for them at the bottom of the staircase.

†

The performance was begun.

†

"Thank you," said Jean de Somme as they approached.

"It was a wish you once had," said Hooke.

"Al-Jinn," said Jean de Somme.

"De Somme," replied al-Jinn.

Jean de Somme smiled at Themis who radiantly smiled at him.

"I was told plums would be served," said de Somme.

Themis took his arm and she led him with al-Jinn and Hooke following after as the others filed behind.

†

After supper, Themis and Jean de Somme regaled them reminiscing of the days of pirates.

Themis told of C. L. Nolan's adventures for which he was chagrined to acknowledge but did correct her on simple errors.

De Somme related his other adventures: the first Chancellor; Dark Arts practitioner who, caused by an unpleasant experience, had misplaced his memory; Priest-Confessor; and, Gardien de Phare de Nuit. It was after his moments with Léviathan he wondered. It was after a Gentlewoman had left him; he had a seizure. He woke remembering. He went seeking his true Love; and, she found him.

"I left the corruption of the Ministry—Jean le Lumineux—behind but it was recently le Lumineux found Contentment. It came after I found Françoise-Pélagie Fayère de Marly and from thereafter I could no longer foretell," said Jean de Somme; "and Jean-Baptiste le Lumineux was finally departed."

Reynaerd entered with a letter on a tray. He went to Nolan. "Sir." He exited. Nolan read the letter and as he did he grew more embarrassed and surprised. They then were silent.

He stood.

"It seems our adventures here with Her Ladyship have garnered attention of our adventures with Her Ladyship. Megan la Fae has requested, by month's end, my return — since as being the member of the Illapses Agency, Ltd. most familiar — to become a ministerial Consul of the Seventy Ninth Congress of Fey, expected to last until 1926.

"It convenes on Samhain."

He was stunned.

"Monaglæd in Barrowcross will be the setting for the realms in England; Corvusweald for the four continents," said Themis.

"Seventy Ninth Congress of Fey."

"My Aunt does not make this offer lightly..."

"I know," said Nolan interrupting.

"...nor was it accepted without concurrence from those you met in the Century House," Themis concluded smiling, "and by those who've been reading thy treatises on Myth and Lore since you began writing them."

"I didn't know," replied Nolan flustered.

"You shall go," said Hooke; "There are still hours left for a few grand adventures in Hades by the Illapses Agency, Ltd.

"There is a ferry from Achéron which will take you as far as the Thames; a carriage from Monaglæd will be waiting. Admiral Paul-Pierre-Clément Duplessis with his dirigible will take you from Barrowcross across the Sea of Gaul to Corvusweald.

"Arrangements to be performed when you wish."

"Thank you," said Nolan as he sat staring at the letter.

The performance was concluded. Coins were given as the audience dispersed.

Hercule approached the Impresario. "Monsieur Claude Étienne François Javelle," said Hercule as he bowed from his shoulders. "It is improved."

"High praise!" said Javelle.

Caroline d'Eirene introduced Mailloche the Dodo and Belette the Monkey to Hercule and Elfriede. They went wandering in the parc.

†

Jean de Somme thanked those three deeply. He exited using the looking-glass in the room above.

✝

Themis, Marcelle, Félix, Nolan, Milot, Fille and Tochi no akaru-sa, and Jules who had been requested were standing on a very large woven rug of Diné design.

"I was asked a final illustration of Place to give you," said Themis. She closed her eyes and breathed deeply; she was smiling.

A compass-rose of glyphs and runes illuminated through the carpet.

✝

They were standing on the rug in a desert at Night above the canyon.

"Where are we?"

"Tséyi' in the desert of Naabeehó Bináhásdzo," said Themis.

"If you listen, you can hear the voices of Spirits antediluvium. Spirits keep to loci they have made sacred by they who keep old beliefs. Hearing and Sight. There is another sense at play."

Milot with his normal curiosity made to step from the carpet: Themis pulled him by his coat's collar.

"If you wander from the diyogí, you would be standing by yourself with no possible way to be rescued or returning.

"Different places; different time.

"A ghost."

✝

Zoë was walking with Mikhail, Orphiel, Erlik Khan, Izanami no mikoto and Ereshkigal.

✝

They were standing on the rug in a desert at Night in the lands of the Hopituh Shi-nu-mu.

"This is Deez'áahjį," said Themis.

✝

"The immediate sense of where one stands and what one sees is a sense of Memory," replied Zoë.

"It is what they see but not perceive," said Ereshkigal. "Commonly."

"Yes."

✝

They were standing on the rug in a desert as l'Aube was rising above the edge of the Earth.

"We are on Hiŋháŋ Káǧa in the Ȟe Sápa."

✝

"The sense of Marvell," said Zoë, "would be the glade that was felt in Memory soon overwhelmed by the sense of the woods seen beyond the clearing."

"Less common," said Ereshkigal.

"Yes."

"We view Waikaremoana in Te Urewera," said Themis.

†

"The sense of Wonder is knowing the glade is in the woods," said Zoë, "to be known by the mind but not the senses, in a country, that, in the far distance, is in confluence with Skylands.

"Their sense of Perception allows this state."

"Perception allows which of these three states they find themselves?" said Ereshkigal.

"Yes."

†

They were standing on the Diné rug set on the Highlands in the Kingdom of Armenia. "We view the mountains of Masis."

†

"There remain those who believe these mysteries to be visions for which others proclaim these visions are deceptions employed by le Malin Génie," said Orphiel: "The first are lunatics; the second are theologians: they are victims of Descartes writing in his *Méditations métaphysiques*, 'I shall think that the sky, the air, the earth, colours, shapes, sounds and all external things are merely the delusions of dreams which le Malin Génie has devised to ensnare my judgement.'

"And, the third are those who have clarity of Perception."

"*Meditationes de prima philosophia, in qua Dei existentia et animæ immortalitas demonstratur* was interesting," said Enma-Dai-Ō who had joined them. "The passage you choose 'The Delusion of Dreams' is fanciful, isn't it? Le Malin Génie cannot devise dreams."

"That is true," replied Orphiel; "however, an Evil Demiurge could influence their dreams if Descartes had believed le Malin Génie as demiurge exists.

"It is that he acknowledges he dreams; that these dreams may be delusional ensnaring his judgements; that his judgements, made in delusional dreams, may be false, even if he knows them to be truthful, when they are of external things yet he concedes external things are found in dreams. For all his meditation, he only proves Existence keeps le Malin Génie or demiurge."

"Every plot to each," offered Mikhail.

✝

They were standing on the ridge of Gulaga with the Ocean before them.

✝

"Even so, I would prefer 'I dream therefore I am' were used," said Orphiel.

✝

They were standing on the ridge of Manaslu.

✝

"If external things are found in dreams, and merrily Life is but a dream, does it then become lunatics are theologians and theologians are bound by Lunacy?" said Zoë.

"Aye, Ma'am, it does," replied Mikhail.

✝

They were standing on the snow of Mauna Kea.

✝

Orphiel began whistling *The Rowing Boat* song followed in order by Mikhail, Erlik Khan, Izanami no mikoto, Ereshkigal and Enma-Dai-Ō as they continued on their promenade with Zoë.

✝

They were standing in the great room of Lugosdunon. The compass-rose of glyphs and runes illuminated through the rug faded.

"What did you experience standing in those places?" said Themis.

Marcelle, Félix, Nolan, Milot, Fille and Tochi no akaru-sa and Jules could not say in words what they felt. They agreed they could sense nothing standing on Mauna Kea.

"It was confluence. All of the oceans are a single body of water. That body of water is what you felt standing on the snow in the sacred locus of Mauna Kea."

"Uncomprehending."

✝

Hooke and al-Jinn were standing on the Arch of Woe. They viewed the spectacles of war in the Théâtre over the wastes of snow.

"It was not merely that palace done by la Lumière archaïque," said al-Jinn.

"All Winter palaces," said Hooke.

"I've heard tell of the deafening thunder and lightning rampaging with terrors against maëlstrom of the Clouds over all of Olympe while the palaces fell," said al-Jinn.

Hooke nodded.

†

"They most are unable to see all things?" said Ereshkigal after they had gone a few miles.

"Arrogance, ignorance and fear," replied Zoë.

"Ma'am, you are ever far too kind to them," said Orphiel. "They have, Ereshkigal, a goat's horn endlessly overflowing with psychoses, superstitions and hatred in their thoughts. Arrogance, ignorance and fear amoung them."

"They believe themselves to have the grandest significance of all things in Nature," remarked Izanami no mikoto.

Ereshkigal paused.

"All things," said Izanami no mikoto.

"Those who do not?" asked Ereshkigal.

"They have trespass from resveries and arcades giving them passage to Portul Pădurilor arriving at the territoires," said Zoë.

"Morpruia and Terra'irae are where they wish to be from what I've seen," offered Erlik Khan. "Morpruia has most. Terra'irae has many. Orbisalius has few."

"Morpruia is a wondrous place after all," said Mikhail. "Perhaps, Orbisalius shall change."

"Change?" asked Ereshkigal.

"William, Lord Hooke and Themis Fey-Queen," said Mikhail.

Ereshkigal nodded.

"Perhaps," said Zoë.

†

They continued.

†

Themis went to the library as she was concerned with the well-being of Jules. She found him in the Cartographer's Room. She found him lying on the carpeted boards scratching notes, on different papers, of his own cryptic design scattered around him.

"May I?" said Themis as she crouched beside him.

Jules handed her the parchment he was annotating and pointed to a sign writ with red ink. "This..." he began pleased: "No!" whispered Themis gravely and said with a normal voice. "That's his curious study, *tu*."

He nodded.

"Do you eat?"

"I've taken sustenance from the lounge on the Quay."

Themis escorted him to the Quay. The large goblin-troll at the chromium door bowed as he opened it for her. They entered Calliope's Lounge.

"Themis!" exclaimed Beatrice as she went to Themis and they hugged exchanging heart-felt greetings.

Themis formally introduced Jules.

"He was 'round a few days ago," said Beatrice. "He sat at the bar telling of an adventure with High Road pirates in the lands of Alcalá de Henares. Charming fellow, are you not?"

He blushed.

"Do you recommend which place for lodging by Monsieur Jules?" asked Themis.

"There are rooms in the Hotel Augustine," replied Beatrice. "Are all these rumours true?"

"I believe so." Themis smiled. "If you wish to hear different tales of High Road villains which may address those rumours, you should come this evening. Do you know of one who could govern this place in your absence?"

"Melpomene would be happy to do so," said Beatrice. "She does when she's bored. His Lordship?"

"He's become thoughtfully quiet again," said Themis. Beatrice frowned. "No; not frightening: his 'Mirthful-eyes-lit-if-interrupted' quiet."

"I like that one," said Beatrice. "I'll come." She turned to Jules. "Do you attend?"

He flustered stood.

"He doesn't," said Themis. "I shall pay whatever he wishes in what ever matter he does."

They went from the lounge.

"Why do you do this?" asked Jules.

She smiled.

They went to the Hotel Augustine. It was antiquated but still regal. Jules was happy.

"Your things will be here by afternoon."

"If I may, I should like two glass panes." He touched the larger window of the hotel and he touched a small window. "I would like them, if possible, to be the sizes of these two windows."

She nodded.

†

She walked him back to the Library. She touched his breast bone with the fingers of her right hand; he shivered. He peered down to see faint light shining through his clothes: it was a sigil. It faded. "It protects you."

†

"He's found something," said Themis as she entered and sat on the unused arm of the couch.

Hooke frowned. Hooke had not moved lying on the overstuffed couch in the great room with his boots resting on the arm of the couch while staring at the fan vaulting with his fingers laced on his breast.

"Beatrice comes this evening," said Themis as she looked, "since you're not frightening."

Hooke tilted his head backwards so as to see her.

"Do I frighten you?"

"No," she replied smiling. "Though, if you did, it would be in a duped sort of way. Do I frighten you?"

"I am far too beguiled to know," Hooke replied.

"All things are well."

†

Jules, after attending his Mystery, went to the hotel after taking a very late supper with Melpomene who told tales of Hooke when thoughtful in silence. The two windows he touched were boarded

He went to his rooms. His things were there placed in his rooms as he had done in the manse of Hooke. The two glass panes were there.

†

Tochi no akaru-sa, Fille, Félix and Marcelle were standing on arête – Arch of Woe – as it had been named after l'affaire du Serpent et de l'Archange.

They were watching as Authorities were crawling up the wall from Nubilus.

The enenra, who had taken to Marcelle, and the frolicking ubagabi, who had made Félix their favourite of the four, flew amoungst those assailants causing them their death falling on to the wreckage of the arête far below.

Four Ten no tsukai flew from the sky and stood before them after watching the defeat of those warrior angels.

"These are my Sisters," said Tochi no akaru-sa introducing Marcelle, Félix and Fille.

Tochi no akaru-sa, Marcelle, Félix and Fille sat on the crenellated parapet with their backs to the battlefields in conversation with the Ten no tsukai standing while enenra and ubagabi were frolicking about the Arch of Woe.

✝

Hooke and Themis had fallen sleeping in the Garden of the Hesperides in Bracara on the Gallaecia peninsula.

They were guarding the grove while Ladon was gamboling with his cousins and the Evening Daughters of Night—Aegle, Erytheis, and Hesperarethusa—were assisting those they could in Limbe.

They were lying down: he was slightly inclined by roots of the ancient tree and her head was on his chest.

Malevolences and géants were approaching the edges of the grove.

A great shadow rose encircling the tree of golden fruit. It was Tenebris the Ghôle King with his court guard, les Insurgés.

The villains halted.

Hooke tapped the leg of Tenebris King.

"Dis manibus sacrum," said Hooke looking sadly from the withered arm to the face of the king. "My apologies."

"Fool!" Tenebris King laughed. "I have told none thy curse was taken from me. I am well left to my thoughts. They believe this was all you could do against their king. I do not trouble them with thy fury." He laughed. "I did inform them that even if you could only inconvenience me they would die.

"They come for you.

"Keep my Conseillère safe."

"She's duped thee, too."

"Wisdom and Grace in a child so young." He smiled at her. "Sir," said the King who bowed from his shoulders. He ran with his sword lighting all before him: the Malevolences and géants would not enter the grove nor return to where they had come.

"He thinks me a child," said Themis with her eyes closed.

"An endearing one."

They returned asleep.

†

Hercule and Elfriede were attending the grand spectacle of Féerie in the small théâtre.

Henri Rivière's Ombre
La Fille de Fantômas
Féerie à grand spectacle
En 3 actes et 29 tableaux

Musique nouvelle et arrangée de Claude Debussy

après la performance

La Fille aux Cheveux de Lin,
La Cathédrale Engloutie
et

Un Coup de Dés Jamais N'Abolira Le Hasard

par

Mon. Debussy

†

Hooke was leading Milot, Nolan and Jules through High Achéron. They were walking on Ploutos Street.

"Charon had a steamboat—Pyroscaphe—on the Achéron river in 1784," replied Hooke. "He purchased a second—he named Shirazad—in 1816 from a company on the Mississippi. His last is the showboat—he named Lyon—on which you've ridden, from 1883." Jules was perplexed. "If one knows where," said Hooke, "on the river Saône and of the Mississippi River, the passages to the river Achéron are found, transport is simple." He smiled. "Not all things are by magie done."

†

"I've seen ghosts here," said Jules. "I was returning from one of the places recommended by Her Majesty and saw five of them."

"Ghosts in Hades?" said Nolan.

"Certainly," said Hooke. "Where?"

"There," said Jules pointing at the Iron Bridge crossing over the river of Acheron. "It was a ghost driving a ghostly coach and four from the past. 1700s by carriage, I think."

"A ghost coach from the 1700s riding on the Iron Bridge?" asked Milot.

"Yes."

"Did you notice the surroundings?" asked Hooke.

"Pardon?"

They crossed over the Achéron on the Iron Bridge.

"You saw the coach and coachman," said Hooke; "but did you see the background? Did the avenue look the same? Or, the bridge?"

"I didn't notice. I was stunned it saw me."

"The first bridge was a passerelle and was constructed in 1729," said Hooke. "It was a foot bridge not wide enough for coaches. The second Iron Bridge - This - replaced the passerelle in 1833. What did you notice of the driver?"

"He was singing. He tipped his hat to me as he passed."

"It was not a ghost," said Hooke; "but the actual coach passing faded and transparent because it has not fully entered this century and you had not fully entered it's century. You and he saw each other as Ghost."

"Are not ghosts from a different realm?" said Nolan.

"A different realm is the standard belief; but, No. Your encounter with it was not of a different realm but of different years."

†

They were at the crossing of the boulevard la Croix-Rousse. Hooke paused. He viewed to the West; he viewed to the East.

Hooke strolled across the boulevard causing the traffic of automobiles, and lorries and carriages drawn by horses to stop; Milot, Nolan and Jules—who were now accustomed to his manner—calmly followed. They waited leaning against the vitrine of a Telesphorus and Hygieia Elaboratory while Hooke perused the affiches pasted on the brick wall beside it.

Hera, Perseús, Artemis and Athene cured from the curse of reflection from the West were coming on the pavement to where they stood. "Marquess Naberius." Hooke pointed to the demon with three heads of dogs on a raven body who was staring determinedly while striding hurriedly to the deities. "Watch." Marquess Naberius passed them shouting. Hera, Perseús, Artemis and Athene professed innocence. Hera, Perseús, Artemis and Athene transformed: they were seen as angels before becoming homunculi.

"Obfuscare," said Hooke. Marquess Naberius overheard; he turned and menacingly approached them. Hooke caught the demon by it's outstretched arm twisting it causing the Marquess to fall to his knees. Marquess Naberius transformed into itself: a malebranche.

The Mortality Brigade arrived behind the malebranche. Hooke shook his head at Tempérance Hiolle. A crowd was forming blocking pavement and streets. Several constables arrived dispersing the crowd. The Senior Constable approached Hooke.

"Four nephilim," said Hooke; "one traitor."

"Who might you be?" asked the Constable suspiciously. Hooke unblinking stared at him.

"Oh," replied the Constable. "Take him."

The malebranche protested as he was set with manacles and leg-irons.

"These noteworthiest gentlemen—by my request—are come from the Illapses Agency, Ltd. and shall accompany you as witness to this affair in my stead," said Hooke looking at those three; they nodded. Hooke gestured to Hiolle who sent one from the brigade. "Brigadier Fontaine shall be their escort afterwards."

"Bonhommes," said Hooke.

The Nine Ravens appeared. "They've begun. Please alert all. Le Maréchal, al-Jinn first. Hades finally last." Hooke pointed; eight left.

"Sir?" asked the Constable.

"La Ruse de l'Imposteur," said Hooke. "Shape-shifting. Those four were High Deities transformed. The malebranche transformed as Marquess Naberius cursed them; his master would have taught the curse and transformed him into the Marquess. You shall find this master; and, when found, please inform Minister Thoas who shall inform those waiting."

Hooke and Hiolle left leaving those three with Brigadier Fontaine.

"Right," said the Constable genially as he led the three members of the Illapses Agency, Ltd. "Names?"

The Minister Thoas and Brigadier Fontaine followed discussing the recent festivities for Chang'e.

†

Zoë was walking with Mikhail, Orphiel, Erlik Khan, Izanami no mikoto and Ereshkigal.

Ereshkigal had commented on how even in the Third Dynasty of Ur, Nobility was solely capable of attaining Kingdom Come as lower classes specifically Impoverished would be sent to the Netherworlds.

"Nonetheless, funerary evidence indicates," said Erlik Khan, "that some people believed Inanna, your younger sister, had the power to award her devotees with special favors in the afterlife."

"Oh, yes," said Izanami no mikoto; "A sumptuous Life in Afterlife is asserted on the grounds of how one was buried: sumptuous burials would cause a sumptuous Afterlife; simple burials cause impoverished states in the Hereafter. Historical precedence. Church and State."

They laughed.

"Think of how many deities exact by menace tithes of blessedness by sacrifice and graves. It's a confidence trick," said Orphiel.

"Inanna has confidence," said Ereshkigal.

"Those stately monuments, crypts and tombs are sumptuous," said Zoë, "but are they proper tithes to the extortionate deities?"

"There you are," said Mikhail; "Those ain't, are they. They are, over earlier Modern Ages, edifications of grandeur for them what were wealthy or Bourgeoisie who wished higher station after Death. Deities wither."

"Historical precedence," said Zoë: "Withered; but not departing."

†

Athene and Aphrodite were arguing with Fille. Lady Constance was waiting.

Fille coruscated. Fille, Athene and Aphrodite were startled. Lady Constance was amused. They heard noises of whimpering. They turned: it was Discordia who had been changed into an imp from the Cocytus eddy of the Great Marsh where Fille as a child had played.

"I was going to curse her!" said Athene. "That could have been me!"

"And, me!" shrieked Aphrodite. "Lord Hooke's doing!"

"Themis Grey-Witch," said Fille.

"She's Themis Witch-Queen, deary," said Aphrodite.

"I prefer Themis Grey-Witch because that is she who I know."

"You don't know anything do you," said Athene who pinched Fille's cheek: Athene screamed.

The middle finger and thumb on that hand grew elongating becoming thorny blackberry stems; the other fingers partially grew.

"Fix this!" screamed Athene as she waved her hand in front of Aphrodite.

"I won't be turned into anything for anyone," shouted Aphrodite. "Not even you."

Athene waved her hand in front of Fille's face.

"Lord Hooke did this!"

"I don't know anything as you did so acutely say; but I do believe that to be Lord Hooke's work and you must ask him for a cure. I must thank him," said Fille. "Mesdames." She left.

Aphrodite and Athene, whose finger and thumb were three-feet-long, went screeching off in search of a remedy.

Lady Constance nodded approvingly. She went to Fille. "Might I have my walking cane?" Fille handed it to Lady Constance who hooked Fille's arm with her's as they would strolling go.

"Actually, dear," said Lady Constance, "it was you who did that curse on Discordia." Fille wondered. Lady Constance tapped her cane with her forefinger: it became a wand. "Your's." Fille was astounded. "Just tuck it away for the while. They'll know soon enough."

†

Zoë was walking with Mikhail, Orphiel, Erlik Khan, Izanami no mikoto, Giltinė, and Ereshkigal.

"How so do you mean?" said Erlik Khan.

"Lesser entities will be forever punished for the infamous wiles of Nobility," said Giltinė.

"Tityus son of Elara fathered by Zeus," began Giltinė. "Elara was set far below beneath Terre - Hades, maybe - from Hera. He was birthed by Gaia after he ruptured Elara's womb. Hera seeks vengeance against her consort. She influences Tityus to rape Leto who was also impregnated by Zeus giving birth to Apollo and Artemis, who were thus Tityus's half-brother and half-sister.

"It was written Artemis and Apollo slayed Tityus. It was further written Tityus, in Tartarus, was feasted upon by two vultures who did nightly dine on his liver.

"The sins of that Wretch and the sins of Her Wretchedness were unrecognized yet Tityus is punished. Apollo and Artemis were unbothered.

"That becomes metaphor of States and Citizens, Nobility and Citizens, Church and Citizens, Wars and Citizens."

"Ah, Tityus," said Mikhail. "He was neither slain nor tortured. Public announcement was all. Granny Morgue intervened." He sighed happily. "Granny Morgue." He laughed wickedly. "Granny Morgue visited with Hera who after which was not seen for several years. Granny Morgue visited Zeus who then suffered from his appendage being five feet longer than that of Priapus. It was only known after he was seen wandering in Hera's orchard with it fastened on a wheeled-contraption. He was not seen for several longer years."

"That was the reason for that sedateness of Life," said Orphiel.

"Themis Queen is like her Granny Morgue these days passing," commented Izanami no mikoto.

"She's happy," replied Zoë.

†

Fille related to Themis and Hooke how Discordia changed into an imp from the Cocytus eddy, and of Aphrodite and Athene.

"Worry about none of them," said Themis as she held the wand of Fille. "It is very old. It was once belonged by a Sorcerer who happens to be my great-great-great-granduncle. He was the Witch-King."

"Thank you," said Fille as Themis returned her the warty and burled wand of silver birch blackened by fire.

"One day you will meet him and you can thank him for having the wand made for him."

"These are thine," said Hooke as he handed thirty gold pieces to Fille who baffled took them. "Your ill-gotten gains. It was a bet I placed in your name against Athene for not being the first to curse you since she was expected to do so because of loathing you more than Hera."

"Thank you?" said Fille.

✝

Fille, Marcelle and Félix were wandering in the sixth arrondissement, l'Hôtel-de-Sens.

✝

Citizen Jean d'Aquitaine had woken from his coma. All his memories of Life were unremembered. He was become an Unfortunate: a Fée humain.

✝

Reynaerd was walking with harried haste on the rues of the le Marais quartier in the sixth arrondissement. He was searching.

✝

Fille, Marcelle and Félix were standing in a magasin on rue de la Gaîté. Hooke abruptly entered.

"Stay still!" Hooke said with his commanding tone. He pressed the index finger of his left hand over his nose and mouth.

They did.

Reynaerd entered. He raised his hands with fingers pointing at them as he would approach Fille, Marcelle and Félix.

Hooke stepped behind Reynaerd as he passed. Reynaerd collapsed. He changed.

The Nine Ravens entered. "Take them!" Fille, Marcelle and Félix were shaking. "Go!" They ran from the magasin surrounded by the nine large ravens.

"Please telephone the Mortality Brigade," said Hooke as he left.

†

Hooke was speaking with Hercule and Elfriede. They were seated in the caravan of Hercule in the parc.

"Imposteurs malefica are attempting to kidnap or kill Marcelle and Félix. They know of the protection given by the Fey-Queen and are adjusting their schemes. No place is safe for them.

"These felons may attempt influencing all who know them which is insidious and possible.

"Moreover, Imposteurs malefica have appeared at the house. It is no longer a game of defense I wish; it is one of provocation. Marcelle and Félix wish to remain in Hades which is much better than to allow them wandering.

"I would like, if you wish, because your last chivalrous act was indeed to be thy final act of chivalry, for you to perform a second last final act of chivalry. You and Marcelle and Félix are remained in danger because of what you three did in that mithraeum; all have heard of it. Thy Venus is no longer in danger; her station is known. Marcelle and Félix remain dangerous to them. Thou art mystery."

"Damaged," said Hercule. Hooke smiled. Hercule nodded.

"Hercule!" cried Elfriede. "Damaged?"

"An Équivalence," said Hooke gently calm: "No, Hercule remains Hercule."

She clutched his hand.

"It is my intent that you three are seen by all. They know little of thee. And, those who may know more, are dismissive.

"Marcelle and Félix have been given wands but they lack knowledge for use of them. They must forego all other things; instead, in these hours, they are learning the formidable arts of Sorcerie.

"They're art none other than thee I ask."

Hercule was fraught with indecision.

"Do you wish to go with them? or, wish to stay?" said Hooke gently. "It is welcomed as much if you choose to stay instead of go with them. Arrangements different will be made. That adventure in the chamber was done and so none would think—*None*—less of thee should you wish to stay with your Elfriede."

Hercule peered at Elfriede. She smiled broadly, nodding. "All is well." He thought. "Yes."

Hooke went to the table where the long polished black wood box with silver inlays he had brought with him lay. "Al-Jinn returns this." He presented it to Hercule.

Hercule opened it. It was a long thin sword. Hercule looked sadly at Hooke. "It is not your's?"

"Thine," said Hooke gently. "Remember it's name."

Hercule thought long. "I remember!" said Hercule as he gazed at Elfriede. He smiled. "It is mine." He faced Hooke. He bowed low so that his beard bent on the carpet.

"Damaged?" said Elfriede with an exasperated curiosity.

"He is fine. Her Ladyship will explain if you care to come with us."

Hercule encouragingly nodded at her. "Yes," she said smiling at him.

Hercule grinned.

Mikhail, Erlik Khan, Izanami no mikoto, Ereshkigal, Enma-Dai-Ō and Zoë were joined by Rhadamanthus.

"How came you here?" said Zoë.

"Envoys have come," said Rhadamanthus. "They are bidding on citizens to enlist in their efforts for War. Kingdom Come offers Indulgence; Hades offers amusement.

"We were dismissed.

"I thank you, Ma'am, for the recommendation of *De Caelo et Eius Mirabilibus et de inferno, ex Auditis et Visis* by Swedenborg.

"I shall have my first Holiday; and, I shall, after having begun my first, take more."

"Interesting to note, isn't it," said Enma-Dai-Ō, "how he was deemed Lunatic from visions, dementia præcox and delirium."

†

Hercule, Marcelle and Félix were in flâneries through all of High Tartarus. Marcelle wanted to view the magasin with eyes of all sizes and shapes displayed. They entered with Hercule who remained standing by the door.

"What is that?" asked Félix as she pointed at an oddly shaped eye-piece hung from the ceiling.

The proprietor—Théophile-Raymond d'Aveyron—retrieved it by use of a long pole with a hook on the end. He gestured for Félix and Marcelle to approach the vitrine on which he had set the object. It was a monocle with a stem. He twisted the bottom decoration; he twisted the stem; he slid a decoration from the side to the top of the round sterling piece holding the glass; he held it to his left eye; he adjusted a decorative bulb on the top.

Théophile-Raymond d'Aveyron handed it to Félix; she viewed the milieu of the boulevard and was increasingly stupefied.

The scene Félix viewed through that glass was rendered in light greys. Six small dark shapes were flying overhead; two darkened figures were running through the crowd.

"Spectres?" replied d'Aveyron.

"Six," said Félix.

"Likely eight," said d'Aveyron; "Those six are bluffing; another two are blind chasing."

"Two chasing," said Félix.

Félix offered the eye-piece to Marcelle.

"By setting aperture and ranges and convolutions, you may see all things which are."

"Can we do that without the eye-piece?"

"Yes, but you would have Röntgen-Ray eyes."

"A spectre is coming."

Three things happened in that instance: Hercule opened the door and flung his sword piercing the wooden boards of the floor; Félix happily exclaimed: "It's Fille!"; the movements of the character of Fille were arrested who began shrieking in the highest of woeful pitches.

"It's not," said Hercule.

Marcelle and Félix were stunned by her behavior.

"May I?" said d'Aveyron as he gently took the eye-piece from Marcelle. He twiddled the knobs; and, he peered through the glass. "Cherub."

"Cherub," agreed Hercule as he watched it.

D'Aveyron returned to the eye-piece to Marcelle who said: "Cherub."

"What should be done?" said Félix who declined Marcelle's offer of the eye-piece.

Hercule gestured them patience.

The cherub caught fire but smokeless turning into vapoury ashes.

"It's master's work," said Hercule.

†

"How fares Paris?" asked Zoë.

"The streetcars in Paris were made electric and the last horse-drawn streetcar was sent to meadows. Prime Minister Raymond Poincaré was elected as the new President of France. Aristide Briand was selected as the Prime Minister of France. The Question Roumaine remains. Tuberculose has become uncontrollable. Bulgares and Grecs are at war. Les Priseurs de Cocaine rise. Snake oil cures are popular. Séances are popular. Dames blanches are popular. And, most importantly, les Maladies de la Femme continue unabated since before Chronos," replied Giltinė.

†

They were surrounded in a ring of malebranches with axes and knives. Arrows from rooftops rained. Hercule held his sword above his head and the arrows caught flames immediately disappearing.

The malebranches were howling.

"You are safe," said Hercule peering at Félix and Marcelle who were smiling at him. He nodded.

Hercule drew a large ensō with his sword in the air above them. The bricked lane rippled from a radiance from those three. The malebranches ceased their cries.

Darkness seeped from the shadows in the darkened square. Ghôles took the assailants screaming into the sky.

"They were not requested," said Hercule perplexed.

"So now we know who watches the Night Watch," said Marcelle.

Hercule blushing smiled.

†

A gathering in secrecy of those most trusted who could attend by Themis and Hooke was held in Hooke's grand salon.

Al-Jinn, le Maréchal, Hades; Prometheus, Hypnos, Pasithea, Dolos and Hermes; Ivos; several of the officers of le Maréchal; Marchosias, King Belial, Baell, the three Kings of Hell, and Andromalius the Earl; Azazil, Orphiel, Samael, Ursumael, Cestisael, Maliqeel and Shamazya; Queen Joan, Maeve, Titania and Obéron; Fille, Tochi no akaru-sa, Marcelle, Félix were seated together with Elfriede and Hercule who was seated beside her at the end.

Milot, Jules, Nolan and Tempérance Hiolle were seated in the center. The Head Constable stood beside them for wont of familiar faces.

"Marcelle. Félix." Hooke politely gestured for them to stand.

They stood embarrassed.

"These are they," said Hooke. "Thank you, Mademoiselles."

They sat.

The Head Constable stated there were two suspected: Auns and Cimeries. "They cannot be found."

"We have begun," said le Maréchal. Cestisael said les Tempéraments would search for them as well.

"We will search the territoires, but it is doubtful," said Maeve. "We know none of those are in the kingdoms."

"All the more reason it must be thorough," replied Hooke. "Milot l'Historien, Jules le Cartographe and C. L. Nolan–the Illapses Agency, Ltd.–with assistance from Hiolle have uncovered another possibility," said Hooke. "Gentlemen?"

Milot, Jules and Nolan stared at Hiolle who stood, smiling.

"It appears a deity is involved somehow in this affaire," said Hiolle. "Messrs. Milot, Jules and Nolan were in the saloon–Conteville–Brigadier Fontaine had taken them after their visit with the Constabulary. They overheard a conversation sporadically, with great difficulty, amidst songs sung and the common raucousness of that place. Those who spoke spoke in harsh tones but unnaturally which further made foreign words and names unintelligible. Minister Thoas said that the large figure cloaked smelled of Nubilus but from the East; he immediately left. Brigadier Fontaine concurred and also noted that the smaller cloaked figure spoke a recitation on the act of castration.

"Milot understood some words; Jules recognized the place they secretly spoke in cypher. Nolan remembered a mysterious visitor who was standing with another in the Library of Achéron; it was similar words: 'curse,' 'conjuration,' 'invocation,' 'purify,' 'eminence.'"

Hiolle pointed at Milot. "The words?"

Milot stood and read from his small calepin: "'Holiness,' 'children,' 'dark,' 'Chang'e,' 'imperative,' 'lord,' 'queen,' 'treachery,' 'treason,' 'sickle,' 'castrate,' 'urinate,' and 'vengeance;' Minister Thoas informed me of these: 'purificabimus,' 'Ἄρης,' 'Nestis,' 'voyageur waits.' Brigadier Fontaine informed me of this: 'Munkar Nakir wait.'" He sat.

"The place?"

Jules stood and said: "Elysion pyr." He sat as an audible murmur filled the salle.

"You are without doubt of this?" said Ursumael.

Jules stood. "Yes, Highness. An archaïc name never to be known was spoken heard."

Ursumael nodded. Orphiel smiled. Ursumael, Cestisael, Maliqeel and Shamazya whispered amoungst themselves. Jules sat.

"Your remembrance?"

Nolan stood. He explained he had been reading a national newspaper while seated at the station. "It was an interesting article about the rise of Spiritualisme in the colonies on Speculae. It reminded me of the conversation in the Library when we had gone several days after our arrival at Lord Hooke's request finding answers for a question he had. I was seated at a table; those conversing were standing in an aisle. One had a voice I somewhat recognized in the saloon Conteville. They spoke about a great Spiritualist seer I did not know of– Orobas."

He was interrupted by the cacophony of the angels and demons laughing. Nolan stood uncomfortably embarrassed.

"No. No, it's not you. Orobas is a charlatan," said Marchosias. "That a deity would believe those words of his is laughable."

Hooke gestured for Nolan to sit; he gratefully did.

"Our ploy."

All were intrigued.

"Her Majesty, al-Jinn, le Maréchal d'Empire and I are engaged. Hercule is the only other I consider entrusting their Fate. Hercule is their protector." Hooke peered at them. "Le Trio diabolique return." Al-Jinn laughed; le Maréchal chortled; Ivos smiled. "However, if le Maréchal has an expert in skullduggery, we may bait for something greater with the assistance of Dolos."

Dolos, amused with subtle malice, nodded.

"Ivos," said le Maréchal. "How long before the lads can be assembled dressed the same as on Terre at camp?"

"They've gone scattered over the four different lands," said Ivos standing. "Half and a day? Three?"

"Very good," said le Maréchal. "I shall look for you and your lads in six hours."

Ivos saluted and hurriedly took his exit.

"I request," said Hades as he stood facing Hooke and Themis Queen, "I request — I do not command, I do not order — I request those caught in this act of Villainy are given sentence so that others may be terror-filled by it from the evils committing these crimes referred on these Sphæres."

"Your Majesty," said Ursumael as he stood; "We do wish as well this regardless of station."

Hooke stood. He faced Themis who nodded in her capacity as Queen. He bowed from his shoulders. "'Tis done."

"What do you propose?" asked Hades.

Hooke smiled.

✝

Hercule, Félix and Marcelle made a habit of walking to the square where they took leisure at the Miser Abels statue in the fountain of Persephone in Lower Tartarus before wandering off into the Night.

✝

The Flying Squad found Orobas. They studied his habits. He frequented with precise regularity *l'Arbre Chantant* in the Bilooghedeop quartier in the département of Tartarus; Dolos composing set the ruse.

One night, two of the Squad were seated in a booth next to the table at which Orobas was taking supper. They spoke of innocuous things until lowering their voices to speak about rumours of two girls with the powers of the Deity. Orobas listened closely. A third from the Squad joined them.

"Those girls were seen in Artuaś. They destroyed it."

"I heard that spirits came taking the ghosts of everyone."

"Inspectors - though this hasn't been made public - found teeth all over the hamlet but no bodies."

"One of Lord Hooke's contes!"

"Likely taught them that, No?"

"A mate who'd seen it told me 'fore they vanished those two were surrounded by black and green flames."

"Scary."

"Why?"

"Witch-Queen does that."

"She was there?"

"Girls alone."

"Lord Hooke and her taught them well."

"Terrifying, ain't it."

They spoke of other things.

Orobas sprinted to the telephone; he spoke a number. He waited. "I have visions." He related the stories of mayhem.

Orobas drove his curricle there to Artuaś where he collected handfuls of teeth. It was as spoken in *l'Arbre Chantant*. He frantically drove to the gates of Dis. A figure was waiting in the shadows.

"I came to tell you they were truthful," said Orobas as he presented those teeth. "My visions cannot lie."

†

Hercule, Félix and Marcelle continued their habit of walking to the square where they took leisure at the fountain of Persephone before going elsewhere from where they had come. They would come by way of the Well; or, they would come by way of the Pier with a Lamp; or, they would come by way of the Drawbridge.

They always lingered at the fountain.

†

Ivos was speaking with Hooke who was idly standing on the grand staircase beneath the arch with a shell ornament in Lower Tartarus. He spoke of the adventure of Theodosius Hallow and his conspirators who would perform as haruspices inspecting those with la Supériorité humaine.

"Even jelly coals," repeated Hooke.

"That's what he said," replied Ivos. "He's been rightly asking permission since that first encounter in the county."

Hooke thought. He suddenly began laughing.

"Sir?"

"Yes," said Hooke, "they are the ideal of la Supériorité humaine beffiting."

Hooke explained.

"Charity personified," said Ivos. "They'll be pleased." He bowed and went.

†

Orobas was seated in *l'Arbre Chantant* listening to the conspirators at the adjacent table. Two more joined them with news that those girls were seen wandering near Speculae.

"They're intended destroying it!"

Hermes appeared. He went to Orobas.

"You are Orobas?"

"Yes."

"The Queen has summoned you."

Orobas paled.

"What is it?" demanded one of the Flying Squad.

"Orobas foretold, in a state of enthusiasmos, Mœrae would be transformed into... hat-boxes. They were! They sit on the mantle of the Queen yet have no hats!"

"I do not remember saying so," protested Orobas.

"How could you!" retorted Hermes; "You were in a state of enthusiasmos! Four nights from this!" Hermes handed Orobas a card; it was from the Queen.

Hermes left.

"I'm glad I'm not going to see her after what she did to the traitor Glasya-Labolas."

"What did she do?" asked Orobas.

"He's a doily on her royal foot-rest!" shouted Ivos.

Orobas thanked them as he staggered away.

"Doily?" declared one the squad while all did uproariously laugh.

"Why not?" said Ivos. "My Gran's got one on her's."

†

They were accosted as they watched the Smoking Fire.

†

Mikhail, Izanami no mikoto, Ereshkigal, Enma-Dai-Ō and Rhadamanthus were conversing with Zoë for Erlik Khan had made his farewells departing.

"There are few in the meadows of Asphodel who have taken draught from the Lethe," said Rhadamanthus; "Those Odysseus met were common folk besotted on Ignorance; their true form shown."

"Much like Thyiades taken ritual into their murderous euphoria where their true form is seen," said Ereshkigal.

"There is a singular aspect of ignorant folk in Asphodel and mænads set in euphoria by Dionysus which you do not appear to acknowledge," said Zoë.

"Ma'am?"

"Ignorant folk are driven into mænadic frenzy when their Dionysus wishes they be so," replied Zoë.

"Aye."

They were accosted as they paused at the Pier with a Lamp.

✝

Orobas entered *l'Arbre Chantant*. All in that place were speaking different stories of what they'd heard or seen. The girls - Félix and Marcelle - were Titanesses. They had made sacrifices of the angels who lived in the territoires. They discussed feats of horror not ever before seen.

One of the fellows went to Orobas.

"Pardon, sir. I've been told you are the Great Orobas the Seer."

Orobas stood and melodramatically bowed.

"Do Psychics know of Physics and Physis?"

"The Pythia and myself are those single two who do."

He was asked to join. They discussed with him the events unfolding.

"They've crossed the boundary of the territory and were seen wandering in the snow deserts seeking victims for sacrifice."

"I wager they're intending marching right up on to the tenth circle."

"Yeah. Lucky for them les Īnsēparābilis only do their damage every three nights."

"Do you know where they next go?"

"I shall know," said Orobas as he rose from the table. "I must consult."

He hurriedly left.

✝

Orobas sped to the rendez-vous.

"It was agreed that it must end this before the third night rises," said the figure. "The visions of Orobas are nothing but triumph and truth."

†

"That?" said Fille after two Serpents flew down to an angel amidst the battle decapitating and rending it's body into mince.

"Theurgy," replied Themis. "Theurgy and Goëtia are forbidden during this amusement. There have been many punishments meted on the sides of these two nations. That explains your next query of why have those Seven not appeared."

"Oh."

†

Hercule was walking with Marcelle and Félix. They entered the square with the fountain of Persephone. Marcelle and Félix fainted. They were confronted by a Hallow malveillance and a deity.

There was a great commotion surrounding them. They were encircled by the sounds of battle.

Hercule drew his sword slashing at the head of the Hallow.

The Saint stumbled as the left side of it's face was set afire; it's breastplate shattered by the trailing blow: it fell onto one knee.

The deity, by the arc of the blade of Hercule, was fatally wounded and fell backwards.

Angels, demons and ghouls were being wounded and killed by the forces Hooke and le Maréchal had assembled: angels, demons, géants, Fey, and a few deities.

The deity was attempting rise but al-Jinn stepped from the shadows and lifted with his left hand the deity by the throat. "Phobos."

Le Maréchal confronted l'Hallow malveillance.

"I will not be taken," said l'Hallow malveillance brandishing it's sword.

"Maliel-pyr," said le Maréchal as his harpe with fury severed the left arm of Maliel-pyr which dropped it's sword and held it's bleeding shoulder. "Aye. I cannot render you as eye and teeth like they; but thy head lofted I can do." Le Maréchal, with the hilt of his sword, struck l'Hallow in it's throat: it staggered blindly until it fell.

Al-Jinn flung the body of Phobos on to the collapsed Maliel-pyr.

Prometheus stepped forward. He cauterized the wound of Maliel-pyr and resurrected Phobos. Hypnos stepped forward; he placed them in a faint trance of sleep. Pasithea stood from the crowd; she cursed them with visions. Hooke went to them; he stared with curious thoughts of Reason and Logic before he shrugged and walked from them: they wavered transparent in faint faltering light before vanishing.

"Where?" asked Pasithea of Hooke as he passed through the lane the crowd had made for him.

"Malevolences."

†

Fire-brigades, ambulances, doctors and nurses had been alerted before that scene began; they rushed to the areas on fire and to those in caught in the Inferno.

The doctors and nurses from the Sanity Corps were flying about assisting and attending as they may those who fainted when the archange of Pyr appeared.

Hooke stood beside Hercule as Marcelle and Félix were sitting but swooned, tended by Themis and Lady Constance, were recovering from the appearance of the Saint. Hooke was smiling. "'Tis over," he said as he leaned close to those three.

Marcelle and Félix were assisted in standing; and, did silently stand in wonder.

Hercule smiled.

†

The legions of le Maréchal caught all who would flee. All were made exemplars regardless of station.

†

Hooke, Themis, Marcelle, Félix, Fille, Tochi no akaru-sa, Elfriede, Hercule, Hermes, Ivos and al-Jinn were standing at the fountain of Persephone.

"If Phobos had not been with that Saint of Pyr, you would have done greater damage to it," said Ivos. "The fact you could make stumble the Saint was remarkable. I've seen no other do that." He bowed from his shoulders, grinning.

"You knew I could that do?" said Hercule gazing at Hooke.

"No. I suspected; but did not know," said Hooke. "I knew you would protect them."

Elfriede squeezed his hand.

"He knew," whispered Hercule smiling at Elfriede.

"Those teeth?" asked Hermes.

"Skulls, calvaria, dentists, all manner of teeth. All manner of Fauna provided," replied Themis. "It was sprites who laid the teeth and sylphs who carried the folk from the villages."

"Black and green flames?" asked Tochi no akaru-sa.

"We did that! Except it wasn't what she did when she does it," said Marcelle as she pointed at Themis.

"Side-Show trick," said al-Jinn. Themis nodded.

"We did set fire with our wands," said Félix.

"Not fire really," said Marcelle. "It was like a lava-fire we did."

"Lava covered everything," said Félix giggling.

"Why couldn't anyone approach?" asked Fille.

"Cardinal points," said Themis. "His Lordship at the West and I at the East stood ghost-like facing each other: we created a one-mile wide dome over them and us so none could come."

"How did you know?" asked Fille.

"All of what Misters Nolan, Milot and Jules noted were of importance," said Hooke. "However– vengeance, Ἄρης, Nestis, Elysion pyr and Orobas were most informative.

"Those others were concerned with Her Majesty and myself. We were to be purified by Death: Munkar Nakir wait, lord, queen, treachery, treason are so. Purificabimus is a common word amoungst Hallows. Holiness is a common word amoungst deities when referring to Hallows.

"Children, dark, Chang'e, imperative, purificabimus were related with Félix and Marcelle. They were to be Oblivion sent during the full Moon of Chang'e. For what reason they did not murder you, we shall not know; but they had been seeking you ever since.

"Vengeance, Ἄρης, Nestis, and Elysion pyr indicated who would be in league with the deity acting in vengeance.

"Ἄρης–Ares–had lost in his attempts raping Nestis, Persephone. It was an act of vengeance to be performed by one of his children who believed she had with Ares performed the act of castration that was done to Ouranos."

"Sir?" said Ivos.

"Sickle, castrate, urinate, vengeance."

"Urinate," said Themis incredulous.

"It's very simple," said Hooke merry. "Milot heard Ouranos in the saloon. He wrote in his small calepin 'Ouréōanos.' Ouréō – 'to urinate' – is what he spoke when standing in terror in that hall of formidable Wights."

"How did you deduce that?" asked al-Jinn slowly with humourous suspicion.

"After removing all things not possible, that final possibility - no matter how fanciful, improbable, ridiculous or lunatic - is the answer," said Hooke. They stared. "I asked him."

"Orobas?" asked Fille.

"Orobas was the dupe," said Ivos laughing still from Hooke's reply. "He demanded payment for his clandestine performance in apprehending the villains; he, at present, has a shoe-shine stand in the vilest of quartiers in Tartarus on Irae."

"All was revealed," said Hooke. "Marcelle and Félix are safe. Marcelle's exploits with Dionysus are still witnessed by many so that they are not doubted for their acts of vengeance, as adroitly rendered by Ivos and his fellows, on behalf of Limbe, since they, Marcelle and Félix, are believed to be two of the same. Hercule is safe not because ghôles were seen in his company but for his duel with the Saint of Pyr and the death of Phobos: his mysteriousness has towering grown.

"All is done; and, so ends all."

Themis and Louis-Aldonse Milot were walking accompanied by a woman pushing the wheelchair of a stern-appearing gentleman who was agog at all that was to be seen—meandering pleasantly in the park in Bucarest.

Mr. Frederick Hills, Bedellus was stately promenading on the High Lane. He spied them; and, waited. "Ma'am?"

"Beadle Hills!" said Themis in her good humour. "You are—it does seem—goodly well and well met, my dear sir."

"And you Ma'am are as gracious as ever!" he laughed. "You've not been to this place before."

"I have twice," said Themis; "but was not accompanied by one who is familiar."

"Well! May I escort you and these fine guests for a proper excursion?"

"Our pleasure," she replied delighted. She introduced Milot; his mother, Béatrice Étiennette Milot; and his father, Christophe-Victor-Louis Milot.

"Lovely," said Beadle Hills as he began walking with them.

Milot viewed Beadle Hills with piqued curiosity. "Good Sir," said Milot, "If I may be allowed, I would ask of you a question with impertinence in this our mere introduction."

"By all means," said Beadle Hills.

"I read a short article in the *Hookland Standard* and, in that article, it stated you were once the beadle in Hook until 1838 last seen, according to the written accounts of witnesses interviewed, speaking with a regal woman dressed in grey," said Milot; "Have you been here since then?"

"No," replied Beadle Hills.

"If I may," continued Milot; "The *Hookland Standard* also noted an apparition of you was briefly seen walking on Thorn Street in 1911."

"Oh?" said Beadle Hills interested: "I have been here since 1911."

"It went further to say you were no longer seen after 1917," said Milot.

Beadle Hills thought.

"Perhaps, you thought of that place longingly or fondly while making rounds here," suggested Madame Milot. "It was the strength of those thoughts which caused a ghost of yourself to appear in that remembrance."

"I do quite often," said Beadle Hills. "Fifty years I made those walks in Hook. One does not readily forget fifty fond years of memories."

"Senses," said Monsieur Milot, "work in mysterious ways, do they not. I am bewildered here but in a highly delightful manner. It's as though I have been here - I cannot say that I have not but I cannot recall - but it is not someplace I would have ever thought to visit."

"Then," offered Madame Milot, "after 1917, this place replaces Hookland as home."

"My pleasantness's returning," replied Beadle Hills. "So— Yes, slowly and surely I believe it will."

"Mrs. Hills?" asked Themis.

"She was endeared the moment she arrived!" said Beadle Hills. "She formed a Ladies Voluntary. Most formidable they are."

"Aren't they all," noted Christophe-Victor-Louis Milot.

Madame Milot winked at Themis who nodded smiling her reply.

†

Mikhail, Izanami no mikoto, Ereshkigal, Enma-Dai-Ō and Rhadamanthus were continued on the High Road with Zoë.

Orphiel returned with Morana whom he had met at the demise of Phobos and Maliel-pyr.

"Dolos and his trickery," said Orphiel, "had exposed Phobos in that plot against those damsel-witches. Maliel-pyr was known only after his appearance at the miserable fountain."

"Maliel-pyr," said Mikhail. "He's gone where?"

"Abyssal Dark," replied Orphiel.

"His Lordship has been roused," said Mikhail.

"Yes," said Zoë; "but fury incensed is much more accurate for his state in these hours."

Mikhail stared at her.

"The Seven Palaces of Depravity he laid waste and ruin," replied Orphiel. "Les Dépravés were sent for Penance or they may stroll to the river Lethe was told to me by Gēnijssgoinneil. Olympe was forewarned by a terror of lightning and thunder."

Mikhail, Izanami no mikoto, Ereshkigal, Enma-Dai-Ō and Rhadamanthus stood shocked with amazements.

"How many others I should wonder," mused Mikhail.

"Les Tempéraments search," said Orphiel. "We should go."

"Let us tarry a few more leagues before we do," said Mikhail.

Orphiel agreed.

†

"I want you to keep this for me," said Hercule as he would present Hooke with his sword.

Hooke smiled.

"If you could," said Hooke as he gestured Elfriede and Hercule to follow him. He led them down one floor and through a long corridor which ended at a wall. A door appeared as Hooke drew near. It opened. He gestured for them to enter. They were standing in the foyer of the Théâtre Hercule and Elfriede had known on Terre.

"I do not; but there is one who does."

They went to the statue. It was leaning holding it's empty hand down to Hercule; the other hand still clutched the dagger of Hooke.

Hercule presented the sword to the statue which took and held it and crossed it's arms over it's breast. It stared at Hercule until—Finally—it closed reopening it's eyes slowly. It resumed it's proper countenance and demeanor.

Hercule bowed.

"Which way?" asked Hercule.

"This way," said Hooke as they returned to the alcove through which they stepped. A passage was revealed.

They entered.

They were standing in Hercule's caravan.

"If I should need use of it?" said Hercule.

"It will show you," said Hooke fondly as he looked around the caravan; "but that day shall never come though Tenebris may well be visiting when in need of a worthy opponent for a game of chess."

"How do you return, Sir?" asked Elfriede.

"I shall find a way," said Hooke merry; "but for now, I have an engagement in the parc." He went and opened the door of the caravan. Themis was waiting at the bottom of the steps. He turned. "If you should like, we are staying at Bra\ele Silen\ioase in town and would very much welcome your company later this evening." He bowed and descending went with Themis arm-in-arm through the parc.

"He knew," said Elfriede.

Hercule nodded.

†

Huillard le Sénateur-Maire was discussing the parc with Hooke, Themis, Elfriede and Milot.

"The boulevards here and in the cité are electrical with Yablochkov candles. All electrical things are worked from Gramme machines and dynamos.

"Gas lit lamps are standard on other lanes of passage. Lamps in windows are still required by law.

"Carré ice-making machines are popular."

They continued as Huillard continued speaking on the amenities of Modern Age used in the earlier epochs.

✝

They passed an arcade where Fille, Félix, Marcelle and Tochi no akaru-sa were in fits of laughter.

The Daedalus Flying Academy

It was a six-storey structure with numerous huge iron flowers not unlike a hearing trumpet or fluted sound horn on a record device set on the exterior.

It was open during Winter only when the North winds were blowing into the trumpets and exiting by way of jets aligned upwards enabling courageous visitors wearing large bat or bird wings to experience flying unattached by wires and pulleys.

"The Icarus Academy is that balloon," said Huillard as he pointed to the large Rozière balloon suspended three miles in the sky. "Hercule?"

"Hercule was uncomfortable as a Gentleman-of-Leisure so he became the Constablery of the Parc," said Elfriede.

The long line of schoolchildren from the l'Hôpital Titania were waiting patiently to fly: Boreas had come so they could fly.

"How very odd," said Milot as they passed. "I would never have believed fairies could be so suited to have deformed children. All the while living in Nature."

Immediately, Hooke turned and, with his right hand, took Milot by the lapels of his coat. He turned to face an appalled Themis. "Excuse us." They vanished.

✝

Mikhail, Orphiel, Izanami no mikoto, Morana, Ereshkigal, Enma-Dai-Ō, Maeve le Dullahan, and Rhadamanthus were promenading with Zoë.

"Collective consciousness," said Mikhail.

"Totems," said Izanami no mikoto.

"Anthropomorphism," said Ereshkigal.

"Apotheosis," said Enma-Dai-Ō.

"Subdued hysteria of Masses," said Rhadamanthus.

"Speculative Madness," said Zoë, "where they, it may be noted, have invented a myth, which we call an illusion, in the vain hope that their superior judgment will make it disappear. It is the time-hallowed archetypal dream, which may or may have not been given them by Génie, of a Golden Age or Paradise, where everything was provided in abundance for everyone, and a great, just, and wise Mystery rules over them."

"Ma'am?" said Morana.

"Innate knowledge is as clever as it is insidious," said Zoë. "They knew nothing of Physics or Physis so looked amoungst themselves with curiosity and they looked about their places with curiosity until they, by inventions, invented wise Mysteries spread by words until they, with persistent propaganda, had resolved all mysteries.

"The spectacular théâtre of Myth is far more beguiled and captivating than Nature with it's simple laws of Mechanics and Physics, isn't it."

Huillard and Elfriede had departed with Heads of State desirous of their expertise. Hooke returned to where Themis had remained.

"He is in the Titania Hospital where she is leading him through the wards of Unfortunates who were formed by the whims of heredity as well as those poisoned in vivo by Man," said Hooke. "He did apologise." Hooke sighed. "He said: 'I only meant to say that they must have done something to cause such things.' I could not speak."

"Titania sadly loosened your hand and sent you away," said Themis.

Hooke nodded.

They strolled aimlessly.

"Why was Hercule's sword kept from him?" said Themis.

"Long ago," said Hooke, "we realised he had found contentment as that wight he had become. Al-Jinn was first to worry he would remember all things that he no longer was and no longer wished to be should his sword be returned. And, so— my dagger replaced his sword."

"What changed?" said Themis.

He abruptly stopped. He attempted not to laugh while she did so too not attempt to laugh.

"Well!"

"He does wear the delicate culottes his betrothed sewed for him," said Hooke. "So?"

"He found joyful contentment," said Themis.

"Verily," said Hooke.

They strolled happily.

†

"Ferris Wheel!" said Themis as she grasped Hooke's hand and began running with him running beside in her laughter.

†

Hooke and Themis were wandering when they spied Hades standing in the lane. He looked up.

"Thank you," said Hades.

"Why are you standing here?" said Hooke.

"I was told you were here," said Hades, "and thought, before Percy and I should be away from the kingdom and it's indignant war for a length of time, I would say that to you. We go to Paris."

"Dame Hades?" asked Themis.

"She's conflicted. She is pleased that that vengeance was made against those two girls in the honour of her because of *her* refusal of the advances of Ares; yet guilty for being pleased that that vengeance was against those two girls who are to be Sisters of Benevolence. Sweet and bitter are her thoughts these days."

"And, you?" said Themis.

"Pleased," replied Hades.

Themis nodded; but was puzzled by his reply.

"Where do you go?" asked Hades.

"Zhį'ii-tsintah," said Hooke.

"After war ebbs?"

"We haven't thought so far."

"You are welcome to visit during your self-imposed exile."

"We may," replied Themis.

"Madame Hades had wished that for centuries," said Hooke. "It was opportune that she could do so."

"She is pleased," said Hades. "Madame?"

"Themis Witch-Queen has deceased; she believed it unwarranted was. She resides as Queen," said Themis. "Caroline d'Eirene concerns herself with the lands in the oceans and Asia; Dame Hinojosa and Dame Gallardo, America. Mary la Toute-Douée and Guenevere de Sens, Europe and Africa. All will assist them with common tasks.

"The intrigues ended and this one-hundred and fifty year war have brought calm."

"Thee?" asked Hades.

"Foolishness," replied Hooke.

"Reasonable."

They continued strolling with the silence of their thoughts.

†

Themis and Hooke were at playing in a billiard hall.

Athene entered and she went to Hooke who stood with a very faint smile as she began poking his chest with her healed finger.

"I am cured!"

Athene continued poking and jabbing Hooke with her finger. Hooke stared with mild amusement at her.

Athene watched her finger metamorphose; none but her could see. She fled, screaming.

"Why?" asked Hooke smiling as he and Themis turned.

"Why?" replied Morgause as she thought with one eye closed frowning. "I haven't a clue." She laughed.

"Those are best," replied Hooke.

They exited.

"Her spells'll be faulty."

"I imagine so."

"Where's Father?"

"Shall we see?"

†

"We thank you, Ma'am," said Orphiel as he and Mikhail bowed before Zoë. "We must away to Orbisalius."

Zoë nodded, smiling.

They departed.

†

"How did you know we were playing billiards?" asked Hooke.

"I overheard Murmur le Duc tell Athene he had seen you. I followed her since I was looking for you.

"Sumōkusunēku is an interesting spell, isn't it," said Morgause. "An illusion formed by the thoughts of those enchanted."

"Where do you take us?" asked Themis.

"Your Father wished less of Seer telling," said Morgause as they went on rue Na'iidzeeł. "He has been kept with that thought for some while; and, when he learned of this impending parc, he wished to participate in a fashion suited for Common folk."

†

They had come to the simple arcade.

Moemoea Scrying

By Appointment Only

They entered.

†

It was a sparse setting. Seventeen steps led to an elevated rectangular base on which was a couch, a partitioning screen, and a comfortable club chair on the opposite side of the screen. Scrims were hung along the walls.

He was dressed in a simple suit of black with a well-starched white shirt.

"It is grand Théâtre," said Virge as he sat on the steps. "They expect something arcane. Illusionary. I'll show you."

He went to the back room. He pulled levers and turned knobs on the panel. He illuminated the stage lights. Mirrors on the ceiling were exposed. The room was darkened by shadows. They fluttered. His shadows on the scrims wavered from breezes unfelt.

The chamber grew cold from hidden vents fed by a Carré ice-making machine.

"It's effective," said Virge as he returned sitting on the couch beside Morgause. "The room is set before they come. I escort them to the couch. We chat. I explain the process occurring; and, I ask what they wish. Great wealth is common; riches is scarce; simple happiness is rare.

"I inform them I must sit behind the screen so my true self may not be seen. It's different for everyone.

"Air jets and fans move the curtains so the silhouettes can move.

"They tell me things of dreams they've had.

"'Portendo!' A puff of smoke. These lights dims. I hurry to the back room. My note flutters down from above them. They take my note.

"I pull a lever opening the front door.

"They exit.

"I pull a lever closing the door. I pull a second lever bolting it.

"I choose what I believe will better their lives. It is those fateful encounters given by fleeting thoughts most have ignored I offer them with engagement. I warn them. It is written on a card. If they remember or ignore it is up to them.

"One of my first guests – a stone mason – wanted something he could not articulate as much as he tried to say. His was quite simple: 'Jongleurs Arcade. Night. Thursday. Outside remain. Apprehend who runs.'"

"What did happen?" asked Morgause.

"I waited at the arcade on that Thursday. I stood in the shadows to see.

"He did so and waited. A pickpocket stole an object from a widow in the arcade. She screamed. The mason caught him as he was fleeing from the entrance. Patrons came. The widow followed. Her memento was returned. She thanked him. The mason and the widow are happily ever after."

Morgause turned embracing him; and, kissed his cheek. "My sentimental darling."

†

Hooke and Themis with her Mother and Father went passing by an arcade of dreams as they went to Brațele Silențioase in town.

†

They continued on their way passing by an arcade where dreams were photographed.

Spectralröntgenphotography

For time-resolved refractions of the séance-induced

By the reknowned Sephosupholeme Method
Hereforeto Unknown and almost Incredible
Monolithic Platinotypelumière Images

Under the distinguished guidance of Professor Grieves
Extraordinary Event at an Enormous Expense of

Marvells
Revealed

By particular request, Messers G & Co., will after the public display, give a private Séance in the manner of their Studies.

†

Hercule and Elfriede were strolling through the parc on their way to visit with Themis and Hooke at Brațele Silențioase in town. They passed the wight that stood on the avenue with the letter-pressed panels of advertisements over his shoulders. The panels stated:

A
Delightful – DISTINGUISHED – Delirious

Absolutely Unequaled
ARCADE
The Witch's Triumphant Sabbat Ride
It relieves Distresses from Mental and Physickal Exhaustions
&
'tis warranted to be indispensable
against Pychosis'd Anima
at Every Individuals Performance
of
Life Passage
6c

†

They ascended the traboule in the Montée du Cascade quartier of the parc to the arcade Elfriede did seek.

The arcade was a very large hall with a twenty-foot-high ceiling. The glass-paneled doors had been unshuttered so all passers-by could view the splendour of the arcade.

The Flights Nocturnus

They were greeted by the Proprietor, Alfonso Margrave. The placard at the entrance was painted:

Entrance, 6 c
Bat, 10 c
Raven, 20 c
Black Cat Familier, 10 c
Black Silk Conical Hat, 50 c
Witch-Queen Crown, 10 fr.
Flying Ointment, 20 fr.
A Photograph [Gratis]

The backdrops were changed for preference: a full Moon in the Spring; a full Moon in Winter; and, a dark night of lightning and thunder and rain.

Two methods of flight were given: a giant taxidermied bat with saddle and reins; or, a giant taxidermied owl with saddle and reins. A black cat would sit behind them.

The bat and owl were suspended by wires from mechanisms of clockworks and tracks and springs. They circled the arcade with a gentle rolling as if flying over the swells and downs of the sea.

"If I may, Madame, who has sent you to this place?" asked Alfonso Margrave, Proprietor.

"Madeleine Brune," replied Elfriede, "who was a visitor."

He gestured his ignorance.

"She is a chambermaid who keeps in the company of Her Sorcière Majesty."

He blanched. He made his obsequience saying "Enter" with his face faced to the ground.

They entered.

The Ticket-Attendant frowned; the Photographer blustered; and, the Advertiser set aside his boards and would hastily flee from the quartier Montée du Cascade.

"It is a simple affaire: you select an owl or bat," began Margrave.

"No side-saddle?" interrupted Elfriede.

"No. Witches are immoral. The naked witch places flying ointment on the saddle they sit astride. That is how they take flight."

Hercule frowned with severe deportment.

"You disrobe and choose the conical hat or crown," continued Margrave; "You decide if a black cat should accompany you. All femmes have chosen flying ointment. The photograph is exposed."

"What purpose?" asked Elfriede.

"Discreet memento."

"If I wished would you wish to have me seated naked on a bat or an owl photographed for you?" she asked Hercule.

"No."

"Why?" asked Margrave.

"I shall not forget," said Hercule. "I have watched Beauty bathing rising from the Ocean as Venus does at the rise of twilight from the waves of Marvells in the light of the jealous Moon."

Elfriede blushed. She composed herself.

"You sign a single carte of name and adresse," continued Proprietor Margrave. "Secrecy given. Payment is received. The package is sent by messenger; or, it may be taken after printing from here. Most delicate."

"Mademoiselle Brune was sent letters of delicate extortion with a series of indelicate photographs she could not remember posing. Others were sent letters as well. This is not to be allowed."

"Who might you be?" asked Proprietor Margrave with grave reluctance.

"This suffices," said Elfriede as she presented Margrave with a twice-folded paper.

"We did not know," groveled Proprietor Margrave after reading the paper signed by the Provincial Gouverneur; and, marked with the sigil of the Queen.

"It is well that femmes - admirable femmes, pretty femmes, naughty femmes, noble femmes, all femmes - would want to ... perform ... here for the delight of themselves and others. That is their's."

"This affair Nocturnus cannot continue. The arcade will be closed and open later. Properly."

She went to the street with Alfonso Margrave, Proprietor. Honos the Brave was holding the Sandwich-Board Fellow. The Photographer and Ticket-Attendant were apprehended exiting by a malebranche waiting behind the structure for them.

The arcade was shuttered and locked by Hercule who had pick-pocketed the keys from Margrave. Those four were led away by Honos the Brave and Brogilos the Scirgerefa.

Hercule and Elfriede went with the black cat following after.

†

Hercule and Elfriede were standing on the pavement across the rue from Braţele Silenţioase.

"Do you know what I see when you stand from your bath?" said Elfriede.

"My scars."

"Yes, they are there. No— I see a knight-errant of noble ways who has come from a river of Enchantment after defending a kingdom from foul things."

They kissed.

Hercule turned to the cat and gestured for it to wait. It tilted it's head before it lept on to the low wall, curled and went to sleep.

Hercule and Elfriede crossed the rue.

"What is it's name?" said Elfriede.

"I will ask on our way home."

†

Hooke, Themis, Morgause and Virge with Hercule and Elfriede had had a wonderfully merry evening.

†

Zoë with Morana, Rhadamanthus and Hine-nui-te-pō were seated in the coach while Mors and Thanatos sat on the back bench as they went in Rhadamanthus's traveling coach-and-four.

"For centuries, on the four continents, of persecution has Man engaged xenophobia on they deemed barbarians and savages in Terra nullius, because of their sacred beliefs, profane beliefs and heritage; and, so— they were born to be enslaved.

"And, for those who would not be enslaved nor colonised with the systematic suppression of ideas on the basis of their origin, the systematic murder of all possible folk in that Terra nullius commenced.

"Fey have experienced Man's xenophobia.

"There is a divine all-consuming hatred which hasn't a name. Some respond to trespassers with cautious kindness; some, self-seclusion; some, murder.

"Those who are vengeful were once kindly but Man's efforts for their demise continued until all Man was villain.

"For those of Fey vengeful, they often will be calm or kept under watch by less vengeful - all Fey are vengeful - to keep Man and Fey safe from harm."

"It's quaintly charming," interjected Rhadamanthus, "how bones are deemed significant when they haven't clues of who was - Actually - buried."

"I was once told by Themis Queen," said Morana, "they once buried an Irish goat who died of very old age in a grave with a stone identifying it as a witch. Men graverobbed it. They were triumphant in their beliefs it was a witch. Her true shape was revealed. That skeleton is in a museum somewhere as proof of knowledge witches exist." She sighed. "Ignorance must be a blessing since most are esteemed by Ignorance. Covetous and fearful they are which is such an amusing pair of Senses for these masses to hold dear."

"Fey have often cast spells on those who would be Inquisitors. Morigena was ruthless against them. She allowed herself to be caught. They became lunatic in their speech and act but clarity of thought remained: they - hopeless and helpless - witnessed their own demise. They themselves were tortured for confession and burned.

"Those gentle souls who would meet them in kindness are treated by vengeful Fey to death: their rage no longer knows differences between the good or the depravity of evil found in Man; or, Celestes."

"They cannot be blamed but should be forgiven," said Zoë: "it has become the systematic murder—by the Avaricious—of all folk on Terre all the while knowing it shall become existing in Reality as Terra nullius."

†

Hercule and Elfriede were being led in procession to the caravan of Hercule by the black cat.

"Moritasgus," said Hercule.

"What does it mean?" asked Elfriede.

"It is Gaulish. Great Badger."

Moritasgus paused and turned to face them. It nodded knowingly.

They continued.

†

Jules was in attendance with Themis and Hooke in the chamber of Sarapis far below the Library of Alexandria Hooke had requested for use by Jules.

"You stay here?" asked Themis as she viewed the vault.

"The Librarian has been most generous. Beatrice has been most wonderful: she sends my meals of supper and breakfast to the front desk which they place outside the door."

"Do you sleep?"

"I have," he replied to a suspicious disbelieving Themis.

Hooke had sent a large map of the three Sphæres with their four continents precisely rendered on the river Oceanus; it was laid on the table with Limbus to the right, Nubilus in the center and Hades to the left.

Jules had a small map of the Principality of Liechtenstein, his large glass pane, and the small pane of glass.

"I found this,

To depart the gate that crosses o'er the gate

cross the gate that ends the gate

penciled as marginalia on a map from Olympe. "If the box were ferried it would have begun in Olympe." Themis nodded. "I searched all of the known maps and found it. It is a simple matter of finding charts for things; it is difficult assembling all of the pieces once commonly known but forgotten in History. Secret places are assembled by skill; and, Chance. That line was found by Chance and, from there, I simply followed Chance."

He took from his small wooden box of chess pieces a red knight setting it on the place the Citadel of High Olympe on Empyreus Minor of Nubilus would be.

"Red knight?" asked Hooke.

"There is a black knight, if you prefer," said Jules as he showed them his red and black chess pieces.

Hooke smiled. "No."

Jules placed the map of Liechtenstein on the large map where the eastern continent of Hades would be so that the Rhine was perpendicular to Oceanus and Türtsch was in Oceanus.

He placed the black queen where the cottage would be near Türtsch in Liechtenstein. He placed a black rook apart from the queen.

"The cottage."

He placed haphazardly red pawns and black pawns in a line from the citadel to the cottage.

"That is the approximate route originally taken after reading annales libri, the written works of Javelle, chronicles, life histories of possible couriers and tales from observations by elder writers; principally: Gaius Lucilius, Decimus Iunius Iuvenalis, Gaius Petronius, Ploútarkhos, Hêródotos, Thoukydídēs, Thallus and Aristophanes; and, Ovid's *Metamorphōseōn librī*.

"Then—Finally—Láthebiosas."

"Láthebiosasmagne?" asked Themis.

Hooke gestured to Jules.

"Láthebiosas was unknown. He wrote an unknown number of volumes. All satires. All of the lives of the Olympes were presented in minutiæ. All scathing. Purportedly, he wrote them in Duvarthim Visadahyum.

"All his works were sought and burned for the obvious reasons.

"The texts have been authenticated; they were written by a single hand. The author has escaped exposure."

"It may be a single historian composing observations," said Hooke. "It may be a single chronicler using words provided by others. It may be both."

"You know," said Themis in her tone of amused scolding.

"The author," replied Hooke grandly smiling at her, "is a single satirist who is a single chronicler who is known by the name of Hermes."

"Of course," said Jules laughing.

"Very amusing," continued Hooke. "If one reads them excising preposterous embellishments, they are merely journal entries.

"The passages taken, as you have established, would have been the most expeditious. There wasn't secrecy involved since none believed their plot would be discovered as well as their arrogance being deities. Hence, this first simple route.

"There are several of these in Olympe. It is the matter of finding which was taken.

"It could have been Hermes, but I do not believe so. He could know who was that courier but I think not."

"It was not the Loathy One," said Themis.

"No," said Hooke laughing. "'Twasn't he."

"Are they not suspicious of Jules le Cartographe?" said Themis.

"No. They do not know his ways. They do not seek understanding. They believe Her Majesty is set on vengeance for the justice of their wickedness and art using him for obvious but nefarious purposes."

"I endeavor," replied Themis.

"We have two difficulties," continued Jules. "Where are the gates? Where is the cottage?"

He placed four large books at the corners of the large map. He placed the large glass on the tomes. He placed a queen and a rook on the glass; the other chess pieces were seen beneath.

"Where is the cottage?" asked Themis.

"That I do not know," said Jules. "His Lordship – during a conversation about Reality – elucidated probabilities. It is not on Terre."

"You visited for three days returning three years after," said Themis; Jules nodded.

"Do they know where is the cottage?" said Themis.

"No," said Hooke; "By their acts and by their very nature they would never have thought to know where they that mystery set."

"Do you know?"

"Perhaps," said Hooke thoughtfully. "Monsieur Jules, you were intending to say?"

"I was told a gentleman from the Swiss Confederacy, before it fell to invasion by the l'Armée Révolutionnaire française in 1798, would be waiting for me in the shadows of the castle Vaduz. Very specific. I had originally thought I was standing in the year of 1789 when conversing with that gentleman from the Swiss Confederacy."

He placed four die on the large glass and placed the small glass on the die. He placed a red rook on the small glass. He stared at them as he moved his head from side to side in contemplation.

"If, however, I was in a year before 1789 it goes to the point that my travels in the Principality of Liechtenstein were also made in a year before 1789 yet my days in the Principality did not affect the length of my stay. I was in a year *before* 1789 but remained in 1913! We were Ghost."

Hooke smiled.

"Which year?" said Jules. "It has negligible significance but one absolute truth."

"That would be?" asked Themis.

"They neither were in the decay of Chronos," said Hooke.

Jules nodded to Hooke's reply as he touched the rook on the small glass. "This is Alcyonian Lake in Hades on the continent of Speculae where, from Alcyonian Lake, one

458

would venture to Oceanus and, by the Rhine, reach the place of salt offering during my first adventure.

"Three rooks, three gates.

"I have opened the gate of the clearing. I needn't do so again since it would remain open after opening the second to last entrance."

He exhaled relaxing himself.

"'To depart the gate that crosses o'er the gate cross the gate that ends the gate' was written centuries after the original passage took place. We needn't follow that first made route."

"That clue?"

"This," said Jules pointing at the rook over the citadel in Olympe and dragged his finger across the rook over Alcyonian Lake to the rook where the cottage would be, "is the gate."

"'To depart the gate,' is the cottage. It is the exit. Rather, my surmising, to enter the cottage is to exit the gate; 'that crosses o'er the gate' is Alcyonian Lake which one must not enter; 'cross the gate' is in the citadel of Olympe; 'that ends the gate' is trickery. It is the entrance."

"Not necessarily trickery," interrupted Hooke. "There are two doors. They are identical. One has 'Entrance' on a brass plate; one has 'Exit.' Which would you choose?

"'That ends the gate' could mean exit from Olympe in that Reality and enter the cottage in a different Reality." He thought. He stared at Themis in his sudden realisation. "Or... or, it could mean that the cottage is the entrance and Olympe is where one exits."

"Someone in the cottage could have voyaged to Olympe," said Themis.

Jules was becoming despondent.

"We cannot know until one visits that place," said Hooke. "My apologies, Monsieur le Cartographe. 'Tis too early for despondency caused by my idle curiosity." He smiled at Jules. "Please continue."

"'One cannot arrive at the cabane by treading with legs of two - or, four since four has a pair of pairs; it must be an odd number of legs - on land but by those of the Æther must be done yet none with wings may fly,'" continued Jules after composing himself.

"To cross o'er the gate is to fly.

"'Those of the Æther must be done yet none with wings may fly' is a thing with wings and three legs."

"What?" said Themis.

"Celeste having a single leg walking on crutches," mused Jules, "would have been who went first."

"Bardos the Lame!" Hooke declared.

"Aži Dahāka, Zhulong and Seiryū have requested us," said Themis. "They would know."

"Bardos the Lame?" asked Jules.

"You cannot walk; you cannot fly," said Hooke. "Then as noted 'none with wings may fly' you shall each do."

"My pardon," said Themis interrupting as she pointed along the length of the pawns. "This is the route taken by courier yet you have a secondary passage with these castles as gates. Does that imply two voyages were taken?"

Hooke laughed delighted. He shook his head laughing as he gazed at Themis. "Monsieur le Cartographe?"

Jules stared blankly at the ceiling; his despondency returning. He viewed the table. He slowly moving his head followed the voyage from the first gate across the pawns to the cottage. He returned his viewed to the first rook slowly moving his head then raising and lowering it as he flew over the middle gate until he reached the cottage.

He shook his head with a pained expression.

†

Sénateur-Maire Huillard was showing Elfriede the second flying academy of the parc.

The Icarus Flying Academy

"Passengers are, as you see," said Sénateur-Maire Huillard, "raised in a Rozière balloon enabling courageous visitors wearing large waxed-feather bird wings to experience flying unattached by wires and pulleys. They leap from the gondola ascended to the height of a league soaring until the waxed-feather wings are caught fire and they fall. Harpies safely collect the courageous visitors before they plummet ending in the manner of Icarus."

"Despondents?" asked Elfriede.

"The harpies keep a Very gun carry which is fired when an Icarus may wrestle themselves free from the grasp of the harpy; and, Madame Szélanya's name is spoken. Szélanya appears and she invokes a columnar vortex beneath them gently setting them on the earth. That Icarus is led from the parc by a nurse from the hospital of Titania escorted by the Constablery.

"And then we have those unbeknownst who are weightless in flight carried off by zephyrs. They are later found. Often."

Elfriede wished visiting the al-Kīmiyā Hermetica arcade.

"Do you not wish to fly?" asked Huillard.

"One day," replied Elfriede.

†

Zoë, Rhadamanthus, Hine-nui-te-pō and Oom Hendrik were seated in the coach while Mors and Thanatos sat on the back bench as they went in Rhadamanthus's traveling coach-and-four.

They had come upon King Paimon strolling on the High Road.

"My Good Sir," said Zoë with surprise. "I cannot remember you without dromedary led by a vanguard of musicians accompanying you."

"It was a lovely evening for a quiet stroll, after the beginning of the War of Indignants, on my way to l'Abbaye Sainte-Marguerite."

"We should take you," offered Rhadamanthus.

"Unlooked-for charity is always welcomed," said King Paimon. "I sit aloft."

He did.

They continued.

✝

Hercule as Constablery was standing facing a line of urchins. They were inside his caravan.

"I would like to know if you would care to be in my Extraordinary Flying Squad of Thieves?"

They protested.

He peered at them.

They quieted.

"You are very good at what you do for the things you wish to take," said Hercule. "Wilhelmine likes watches."

Wilhelmine stared at him. He showed her three pocket-watches. She instinctively touched the sleeve of her left arm.

The other eight urchins barely suppressed their snide laughter.

"Leopold likes spoons," said Hercule as he took several ornate sterling spoons from his own coat pocket.

The other eight urchins barely suppressed their wonder.

"Oksana takes silver things; Sigismund takes stick pins and hatpins; Beatrix, silk handkerchiefs; Jefimija, wallets; Nicola, watches and hatpins; Umberto, canes; Garibald, all things with gems." He took those various objects from his pockets as he spoke; he removed the stick pin stolen by Sigismund he was wearing.

They stared.

"I know what you do here," replied Hercule. "If I know what you do here, I deduce I know what you do there." He pointed in the direction of Portul Pădurilor. "I have not seen all the thefts you have taken but I did return the articles taken when I did see."

"That's why!"

"That's why," said Hercule, "you did not have them when you left from the parc."

"What do you want us to do?" said Jefimija.

"Steal from thieves stealing in the parc."

"We can still steal from them in Portul Pădurilor," said Umberto.

Hercule shook his head.

"What if they're better than us?" said Beatrix.

"Practice. Practice stealing from them which they've stolen. If you believe they are better than you, use each other in the act of pilferage."

"The difficulty?" said Umberto.

"I would obligated be informing magistrates and they would send someone for you."

"Snitch," said Umberto.

Hercule nodded.

"You're threatening us!" stammered Sigismund.

"No," replied Hercule after a long length of thought with furrowed brow. "It is not a threat. It is a choice you choose. Either ... Or."

"If'n we do?" asked Nicola.

"I have no obligated informing. I will snitch if I know you have stolen when in the Flying Squad. They will send someone with you."

"Who is the someone?" said Umberto.

"Honos the Brave."

"Who's he?" said Oksana. "I have heard his name sometimes when I am here in the parc but I haven't seen him."

"He is the tall gardener you have met in the Woods. He gardens here, too."

"He's not scary," Umberto pronounced.

"No," said Hercule in agreement. "If you wish, I shall inquire with Madam Navjaci la Alkonost if her children would care to watch you. She is thought scary, isn't she? We'll see who has interest since you want scary watchers guarding over you." He went to the open door. "Thank you. Please tell me in the last hour before the parc closes." He went.

They furtively spoke. Those nine descended the steps.

"He'll never what's gone know," said Umberto as he and Sigismund examined the snow globes they had taken.

"Master Hercule will know when he returns," said Oksana; "but he won't know who took them and we'll all be suspects and I don't want to be suspect."

"He won't know if you don't tell him," said Umberto threatening her with a knife.

"That's bad," was heard a femme's voice.

They looked around.

"Very disappointing." Madame Navjaci was seated on the roof of the caravan. "Shall we take you places?" She opened and closed the talons of her right claw. They looked around. Twenty-three of her grandchildren were waiting smiling. "It is fortunate for you it is Master Hercule's decision what happens with you two boys.

"We were late arriving to find him instead we find this and so we go to find him."

Madame alighted on the ground. She led her grandchildren away from the caravan as they were prepared for the indulgences of their grandmother in the parc.

The fledgling pickpockets—Oksana, Beatrix, Jefimija, Nicola, Wilhelmine, Leopold and Garibald—went from the older two cutpurses.

"We don't need them anyway," said Umberto. "Bucarest."

Umberto and Sigismund ran from the parc.

✝

Two figures were standing in the dark of the ruins.

"Do you perform Sabbaths here?" asked Philibert Beyle.

"No. I like ruins. Aesthetics. I find calm in them," said César-François Collot.

The carriage came.

They entered—Zoë with Rhadamanthus, King Paimon, Hine-nui-te-pō, Oom Hendrik, Thanatos and Mors—entered the ruins of l'Abbaye Sainte-Marguerite founded in 1100 in the high valley in the village of Bouilland by l'Ordre Hospitalier de Saint-Antoine who tended those afflicted with la Peste and the sacred fire of Saint-Antoine.

"My apologies, King Paimon," said César-François Collot l'Adepte de Occultisme as he hurriedly went greeting his arrival of King Paimon. "I have to wit's end gone."

"What is Existence?" said Mors.

"I no longer know. My faith in the philosophies and Myths left me," said Collot l'Adepte de Occultisme: "My belief is shaken."

"Science and Enlightenment disapproved of the existence of Myths," Hine-nui-te-pō did in humour retort.

King Paimon asked Collot to introduce his companion.

"Monsieur Philibert Beyle was here when I came," said Collot. "We have been talking in admiration of this structure. It's most enchanting."

"Myths," said King Paimon. "Science has proved cause and effects of most things occurring in Existence. Science has never disproved Existence of beings which may or may not be responsible for the cause of those effects in Nature nor those which they have never seen except in dreams and reveries. How does one scientifically disprove Fey of their existence when one does not believe they exist?"

"Enlightenment from knowledge they profess," said Zoë; "In centuries Past, Modern Age Enlightenments have denigrated and traduced antique beliefs a posteriori yet not with empirical evidence."

"And those having met in Existence Fey are known to say Science lies," offered Mors.

"It is not secret Knowledge," Monsieur Collot. "It is Mystery."

†

Les Mademoiselles were walking in the parc. They paused.

It had wooden signs of various sizes each painted with a single eye adorning the façade of the arcade.

A gentleman was approaching from the opposite direction.

They read the advertisements of the arcade which was closed. The proprietors were on Holiday. The signboard at the entrance read,

The Heart Purloined
By DESIRE
The Thieving Airs spirit-dreaming
of the Fairy's Kiss:
Spring arrived

with

Spectacular Specular Seeing Ghosts
for all

to

Sea

Théophile-Raymond d'Aveyron greeted them as he was opening the exterior of the arcade. "Mademoiselles, do you come for the Specularities? in thy glass to see the spectres of cherubs?" They merrily declined.

✝

"They are in horrific pain of the body," said Mors. "Memories are gone. They have no mind. Echoes of emotions of what they once felt are what remain. Terror, Fear, Sorrow. The pain they feel is augmented by those emotions. It never wanes. It is always felt; it is always remembered. It does not dull; it is always excruciating."

"It cannot be ended like Sisyphus," said Thanatos, "who, bored of his punishment wagered Hyperion, who often walked in the Salles of Arrogance, that he - Hyperion - could not make his punishment worse. Hyperion broke the boulder into smaller stones. Hyperion pleased went laughing. Sisyphus broke the rusted iron shackle fastened on his ankle to the long iron anchor chain with a smaller stone. He went finding Hyperion, paying his lost wager, and left."

"That river in your dream was poisoned," said Mors.

"What do you believe?" asked Collot.

"Amorphousness existed; Nature followed. Demiurge—or, Dæmon—brought forth Fauna," said King Paimon. "I find this more in keeping with my senses of Reason and Logic. Though, in those earliest Myths they were different named."

"I prefer Ex nihilo," said Mors. "Simplicity absolute."

"You will find, Monsieur Collot, Fey tend towards those two possibilities."

"It is here you find goddesses and gods of Creaturae are prevalent since that is what Man has been taught by religio and superstitio and superstitionis in the myths of Existence.

"An assumption Man makes is these Creator Deities created lesser deities simultaneously; Olympes in particular.

"The introduction of Man was last.

"It is from these two parts we get to Existence."

"Whose Existence are we speaking of?" César-François Collot said after much thought.

"Man's sense of Existence," replied King Paimon; "Fey do not have a word for 'Be-ing.' 'All things are therefore I am' is what they would say if pressed for reply. This Existence — Perhaps — in this place - le Parc de Terre naturel - for those not of Fey, is simply a Théâtre-pièce: a play performed being for the benefit of César-François Collot," said King Paimon. "And, if this were a Théâtre-pièce, Then— one-hundred, two-hundred years from this day, someone will know all of the scenes in the Acts preceding our scene in the ruins of l'Abbaye and shall be reading this our conversation as we are speaking of Existence.

"Or, it is — Perhaps — a guignol Amusement set by those in Empyreus Minor.

"Or, it is a Conte d'Homme viewed as Raree Show projected by lanterna magica for the benefit of viewing by the Idôla'wiyákpa; or, if one believes: Deus absconditus and the Dæmiourgos of the Phenomena; or, Deus otiosus; or, Mortal apotheosis: or, Transcendence."

"Or, cacodaemon on occasions," said Thanatos, smiling.

"My pardon," said Oom Hendrik. "Phenomena is all things seen in Nature; but Nature, by arch-dualists and others, is thought evil."

Zoë smiled.

"That is reasonable they would assume such," interjected Mors; "Eudæmonia could only be achieved after entering, in their Existence, the Otherworld in the manner proscribed by the Stoics preferred.

"By having Earth and Otherworld, you have a plurality of worlds within Existence. All things forever return to substance and essence. Monism and all those others.

"Moreover, what if amorphousness was sentient?"

"By words, Existence could be anything in Life and Death," said Collot bewildered.

"Existence is of the Past, the Present and of the things to Come," said Mors. "It is a persistent illusion to believe Existence ceases after Death departs."

"It is for you to decide, Monsieur Collot," replied Zoë, "for as you said Existence could be anything."

César-François Collot thought but could no answer give. He shrugged. "Then I shall keep my thought of incarnations, with innate knowledge, in the length of Eternity, for however long that may be."

"Monsieur Beyle, what is Existence for you?" asked King Paimon.

"I do not know," replied Philibert Beyle sadly. "I don't believe I do."

César-François Collot effusively thanked King Paimon for his visit. Philibert Beyle and Collot would remain even though they were invited to travel by coach wherever they wished as Zoë, Rhadamanthus, King Paimon, Hine-nui-te-pō, Oom Hendrik, Thanatos and Mors took their leave.

†

"Let us decide that—Momentarily—we have two possibilities," said Hooke: "a single voyage but someone later discovered a simpler faster passage by flying over the middle gate as an elementary exercise; or, a second voyage was made after someone wished to know of a simpler faster passage to be taken in haste for retrieving what was originally left or for placing a second object in the cottage. Regardless of which possibility, they each began in Olympe."

"Who would have first known to set this act in that numinous place?" asked Themis.

"There are a few," replied Hooke contemplatively.

Jules collapsed himself seated on the floor.

"We are concluded," announced Themis. "We shall discuss these mysteries in some other place. What's intended?"

"I would like to let this remain as you see, return to the hôtel and sleep."

"And then?"

"Once arranged, it is a simple task finding passage. There are common practices for all passages. The entrance should be simple enough found. The middle gate I do not know where it lies. I do not know how tall it is. Nor wide. Standard; or, from Hades to Limbus high since the lake is in the Territory; or, higher."

"If you'd please, collect all papers of this high gate and inform me when we may come to read them."

"Eh?"

"Depending on what is read and seen, you may need only go under the gate."

"Oh?"

"Perception," said Hooke. "After we have decided, and Bardos the Lame has been found, you shall be escorted by the Thirteen and Nine to Olympe; and, so discover the end of the gate."

"That would be first, Yes." Jules stood.

"May we escort you to the hôtel?" asked Themis. "Thank you, Monsieur Jules le Cartographe, for all of this your remarkable work. Thank you."

"Please."

✝

Oksana, Beatrix, Jefimija, Nicola, Wilhelmine, Leopold and Garibald—the fledgling pickpockets—were standing with Hercule at the parc's entrance.

They explained what happened after he parted.

"They were pretty," said Hercule. "Not sentimental. Just pretty. I will inform the Mayor in the morning and he will speak with the Mayor of the Harbour."

"Shouldn't we do something about your snow globes?" asked Leopold.

"Just pretty," replied Hercule.

"So, we sign papers?" said Wilhelmine.

"No."

"Swear an oath?" said Garibald.

"No."

"Blood vow?" said Oksana.

Hercule stared at her before he shook his head.

"What do we do?" asked Leopold.

"You came," said Hercule.

"You trust us," said Jefimija with disbelief.

Hercule nodded.

"You trusted Sigismund and Umberto?" asked Nicola.

"You were invited not trusting not distrusting."

"Are you trying to save us?" asked Beatrix who had been keenly staring at Hercule.

"No," said Hercule. "I can keep others safe; but not save someone from what they do." He looked at them: a few nodded but the others were confused. "They may perhaps save themselves. I..." He thought. "I... only offer opportunity ... to those ... who ... would like to ... change ... themselves." He thought. "Yes." He looked at them; they nodded. "Please come before the hour of opening. We shall meet at the cafe Asio Stygius to have breakfast to speak of many things."

"We have this question," said Oksana gesturing to Leopold.

"Did you battle Malevolences at the Miserables fountain?" asked Leopold.

"No."

They were relieved.

"I wounded mortally Phobos the Deity. I stumbled a Saintly Holy to the ground; an eye was taken," replied Hercule dispassionately; "No Malevolences." He bowed from his shoulders; and, went.

They paled.

✝

The courts of Hades and Nubilus were in upheaval for Hera had disappeared after visiting in the county of Lucidusmons.

✝

There was a pause in the War as belligerents celebrated the Autumnal Equinox together on the battlefields.

†

The Parc was celebratory.

†

Les Mademoiselles were now four. Elfriede de Vienne had been installed by Themis Queen as Madame Conductrice in that her duties she improved by acting as psychopompe which none other had ever thought to be.

Les Fées marraines — Theresa Aurélia de Phaenna the Violet Witch, Mary la Toute-Douée the Red Witch, Snježana de Pasithea the Blue Witch, and Shiretoko-hantō Miyabiyaka the Brown Witch led by Caroline d'Eirene the Orange Witch — appeared often assisting them. Fille was often with Lady Constance.

Tochi no akaru-sa, Fille, Félix and Marcelle were understanding their wands spending a goodly amount of their hours at the battlefields tending those fallen wounded and protecting those they could.

On the hours they were not on battlefields, they went sightseeing in the territoire and were much surprised by how many from Terre had been given residence.

Themis was visiting with them less.

At one village, Tochi no akaru-sa, Fille, Félix and Marcelle were ambushed while tending those fallen and wounded. Félix and Marcelle caused far less destruction than previously. Caroline d'Eirene complimented them.

Félix and Marcelle sent Themis a telegram.

Zoë with Maeve le Dullahan, Mors and Thanatos were strolling after Rhadamanthus would continue with King Paimon, Uncle Henry and Hine-nui-te-pō on to Troyes.

"It was Olympiodorus who wrote Humanity rose from the smoke of burning fat of the Titan corpses. The Titan was the body of Man, the soul was the divinity," offered Mors.

"Terre'eden ex Nihlio," said Maeve le Dullahan: "It's simplicity. A garden with flora and fauna is created for first Entities. A man and a woman are created from clay. She departs. The fellow creates a woman from a bone. All those miraculous births in Myths."

"The first entities *were* the Autochthones immortalium rising from pitch and tar after rain," said Zoë. "The Dark Elves."

"Yes, they were," replied Maeve. "I forget the goblins."

"Man rising from smoke of Titan corpses in that Eden is plausible. They were the last of the fauna; they were the weakest. Azazel and other Watchers took pity on those for having drunk of Lethe as did affable Olympes and others of Fey," said Thanatos.

†

Félix, Marcelle and Fille were strolling on the avenue with Lady Constance as their chaperone. They were come across a gentleman with a peep box on his back.

The Wonder Show

"Jacques l'Aveugle de Vincennes was tall. He was thin and frail. His face had been set in an ancient rictus of his laughter. His white eyebrows were large and bushy. His whitened beard was tucked beneath his wide belt and his whitened beard fell to the length of his knees. He was dressed in fancy dress à la Turque of 1750.

"Ladies and Gentlemen, this *sanduk al-ajayib* was found as displayed in this during an expedition into the dark land of Death for it was taken by Genghis Khan from an ancient Mystical and from him was given to a most Venerated Wazir until it was obtained by I. All my companions were murdered by the Dark! It was by Fate that I alone escaped! Escaped!"

The Maestro had composed the box on the stand.

"View our performance that not even Heads of State have seen!

"C'est Triomphe l'œil!"

He strode closer to those gathered on the boulevard.

"Mesdames!" He waved Félix, Marcelle and Fille to approach and view. He bowed as they approached him merry.

The box had six holes through which they could see the scenes performed lit by a single candle. When they each peered inside the box it was very much larger than the size of the box: it was a théâtre proscenium arch with the scene performed inside of it.

"Mirths! Merriments! Merry entertainments! for our blessèd invited Guests! Enlightenments! we offer for all in attendances! Simple tales! Sacrèd tales! and we all know that sacrèd is merely variously spelled Entrancements! we offer for all in attendances! Mirths and merriments and merry entertainments that are to be seen: Paradise and Hades, exotic views in the lands of the Past, farces and masques, court ceremonies, conclusions found in the days yet come; and of course, lewd tableaux."

✝

"I must attend a service in Quarré-les-Tombes," said Thanatos as he bowed saying his farewells before Zoë for they were arrived at the crossroads.

"Thank you for accompanying me," said Zoë.

He departed.

✝

Lady Constance was standing watching the entertainment before her of Marcelle, Fille and Félix peering through the Wonder Box.

She smiled.

✝

"Who shall know of what they see?" said Maestro de Vincennes with enticement. He paused dramatically. "Entr'actes, perhaps," he said in a tone of beguiling wonder: "Of Ecstatic Wars; of Sixteenth Century voyages; of Life's marvellous spring-balances; of future rendez-vous by those bewitched; of the risen ghosts of Hope; of guileless cotillion with Nature." He paused before he said in near whisper with his eyes lit brightly: "Or, Trysts éternel."

The scenes concluded.

They stepped away from the box. Félix, Marcelle and Fille were smiling.

The Maestro thanked them; they thanked the Maestro.

"Who would peer!" said the Maestro.

All of the others wanted viewing. He selected six. They gave him coins. He began his recitation, but it was different from the first.

Those four went continuing on their stroll.

✝

Hooke was seated, in his cabinet, with his legs on the ottoman, caressing the hair of Themis who lay on the couch with her head on his lap.

"What troubles you? about this voyage to be taken by Monsieur Jules," said Themis.

"'To depart the gate that crosses o'er the gate cross the gate that ends the gate' was written *after* the first trespass by Monsieur Jules. Whomsoever scratched those words knew that the gate of his first trespass was under watch; it is not the entrance. It has all been stage-craft."

Themis sat up.

"The gates are locks."

"Over or under," said Themis. She thought. "Praesens."

Hooke nodded.

"You asked if Olympe knew where the cottage would be," said Hooke. "I gave an imprecise reply. They do not know because the avenues and relic-stones were moved; entrances never move."

"Persephone's Gate," said Themis musing.

He nodded.

"They are not kept by secrecy."

"No. However, they are kept secret by being forgotten which is the grandest form of secrecy."

"Neither Olympe nor Fiend know where the entrance waits."

"No."

"Jules?"

"Years of Coincidence," replied Hooke. "Jules stated he began searching in 1781. His efforts lasted 93 years. The beginning would have been feverish and then become increasingly dwindling less frequent as the years progressed until he truly abandoned his quest in 1874. However, during those next four years, he, by happenstance kept finding clues. They were given. In 1878 after being informed under mysterious - Suspect! - circumstances, he continued with his quest.

"Jules states he met and spoke with a gentleman from the Swiss Confederacy in a year before 1789. He was asked if he still carried salt from Lunéville Saltworks. They knew.

"L'Invalide was known in 1794 but came earlier; he departed Saint-Lazare in this year of 1913. L'Émissaire would have been in 1794 but came earlier. Where had it been for those missing years? before appearing in this year of 1913.

"Reverie," said Themis.

"Yes. Yet... Monsieur Jules remembers he is from a different year when he said to us, in the chamber of Sarapis, those few nights ago, 'I was in a year before 1789 but remained in 1913.'"

"They neither were in the decay of Chronos," said Themis.

"Thirty five years ago, Jules le Cartographe steadfastly remembers — Steadfastly — he is in the year l'Hallow Malveillance — l'Invalide and l'Émissaire — are acknowledged:— 1913."

"What does this mean?" said Themis. Hooke gazed at her with his beguiling smile. She thought until she shuddered. "Resverie."

"Elysion pyr," said Hooke. "It was l'Émissaire who met Jules at the castle in a year before 1789. They would have known his true character. He had disappeared from them; they found him. Milot had written 'Voyageur waits' when told by Chthonius. Their prey was Jules. Their plot was altered when we prosecuted our snare; and, thus were twice exposed: Horrors and their intrigue for a treasure.

"Maliel-pyr," said Themis.

"Aye."

"What is it that Olympe has done!" said Themis. She faced him. "They cannot go!"

Hooke frowned with eyes of sublime menace.

"Thy intention?"

"Thirteen Kings."

✝

Madame Dewognata had volunteered to accompany Fille, Félix and Marcelle through the wax works,

Les Litanies d'Ḩomme

Two Porters diminutive passed behind them carrying a sedan chair without it's sedan box on which was seated an Ange blessé.

They entered to find nurses attending fainted malebranches and demons who had not traveled ever to the land of Terre.

"You are not horrified by these savageries," said a Zabaniyya as they went.

"No," said Marcelle. "These are prurient vignettes of larger authenticated villainies. There are worse."

"Kanryueki - Taru-Oni - are returning," said Madame Dewognata. "It is much worse than these."

They did view all of the arcade; and, did exit.

✝

Mors, Maeve le Dullahan and Zoë were lounging at the crossroads.

"When comes Queen Aoibhell?" asked Mors.

"She did not say," said Zoë.

"If you would excuse me, Ma'am," said Mors: "I make my way to the commune of Châtillon-sur-Seine."

He bowed and wandering went from them.

"Fey are not blameless," continued Zoë. "It was their cunning with Humanity which assisted the wasting of Terre.

"Deities, Demons and Féeries all took part.

"Deities with their need for sacrificial offering. Deities destroying all things when not given proper sacrifices. Why? Why would Celestial entities seek such things? Effronteries? Jealousies? Vanities? Ignorance?

"Deities by the acts of patronage influencing History.

"Demons with their amusements against lesser beings. Demons giving archaic knowledge to all requesting.

"Féeries with their helpfulness to creatures born of blood or from bones of Titans who were cruel and vindictive against themselves and deities.

"Man was given knowledge; avarice and covetous thoughts of the Aristocracy of Wealth swayed them from Nature. Man's baseness won.

"There are those of Fey who are saddened remorseful by their acts. Most set all blame on Man. It does not matter if the parts played by Fey were minor, insignificant or given in the spirit of Benevolence corrupted by Man: they still assisted.

"The Long Withering of Terre was in large measure encouraged by Fey. Man could not have done so without their meddling; Fey caused acceleration of it's demise.

"All are culpable."

They began strolling on the High Road.

"Whiro, Angra Mainyu, Typhoeus, all of the Lords of darkness, all of the embodiments of all evil, are the corporeal personifications of the villainy and vices found in Deities and Demons; and, later grown by magnitudes when was come Humanity.

"Théodicée is interesting. Nothing more. Deities are known of evil.

"Eblis and Satan did travel in the realms of Fey, before Man magically appeared, yet their sway was insignificant when compared with that of the understudies of Satan: Mephistophilis and Devil.

"That evil, from which suffering is necessary for the growth of the Spirit before it may find pacific salvation in Kingdom Come, is as banal as it is lime-washing the evils they do: that the necessity of evil must be to counterbalance good; original sin was the cause; evil wends to a greater good; absence of morals finds evil; evil is an innate knowledge."

Zoë was concluded.

"My apologies, cher Maeve," said Zoë laughing as she paused their promenade.

"I enjoyed it," said Maeve. "It was a History Lesson and of things I had forgot. A thoughtful disapprobation."

"Your patience was of benefit."

They continued.

✝

Zoë and Maeve le Dullahan had come to a gentleman – Paul Laurent Merlin de Théophilanthrope – who was standing on the railway tracks and pondering the setting Pale.

"It is a lovely morning," said Zoë after they had stood near the Théophilanthrope for several minutes.

Paul Laurent Merlin de Théophilanthrope was startled.

"Death-in-Life and Life-in-Death are the same facets of Life," said Merlin de Théophilanthrope.

"Yes?" said Maeve.

"Simple perspective," said Merlin de Théophilanthrope matter-of-factly. He took a piece of blue chalk and inscribed on one railway track–

LIFE

And Merlin de Théophilanthrope inscribed on the other railway track–

DEATH

He faced DEATH and pointed with his left hand to the word scratched in chalk on the track to the West as he faced North and said: "There at the confluence of single DEATH with the other, at the horizon, it is DEATH IN LIFE."

He faced LIFE and pointed with his right hand to the word scratched in chalk on the track to the East as he faced South and said: "There at the confluence of single LIFE with the other, at the horizon, it is LIFE IN DEATH."

"Why in this order?" asked Zoë.

"We read from left to right! Top to bottom!"

She nodded.

"Does North have significance in this argument?" asked Maeve.

"Naturally."

"When we stand at this perspective, along the curvature of a sphere, the tracks are parallel curves which are a simple line at the horizon," said Zoë.

"Yes?" said Merlin de Théophilanthrope.

"How does that twined track at the North become twain again approaching from the South?" asked Zoë.

"Sooth! Empirical Knowledge 'tis illustrated!" said Merlin de Théophilanthrope. "Do you not believe thine own eyes: peer backwards and they are converted; peer forwards and they are converted.

"They are apart herein where we stand because we cannot comprehend unless from afar in the distance."

"You mean to say that if we travel North we have Death-in-Life but if we travel South we have Life-in-Death," said Maeve.

"Yes."

"What then is the riddle for which you have this answered?" asked Maeve.

Merlin de Théophilanthrope would reply but abruptly he could not and so stared at the tracks. He stared North; he stared South. He paced. He stood staring at the earth on which the tracks were resting as Zoë and Maeve departed.

"Do they not suffer both that girdle this sphere?" said Zoë.

Maeve nodded.

†

Tochi no akaru-sa, Fille, Félix and Marcelle were resting on the steps of the library in the commune of Tahungamarire after assisting Fūjin, a few shaytan and a company of wanyūdō defend the town from an attack by géants, thrones and cherubs when a messenger brought Marcelle and Félix a telegram.

Félix read it; she was stunned. She handed it to Marcelle and Marcelle read aloud:

My dear Mademoiselles—

As to your request, in the telegram you sent to me, it was
evident long ago, for those with knowledge given by Ghosts,
as well as encompassing all of the things we did speak for
which you addressed succeeding, disencumbrances would be
taken earlier and thus did occur in the days before your
adventure with the flock of Putus inexplebilis and that Géant;
so, it must be noted— it was you alone performing magie.

Ŧ

"We've been wandering around naked for seventeen days!" declared Félix who
moaned.

"She trusted you," said Tochi no akaru-sa.

"How?" said Marcelle.

"I imagine," said Fille, "she trusted you would not let yourselves be murdered."

"You were not," said Tochi no akaru-sa.

"Sea-born," mused Félix in her reverie. "My Father held me on the surface when I
swam. Every morning. My Mother would wait on the beach. One day, he removed his
hands. I didn't know he did. I didn't know I was swimming farther from the cove. It was
ocean. I stopped. They were still there. Standing where we were. They were smiling."

"Weren't you scared?" asked Marcelle.

"No," said Félix calmly. "Terrified. I could see the sand beneath the water in the cove.
I couldn't see the bottom of the ocean. But I was swimming and they were there. I swam
back. He took my hand. She took my hand. We went home."

"Her Majesty and His Lordship may be gone but they're still there," said Fille realising
the situation of things, "aren't they?"

"They're all still there," replied Marcelle in her reverie thinking of her parents, and
those she had met during these their adventures voyaging.

"They are," said Tochi no akaru-sa in her reverie.

Fille silent nodded in her's.

"Yes," said Félix.

They each were gone to a different place at a different time.

†

"I have not been able to deduce if anyone left the cottage or if there was a second passage from Olympe, so I shall go and see," said Jules.

"I have decided on the type of gate they used: it is not Nature-alchemic, Moon-alchemic nor charmed but a common passage from those years they would have taken passage. The command word may take time: commence, begin, enter, entrance; all those sorts in the present-perfect tense."

"You may wish to try Šoru'kardé-im – 'I have begun' – first," said Hooke. Jules wrote it in his book. Hooke faced Themis saying, "Persian and Asian were considered mystery languages; hence– Secrecy." She smiled.

"There are several of them," said Jules.

"Which of the twelve?" asked Hooke.

Jules pointed to them. Hooke peered. "It is not this," Hooke said pointing, "because it lies in the middle of Oom Hendrik's sulfur baths." He peered. "It is not this," he said pointing, "because it is in the Loathy Archaïc's closet and he would not have used his own: he'd have rather set blame on some other of lesser import." He peered. "This goes to Terre; this goes to the county of Stella in the southern hemisphere of Virtus Minor; this goes to the outer court of Hades." He stood. "Two."

Jules scratched those from his list.

"If you'll indulge me," said Hooke as he went and opened the doors of the casement window stepping on to the terrace. He stood with his hands in his trouser pockets, staring.

"Let us tarry elsewhere," said Themis as she wrapped her right arm around the left arm of Jules. "I have things you may later wish to have taken with you." She led Jules from the withdrawing-chamber. "He's pondering."

✝

Themis and Hooke had waited until Aži Dahāka, Zhulong and Seiryū summoned them; Bardos the Lame preferred seclusion and so was difficult to find. They were trysting with secrecy in the vale—Öndör-mo'tóyaohkii—of the highest range of mountains in Limbe, Taj'wóištiŋme.

Bardos the Lame rose himself on his tail when Themis and Hooke entered; he bowed with his left claw over his breast. Bardos the Lame was a wyvern.

Hooke solemnly bowed from his shoulders to which Bardos the Lame replied: "Sire." Hooke formally introduced Bardos to Themis. "Majesty," said Bardos.

"Sir," began Themis, "His Lordship and myself thank you for accepting to speak with us. It is - I confess - a whim of mine this adventure in which you are requested to participate with a Bonhomme of mystery who finds things that are not meant to be found. It concerns the box of Pandore in a place that does not exist."

Hooke explained unfolding all facts and possibilities surmised by Themis, Jules and himself.

Aži Dahāka, Zhulong and Seiryū asked many questions Hooke did reply; Bardos the Lame lay silent.

"You trust this wight Jules le Cartographe," said Bardos with half-closed eyes.

"Vehemently," replied Hooke.

"I as well," said Themis

"It is an honour for me," said Bardos. He rose and bowed with merry bright eyes. "I have not been before to a place that does not exist. I should like visiting it."

"Thank you," said Themis.

✝

Tochi no akaru-sa, Fille, Félix and Marcelle were seated on the Arch of Woe. They had visited with their newly discovered friends who left returning to their homes after receiving acceptance of visits soon from them.

Tochi no akaru-sa and Fille would soon be leaving, too.

They themselves pondered, on the things to come, with conflicting emotions after the Mœræ gave their benedictions.

✝

C. L. Nolan, after all was done, had come to find he missed his house in the established pandæmonium that was the county of Hookland as he sat waiting with Milot and Jules on Achéron Quay for the ferry that would take him as far as the Thames to dock.

Themis Queen and Hooke had made their farewells on the previous night. Tochi no akaru-sa, Fille, Félix and Marcelle made their's after breakfasting.

He believed the Seventy Ninth Congress of Fey would be welcome sedation after his hours in Hades; but realised — Unfortunately — it may become dull after his hours in Hades until Themis Queen did explain that, on occasion, unexpectedly, blood was shed during those congresses in a fashion which would make the belligerents in the War of Indignities pleased.

He amused himself as they waited discussing future escapades of the Illapses Agency, Ltd. with thoughts of writing a three-volume conte de fées of their adventures. "*Les Trois Mousquetaires* for the Future," he said to himself pleased as he waited on Achéron Quay for the ferry that would take him as far as the Thames.

✝

"All these mementoes mori," said Maeve le Dullahan as she viewed those places of Nature she saw from the High Road accompanying Zoë during the partial solar eclipse.

"Mori is a word which sets words differently, if one knows," said Zoë. Maeve le Dullahan waited. "'Sea' from early Celtic language of that First Language is 'mori' whereas 'mer' from that First Language is 'to die.' So, 'memento mori' is either 'Remember Death; Remember that you have to die' or 'Remember that you are of the Sea.'

"I prefer the latter."

"Oh," replied Maeve le Dullahan.

"Mer-femmes and mer-hommes," continued Zoë, "are different too if it were known those words but they are'n't."

"Lord Hooke's influence," said Maeve le Dullahan.

Zoë raised her eyebrows with a mischievous smile.

"The Sea is encased in les Mémoriaux."

✝

Hooke, Themis and al-Jinn were speaking of the Night Horrors, the two Pyracanthes and one of les Enragés who from the Théâtre vanished.

"Simple ruse. Those three were found. They are watched."

"Where are they?"

"Orbisalius. L'Hôpital de la Divinité Bienveillante. They are harboured by le Directeur Mortuorum."

"Do you come?" asked al-Jinn.

"Queenly things pressing," replied Themis. "I take part in this clandestine by going to stay with my Aunt Meg until November."

"What do we do?" asked al-Jinn.

"We shall take a private train through Morpruia until Morpheús and so enter Limbus away from all things which could be damaged. And, take steamships and dirigibles to the territoire. A quarter's journey."

"Are we?" said al-Jinn laughing.

"No. Reynaerd shall appear as myself and who ever Reynaerd suggests in your guise does take our places in widely heralded secrecy. We go via the amusement in the fields of Ēlýsion. The carriage shall go to the fields, waiting. Decipio.

"Le Maréchal has closed the amusement due to intelligence rumours of an angelic press-gang coming for volunteers.

"A pleasant walk, a pleasant talk amoungst the briny beech."

"Why this subterfuge?" asked al-Jinn.

"Spies. I do not know who."

"Spies," said Themis.

"Yes. Hades it could be. Marquess, perhaps. A few others. The spy or spies are from the lands of Hades. It could be an intrigue set by Persephone which would explain my reluctance to engage with Hades in these hours. It could be Cartouche the Imp.

"It may be one of my lowest household staff. I do not know."

"You do not know if spies are in thy employ?" asked al-Jinn.

"No," said Hooke.

"I would like to see a fellow in the Duchy of Montmartre before venturing onward to the places of Orbisalius," said al-Jinn.

"I'll inform Reynaerd," said Hooke. He paused. "An entertainment, too."

✝

Zoë was approaching the carrefour of the road. Two Gentlemen were waiting: one whose colour was red was dressed in clothes of mourning; one was dressed in morning clothes, wearing a broad brimmed straw hat and smoking a pipe as he leaned on his cane.

Maître Carrefour offered Zoë a sip from his glass. "Gunpowder rum?

She graciously declined; and, so— conversing they went on the road of the Kings.

✝

Zoë went on the High Road.

COLOPHON

The Théâtre Optique icon was designed by Pochih Chang.

Typesetting utilises the structures found in 3 different printed works, ca. 1910.

Alcoholica by František Štorm/Storm Type Foundry ⟦Špálova 206/23, 162 00 Praha 6 Czech Republic⟧ has been the preferred text type since '00.

Aeronaut by the FaceType Foundry ⟦Otto-Bauer-Gasse 24/3/27 Vienna, 1060 Austria⟧ is used for the covers, half-title page, title page, and chapter names. AeronautBase is used for the title of the tales, characters, and venues.

NicolasCocTReg by (URW)++ is used for printed and engraved texts.

Didot by Linotype Library GmbH/Adobe Systems is the dagger.

Goudy Bookletter 1911 by Barry Schwartz was used on sundry pages and are page numbers.

Greature published by Uncurve was used on the cover.

Blackoak Standard was designed by Joy Redick and used on a signboard.

Boswell published by Scriptorium was used on a book cover.

The cover was written and set by the Author.

"All voyages are fraught with peril for therein lies Knowledge."

L - #0157 - 050321 - C0 - 254/178/26 - PB - DID3037751